W9-ASQ-088

PERFECT SWITCH

Lisa Plumley

WHEELER
PUBLISHING

Published in 2004 by arrangement with Zebra Books,
an imprint of Kensington Publishing Corp.

Wheeler Large Print Hardcover.

The text of this Large Print edition is unabridged.
Other aspects of the book may vary from the original edition.

Set in 16 pt. Plantin by Al Chase.

Printed in the United States on permanent paper.

Library of Congress Cataloging-in-Publication Data

Plumley, Lisa.
    Perfect switch / Lisa Plumley.
        p. cm.
    ISBN 1-58724-829-8 (lg. print : hc : alk. paper)
    1. Twins — Fiction. 2. Sisters — Fiction. 3. Housesitting
— Fiction. 4. Impostors and imposture — Fiction.
5. Television actors and actresses — Fiction. 6. Large type
books. I. Title.
PS3616.L87P47 2004
    813´.54—dc22
                                                            2004057213

Thanks to all the readers who wrote to me asking for Meredith's story. Here it is! I hope you enjoy it.

And to my husband, John, with all my love. Happy Fifteenth!

As the Founder/CEO of NAVH, the only national health agency solely devoted to those who, although not totally blind, have an eye disease which could lead to serious visual impairment, I am pleased to recognize Thorndike Press* as one of the leading publishers in the large print field.

Founded in 1954 in San Francisco to prepare large print textbooks for partially seeing children, NAVH became the pioneer and standard setting agency in the preparation of large type.

Today, those publishers who meet our standards carry the prestigious "Seal of Approval" indicating high quality large print. We are delighted that Thorndike Press is one of the publishers whose titles meet these standards. We are also pleased to recognize the significant contribution Thorndike Press is making in this important and growing field.

Lorraine H. Marchi, L.H.D.
Founder/CEO
NAVH

* Thorndike Press encompasses the following imprints: Thorndike, Wheeler, Walker and Large Print Press.

ONE

"Whenever I'm caught between two evils, I take the one I've never tried."
— Mae West

As far as escorts to a fantasy getaway went, he was perfect. Brawny, well-dressed, quick to smile — and to lend a hand into the evening's limo. At his first touch, Meredith Madison knew she was going to enjoy herself with him.

Mostly because he had no idea who she really was.

That was exactly the way she liked it. The hunk who'd arrived to pick her up just a few minutes earlier had never seen her before. After tonight, he'd never see her again. The realization felt unexpectedly liberating.

She could do this. Swapping places with her glamorous sister Marley wouldn't be easy, but she could do it. No one would be the wiser.

Feeling more sure of herself, Meredith smiled. In the sleek black stretch of leather, steel, and chrome she and the hunk shared, she watched him lower his broad frame onto the seat across from her.

The natural athletic grace of his movements intrigued her. So did his hands. Big, square-fingered, and wholly masculine, they were made for fixing things. For laying out maps of conquest. For caressing the small of a woman's back while escorting her into a room, or cradling her cheek while kissing her.

Not that *she* needed to be fixed. Or conquered, Meredith told herself as she swung her feet onto the limo's cushy upholstery in her favorite casual pose. She'd never allow anyone to tell her what to do. But this adventure included an escort. If he wanted to kiss her later, who was she to argue? After all, the invitation had promised her "the fantasy of a lifetime." That's what she was here to claim.

The limo driver closed the door with an expensively subdued *thunk,* then stowed her borrowed overnight case in the trunk. In the interest of being prepared, Meredith had brought a change of clothes and some toiletries. The fact that the driver hadn't even blinked when she'd handed over the case had only confirmed her suspicions.

The invitation she'd co-opted from Marley must have been for a comped stay at a new luxury resort, just as she'd thought. Her twin sister had enjoyed countless such perks from various places, all hoping she'd lend her famous starlet charisma to their let-us-pamper-you atmospheres.

If she didn't like it, Meredith reasoned,

she'd simply cut her stay short. If the place turned out to be as showy and pretentious as the luxe Hollywood bungalow she'd been house-sitting for Marley for the past few days, she'd bail out and spend the weekend fighting for a place to stow her ratty old sneakers in Marley's sequin-spangled closet.

The overall gorgeousness of the man who'd arrived to take her to the resort boded well, though. Dark-haired, dark-eyed, and possessed of a manner undoubtedly meant to put skittish guests at ease, he gave Meredith a distinct sense of being in capable hands. Warmed by his influence, she relaxed.

So what if she wasn't a star actress like her sister, Meredith thought defiantly, hugging her knees. She deserved a little downtime, too. She'd spent the whole day at the museum, cataloguing pop culture reference materials — the dustiest, most thankless part of her job as an advertising historian. Now it was time to cut loose.

As if in accord with her thoughts, the limousine accelerated along the drive and left the house behind. It began the winding descent through the Hollywood Hills toward the L.A. basin, bearing her toward her mysterious destination like a modern-day Cinderella's pumpkin-turned-limo. Sure, she didn't have a fairy godmother, and Meredith was more likely to wear Tevas than glass slippers. But the analogy felt apt, all the same.

Through the tinted windows, flashes of vibrant summer sunset came and went. So did Meredith's bravado. She couldn't help it. Kidnapping someone else's identity — even temporarily, and just for the fun of it — wasn't an everyday occurrence for her.

Her escort turned his attention to her again. "Sure you're ready for this?"

"Of course. I was born ready."

"Good. I'm glad to hear it." He clasped his hands loosely between his spread knees, the gesture both confident and relaxed. He nodded toward her arms-locked-on-knees pose. "Because you look a little uneasy. For a minute there, I thought you'd changed your mind."

Great. He was handsome *and* observant. If he guessed somehow that she wasn't really who she'd claimed to be. . . .

"Me? No!" She unclasped her knees, realizing for the first time exactly how tightly she'd been hugging them. Maybe she *was* more nervous than she wanted to admit. Deliberately, she sprawled sideways on the limo seat and gave him a provocative look. "I'm yours for the night, Prince Charming."

"Tony," he reminded her. "Tony Valentine."

Tony Valentine. That's right. He'd told her that when he'd arrived.

Disappointment stole over her. She didn't want to be reminded of who he really was — a man with an identity, a past, and a job to do. In her mind, "Prince Charming" worked

10

perfectly well as a nickname. It synced up nicely with her Cinderella fantasy. So did the even more appropriate "Hottie." Both monikers kept her macho escort at arm's length, a distance Meredith needed. For tonight, she truly wanted to feel like Cinderella — a naughty, punk-historian Cinderella — removed from her ordinary life for as long as the fun lasted.

But apparently, Tony wasn't the kind of man who would let himself be generalized. Probably, he saw himself as a *unique* version of super-stud escort and liked to be treated as such. She wondered how he saw her. Unlike her absentee twin sister, she wasn't exactly —

No. Making comparisons was *not* what she needed.

"Okay. Tony it is. We might as well get started," Meredith announced instead. She swung her feet from the seat and faced him. In the confined, vaguely rocking limousine space, their knees nearly touched. "What happens next, exactly? I'm new at this."

For a moment, he only continued to watch her. Thoughtfully. His gaze hadn't left her since he'd sat down, she realized then. The whole time she'd been classifying his attributes like the trained academic she was, he'd undoubtedly been studying her, as well. The man was *good*. Not to mention uncomfortably observant.

"You thought this was for just one night?" he asked.

"Okay. I'm yours for . . . as long as it takes!" Meredith returned gamely. Never let it be said she wasn't up for adventure. "Now that I've met you, I feel much better about this whole idea."

That seemed to please him. He delivered her a devastating smile, one that actually made her heart pound a little faster. Placing her hand automatically over her chest, Meredith smiled back. This man was even more charming than she'd thought. His interest in her felt remarkably genuine.

Wherever this resort was, she *had* to recommend it to her friends. So far, just riding in the limo with this guy offered more excitement than her Friday nights usually delivered.

"That's good," he said, nodding. "I do want you to be comfortable. You're our star attraction, after all."

"I *feel* like a star attraction."

"And you look —"

He broke off, his dark-eyed gaze darting to her feet. It skimmed over her flip-flops, traveled along the comfy, utilitarian-pocketed length of her khaki cargo pants, snagged on her T-shirt and the L.A. museum sweatshirt tied around her hips. Finally, it wound up on her Dodgers baseball cap. A smile quirked his lips.

Inwardly, Meredith cringed, half expecting the inevitable comparison.

"Great," he finished, seeming to mean it. "Really comfortable."

She shrugged. "All of my ball gowns chafe."

"Ahhh. I see." His smile widened. "I have the same problem with my tuxedos. They rub my sense of machismo raw."

"Hmmm." She pretended to consider it, letting her attention roam upward from his large, leather-clad feet to his L.A.-casual pants and knit shirt. Both were dark and well-fitted. "Your machismo seems to be limping along okay to me."

"Maybe." He offered her a good-natured grin, leaning closer as though confiding in her. "But you haven't seen the Victoria's Secret number I've got on underneath this."

Meredith froze. Was he . . . serious? She'd been on dates with some unlikely candidates before, but this — she'd thought — was different. Oh, God.

"Kidding." Tony grabbed a fistful of knit and lifted his shirt neck-high. The motion revealed a tantalizing flash of taut abs, muscular chest, and a smattering of dark hair. Too quickly, he covered himself again. "Sheesh, you're easy."

"Easy? You haven't proved a thing," she shot back, raising her eyebrow. "For all I know, you're wearing a thong."

"For all I know, *you* are."

"Maybe you'll find out," Meredith purred. "Later."

"That sounds like a challenge." He paused, regarding her with blatant masculine interest. "I enjoy a challenge."

"Most men do."

He shook his head. "Not like I do. Otherwise, I'd never have taken on this job in the first place."

Something rueful flashed in his eyes. Meredith wondered at it. Ordinarily, she loved her own job. But she couldn't imagine having one like his. Being an escort to spoiled actresses and other Hollywood types couldn't be easy.

"It's not so bad, though." Releasing a pent-up breath, he finger-combed the wavy brown hair away from his forehead. He scanned the bulging manila file folders, cell phone, pager, and sunglasses arrayed haphazardly on the limo seat next to him, then brightened. "I'd been warned you might not even show up."

"I'm glad I did."

"Me, too. The night's looking up."

"I'll say."

Something about him appealed to her — something beyond his remarkable good looks. His cockeyed point of view? His easy laughter? His teasing ways? Meredith wasn't sure what it was . . . but she *was* sure she wanted to make the most of her time with

14

him. Now that Tony had accepted her as Marley, the liberating effects of being incognito were kicking in. He thought she was someone else — which left Meredith free to be as wild as she dared.

After all, nobody would ever know what she did tonight. Nobody . . . except her and the hard-bodied hunk seated across from her.

He took out a clipboard. Poised a pen over the sheet of paper fastened to it. Fixed her with a businesslike look.

"Humor me with some preliminary feedback," Tony said, rubbing his thumb up and down his pen. "What do you think of the experience so far?"

Reluctantly, Meredith lifted her gaze. She'd never before longed to morph into six inches of plastic and ink. But watching Tony stroke his pen, so slowly, so provocatively . . . *Criminy!* What was she, some kind of ballpoint fetishist?

"It's very . . . stimulating," she said.

He didn't so much as quirk an eyebrow. He scrawled *stimulating* on the paper. "The limo pickup is meant to set the correct mood for the experience to come. Do you like it?"

"The mood?" *Sexy, flirty* . . . "Absolutely."

Tony scratched a check mark into the designated box. Meredith leaned over, squinting at the remaining questions. A dispiriting number of them filled the page.

"Aren't opinion surveys usually reserved for

after a guest's stay?" she asked.

"Ordinarily. But you're not just any guest." He checked his watch. "I'll want your opinion on the arrival process, too. We ought to be there in fifteen minutes."

So soon? Impatiently, Meredith frowned at the clipboard. Her whole life was ruled by clipboarded lists, museum pieces to be archived, and the other demands of her job. Tonight, she intended to break free.

Still concentrating on his list, Tony glanced up. "Our guests are meant to experience 'the fantasy of a lifetime,'" he said. "Are we off to a good start on that?"

The fantasy of a lifetime. His words echoed the invitation she'd snagged. They also served as the best opening she'd had since stepping into the limo with him. Meredith seized it.

"No."

Tony frowned. "No?"

"No." In as fluid a movement as her cargo pants and hip-tied sweatshirt allowed, she slid onto the limo seat beside him, into the space unoccupied by papers and gadgets. His body heat touched her. His presence enveloped her, even more strongly than it had before. She drew in a deep breath. "So far, there's too much talking. Not enough touching."

His eyes widened.

Thrilled with her own audacity, Meredith put her hand on his knee. "You know . . . touching. Like this."

16

His leg tensed, muscular and strong beneath her palm. She would enjoy that strength if things went well between them, Meredith mused. Maybe she'd invite Tony to dinner at the resort. See what developed. Canoodling with a hottie like him would sure as heck beat lounging poolside.

He nodded, staring transfixed at her hand on his knee. "I know touching," he agreed.

His voice sounded deep. Undeniably sexy. As sexy as Meredith felt while undercover as her glamorous twin. She'd never been timid. In fact, she prided herself on being up-front. Unconventional. Occasionally rebellious. But this . . . only giddy momentum could have carried her through it.

"Touching, touching . . ." Tony pretended to scan his clipboard, then raised it with a manly shrug and a teasing grin. "Nope. That's not covered on the opinion survey."

"To hell with the opinion survey." Meredith seized it. She tossed it onto her just-vacated limo seat. "I don't need prompting. I'm perfectly capable of telling you what I think."

His look of interest returned. "I like a woman who speaks her mind."

"I like a man who recognizes a come-on when he sees one."

"Are you suggesting I don't?"

She squeezed his knee. "Let's put it this way . . . I'm not evaluating the flexibility of your anterior cruciate ligament, here."

Tony raised his eyebrows.

"My favorite tight end nearly missed the playoffs last year because of a torn ACL."

That stopped him. "*You're* a football fan?"

Whoops. Her sister Marley didn't know a quarterback from a Quarter Pounder. Scrambling to cover, Meredith shrugged. "I learn all kinds of things researching roles. Acting is my life's work, you know. I take it seriously."

Tony stilled. One moment, he was right there with her, enjoying the banter between them. The next . . . whoosh. He was gone. What had she said?

"I take my work seriously, too." He eyed the clipboard, preparing to reach for it. "There's a lot at stake here."

Damn. She'd gone and reminded him of work. There went her first opportunity to be TV-starlet wild. Unwilling to quit so easily, Meredith lunged sideways, intercepting his grab for the survey.

Tony's chest met her shoulder; his arm brushed hers, almost cradling her from behind as they both reached across the limo. They were as close to indulging in vertical "spooning" as possible while still sitting side by side, Meredith realized. But his arm was much longer than hers. He could still reach the clipboard, even though she couldn't.

He didn't, though. Instead, Tony paused. He looked at her, then smiled. The space between them grew taut with expectation.

18

She canted her head toward the clipboard. "Write down an A-plus for everything," she suggested, giving him a saucy look. "I'm wildly optimistic."

His gaze dropped to her lips. Poised with his arm still outstretched, Tony slowly brought his hand up to her face. He skimmed his fingertips along her cheek. His touch felt every bit as sure and pleasurable as she'd imagined it would. Purposefully, he lowered his head.

"You have reason to be optimistic," he assured her.

A kiss felt inevitable. Waiting, Meredith held her breath. Crazy as it was, she wanted this. Wanted *him*. Yes, *yes*. . . .

Into the silence, intercom static crackled. "Five minutes, Mr. V.," the driver announced.

Meredith started. Tony blinked. The spell between them scattered. He grabbed his clipboard in one swift motion, then shoved it amid the rest of his belongings. "That warning's for you. I thought you might want to get ready for your entrance."

Puzzled — and yes, okay, disappointed — Meredith stared down at herself. She gestured toward her casual clothes. "Do I look like I'm into making an entrance?"

His perplexed expression matched hers. "You did last month at the premiere of that new Jennifer Lopez movie."

Arrgh. Another forehead-smacking moment. She was supposed to be Marley. She had to remember that.

"I decided to go for the celebrity-caught-by-surprise look," she ad-libbed. "You know, like in paparazzi shots."

"How appropriate." Wearing the expression of a man with a private secret, Tony tugged the brim of her baseball cap. Then he gestured toward her cargo pants, T-shirt, sweatshirt, and flip-flops. "Just so long as all this is gone by tomorrow."

"Tomorrow?"

"Right. Just like me, you have a job to do here. Remember?"

Openmouthed, Meredith stared at him. "A *job?*"

Tony grinned. He rolled his eyes, as though she really *were* her famously flighty twin sister. "Never heard the term, princess? J-O-B. It's the thing Valentine Studios hired you to do at this shindig. I've got the contract right here."

He reached for the manila folder beside him, leaving Meredith gawking. What did he mean, a job? Why hadn't Marley warned her about this?

Oh, yeah. Because Marley didn't know she was here. She didn't even know Meredith had accepted the invitation on Marley's behalf. Because she *couldn't* know, ever, or Meredith would never live it down.

She summoned her wits — and the original invitation from one of her cargo pant pockets. She waved it toward Tony. "What about this? This isn't a contract. It doesn't say anything about a job."

"That's a courtesy invitation." He didn't even glance up at the heavy cream cardstock, engraved in sensual, bold-faced script, which had enticed her into this whole mess. He rifled through his file folder. "Similar to the ones sent to the registered guests you'll be responsible for teaching at Valentine Studios' actor fantasy camp."

Teaching? "Actor fantasy camp?"

"Yes. Didn't your people brief you?"

Mutely, she shook her head.

"Figures." He made a face, his impatience with her supposed entourage plain. "The short version is, actor fantasy camp is like a live-in studio tour. The idea originated with baseball fantasy camp. Only ours is done Hollywood style."

Okay. Baseball fantasy camp she was familiar with. That, she understood. She'd spent much of her teenaged years watching televised MLB games with her dad while her mom ferried Marley to one audition after another. But the rest. . . .

Efficiently, Tony plucked a glossy tri-fold brochure from the file. He pressed it into Meredith's grasp. "The Valentine Studios' camp is debuting this weekend, featuring our inaugural celebrity attraction: Marley Madison. AKA, *you*."

Her? This just got worse and worse. Holding the brochure, Meredith blinked at her sister's glamorous likeness on the front cover. Set against a background of the usual images — the Hollywood sign, a director's chair, glittering stars, and a marker slate — the photograph showed Marley at her starlet best: decked out in designer duds, expertly colored blond hair, and artfully enhanced breasts.

"We have guests booked from all around the country," Tony continued. "Classes ranging from Diva Dramatics to Tabloid Tattling to Star Schmoozing 101 — ahhh, here it is."

He brandished a contract. Meredith snatched it. After scanning several pages of legalese, she recognized Marley's loopy signature on the final page.

Apparently, her sister had agreed to a two-week "actor fantasy camp" appearance — and then conveniently forgotten it, probably in the midst of planning her recent wedding. Meredith had unknowingly stepped smack into the middle of the whole mess.

She shoved the contract and brochure back. "I can't do it."

"Nerves? I expected that." Tony grabbed something else from his pile of things. He offered it to her. "Here. Breathe into this."

She stared. "A paper bag?"

"Best thing to cure hyperventilating."

"Trust me. I am *not* the type of woman who hyperventilates."

"You might be." Grinning, he gave her an exaggeratedly lascivious eyebrow waggle. "Given the right stimulus."

"Oh, puh-leeze." She was in enough trouble already.

"So distraction doesn't work for you, then. Fine. Try the bag."

"No." She thrust the brown lunch sack into his hands. "This is ridiculous."

"It's effective." Stuffing away the bag, Tony scrutinized her. "Would it ease your mind if I told you the real reporters and potential investors aren't arriving until later?"

He looked at her hopefully.

She hated to disappoint him, but . . . There would be reporters there? Yikes! Marley was going to kill her! Sure, they were twins. But where their lives were concerned, Meredith and Marley couldn't have been more different. She was not cut out to take her sister's place — not for an event like *this*.

"Reporters?" She swallowed hard.

"At least one. From *Inside Hollywood* magazine. He — or she — will be posing as a guest in order to write one of their 'Insider' profiles." Tony glanced out the window as something flashed overhead — the Valentine Studios gates. "Hell, I'm running this thing,

23

and even I don't know which journalist has been assigned. It's a gamble, all right."

He chuckled, apparently unconcerned. The big galoot.

Trying not to panic, Meredith analyzed the situation. She'd gotten into this. But there was still time to get out. Once Tony knew who she really was, he'd realize he had to change his actor fantasy camp plans.

"Tell the driver to circle the block." She slapped her hand over the limo's control panel, looking for the intercom button. "Driver! Go around the block, please."

Tony removed her finger from the button she'd chosen. He looked amused. "That's the cigarette lighter."

"Well, we can't go any farther." Meredith twisted. She rapped on the partition. It summarily slid down. "Driver, please stop the car."

"Harry, stop this car and you're fired."

The partition noiselessly rose again. The limo prowled through a shadowed pathway between two enormous soundstages, just as though she'd never spoken.

"Arrgh!"

Tony cupped her face in his hands. Kindly, he studied her. His air of calm reached out to her. It nearly succeeded in lulling Meredith into forgetting the snafu she'd gotten into.

"Relax," he said. "I know you're nervous.

Once you make your entrance, you'll feel fine. All actors are that way."

She nearly sighed. He really was being sweet — for an unreasonable, misguided, know-it-all actor fantasy camp executive.

She'd liked him better as a fantasy escort.

Still, too beguiled to resist, Meredith curled her fingers around his. Their warmth mingled reassuringly.

She had to play it straight with him. "Listen, Tony. I'm not who you think I am. I'm —"

"Your red carpet awaits," he interrupted, preoccupied with something outside the window. The limo stopped. He twined their hands together, his grasp steady and encouraging, then gave her a squeeze. "Ready or not, here you go."

An instant later, their uniformed driver whisked open the door. The screams of — were they fans? — hurtled toward Meredith, followed closely by a brilliant flare of flashbulbs. Blinded by them, she clung to Tony as he hustled her out of the car.

In a moment, they stood together on the red carpet. A hush fell over the spectators.

It lasted only a second or two. By the time Meredith regained her wits, the uproar had begun again.

"You've got the wrong woman," she said to Tony through clenched teeth, desperate to make him see reason. "I'm an academic, not an actress!"

He cupped his ear. He shook his head, indicating he couldn't hear her in the din. Then, with a cheery smile, Tony held up their joined hands in greeting.

The crowd loved it. The shouts grew louder. The flashes increased.

This was insane. Squinting, Meredith could just make out the scene. Reporters and paparazzi lined the area behind the velvet ropes, which separated the rest of the Valentine Studios back lot from the red carpet. Along the length of that red carpet more people waited in the post-sunset afterglow, screaming crazily as they waved eight-by-ten glossies of Marley. Fans, Meredith assumed in a daze. There were reporters *and* fans there.

She had to get out of this. Now, before it was too late.

"Marley! Marley! Over here!" someone yelled.

"Say it, Marley! Give us your catchphrase from 'Fantasy Family'!"

"Marley! Can I have your autograph?"

It was all too much. Tugging her baseball cap lower with her free hand, Meredith tightened her grasp on Tony. He offered her another reassuring squeeze, but didn't look her way. Frustrated, she yanked as hard as she could.

That did it. Quizzically, he faced her. "Hey, what the —"

She cupped her hands around her mouth. "I've got to talk to you!"

He probably still couldn't hear her. But whatever he saw on her face convinced him she meant what she was saying — and it was important. Tony took one look and blessedly hustled her into motion.

Sheltered against his chest, held there by his burly arm as they maneuvered the rest of the way down the red carpet, Meredith felt protected. Safe. Indulged. But when they reached Tony's private office and he shut the door behind them . . . Well, clearly the jig was up.

"Okay." Looking aggravated, he shoved a hand through his hair, then turned to face her in the sudden silence. "Exactly what the hell is going on?"

TWO

"Through the turnstile . . . to a land of adventure!"

— advertisement for
Piggly Wiggly stores (1929)

"I'm not Marley Madison," Marley said.

Tony stared. He had to be hearing things. Sure, Marley wasn't anything like he'd expected a celebrated actress to be. She was wearing a Dodgers cap, for Chrissakes. And flip-flops. And in real life, her bombshell figure looked loads less bodacious than it did on the small screen. But her famous features were instantly recognizable: full lips, pert chin, big brown eyes . . . airheaded attitude.

"I'm not Marley," she repeated.

She sounded reasonable. Looked assured — if a little rattled by the red carpet arrival they'd just been through. But Marley Madison was an actress, he reminded himself. She possessed that unique blend of charm and charisma that made idiots like him forget the job at hand the minute she slid into their limo. Marley could probably make anything seem believable. Even the ridiculous claim she'd just made.

28

He decided to play along. "You're not."

"No."

"You look like her."

"I know."

"Sound like her."

"I guess so."

"Act like her."

"Hey!" Her gaze narrowed. "I don't act *anything* like Marley."

Okay. Screw playing along. Hardball was more his style, anyway.

Tony had hoped getting tough with her wouldn't be necessary. He wasn't the kind of guy who bullied the people who worked for him. But he *was* the kind of guy who got results. His legendary business acumen had proved that. He needed results now. A lot depended on it.

"You don't act like Marley?" Patiently, he tallied what he knew of her so far. "Flaky? Check. Irresponsible? Check. Trying to avoid serious work from the minute you arrive? Check, check, check." He shook his head. "I've been warned about you."

She folded her arms. "Those warnings were justified, believe me. But they weren't about me."

He *hmmph*ed in disbelief. What was she going to tell him next, that she was in character already as a ditzy star actress? That not *acting* her part twenty-four-seven would wreck her concentration? That she was a

29

Method actor who delved deeply into whatever role she played?

Tony was familiar with the immersion-acting technique. Growing up in one of Hollywood's oldest and most established families, he'd encountered it more than once. But even the most devout of those Stanislavski disciples dropped out of character when serious business was on the table.

"Look, none of this is necessary," he said, remembering that her inept entourage hadn't clued her in to the details of her appearance at Valentine Studios. "We hired you to be *you*. To play *yourself*. Didn't you see all those fans outside? The paparazzi were hired," he explained, "but the fans —"

"Hired? You *hired* paparazzi?" She shook her head pityingly. "You must not be from around here. Most people try to avoid those guys."

"Fake paparazzi." He leaned on the edge of his desk, ignoring her jab about his supposed lack of Hollywood acumen. "Controllable, *reasonable* paparazzi. They'll give our fantasy camp guests the deluxe 'star entrance' treatment when they arrive tomorrow. Red carpet, paparazzi. It's all part of the experience."

"You can't be serious."

He stared her down.

She rolled her eyes. "Okay. Then those 'journalists' " — Marley made quotation marks with her fingers — "won't be filing reports with the tabloids, or magazines, or entertainment news broadcasts?"

"They're strictly for show."

Exhaling, she slumped onto one of his office's low-slung chairs. She closed her eyes, shaking her head. A sigh rippled through her.

Tony almost would have sworn he saw relief in her face. Experience had taught him to interpret differently.

"Rein in your disappointment, princess. This is a job, not a PR opportunity." He scrutinized her. "That panicky thing you had going on back there looked pretty convincing. Dramatic, I'll give you that. But you can drop the act with me."

Marley tilted her head against the chair. Wearing an inscrutable expression, she leveled her gaze on him. "I liked you better in the limo."

In a flash, he remembered *her* in the limo. Remembered the way the soft leather seat had dipped beneath her weight, urging them both closer. The way she'd looked at him, boldly stating her interest in *touching*. The way her hand had felt on his knee, all warm and feminine and certain. He'd liked it.

He'd liked *her*. Back when he'd thought she was up-front and refreshingly assertive. Back when he'd considered kissing her as an alternative to getting-to-know-you small talk. Back when he'd thought she might be different. He'd liked her and he'd wanted her.

31

But the hard truth was, he had a job to do. One that *didn't* involve getting hot and heavy with his star attraction.

He cleared his throat. Back to business. "Those people outside were here to see Marley Madison, not whatever role you've cooked up. So you can drop your Method training —"

"I don't know the Method."

She uttered the denial as though he were a nitwit to even suggest as much. She tugged defensively at the brim of her Dodgers cap.

Okay. So she didn't want to admit her training. Why should he be surprised? Hollywood was filled with people who wanted to seem like someone they weren't — a natural, unstudied actress, for instance. That superficiality was one reason he'd left when he had . . . and had stayed away, until now.

"And this isn't a role! I told you, I'm not Marley."

Humor her, he told himself. *You need her.*

"Who are you, then?"

She bit her lip. "I'd rather not say."

"Jesus Christ!"

Earnestly, she held his gaze. "If word gets out about this, I'll never live it down."

Great. So that's what she thought of his actor fantasy camp? It embarrassed her? Stung, Tony frowned.

"From what I hear, we didn't exactly have to twist your arm to get you to agree to this."

"What do you mean?"

Folding his arms, Tony examined her. Industry scuttlebutt held that Marley Madison was washed up. Typecast, out of work, and out of demand at the ripe old age of twenty-seven. Which explained why her management team had been so willing to sign her up with Valentine Studios — and probably why they'd soft-pedaled the details of her appearance, too. Probably her entourage had been trying to protect her. They relied on her for their salaries, after all.

He, however, had no such compunction about laying it on the line with her.

At least he shouldn't have.

"Because actor fantasy camp is an innovative idea," he said gruffly.

More apparent relief on her face. "Yours?"

He nodded. "My usual specialty is launching dot-coms."

"Hmmm. I might have to revise my super-stud-escort opinion of you." Her grin teased him. "You might actually have brains to go with all that brawn."

Brawn? He resisted an idiotic urge to flex.

No. This was getting out of hand. *She* was getting out of hand. Again. Tony couldn't allow flattery to soften him. To show it, he scowled elaborately at the wall clock.

When Marley noticed, she got up and crossed to his desk. Her flip-flops slapped against the soles of her feet. Her hip-tied sweatshirt bounced against her thighs. Between her non-starlet wardrobe and the schlumpy way she walked, he almost believed her performance. One look at her face told him the truth.

She was Marley Madison, all right. Despite her denials.

As though sensing his skepticism, Marley amped up her performance.

"I know this must seem confusing to you. All I was looking for was a little adventure," she said wistfully. "I'll admit, it's gotten out of hand. Believe me, I had no idea what I was getting into."

"You mean . . . real work?"

She narrowed her eyes.

He shrugged. "Those of us who aren't stars have to take life the hard way. Dead-on. With no favors, no favorites, and no special privileges."

Her lips tightened. Probably she was envisioning life on set without a team of flunkeys to buff her toenails and peel her grapes. Poor baby.

"Don't worry," Tony said, reassuring her for reasons he didn't quite understand. "Your star trailer is the deluxe fifty-footer. You won't be roughing it too much while you're here."

She wasn't mollified. In fact, she looked fit to pound him with the *I love NY* paperweight on his desk. What had he said?

"You have no *idea* what my life is like!"

"Oh, I think I do." He remembered the warnings he'd received about Marley's notoriously flaky behavior. Her spoiled-starlet shtick. Her tendency to wrap well-meaning directors right around her manicured finger. He wasn't falling for this little-lost-actress routine. "Meeting you has confirmed everything I ever suspected."

"The joke's on you, then. Because —"

He held up his hand. "Don't bother saying it again. Any idiot can see you're Marley Madison."

At that, she seemed amused. A definite know-it-all gleam came into her eyes. She paused, looking him up and down.

She quirked her brow. "Apparently not."

He had the uncomfortable sensation the joke really *was* on him. Tony refused to allow it. "Look, I'm not some kind of La-La Land pushover. I flew in from the East Coast a week ago, and I'm flying out again two weeks from now. I don't have time for actressy bullshit. If you don't feel like working, that's too bad. I don't have time to waste."

Her mouth dropped open. Good. He was getting through to her.

"I won't stand for the kind of stunts you've pulled on other people's projects," he warned. "Impossible demands. Temper tantrums. Meltdowns. Whatever your problem is" — What could it possibly be? A pantyhose crisis? — "just pack it into your leopard-print bag and keep it there."

Marley's gaze snapped to the overnight case Harry had delivered from the limo to Tony's office. At the sight of it, a certain stubbornness sharpened her expression. She opened her mouth to speak.

He interrupted. "You have a job to do. Period. I'm here to make sure you do it."

"Gee, how do you find the time?" Marley pretended to study the plain-banded Timex on her wrist. She widened her eyes with sham innocence. "You seem so busy jumping to conclusions."

He gave her a grin. "Purely preventive measures, princess."

Ready to move onward, he strode across his office's aged linoleum. He passed the ever-present framed posters of Valentine Studios' bygone triumphs without looking at them. Then he snatched up her bag and plunked it into her arms.

"You might as well know this going in. For me, actions speak louder than words. So save your breath. Excuses won't work. Cajoling won't work. *Work* will work."

"All business, hmmm?"

"You bet."

Unlike the rest of his starry-eyed family, Tony had spent his whole life focused on business success. He'd achieved it, too. He'd temporarily left his various e-commerce ventures in the capable hands of his second-in-command, Jim Woodwiss, in order to come here. Now, charged with the unwanted task of resuscitating the family's faltering studio, Tony intended to succeed again.

To do that, though, he needed Marley Madison. Needed the cachet she'd lend to his actor fantasy camp, the draw she'd prove to tourists . . . the expertise she'd share, however grudgingly, in the classes she'd teach. Valentine Studios had promoted her appearance extensively, with tourism agencies and investment partners alike. She was the lynchpin his whole revitalization scheme depended on.

Marley gave him a once-over. "All business . . . except when it comes to limo rides."

He frowned. She would have to remind him of that. The woman was a complete pain in the ass.

"What happened in the limo was a mistake," Tony said. "It won't be repeated."

"Says who?" Her expression turned flirtatious. "I've just been gypped out of the 'fantasy of a lifetime,' remember?"

Tony remembered. She was referring to her courtesy invitation's racy-sounding promise — "the fantasy of a lifetime." Since it would be strictly business between them from here on out, though, he didn't need to know where she was going with this. He wasn't going to ask.

He wasn't.

Fifteen seconds ticked past. She appeared to be waiting him out. He added *patient* and *clairvoyant* to her other irksome qualities.

"So?" Tony growled.

She smiled. Triumphantly. "So, how about making it up to me? Maybe this night can still be salvaged. I'll pretend I'm Marley; you'll pretend you're Prince Charming . . . We'll see what happens from there." She ran her hand down his chest, lightly fanning her fingers over the muscles there. "The night's still young. What do you say?"

At her touch, his whole body tensed. Pleasurably. For a nanosecond, Tony actually considered taking her up on her offer — kooky as it was. That's when he knew dealing with Marley Madison would demand even more determination than he'd planned.

For better or worse, determination was one thing Tony had never lacked. Exercising it now, he moved her hand. Squeezed her fingers. Released her. "Let's not complicate things."

Her mouth turned downward. She resituated the overnight case in her arms with a clear air of resignation. "Fine. I can take a hint. Just point me to the nearest exit and I'll catch a bus home."

He blinked. Damn, but she was a good actress. For a minute there, he'd actually believed she meant it. A bus. For a va-va-voom former sitcom starlet. What a knee-slapper.

"You're not going anywhere. Your contract says —"

"That again?"

He fought for patience. It had been said that Tony Valentine had a golden touch with business, with pleasure, even with women. But star wrangling? He wasn't sure he was cut out for this kind of candy-ass ego stroking.

"Leaving the studio now would violate the terms of your contract," he explained. "I think we'd both rather avoid litigation over all this."

The reality of her situation swept over Marley's face. He could tell the moment she realized her get-out-of-work-free scheme wasn't going to work. She tugged her Dodgers cap again.

All the same, she made one last stab at rebellion.

"You wouldn't dare sue. Over a has-been studio?"

Tony winced inwardly at her words. *Has-been studio.* That's what Valentine Studios was. She'd nailed it. But it was *his* has-been studio. His and his family's — for several generations now. He'd promised to try to save it, and he'd damned well do it.

"Don't make me laugh," Marley goaded.

He looked at her. She waited for his reply, clutching her ridiculous leopard-print bag against her middle, clearly trying to show that his threat hadn't scared her. Her chin jutted upward at a defiant angle. Her gaze dared him to disagree.

Her trembling lips betrayed her worries.

Unreasonably, her bravado touched him. Tony looked away.

"There's a welcome party for the cast and crew at eight. Across the lot, in Bayberry." Bayberry was Valentine Studios' "small town Americana" set, straight out of its earliest silent films. The location had seemed a fitting place to begin the studio's revamped future. "Be there. On time."

He turned to leave, intending to find Harry to show her to her trailer. Marley's voice stopped him.

"Or what?"

Tony paused. Against all reason, a smile burbled up from inside him. She gave as good as she got, that was for sure. He couldn't remember the last time anyone had dared to needle him on purpose.

"Be there or what?" she repeated.

He sobered his expression. Turned. "Or I'll hunt you down," he said, taking a few steps nearer to her. She didn't so much as flinch. "Take you to the party myself. And subject you to the worst dance moves known to mankind."

Her eyes sparkled. "Awww. Your moves can't be that bad."

This time, his smile broke through. He

couldn't prevent it. "Wear combat boots," Tony advised, then went to locate Harry.

Left alone in Tony's office, Meredith hugged the gaudy bag she'd borrowed from Marley. *Wear combat boots.* Tony might not want to admit it, but the guy had a sense of humor — along with a truly wicked smile. Something about that smile made her usual clear-headedness hike up its sensible skirts and run away. In its place arrived a silly sense of audacity and a huge amount of sheer stupidity. How else to explain that she hadn't revealed her true self to him?

Okay, so for starters there was the fact that it was embarrassing to have been caught in her Cinderella fantasy. Then there was the fact that if Marley found out Meredith had commandeered that invitation — and her identity — there'd be hell to pay. Finally, there was the fact that she still didn't have all the information she needed to know exactly what was going on here. Meredith never made decisions without having all the pertinent details close at hand.

Sure. Those were perfectly valid reasons for her behavior this evening.

Nodding reassuringly to herself, she strode across the office. She trailed her hands over the furnishings, recognizing them as midcentury modern by their austere lines and square shapes. She bounced restlessly on the severely

41

upholstered taupe sofa. She studied the sculptural hanging lamps with their L.A.-casual pastel shades. She peered at the desk, with its two laptop computers, PDA in a sync cradle, videophone, and other geeky, high-tech devices she couldn't identify.

Except for the gadgetry, the whole place felt as though it had been untouched for decades. Meredith might have stepped back into one of the museum archives' advertisements — say, Spic 'N Span, circa 1955 — and found herself here. It was spooky, really.

All right. So who did she think she was fooling? Not herself, certainly. She'd tried to speak up, but the whole experience of finding herself on the red carpet in her sister's place had seriously shaken her composure.

She didn't think she'd imagined that shocked three seconds of silence when she'd appeared, looking (as usual) utterly unMarley-like. Those three seconds had hurt. During that hushed moment, she'd felt twelve years old again. Gawky. Tomboyish. Left out. She'd been just that age when she'd begun to realize that while her teen-dream sister was becoming a star . . . Meredith never would be. Even in her own family.

But then the red carpet roar had begun again, and Meredith had realized another truth. The public was completely willing to overlook their own perceptions. Despite all evidence to the contrary. Like Tony, the fans and photographers lining the red carpet had seen exactly what they'd *wanted* to see. Ergo, Marley Madison. Nothing Meredith had done had changed that.

It was interesting, she reflected, how easily reality bent in the face of combined wanting.

She should have been grateful. After all, thanks to the mass wish-upon-a-star effect, her spur-of-the-moment adventure hadn't been uncovered yet. But instead, she felt a little disappointed. Tony, at least, should have been smart enough to detect the real her. His insistence on treating her like the bubble-headed actress he thought she was had been particularly galling. Couldn't he see she was nothing like Marley?

Apparently not, the wicked angel on her shoulder replied. *Maybe you can still pull this off.*

Predictably, the rest of her rebelled. The whole idea was nuts. Not to mention risky. Stepping into her sister's glammed-up Hollywood life for the weekend had brought her nothing but trouble so far.

Sure, that devilish angel rebutted. *But going in, you were unprepared. Now you know the score.*

Hmmm. That did change things, Meredith mused. It might be interesting — from a purely intellectual standpoint, of course — to find out exactly how far she could take this ruse. Long enough to steal that kiss from

Tony Valentine? Long enough to see for herself exactly how the other half lived? Long enough to scarf some free munchies at the welcome party Tony had mentioned?

In the end, the possibility of scoring cocktail weenies and maybe a Budweiser settled it. She was *starving*. She'd go on with this charade — just for the night — Meredith decided. She could always sneak out at midnight, Cinderella-style, and go back to her ordinary, books-and-Birkenstocks life. No one would ever need to know.

Besides, from where she'd sat over the past twenty-seven years, being a beloved starlet sure *looked* easy. How difficult could it possibly be?

THREE

"Novelty is always welcome, but talking pictures are just a fad."
— Irving Thalberg

Built in 1921 for a silent feature, Bayberry was at first a ramshackle collection of tall false fronts and narrow, dusty streets. Through the years — thanks to upstart Valentine Studios' rising importance in Hollywood — the outdoor set had blossomed into a gingerbread-trimmed, Technicolor vision of small-town life.

Before long, Bayberry boasted a cobbled Main Street, a general store, a Gay Nineties saloon, several oak trees (potted and wheeled for easy transport), and a grassy central park featuring a white-painted gazebo. To step onto the set was to step into an idealized past. Tonight, Bayberry would host the studio's future, too.

In Tony's earliest memories, Bayberry was simply the most awesome place he knew to play hide-and-seek. The buildings here had all been boarded up when he was a kid, casualties of the post-*Star Wars*, post-*ET* boom in filmmaking. As a consequence, he'd been set free to roam among them, just so long as he stayed out of the way of whatever production had been going on at the studio's more urban and futuristic sets.

After school and on weekends, he and his friends had explored every inch of the faux-finished buildings, cobwebbed interiors, and weed-choked raised boardwalk. He'd been an original latchkey kid — except his backyard had been the studio back lot. Back then, he'd never have dreamed he'd want to leave it all behind.

Or that he actually would.

Tonight, though, the buildings in Bayberry stood tall against the deepening night. The tang of recent paint jobs and thorough window scrubbings hung on the summery Burbank breeze. Inside each building, different catered specialties awaited. Cocktails in the dance hall. Hors d'oeuvres at the soda fountain. Sushi in the barbershop and decadent desserts along the check-in desk at the hotel. In each locale, uniformed catering staff bustled to and fro amid the party's guests, ready to meet any request.

Outside, strings of glowing white lights brightened the path from the town itself to the gazebo, where a quintet played jazz instrumentals. More lights wound their way through the repositioned oak trees, illuminating the cobbled "dance floor" at the edge of the grass.

Already, Tony saw, invited guests dipped

and swayed to the music. Others held drinks. A few more curled into the red velvet prop-house settees placed in groupings amid the trees. The murmured sounds of his guests' conversations reached out to him as he passed, punctuated with the laughter of people for whom this was just another party. Just another night.

For him, it was a beginning. A test. A penance, all rolled into one.

His mind on the evening to come, he strode past a cluster of development execs. The pungent smoke from their Cuban cigars trailed him across the town square, where a group of grips, gaffers, and best boys hung out. Tony held up a hand in greeting, then continued on.

Where the hell was she?

All around him, partygoers circulated. Crew members mingled with cast members; fake paparazzi chatted with real experts. He'd hired several of them — a director, a cos-tumer, hair and makeup artists, a screen-writer, stunt people, media and voice coaches, and more — all chosen to teach the classes that would turn tourists' dreams of TV stardom into reality within two weeks. Complete with a live studio audience at the finale and a souvenir videotape to take home with them.

He never should have entrusted Harry with picking up Marley Madison at her trailer. Their star attraction, having failed to get the re-prieve she wanted from Tony, might have whacked Harry on the head, hijacked the golf cart he used to travel across the back lot, and made a getaway. Straight to Rodeo Drive or a club on Sunset, or wherever empty-headed starlet types like her flocked together. Which would explain why there was no sign of her here.

Hell.

No. Even more likely, Marley had simply bamboozled poor Harry. She'd charmed him, disarmed him, and made him happy to grant her every wish. Kind of like Tony had wanted to, back in the limo. Then she'd nabbed his golf cart and driven it to the nearest bus stop — just to prove Tony wrong about her.

The woman was full of surprises. She might already be halfway back to her chichi mansion in the Hollywood Hills, still insisting to whoever would listen that she wasn't who she obviously was.

Irritably, he scanned the crowd. Already, several people had asked him when they could meet their star attraction. Marley's sitcom, "Fantasy Family," had been a top-ten Nielsen hit for years. She, as its most popular performer, had spawned an entire industry. Fan clubs, TV specials, two haircuts, several clothing fads, calendars, pinup posters . . . The mania had gone on and on, culminating in at least one Emmy, a People's Choice award, and God only knew what else.

Tony didn't keep up with industry news anymore. But he hadn't agreed to save Valentine Studios without doing his homework first. The media coverage of Marley and her Southern belle alter ego, Tara, had been both breathless and ridiculously extensive. It seemed the public hadn't been able to get enough of either one of them. They hadn't been willing to let Marley move on, either. Since the demise of "Fantasy Family," she'd made one disastrous feature film, and then . . . nothing.

Tony's actor fantasy camp could be a second chance for them both, he knew. He could offer Marley the additional exposure she needed. She could provide him with the star power to get his attraction off the ground. *If* she showed up.

"She's not coming," said a familiar voice.

Tony glanced over his shoulder. His sixty-two-year-old uncle, Roland Valentine, squinted back in his typically crotchety way. That scowl of his had stricken terror into the hearts of Hollywood insiders for almost four decades.

"She's not coming," he repeated. "I tried to warn you. But would you listen? Hell, no." He slurped up some of his whiskey sour, then tapped out a cigarette from the pack in his suit pocket. "Actresses are flighty by nature. You've got to keep an eye on them."

"She'll be here."

"Ha." Roland gave a rheumy cough. "Women are like reel-to-reel projectors. Touchy, expensive, and harder than hell to get started on time. If I had a nickel for every woman I've cooled my heels waiting for —"

"You'd have an enormous deficit by now," Errol Valentine said, breaking into his brother's conversation with a gleam in his eye and an urbane half smile on his face. He nodded hello to Tony. "You've never waited for anything in your life, Roland."

Roland chuckled. "A hot tamale being the only exception."

"Nonsense. Spicy food gives you dys-pepsia."

"Who's talking about food?"

Errol released a despairing sigh. "It's fortu-nate you lend some class to this operation, Tony. Between the two of us, we might be able to drag Valentine Studios into respect-ability."

"Sure, kicking and screaming, maybe," Roland grumbled. "I'm telling you, there's lots of money to be made in B movies. It's all about quantity, baby." He rubbed his fin-gers together, pretending to handle oodles of cash.

"I'm afraid you're mistaken," Errol dis-agreed. "*Quality* will be our saving grace. A few films and television shows, selectively chosen, will restore our reputation and revitalize the studio. Look how far Bob and Harvey Weinstein have taken Miramax."

"Pornos rake in big bucks," Roland mused. He dragged speculatively on his cigarette. "They're quick to make, too."

"*Pornography?* Good Lord, Roland. Why not just turn the place into a brothel and have done with it?"

"Hey. That's not a bad idea . . ."

Errol turned purple. Ordinarily the epitome of sophistication, the sixty-four-year-old studio executive looked ready to grab the nearest prop lamppost (wheeled, like the oak trees) and wallop his brother with it. The Valentine family squabbles were legendary in Hollywood. Roland and Errol were a big part of the reason why.

Tony stepped in before his uncles came to blows. "We're not doing pornos *or* quality TV. We're running an actor fantasy camp. Remember?"

"Certainly. Of course." Errol patted Tony's shoulder, delivering a final censorious look at his brother. "We're all counting on you, Tony. You know that. If you can work half the magic here that you did on the East Coast . . . well. Let's just say, retirement wouldn't be wholly unwelcome to me."

"God bless the tourists," Roland agreed. He stuck out his tongue at his brother.

"Long may they buy into this bullshit." He raised his whiskey sour in salute.

Automatically, Tony followed the gesture. The sweep of his uncle's arm encompassed all of Bayberry, with its twinkling lights, mellow jazz, sociable guests, and postcard-perfect buildings. The sight reassured him. Everything here was under control. Everything was proceeding exactly as he'd planned.

Everything . . . except Marley Madison. Because just then Tony glimpsed her across the town square, encircled by admirers.

On the plus side, at least she was here. On the minus side, she didn't exactly look ready to dazzle her public. Dressed in a bizarre combination of bikini top, cargo pants, and black suit jacket, she hefted a long-neck beer in one hand and gestured wildly with the other.

As though she'd said something hilarious, everyone in her circle laughed. Looking relieved, Marley lifted her face to the stars and laughed, too. He realized then that her hair — formerly covered by her Dodgers cap — was not the famously golden color he'd seen captured in a million photographs. Instead, her lackluster style was a muddy brown.

That was weird. Tony squinted. A crease dented her tresses at forehead level. Hat head. His glamorous star attraction was sporting hat head, wearing a pile of thrift store rejects, and chugging brewskis like there was no tomorrow.

At this rate, there really *would* be no to-morrow. Not for him, and not for Valentine Studios.

"My word," Errol said. "That's not her, is it?"

"She guffaws like a donkey," Roland observed, not wholly unapprovingly. "Reminds me of my third wife, Fifi. Uninhibited as hell. When you got that woman into the sack — look out! There was no stopping her."

He sighed, obviously lost in fond remembrances.

"Honestly, Roland." Dismay tinged Errol's voice. "Have a little dignity."

"I've got a *big* 'dignity.' That's what kept Fifi happy for so long. Heh-heh."

"*I'd* be happy if you'd keep those little details to yourself."

"Hey, it's not little. That's the whole point. Whoa!"

"You are like a child. Do you realize that?"

Tony frowned, ignoring his uncles' renewed bickering. He had bigger problems. Starting with one uncooperative starlet . . . and ending with making sure that starlet delivered exactly the performance he'd hired her for.

"Excuse me," he said, focusing his attention on Marley. "I have business to attend to."

"That's our Tony." Roland raised a second toast. "Born to take charge."

Tony didn't reply. The only things left to

take charge of were mounting debts, the Valentines' crumbling studio, and the small amount of hope his entrepreneurial experience offered all of them. He felt the weight of his family's expectations keenly.

Roland and Errol had all but raised him. Given his own parents' penchant for traveling to "scout locations" in the Bahamas at a moment's notice, Tony had been left in his uncles' care often, and for long stretches of time.

When he'd reached adulthood, Roland and Errol had stuck by him. They'd financed several of Tony's dot-com startups, giving him the running start he needed to succeed. No matter how he looked at it, Tony knew he owed his uncles too much to let them down now.

He headed toward Marley.

Errol's hand on his shoulder stopped him. "Be easy on her," his uncle advised, his gaze direct. "You're not in New York City anymore."

What the hell did that mean? He could tell by Errol's expression that it wasn't good.

Whatever. He couldn't think about that now.

"Enjoy the party." Tony shrugged off his uncle's restraining hand, then went to deal with Marley.

So far, so good, Meredith thought. This

starlet stuff was a piece of cake.

Already she'd enjoyed one exhilarating golf cart ride through the studio's back lot, shrieking in excitement as Harry careened around the corners of the soundstages. If only he'd agreed to let her drive, as she'd asked. She was sure she could have popped a wheelie over the stunt ramp they passed.

Then when they'd arrived, she'd been wowed by the sight of Bayberry itself. Festooned with miniature lights, perfumed by the scents of food and drink, enlivened by jazz music, it was (to risk a cliché) like something straight out of a movie.

Unfortunately, that movie happened to be *Adventures of a Glamorous Starlet*. Meredith definitely didn't belong in it.

She'd hung at the edges of the party at first, stomach knotted with the certainty that all these people would see right through her. But then Harry had given her a wink and a kind-hearted nudge. Her usual rebelliousness had returned. She'd lunged right into the thick of things. So what if someone discovered she wasn't Marley? What were they going to do? Fire her?

Actually, Meredith thought as she took a long pull on her Budweiser, they just might. She wouldn't put it past Tony Valentine. She couldn't be responsible for getting her sister axed from a job. For now, Meredith would just have to play along.

Besides, enjoying a deluxe welcome party wasn't exactly arduous. She hadn't had this much fun since the opening of the museum's "Trend-Setting Liquor Ads" exhibit. She and her coworkers had gotten pretty wild. Someone had even set up a life-size promo cutout of Johnnie Walker that *didn't* belong to the period on display.

Nobody partied like historians.

A uniformed waiter glided past. Meredith seized the opportunity to first tuck her beer between her elbow and ribs, then pluck a second longneck from his tray. Still nodding at the conversation swirling around her, she took another bite of the tomato-topped bruschetta in her opposite hand. Yum. The tomatoes were a little sloppy, but the basil added just the right flavor. Eagerly, she popped the rest of her snack into her mouth.

"Enjoying yourself?" someone asked from behind her.

She recognized that voice. Rapidly, she chewed and swallowed. "Hmmm. Disapproving tone, complete lack of festive attitude . . . let me guess. Tony?"

"Very funny."

"It *is* you!" Absurdly glad he'd sought her out, she couldn't suppress a smile. She turned. "What, did you forget to give me a time card to —"

His appearance snatched the words right from her lips.

Wow, was all she could think. Tony in casual clothes had been remarkable. Sure. But Tony in a sleek suit and open-collar white shirt was devastating. Machismo on a stick.

Meredith took one look and wanted to lick him all over. Up his torso. Over his chest. Along his neck and across his mouth. She wanted —

She wanted *not* to look like an idiot. She swallowed hard. "— punch?"

"Time card? Something like that."

Reluctantly, she lifted her gaze from the warm golden skin at his throat, displayed to advantage by the unfastened top two buttons of his shirt. *Hubba-hubba,* as they said in the old days. Was he gorgeous. He'd obviously showered and shaved for the welcome party. His jaw looked rugged and smooth . . . and severe. Almost as though he were angry about something.

"You don't look like you're having very much fun at this party," Meredith said. "Here, take my spare Bud."

She pushed her just-procured longneck into his hand.

"You could probably use something to eat, too. I always feel a little woozy if I don't get a snack. I couldn't find any cocktail weenies, but those toast things are pretty good."

She nodded toward a waiter's tray of bruschetta, not trusting herself to pronounce the Italian word. Unlike all the elegant people here, Meredith liked to keep things simple.

Also unlike them, she tended to babble when nervous.

"Have you met everyone? I could introduce you." She inclined her head toward the group she'd been a part of until a few seconds ago. "I have to warn you, though. It's a very insular crowd. Everyone here is in showbiz."

She made a face. He opened his mouth — probably to defend his choice of guests, Meredith realized. At the same time, she remembered she was supposed to be "in showbiz," too. She rushed onward.

"But you probably already know everyone, don't you? In that case, maybe you should introduce me around. It would save me from crashing every crowd."

That had been mortifying. Even while masquerading as Marley she'd been invisible — no screaming fans here. Reluctant to dwell on the way she'd awkwardly infiltrated the cocktail-sipping groups, she hurried to add, "You're the host, after all. It's your job for the evening. It wouldn't be like you to blow off a job obligation."

"Introduce you?" He appeared to think about it. A grin kicked up the edge of his mouth. He shook his head. "Now that I've seen you, I'm tempted to keep you to myself."

Keep her to himself? Meredith wrinkled

her brow in confusion. Was that an insult? Was there something wrong with the way she looked?

Wearing a bemused expression, Tony lifted his gaze . . . from her middle, she realized. From the expanse of bared abdomen and meager cleavage revealed by the bikini top she'd worn to spice up her outfit.

He seemed discombobulated by the experience.

God. Did she look that bad? She fought an urge to wrap her jacket around herself. So long as her hips and thighs were covered, she usually felt comfortable. Getting dressed for tonight, she'd pretty much done an eeny-meeny-miney-mo number with the spare clothes she'd brought and hoped for the best. It hadn't even been until the last instant that she'd realized her Dodgers cap probably wasn't appropriate.

She took a fortifying swig of Bud, peeking at Tony from the corner of her eye. He was staring at her cleavage again.

The hell with it, she thought defiantly.

"It's a bikini top. Maybe you've seen one before?"

"Not like that, I haven't."

"It's the closest thing to evening wear I brought."

"I like it."

She snorted. "You don't have to sound so surprised."

His smile widened. "Did you just snort?"

Arrgh. Had she? How embarrassing. Hoping to finesse her way out of the situation, Meredith gazed at the milling partygoers. None of them, she noticed, were making impolite noises. What would Marley do right now?

Who was she kidding? Marley wouldn't be caught dead snorting. Or drinking beer. Or *belching* from the beer. Or sweating or shaking with nervousness, like Meredith was now . . . all of a sudden.

"At least I didn't fart," she blurted.

Tony laughed. He shook his head, giving her an assessing look. "You're not what I expected."

He meant she was failing. Failing to emulate Marley, failing to make herself stand out, failing to fit in. Meredith knew it.

She had to get away. She wanted to morph into Mr. Clean and whoosh into her Budweiser bottle in a puff of magic, like in the vintage TV commercials. Since the brawny earring-wearing genie was nowhere in sight, there seemed to be no choice but to brazen it out.

"Stick around," she said with an airy wave. "It gets better. Maybe later I'll show you how to burp the alphabet. Or your name. Or mine. Mine's more challenging." She swigged her Bud. "It's got a lot more letters."

As if from a distance, she heard herself actually offer to tutor him in Creative Belching. The jazz music whirled around them, conversations overlapped theirs, mingling people moved past. But Tony only went on watching her, still with that gobsmacked expression. Half fascinated, half shell-shocked, one hundred percent amused.

That look on Tony's face was familiar, Meredith realized. It was exactly the same look her parents had worn, the one and only time she'd borrowed a costume from Marley and performed for them. She'd only reached the second stanza of her opening soliloquy before they'd burst into gales of laughter.

Unfortunately, it hadn't been a humorous piece.

She couldn't stand it. She had to create a diversion.

The jazz quintet kicked into a new song. Perfect. She grabbed the nearest *non*-Tony male, a stunt man with a shaved head and bulging biceps. "Hey, Cody. Didn't you promise me this dance?"

"Uh, sure. I guess so."

He galumphed obligingly toward the outdoor dance floor with Meredith in tow. Offering an apologetic over-the-shoulder glance at Tony, she shrugged and let herself be pulled into Cody's arms. They whirled into motion.

Tony watched them for a moment, his face inscrutable. She saw him linger amid the

61

fancy-dressed guests, catching brief glimpses of his dark hair and strong features. She didn't need him anyway, Meredith told herself as Cody danced her over the cobblestones. Tony Valentine didn't want *her*. He wanted her sister. So long as that stood between them, they were doomed for sure.

A moment later, he was gone. Despite her rationalizations, Meredith felt a lump of disappointment settle into her belly.

Or maybe that was just the bruschetta. You never could tell with exotic food. She should have stuck with the cocktail weenies, like she'd planned, she assured herself. She might as well face it — she was a weenie girl, through and through. A fancy hors d'oeuvres guy like Tony just wasn't for her.

He'd found himself intrigued. Against his will and against all reason. He'd always liked a puzzle, and Marley Madison was a deluxe two-sided jigsaw with a thousand pieces. He couldn't make all her many sides snap together.

She was a famous starlet who chugged Budweiser, who paraded around with hat head, who hooted like a truck driver when amused. She attacked bruschetta with a complete lack of self-consciousness, yet stood with the round-shouldered posture of a woman who wanted to curl inside herself. She was outspoken, cute as hell, and sexy in an all-elbows, don't-worry-about-my-hairdo way. She also had a knack for barely wearing her clothes which was impossible to ignore.

Yeah. *That* again. Tony still didn't know exactly what had happened to him. He'd taken advantage of a lull in the knock-knock jokes to ask if she was enjoying the party, intending to give her hell for being unprepared. He'd been pissed, damn it. Then she'd turned to face him . . . and *wham*. Instant sizzle. He hadn't been able to process a single coherent thought.

Instead he'd stood there gawking, as though he'd never seen a woman wearing a bikini top before. As though he'd never seen a *woman* before. Which was ridiculous. He was thirty. He'd seen plenty of women — several of them up close and personal, and many of them wearing much less than Marley had on tonight.

But something about the way her body curved at the hips, nipped in at the waist, filled out a couple of skimpy fabric triangles . . . Something about *her* was exactly what he liked.

Uncomfortable now with the realization, he swigged more beer. Mixing business with pleasure was always a mistake. Given his past, Tony understood that maxim better than most. It didn't matter how he felt about Marley. The two of them were here to do a job. The sooner he finished that job — the sooner he set Valentine Studios on the path to a revamped future — the sooner he could escape from La-La Land and return to his real life in New York.

With that in mind, Tony scanned the crowd. Time to get on with it.

"I dunno, Mr. V., Marley's just not what we expected," one of the gaffers said. "She's, like, not the way she is on TV."

Beside him, a grip nodded. "I've had that swimsuit poster of hers on my wall since high school. I was psyched to meet her! But now . . . I guess the fantasy was better."

"She doesn't even have any good gossip," one of the wardrobe women added. "I asked her for the latest dish, and she pointed me toward the bruschetta."

More grumbling ensued.

Tony held up his hands. "Hang on a minute. Marley just got here. Give her a chance."

"We did, dude. But those knock-knock jokes? Lame."

"At least you didn't dance with her. I think my big toe is broken."

"Drinking Budweiser is *so* déclassé."

Tony rolled his eyes at the media coach who'd volunteered that last. "I drink Budweiser."

"Sure," she replied. "But you do it ironically. With a sense of the absurdity of it all."

He remembered another reason he'd left Hollywood. No one here was in touch with reality.

"Just give Marley a break." Tony folded his arms and delivered them all a no-nonsense look. "Her entourage didn't clue her in to the whole actor fantasy camp thing."

Derisive snorts were heard. He understood. He'd felt the same way, until Marley had stuck her hand on his knee. Until he'd leaned in to kiss her. Until she'd bewitched him with her smile and her voice and her bikini top.

Damn it. He had to stop that.

Searching for focus, he tipped his head to the sky. He followed a string of lights from his place amid an oak grove on wheels to the gazebo in the distance. He'd waylaid part of his staff here a few minutes ago, hoping to gather feedback.

"I'm sorry. Marley's flaky," one of the makeup gals said.

"She's nice enough, I guess. Just not glamorous."

"Not exciting," someone else agreed. "Not like I expected. It's disappointing."

"Yeah, I'm bummed. I was looking forward to meeting her."

"Yeah. Who's the next star attraction, Mr. V.? Maybe they'll be better."

Tony dragged in a deep breath. "There won't be a next star attraction. Not if Marley's appearance doesn't drum up enough satisfied customers and investor enthusiasm to get the ball rolling. This is it. Our one chance."

Everyone sobered. In the background, the jazz quintet kicked into a rousing song finale. Partygoers cheered and applauded. Here, away from the crowd, the mood felt more subdued.

Some of these staffers had worked for Valentine Studios, in some capacity or other, for years. Others were hoping the actor fantasy camp would give them steadier work than vagabonding from production to production, set to set, location to location. Below-the-line types with families to support valued consistency. Creative types longed for freedom. With this latest innovation of his, Tony planned to provide both.

If it worked, it would be perfect. But at this point, perfection depended on a certain starlet he'd last seen curled up in a corner chair with her high heels in her lap and another beer in hand, singing (badly) to the music. If his paying guests were as disappointed in Marley's performance as his staff and invited experts were . . . Well, he couldn't let that happen. Period.

One of the prop guys spoke up. "After tonight, I don't see what made Marley a star. She seems pretty ordinary to me. At least in person."

"True," the voice coach agreed sadly. "Maybe there's more magic in Tinseltown than we, as insiders, give credit for."

Everyone nodded. Tony's spirits sank.

"Keep an open mind," he said. "That's an order."

Then, setting his jaw, he went to find Marley.

Away from the glow of the lights, Meredith stood frozen with her hand on her beer. She'd lost track of exactly how many she'd had. Feeling a little lightheaded, she'd snuck away to this more-isolated section of Bayberry, hoping to find Harry. Another golf cart trip back to her trailer had sounded pretty good.

What she'd overheard had not.

The fantasy was better.

Just not glamorous.

Not like I expected . . . disappointing.

She wished she'd never heard any of it. Until now, she'd thought she'd been doing pretty good. Obviously, she hadn't been. Humiliated, Meredith slumped against a tree. It wobbled against her back, nearly toppling her over. Through teary eyes she peered at it, then saw the wheeled container it had been planted in. Like her, the stupid tree was out of its element. Stuck where it didn't belong.

She gave it a kick.

Barefoot.

Ouch. She'd forgotten she'd taken off her uncomfortable stilettos, the ones she'd found in her star trailer's closet. On a whim she'd put them on, hoping they'd give her a little extra dazzle — like Cinderella's glass slippers.

They'd probably give her bunions.

Well, she didn't need this. She'd been looking for a weekend adventure, not a personal critique. Not a focus group pointing out all her flaws. If there was one advantage an advertising expert like her had over poor old Cindy, it was that Meredith could recognize false promises when she saw them.

The fantasy of a lifetime. Ha!

Reluctantly returning her skyscraper shoes to her feet, she set off across Bayberry toward the party. She'd find Harry or hijack his golf cart herself. Then she'd drive back to her trailer and pick up her things. Sure, the back lot was big, but she had a good sense of direction. No problem. An hour from now, she'd be on the bus back to her ordinary life.

That was where she belonged, anyway.

The jazz grew louder, along with the murmur of partygoers. Wrapping her jacket protectively around herself, Meredith wove in and out of the throngs, feeling exactly as rejected as she had as a teenager, when boys used to ask her out in the hope of getting close to her famous sister. Then, she'd kneed them in the cojones and told them to drop dead. Now, her defenses weren't what they used to be. She'd fallen out of practice. Years of carving her own non-Marley niche in the world had made her soft.

Vulnerable.

Fighting against the realization, Meredith clutched her Budweiser tighter. She pushed her way past a group of laughing sound operators, her gaze fixed on the wide back of a man who might have been Harry. If only she could reach him. She shoved harder, trying to squeeze past a broad-shouldered man.

He turned. *Tony.*

"Just who I was looking for," he said, his wicked smile vaguely foreboding. "Come on. Let's dance."

Tony's first mistake was slipping his hand beneath Marley's jacket to hold her waist

71

while they danced. His second was enjoying the smooth bare skin, alluring warmth, and nonstarletlike curves he encountered when he did it.

He flexed his fingers, reminding himself she was his star attraction. He'd sought her out to instruct her in what was expected of her at actor fantasy camp. Period.

Better to kick off on a positive note, he decided. Actresses were notoriously sensitive. Hell, *women* were notoriously sensitive. Tony had never met one who could handle straight talk. Least of all Marley, who'd fed him that ridiculous story about not being herself.

"You met a lot of people tonight," he said. "That's good."

She made a dismissive sound. "Good for whom?"

Okay, so much for positive. Puzzled by her attitude, he frowned. "For all of us."

"Says you." She slumped in place, not moving. "Look, can we do this later? I was on my way someplace."

"It can wait." Tony captured her hand in his palm and started dancing again. Looking down at her obdurate expression, he added, "Don't stomp on my feet on purpose."

She wrinkled her nose, meeting his gaze for the first time since he'd whisked her onto the crowded outdoor dance floor. When he'd waylaid her, she obviously hadn't been pleased. As the person with the most at stake here, Tony hadn't especially cared.

"The same goes for you," she replied. "I'm the one who's supposed to need combat boots, remember?"

He glanced downward. "You didn't take my advice. Why am I not surprised?"

A shrug. "You undersold your dance moves. So far, my toes are intact."

Surprised, he realized Marley was right. They'd fallen effortlessly into sync, moving together as though they'd done this a million times. He'd never danced so well. Remembering what he'd witnessed of her moves earlier, he knew there was only one explanation.

"You must have sobered up some."

She gave him a dark look, then walloped him on the back with something. "I ditched my shoes, remember?"

Right. Her high-heeled shoes. She'd slipped them from her feet on the way to the dance floor. They dangled even now from the hand she'd set on his shoulder, thumping him gently on the back as they swayed and turned. Without them, she moved . . . not gracefully, exactly. Adeptly. Almost athletically.

"Ordinarily, I never wear high heels," Marley explained. "Tonight was supposed to be special."

She gazed over his shoulder toward the trees, her expression plaintive. Taken aback, Tony studied her. In the glow of the high-

73

strung lights, her features looked pretty. Fine-boned, flush with vitality (or possibly one too many brewskis), untouched by artifice. Vulnerable, even. He experienced a wild urge to skim his fingers over her cheek, to bring a smile to her face.

The effect must have been an illusion. Marley Madison was a star. Vulnerability couldn't touch her.

"Tonight *is* special for us," he told her. "It's the start of something big."

Her gaze swiveled to his. "You feel it, too?"

"How could I not? I came up with this whole idea." He inclined his head toward the party surrounding them, indicating not just Bayberry, but the entire actor fantasy camp setting. "Nothing like this has ever been done before. We'll be first in the marketplace. Tourists are hungry for something new — something real. We're going to give it to them."

"Sure. Actor fantasy camp. Of course that's what you meant."

He felt her withdraw from him, her remote expression putting the equivalent of three feet of brick wall between them, instead of a measly six inches of summer night. He should have known. The talk had turned to work. Predictably, Marley wanted no part of it.

"Stop fighting it. It's two weeks out of your life."

74

She said nothing. Her silence pissed him off.

"I want what I paid for," he said, keeping his voice low. He pulled her closer, letting her know she wasn't leaving until he'd finished. "I want the TV star I hired. The va-va-voom glamour girl the fans can't get enough of. *She's* the one my guests are coming to see."

His "glamour girl" stiffened. She frowned, moving with exaggerated care — almost as though he'd hurt her feelings. Tony couldn't see how. A man had to call a spade a spade. She hadn't exactly prepped for her appearance at the welcome party.

"Well." A wobble. "Won't they be surprised?"

"No. Not once you pull yourself together."

Her chin set at a stubborn angle. She shook her head. "Nope. I thought I could do it. I did. But after tonight . . . this stuff is hard work! The shoes, the clothes, the small talk. I can't do it. It's not me."

"It had better be you. You, with all your starlet accoutrements."

Marley blinked. "Accoutrements. Big word."

"I learned it from my Word-a-Day calendar," he said dryly. "It was the next entry after 'contract litigation.' "

She peered up at him, wearing the owlish, overly shrewd expression of the very tipsy. A moment passed.

"This is a party, remember?" She gave a flirtatious grin. She dropped her shoes with a clunk, a motion which enabled her to walk her fingers unsteadily over his shoulder and down his chest. "Let's have fun."

"You're drunk."

"No, *you're* drunk." She hiccupped.

Tony clenched his jaw, struggling for patience. This was just one more example of her flaky starlet shtick. "Start living up to everyone's expectations, damn it! This isn't a vacation for you. It's a job. A performance."

A performance whose success or failure meant the difference between satisfied customers and Valentine Studios' shutdown. Why couldn't he make her see that?

He tried. "I don't care if I have to threaten, cajole, strong arm or sue you —"

"Sleep with me?" She blinked.

"— I'm getting the performance I need."

Sleep with me, echoed in his head. They stared at each other, contemplating their miscommunication. Or her deliberate misdirection. He wasn't sure which. The jazz was pretty loud here on the dance floor.

And she was pretty distracting.

"Sue you," he repeated.

But the images in his mind had nothing to do with contracts and lawyers and mounds of paperwork. Instead, they featured Marley, naked. Him touching her. The two of them finishing that kiss they'd almost shared in the limo.

"I want your cooperation." All business. He frowned to show he meant it. "Starting yesterday."

She pouted. He hated pouting. Unfortunately, the gesture did nothing to diminish the sexy lure of her mouth. Determinedly, Tony looked away.

"I want *you*," Marley said. "Even if it's just for tonight. Let's not talk anymore. If you won't let me go, then take me away. Be my Prince Charming, like you were in the limo. Okay?"

Her eyes begged him to agree. Her body brushed lightly against his, offering further persuasion — persuasion he hardly needed, given the bump-and-grind hip sway they'd been indulging in for the past few minutes.

I want you. The feeling was mutual. Closing his eyes, he resisted. Why was it that every time he tried to get tough with Marley, she turned on the sex appeal?

Ah-hah. All at once, he wised up.

"I'm not falling for that one, princess. You might be able to wrap casting agents and directors around your little finger this way, but not me."

She wavered. Tripped. Looked down. "Stupid shoes."

Pausing, she kicked the shoes she'd discarded onto the nearby grass. Then she

77

swiped her fingers over her eyes and faced him. Were those tears he saw?

"I need to sit down," Marley announced abruptly.

She wove between the other dancers, leaving Tony to follow. He found her sitting on the grass near the gazebo, knees drawn to her chest. A cool midnight breeze spun around them.

He hunkered down to peer into her face. "You could have just said you were done dancing."

"You would have ordered me to keep going."

He sat down next to her. "Probably."

"I'm not Marley, you know." She turned her face to his, obviously trying to focus through her Budweiser haze. "I'm her twin sister, Meredith. I'm an advertising historian in charge of twenty-two percent of the popular culture exhibits at my museum. I've never acted in my life — well, except for that disastrous soliloquy, and that doesn't count, because it wasn't even supposed to be funny — and I can't remember the last time I went to a fancy party like this. Never, I guess."

Tony sighed. "A twin sister? Who works in a museum? You're really getting inventive now."

"It's the truth."

He couldn't believe it. He shook his head, then brought Marley's head to rest on his shoulder. "You've had too much to drink."

She resisted for an instant, then snuggled against him. Her acquiescence felt weirdly like a victory. Unwilling to think about why that might be, Tony angled his arm sideways so he could stroke her hair.

Touching her felt surprisingly natural. Beyond them, partygoers danced and schmoozed. He ought to be doing the same, but this was nice. For now. The jazz music continued. Laughter could be heard in the distance.

After a minute, she burrowed closer. "Brrr. Cold."

He eyeballed her bikini top. "That's because half your clothes are missing."

"Mmmm."

It was no use fighting any longer. Not tonight. Giving up for the moment, Tony tucked her jacket closer around her. Tomorrow he'd revisit this. He'd make her understand there'd be no more nonsensical stories. No more excuses. Just work, work, work. He stroked Marley's hair again, finding the hat head lump that encircled her head. He smiled.

He relaxed. Possibly for the first time in days.

"You should have taken the paper sack I offered you in the limo," he murmured. "These actress nerves of yours could have been avoided. Everything would have gone a lot smoother."

He waited for the rebuttal he knew would be coming.

A loud snore rent the night.

She'd fallen asleep. Or more likely, passed out.

Tony checked his watch. Half past twelve. Long past time for Prince Charming duty to be over with. All the same, he got carefully to his feet, propping Marley gently with his hands while he moved. Then he scooped her into his arms. Taking the back way across Bayberry, he ferried her to her star trailer.

Inside, he squeezed through the narrow fifty-by-twenty-foot space, his steps making the whole trailer vibrate slightly as he made his way past the seating area, built-in kitchenette, and bathroom. The lavishly decorated bedroom enveloped him in flowery scents and a profusion of pink in every shade. For the starlet in his arms, it was a fitting scene.

He'd been inside plenty of star wagons in his life. None had been so froufrou as this one. Spending so much time in Pinkville could have a serious shrinkage effect on a man's package. He'd be lucky to get out with his equipment intact. Ready to make his escape, Tony lay Marley on the bed, then turned to leave.

Another snore vibrated through the pink-tinged air.

He glanced over his shoulder. Marley sprawled gracelessly on the bed with her

80

mouth agape and both arms akimbo. Her jacket had fallen open to the sides, revealing her bare midsection and her bikini-covered breasts.

They were cute breasts. Small but pert. He'd hate for them to catch cold.

Tony grabbed a spare blanket from the bottom drawer of the built-in dresser. He noticed how few belongings she'd brought — a book, a couple of T-shirts, sunscreen. Everything else, all the sparkly, spangled, sequined stuff he'd expected, must be being delivered later.

He lofted the blanket over her. Hesitated. Frowned. Tucked it in, then glanced over his shoulder to make sure no one had witnessed his careful gesture.

It wasn't a big deal, Tony assured himself as he let himself out and crossed the back lot. Protecting a nice pair of breasts was for the good of all mankind.

FIVE

"If you keep late hours for society's sake, Bromo-Seltzer will cure that headache."
— advertisement for Bromo-Seltzer (1895)

Telephones had clearly been invented by an evil genius. Right this minute, one of his nefarious creations rang shrilly enough to rattle Meredith's teeth. Worse, she couldn't find the damn thing.

She slapped the nightstand, searching. Nada. Maybe if she actually opened her eyes.

Youch! Sunlight pierced her skull. The impact made her nostrils hurt. She swabbed her tongue around in her mouth, encountering a taste somewhere between cotton and road kill. Groggily, she screwed her eyelids shut again.

The phone kept ringing. Probably it was Marley, calling from her honeymoon to make sure her gardener had color coordinated the hydrangeas. Or wanting to share the *latest* adorable thing her new stepson, Noah, had done. Or checking to see that Meredith hadn't disturbed the just-for-show leather-bound books in Marley's useless, hoity-toity library while looking for something decent to read. Again.

82

Ever since marrying her sportscaster husband, Jake, Marley had loosened up. But not so much that she completely trusted her sister to see to all the details while she was house-sitting. Sometimes Marley could really be a pain. Groaning, Meredith rolled over.

Ring. On second thought, it might be Leslie at the museum, wanting Meredith to stand in for one of the docents who led weekend tours. The last time Meredith had done that, a four-year-old had asked "Why?" so many times, she'd thought her head would explode. But Leslie was her best pal from college. She couldn't leave her stranded.

Only a friendship that had survived dorm life, first jobs, first apartments, and breakups from men whose idea of commitment consisted of peeing with the bathroom door open could have convinced Meredith to try moving again. She sat up, feeling the room spin. She cracked open her eyes.

It was like waking up in Barbie's bedroom. Pink, pink, pink. Frills. Potpourri. A gilt-edged mirror. Ah-hah. Just as she'd thought. She was still house-sitting at Marley's.

Except this wasn't Marley's bungalow in the Hollywood Hills. For one thing, this place was too dinky. For another, it was . . . moving?

A forward jolt dropped her onto the mattress. Muffled by a piled-up blanket, Meredith pushed it away. Then she stared at it. She remembered a man tucking the soft weave around her, recalled his careful touch and the way he'd hesitated for just a minute as though making sure she was cozy. His presence had made her feel protected. Warm.

Nah. That was just the blanket heating her up, she assured herself as she pushed upright. Besides, she had more important things to think about. Like where she was. Why she was there. Why the phone had suddenly quit ringing. And how the room could be in motion.

Ignoring the queasy feeling in her stomach, she lurched to the window opposite the bed. Yup, she was definitely motoring along. New York City passed by, a row of brownstones with charming stoops. Then a corner wended past, and she realized the Big Apple had been a façade. Behind it the buildings were fake, their bricks painted in, the lampposts and trees on wheels.

Meredith squinted at the wheeled tree containers, a remembrance tickling the corner of her groggy mind. A part of her resolutely pushed away the sensation. She examined her more immediate surroundings, fuzzily taking in the paperback book on the built-in bureau, the museum sweatshirt slung over a chair, the hallway leading to a compact, hotel-like sitting room in the distance. At the farthest end a sectional banquette lined two walls; a table occupied the third.

On that table sat a pair of grass-stained high-heeled stilettos.

Seeing them made everything flood back. The limo ride. The red carpet debacle upon arriving at Valentine Studios. The welcome party. The you're-no-Marley focus group. The familiar sense of not belonging. The dance with Tony.

The obvious *lack* of a getaway she'd made last night, despite her plan to find Harry and catch a bus home.

"Aaarrgh!"

An instant later, her trailer jerked to a stop. Great. This was her chance. Hastily grabbing her things, Meredith shoved them into the overnight case she'd borrowed from her sister. Then she zipped it up, blew the hair from her eyes, and tied on her trusty hip-camouflaging sweatshirt.

There. Time to blow this Popsicle stand before things got any worse.

Things got worse. As soon as she opened the door.

"See? This is why I decided to move your trailer close enough to keep an eye on you," Tony said. "Going someplace, princess?"

Meredith whipped her head sideways, locating the source of his voice. She found him standing a dozen feet away, watching a pair of Teamsters climb out of the truck attached to her star trailer.

They started working at unfastening the hitch, which had enabled them to drag her home-away-from-home across the back lot. Neat high-tech design, she noticed. The hitch had an extended pin box and slider, which would allow the truck greater turn clearance while pulling her trailer, and the —

Hang on. She wasn't here to marvel over modern-day feats of engineering.

She reined in her geeky side and returned her attention to Tony, who was currently — and sexily — outfitted in a crewneck, lean pants, and a bad attitude. He cocked an eyebrow and waited for her reply, his legs spread and his arms crossed over his middle as though he were king of the world.

In this world, she supposed he was. She didn't doubt he was just macho and arrogant enough to let her know it.

Naturally, that only made her mad. Tony had been getting on her nerves ever since she'd arrived.

"Yes! I'm going home," she informed him, clenching her fingers on her overnight bag.

"That might be tricky. Since you don't have any steps."

Meredith glanced downward. At least three feet of fresh air swirled between the bottom edge of her trailer and the ground below. As hungover as she was, she felt dizzy just looking at it.

Yesterday, there'd been a set of metal stairs

there. No doubt the Teamsters had removed them before towing her trailer and hadn't replaced them yet. She swallowed, gripping the door frame with her free hand.

Tony continued. "Also since I can sue you for breach of contract if you so much as let the smell of your perfume drift across the studio's property line. I don't think you're going anyplace."

"You can't keep me prisoner here."

He shrugged. Big. Powerful. Manly.

Jerk.

"Sure I can," he said good-naturedly. "If you want to keep your job."

Marley's job. Torn between her natural inclination to help her sister, her indignation at being stuck here, and (let's face it) her hangover, Meredith hesitated. Maybe she should stay. For a few more hours, at least. Long enough to come up with a plan to prevent Tony from suing Marley, for instance.

This wouldn't be the first time she'd come to Marley's rescue. Her sister had a knack for getting involved in impractical, unpredictable messes. Meredith had always had the know-how to bail her out. If she handled this situation well enough, Marley would never need to know it had happened.

Neither would the rest of the world. Including all the people who really knew her and would probably laugh their heads off at the idea of a "glamorous" Meredith.

She considered Tony. He gazed steadily back, his expression daring her to disagree. So she did.

"It's not that far. I could jump."

"You won't. You're not a quitter."

He had her there. Damn him. "You're . . . not very nice."

Sheesh. As a rejoinder, that ranked right up there with, "I'm rubber and you're glue! Bounces off me and sticks to you!" Brilliant. For this she'd spent four years at USC? Two more years in graduate school?

Meredith wavered, searching her muzzy hung-over brain for something snappier. Tony mistook her silence for acquiescence. He nodded to one of the Teamsters, who carried over a set of metal steps. Then he smiled.

"I thought you'd see it my way. Before you head out to your first class this morning, one word of advice: clothes."

She glanced down at herself. Bikini top, rumpled cargo pants, bare feet, wrinkled jacket. She looked as if she'd been Jell–O wrestling. And lost.

What else was new? Clothes didn't make the woman. The *woman* made the woman. Thinking otherwise was just plain immature. Meredith had always prided herself on that viewpoint.

Tony, however, did not. Judging by the way he was looking at her, he was still approximately two years and one ogle away from maturity. She caught him checking out her cleavage again. She slammed the door shut. With dignity.

God, she hated being backed into a corner.

"Don't forget to do your paperwork first!" he yelled. "The business office needs everything before you start teaching."

Paperwork. Now that was an area in which Meredith could excel. Teaching probably was, too. She'd always been a quick study. A straight-A student. And the classes he'd mentioned yesterday? Diva Dramatics? Tabloid Tattling? Star Schmoozing 101? Utterly lightweight. Surely she could bluff her way through those.

Dropping her overnight case, she went in search of the required documents he'd mentioned. She'd show Tony Valentine — and his stupid, cocky attitude — a thing or two. If Marley could be expected to handle this actor fantasy camp thing, then so could she.

Meredith emerged from her trailer thirty-seven minutes later, freshly showered and dressed in her spare T-shirt, a pair of jeans, Pumas, and her hip-slung sweatshirt. Her hair hung in damp strands to her shoulders. She bounced down the steps onto the back lot's asphalt, feeling more alert after a rousing session of paperwork.

Okay, so the personality profile, permission statement, waiver, and other forms she'd completed hadn't exactly been IQ challenging. But they'd enabled her to focus on something besides her pounding head and unsteady legs long enough to feel almost human. For that, she was grateful.

Fully committed now, she'd called the museum to cash in a couple of weeks' vacation time. Then she'd phoned Leslie and asked her to pack up a few essentials and some spare clothes and have them delivered to Valentine Studios. When her best friend had agreed, Meredith had nearly keeled over with gratitude.

At least *someone* was in her corner — even if that someone didn't *quite* know all the details of Meredith's big adventure. Hey, that's what friends were for, right? Camaraderie, encouragement, and company while sitting through a tenth showing of the latest Brad Pitt movie. Later, Meredith promised herself, she'd give Leslie the whole scoop.

Right now, she looked for Tony. No dice, although there was a trailer beside hers which exuded a certain air of machismo. Its awning spread over a rectangle of Astroturf. Atop that stood a pair of battered lounge chairs, a beach ball, and a huge barbecue grill. She'd have bet her last issue of the *Journal of American History* the trailer belonged to Tony.

Harry sat in a parked golf cart a few feet away, his gray hair gleaming in the sunshine.

When he saw her, he raised his hand in greeting.

"Mr. V. says I'm supposed to drive you to hair and makeup," he said. "Then wardrobe."

"Oh, I don't need any of that." She climbed inside the cart, then arranged her stack of neatly penciled paperwork on her lap. She hunched over, covering the papers protectively with her forearms so they wouldn't blow away. "Let's just go straight to the set where my class is being held."

"Sure thing, Miss Madison."

They drove a new route, past Valentine Studios' Old West set, Tumbleweed. There, tall false-front buildings rose from a dusty street, and a saloon and church stood nearly side by side. There were hitching posts and water troughs, batwing doors and fancy, hand-scripted signs. The whole place looked surprisingly authentic — except for the tire tracks and sneaker prints in the dirt.

Harry saw her noticing them. "The tire and shoe prints get smoothed out before shooting. The set decorator's crew drags a piece of plywood on a chain over the street to erase them. I guess you've never done a western before?"

She shook her head.

"I loved those old westerns. Used to watch them all the time." He turned a corner, driving along a realistic-looking creek. "They're not too popular anymore, though."

Harry darted her a hasty look. "I don't mean anything by that. Westerns will probably come back any day now."

So will your career. Don't worry, his anxious expression assured her. He was obviously concerned he'd offended her — Marley — with an oblique reference to her faded career.

"I hope you're right," Meredith said.

He shifted in his seat, keeping both hands on the cart's wheel. He glanced at the deserted set they passed next, a jungle scene with bamboo trees, thick greenery, and the tail end of the creek. She was surprised to see that it, like the other sets they'd passed, was devoid of both people and activity.

How did the studio make any money with empty sets?

"Used to be, these sets were packed with movies and TV shows in production," Harry told her. "You couldn't take three steps without running into some Hollywood hoo-ha."

They both looked toward the jungle set. Its sign — *Acajatuba* — hung crookedly, adding to the sense of abandonment. A feeling of melancholy stole over Meredith. It hadn't occurred to her until now to wonder . . . What had happened to all the people who used to work here?

With deliberate heartiness, Harry went on. "Mr. V.'s going to give the place a fresh start, though. You might think our actor fantasy camp is small potatoes. But if everything goes well, it'll expand over the whole back lot. People will come from all over the place to have a real movie star experience for the two weeks they're here. Mr. V.'s sure of it. All of us believe him."

Meredith hoped he was right. But something else had caught her curiosity. "Why do you call him that? Mr. V.?"

Harry shrugged. "He says it's better we don't think of him as a Valentine at all. So, Mr. V., for short. Course, he's been away so long in New York City, he's hardly part of the family anyway. We don't hold it against him, though."

"That's nice of you."

"Nothing nice about it. He's working hard to bring back the studio. If anybody can do it, it's him. Leastwise, that's what I've heard. Mr. V.'s a regular whiz kid when it comes to business, I guess. Lots of Internet doohickeys to his credit."

They chugged over a replicated covered bridge.

"E-commerce? Dot-coms? IPOs?" Meredith asked.

"Sure. Some of those."

Hmmm. A heavy hitter in the Internet biz. Interesting.

A few minutes later, Harry braked at one of the soundstages. Beside their golf cart, the soundstage's large, garage-door-style rollup entrance was closed tight. A few feet away, a set of steps led upward to the enormous building's other, less imposing door. *Soundstage 23*, Meredith read on the engraved brass plaque to its right. A long list of the classic movies and fifties-era TV shows that had been filmed there made up the rest of the plaque.

The history of this place intrigued her. Until now, Meredith hadn't thought about what *she* might get out of delving into Marley's life. Aside from a chance to hide the embarrassing way she'd stumbled into it, of course. But now, looking at that plaque, she experienced an unexpected sense of fascination.

Someplace around here, Valentine Studios was bound to have archives. Stored collections of props, costumes, movie one-sheets, and legendary original scripts. Items like that were a little outside her field of expertise . . . but they might prove interesting, all the same.

First, though, she had a class to teach.

"Well, I guess I'm off."

Harry nodded. "Break a leg."

Break a leg. The legendary showbiz "good luck" phrase.

Hearing it, Meredith felt jangly with nerves. She was about to give a performance — again. Would it turn out as disastrously as her childhood soliloquy? Would she crash and burn as miserably as she had last night at the welcome party?

No. If her ditzy sister could do this, then so could she.

"Thanks, Harry. And thanks for the ride." She held her paperwork toward him. "Would you mind dropping these off at the business office for me, please? I think I'm already running late for my first class, Diva Dramatics."

"Sure thing," he said. "Remember — if you need a ride and I'm not around, just borrow one of the spare carts. They're all over the lot. Now that you've had a tour, you should be able to find your way around."

The prospect of finally popping that wheelie cheered her up. "I will," Meredith told him. "Thanks again, Harry."

With a wave, he drove away. Standing outside the soundstage with her hand on the doorknob, Meredith waited. An instant later, Harry's bright yellow golf cart turned the nearest corner and disappeared. She couldn't delay any longer.

You're no quitter, she remembered Tony saying.

He was right. Meredith turned the knob and went inside.

The sitcom set was crap.
Standing at the edge of it as the crew bustled past performing last-minute tasks, Tony gave its movable walls and strategically ar-

ranged furniture a critical once-over.

In a few minutes, this set would be used for his actor fantasy camp's sitcom, a twenty-minute companion to the drama being put together in a neighboring soundstage. Guests who'd signed up for either of the TV experiences had already received scripts with their assigned roles. Today, they'd get their feet wet by watching their star co-performer — Marley Madison, in the case of the sitcom — run through an example taping. Tomorrow, they'd begin table reads, with rehearsals later in the week.

Unfortunately, Tony decided, as solid as that plan was, there was no getting around one key fact. The fake sitcom set he'd had designed looked like exactly what it was: a cheesy throwback.

There hadn't been enough money in Valentine Studios' coffers for a new set. Or even a deluxe remodel. Instead, the construction workers and set decorators had been forced to make do with whatever they could salvage around the lot. As a result, they'd created a mutated set that was half "The Honeymooners," half "The Brady Bunch," and one hundred percent bargain basement. It wasn't exactly classed up by the two tons of duct tape holding it together, either.

On camera, though, it didn't look half bad. Even Tony had to admit that. With the right lighting, even the lousiest set looked good on videotape. That was the saving grace of studio budgets everywhere. Expert lighting and quality film were the push-up Wonderbras of the entire industry. They made the most of very little to the appreciation of millions.

"Picture is up," the first assistant director said. "Settle, please."

At the command, Tony stilled. So did the group of actor fantasy camp guests standing just beyond the cables, three cameras, HMI lights, and scrims. They'd be the first guests to see the famous Marley Madison in action, and the first to act with her on-set. Other guests roved elsewhere on the back lot, already packed into classes ranging from stunt work to dialect coaching. Still more guests enjoyed the services of Hair, Makeup, and Wardrobe, or settled into their star trailers — the "hotel rooms" assigned during their stay.

Overall, things were going well. This morning, the red carpet treatment for arriving guests — complete with hired paparazzi — had gone off without a hitch. So had the mimosa reception and the "welcome" brunch afterward. His actor fantasy camp was off to an excellent start.

Satisfied for the moment, Tony crossed his arms over his chest. He nodded to the first AD. Since this was a run-through, meant to give the guests their first glimpse of life on-set, everything would proceed just as it would have at a real sitcom taping. Wearing his requisite headphones, the boom operator held his mic near the place where Marley would make her entrance for this introductory performance.

All the actor fantasy camp guests leaned forward. Anticipation crackled in the air. Tony felt it, too. Marley had conducted her first class already — a session on Diva Dramatics — but he'd stayed away to let her get settled. Now he was ready to see his bombshell actress in action.

"Last looks!" came the first AD's voice again, telling everyone on crew to be sure they were ready. "Roll sound."

"Speed," the sound mixer said.

"Roll camera."

"Speed," the camera operator said.

"Marker."

A sharp clap rang out — the second assistant camera operator tagging the shot with the ubiquitous marker slate meant to synchronize audio and video for editing. At the sound, Tony felt an unexpected — and unwanted — nostalgia. It had been years since he'd heard that clap.

Not that he'd missed it, he assured himself. A marker slate was about as big a Hollywood cliché as they came.

The director straightened. "Action!"

The moment had arrived . . . for a cell phone to ring?

Marley stuck her head through the nearest on set doorway. "Sorry, that's mine."

As the director called a cut, she flipped open the phone, turning her back on the exasperated crew to take the call. Nearby, the boom operator shared a look with one of the grips. Marley had ruined the first take — not a good omen for the rest of the day. Discontent rippled through the crew. Of all the amateurish mistakes, not turning off a cell phone was the worst.

"Okay, ready," Marley called.

She waved, cheerfully shoving her phone into the pocket of her baggy jeans. For the first time, Tony noticed her sloppy T-shirt, hip-tied sweatshirt, and scraggly hair. When he got his hands on the incompetent wardrobe, hair, and makeup people, he was going to make them regret the day they'd ever left beauty school.

Obviously, Marley had ridden roughshod over them, too. She'd probably put her hand on someone's knee, claimed to like "the natural look," and neatly sidestepped a boring hour in the hair-and-makeup chair. Her natural charm let her get away with murder — and with avoiding work whenever she wanted. Obviously.

As the spectators caught their first glimpses of the famous Marley Madison, their murmured comments flowed.

"Looks shorter in real life, doesn't she?"

99

"I didn't expect her to have brown hair. Didn't she used to be blond on 'Fantasy Family'?"

"It's probably for a part."

"Look at her clothes. Those ratty old things probably cost a fortune at some Beverly Hills boutique. You'd never know it to look at them, would you?"

Gritting his teeth, Tony watched as the take began again.

This time, they made it all the way past "Action." Marley hurried on set, galumphed past her mark as though it weren't even there, and then stopped dead in front of the camp guest recruited to be the other principal actor for the scene. She held up her script pages and squinted at them. Visibly. In the frame, where the camera would pick them up.

"Cut!"

"Didn't you learn your lines?" the director asked her. "This demo script is from 'Fantasy Family.' An old episode. It should be a piece of cake for you."

"Sorry. I'm a little nervous. The lights are really bright." She shaded her eyes against the glare, then waved at the guests assembled beyond the scrims. "Sorry!"

They tried again. Once more, Marley tromped right past her mark, stomping over the strip of tape on the floor where she was supposed to stand. She delivered her first line perfectly. While the camp guest emoted over his dialogue, she stared raptly into the camera . . . and became mesmerized.

In the ensuing silence, the script supervisor fed Marley her next line. Marley went on gaping, unblinking, into the camera. A crooked, self-conscious smile wobbled onto her face.

"Cut!" the director yelled.

All the spectator-guests slumped. So did the crew.

Marley shook herself. "I can do it!" she insisted. "Just give me one more chance. This *can't* be that hard."

"Could've fooled me," muttered a soundman. He slapped the switch that turned off the wigwag — the rotating beacon letting everyone on set know sound was rolling.

The crew visibly regrouped. Tony braced himself for whatever came next. He'd spent half his life on sets at Valentine Studios, killing time or working as an assistant to somebody. Every gaffe Marley made was obvious and unprofessional. He couldn't believe she was biffing it this badly. Was she really that hungover?

Note to self: Hide the Budweiser. Beer was clearly Marley Madison's kryptonite.

Wearily, the director waved his hand. "Action."

Marley bustled onto the set. At the last instant, she remembered her mark. She backed up onto the tape with a triumphant look. Then she ran through her lines, delivering each one with thoroughly memorized precision. Her posture straightened a little. Prompted by the script supervisor's hand movements from the sidelines, she jerkily progressed — head down — across the set to her next mark. Her smile broadened when she hit it.

"Why, I *do* declare!" she exclaimed in a truly awful Southern drawl, issuing her character's famous catchphrase. "I do declare, indeed!"

The scene ended. Camera and sound rolled for another few seconds, capturing room tone for use in editing later. Oblivious, Marley punched her fist in the air.

"I did it!" she cried. "I *knew* I could do it!"

The audience of camp guests applauded politely.

"Cut," the director said through clenched teeth.

"Oops, sorry." Marley slapped a hand over her mouth. "I'm supposed to wait for you to say 'cut' first, aren't I?"

"Yes. Yes, you are."

She frowned. "I forgot."

She forgot. Tony could hardly believe it. Marley Madison had been a child actress since the age of four. How could she forget something so elementary as waiting for the director to call "cut"? Something so obvious as meeting her mark?

Something wasn't right here. His instincts told him that, and he'd always been a man who trusted his instincts. Marley Madison was an experienced, world-famous actress. How could she flub her lines, gawk at the cameras, answer her cell phone, and act like a complete fish out of water?

Because she *was* a complete fish out of water, Tony realized with a dawning sense of horror. *Oh, shit.*

Suddenly, it was as obvious as klieg lights to him. The woman he'd thrust in front of his paying guests, the woman he'd paid to tutor them, really *wasn't* his star actress.

She was his star actress's clueless twin sister.

His star actress's clueless, not-an-acting-genius twin sister.

His star actress's clueless, not-an-acting-genius, *nonglamorous* twin sister. Just like she'd said.

And Tony? That was easy. He was screwed.

SIX

"Just learn your lines and don't bump into the furniture."

— Spencer Tracy

"Tony!" Meredith smiled as he approached her between takes, happy to see the person she knew best in this cockeyed environment. "Did you see me? I'm getting the hang of it! I didn't need any prompting at all that time."

Proud of her minor triumph, she bounced up on the toes of her Pumas. Crew members milled around them, moving cables and sliding light stands and carrying props. Tony stepped dexterously between two of his employees as though he'd been navigating the backstage hullabaloo his whole life. He stopped in front of her, tall and serious. His jaw looked stony enough to inspire a whole new tourist attraction: Studhenge.

Well, she didn't care. He could look as foreboding as he pleased. In that moment, Meredith was almost glad Tony had threatened litigation if she — AKA, Marley — left. Otherwise, she might never have gotten the opportunity to show what she could do. To prove that she was just as good as Marley when it came to superficial fluff like acting.

104

"I think I'm a natural," Meredith said. "Don't you?"

"A natural?" Tony flexed his jaw. "My Aunt Esther acts better than you do. Did you seriously think you would fool anybody?"

Shocked, Meredith stared at him. She *had* been fooling everybody. Including him. It was on the tip of her tongue to say so.

"Spare me the tyrannical producer routine. I have an Emmy," she informed him instead, indignant on Marley's behalf. "And a People's Choice award."

"You mean your *sister* has one." He clamped his hand on her wrist. "Come with me."

Oh, God. *Your sister,* he'd said. *He knew.*

She stalled. "You choose *now* to believe me?"

"I choose now to stop being made a fool of."

"But you've been doing such a whiz-bang job."

"That makes one of us. Your skills could use work."

"Are you maligning my acting ability?"

"You'd have to possess some first."

That hurt. "Maybe you can teach me this hardheaded studio exec thing you've got going on." She pretended to consider it. "No, wait. That's not acting. You really are a jerk."

"Beats being a fake."

"Let me go." She tried twisting out of his

105

grasp. No dice. He was too strong. "I have a job to do here."

Fury stamped hard angles over his features. "You just got the morning off."

Before Meredith could cook up another retort, Tony hustled her around the back of the set. On the other side of the wall, she heard the director's voice, followed by the sound of all the assembled actor fantasy camp guests talking at once.

"Listen." She dug in her heels. "They need me!"

"They're fine without you."

"They're mumbling!"

"They're doing wallas. It was all I could think of to keep them busy while I figured out what to do with you."

He towed her farther. Foreboding surged inside her. She hadn't seen this side of Tony before. Apparently, he wasn't big on surprises. Or on fake actresses. Would he sue her, too? Get Marley into trouble? Tell the press, or reveal her imposter status to the crew?

She'd die if he did. She hadn't survived this morning's Diva Dramatics class — not to mention last night's welcome party — just to be mortified now. She'd thought she was doing well.

"Wallas?" she hedged, needing time to strategize.

"Looping voices for background ambiance.

Lots of voices talking at one time sound like 'walla, walla.' Usually the ADR editor does it in post, but I asked the sound man to do some impromptu taping while I have you arrested."

She gave him a look.

"It was a good diversion."

She couldn't believe he thought she was criticizing his choice of diversionary tactics. "Not that. The 'have you arrested' part."

He remained silent, increasing her anxiety. She should have known nothing good could come of snatching Marley's invitation and pretending to be her glamorous twin. At twelve, Meredith had tried to score take-home privileges to the special research section of the city library by pretending to be Marley. The librarian had responded by offering her patrons an impromptu "Marley Madison" autographing session, a session that had quickly turned into a marathon. It had been days before Meredith's fingers had worked well enough to hold a book again.

Tony dragged her out of soundstage 23. Sunshine prickled her eyes as they crossed the back lot, but he seemed oblivious to the brightness. Probably he'd ordered it for the occasion, just to annoy her. They went into another building, this one musty smelling, dimly lit, and silent. He flipped on a light switch. Slammed the door.

Then he leaned on it, blocking the only exit.

Meredith looked around. Piled-up crates, slip-covered furniture, cardboard boxes, and skinny mailing tubes surrounded them. Heartened, she perked up. This obviously wasn't a holding cell. He hadn't called the police yet. Or studio security. She could handle things from here. Thinking on her feet was a snap.

"If you wanted to go someplace where we could be alone, you could have just said so." She winked, hoping to set him off balance. "I might even have agreed."

It didn't work.

"The fewer witnesses to this, the better," he said.

"Ooh, threatening."

"It's not a threat. It's damage control. I don't plan on 'bankruptcy' being the next entry in my Word-a-Day calendar."

That got her attention. Meredith gazed up at Tony's angry face. There were a lot of Hollywood professionals here. Did Marley's appearance at his actor fantasy camp really mean that much to him? She hadn't thought so, but . . .

"Where's your cell phone?" he asked. "You have a call to make."

What, to her attorney?

"No." Meredith wasn't doing anything until she had more information. "First tell me what you plan to do."

"Have it your way."

He released her wrist. Before she could spare a grateful breath, he invaded her personal space completely by patting down her jeans pockets.

What was he doing? Frisking her? Too surprised to react at first, Meredith stared as Tony spanned her waist with his hands. He untied her sweatshirt from her hips. It landed on the floor beside her sneakers.

"Hey!" She needed that sweatshirt. Without it, she might as well wear padded clown pants. Her hips demanded center stage no matter what else she did. She moved to retrieve it.

Tony blocked her. He crouched to slide his hands down her left thigh, patting and squeezing. Strong fingers touched her knee. Through her jeans, his palm stroked her calf.

Meredith choked out a laugh. "That tickles!"

"Try to control yourself, princess. This is strictly business."

"I'll bet you say that to all the girls."

"Only the pain-in-the-ass ones."

"What about the rest?"

"The rest?" He glanced up with his hands on her right knee. A dangerous-looking smile enlivened his face, just for an instant. "They can't control themselves at all. Not once I start doing *this*."

He stroked her, his touch subtly changing. Where before his hands had felt purposeful against her leg, now they felt . . . *seductive* against her thigh. Erotic. Captivated by the change, Meredith stilled. Tony's palm slid upward; his deft fingers grasped the back of her thigh. A little higher . . . now he let his other hand join in, bringing heat and a firm caress to the outside of her thigh.

She stifled a gasp. Another few inches, and she'd be just like all those other women he'd mentioned. The ones who lost control when Tony touched them.

He plucked her cell phone from her jeans pocket, then straightened. He handed her the phone. "Call your sister."

Moronic disappointment filled her. She pretended indifference. "First, are you sure you're done feeling me up? I wouldn't want to miss anything."

He whisked his gaze over her legs, lingering for the barest instant. Beneath his perusal, Meredith felt naked. Naked, and hot. She couldn't begin to guess what he was thinking.

Probably that she had on clown pants. She sighed.

He mistook her exhalation for resistance. As if she'd demonstrated much of her usual rebellion a few seconds ago. Ha. Apparently, all her contrariness dissolved when it rubbed up against a tantalizing touch and a macho attitude.

She ignored her phone and examined him with as much nonchalance as she could manage. "It would only be fair if I got to pat you down, too. Who knows what you've got hidden in those pants?"

His mouth quirked. Begrudgingly.

"More than you can handle. Now call your sister. Whatever game you two have cooked up, it's finished."

"Marley's got nothing to do with this."

And wouldn't, if Meredith could help it. For twenty-seven years now, she'd forged her whole identity to be as opposite from Marley as possible. As far as the world was concerned, Meredith was the anti-Marley. To think her sister might discover that teeny, tiny, barely noticeable part of Meredith that longed for a spotlight of her own . . . She couldn't stand it.

"Besides, she's on her honeymoon. She can't be reached."

"Very convenient."

"Funny. I find it just the opposite."

"I'll bet you do." Tony circled her, giving her a speculative look. "I'm not kidding around. Without your sister here, my guests won't stay. They paid to hobnob with a celebrity starlet, not a —" He raised his eyebrows.

"An advertising historian," she supplied helpfully.

"That's what you told me yesterday. When

you also told me you were Marley. How stupid do you think I am?"

She blinked. "Do you really want me to answer that?"

He waved away her wisecrack. "Advertising historian. That's not a real job. You're making it up."

Meredith crossed her arms. "The first paid advertisement in the American colonies appeared in the third issue of a newspaper called the *Boston News-Letter* in 1704. It offered a plantation for sale on Long Island."

"You're making that up, too."

"During the Victorian era, printed advertisements became increasingly overelaborate, with extravagant typefaces and cluttered graphics. Euphemisms abounded: 'limb' for leg, 'departed' for dead, 'white meat' for chicken breast."

"So *that's* where that comes from!"

As though realizing his outburst ostensibly proved her point, he clamped his mouth shut. Stubbornly.

Meredith went on. "Brillo's S.O.S. pads stand for 'save our saucepans.' The Jolly Green Giant was created in 1925 to sell peas. Lucky Strike cigarettes were once promoted as diet aids. A copywriter invented the concept of halitosis to sell Listerine as a bad-breath remedy in 1922."

He scoffed. "Bad breath wasn't invented in 1922."

"Tell that to Madison Avenue." She was in her element now. Facts. History. Popular culture. Just to show off a little, she offered, "In early ads, Listerine purportedly worked as an aftershave tonic, antiseptic, and deodorant. And it cured dandruff, too."

"Ewww." Tony shook his head. "No sane person would pour mouthwash on his hair. I'll admit, you have a head for trivia. But your cover won't wash. I'm not that gullible."

Graciously, she let that pass. "My thesis was on the changing impact of advertising mascots on modern society. It was fascinating."

"Now you're yanking my chain."

"Fine." Time to break out the big guns. Meredith put her hands on her hips and delivered the pièce de résistance she knew would impress him. "Captain Crunch's full name is Horatio Magellan Crunch. He sails the S.S. Guppy with his mate, Seadog."

That got him. He tilted his head, studying her. "How the hell did a brainiac like you survive in La-La Land?"

"What's the matter?" She grinned. "Never felt up a girl who'd read a book before?"

Tony looked stunned. He sat on a nearby crate. "Not knowingly."

"I'll bet." She pocketed her phone, then scooped up her museum sweatshirt from the floor and tied it around her hips again. Ahhh. Much better. "Are you still planning

113

to have me arrested?"

"Nah. Just roughed up a bit."

"Because if you are, I might need a head start on running away." She climbed onto the crate beside him, knees drawn to her chest, uncomfortably aware of his continued scrutiny. "Those high heels really wrecked my feet last night. I'm not my usual Speedy Gonzales self today."

He gave her a once-over, looking handsome and a little dumbfounded. He'd see her differently now that he'd discovered who she really was, Meredith knew. She wished she didn't wonder exactly *how* differently, and whether or not he'd be disappointed in what he saw. She wished she didn't care.

She glanced down and curled her fingers into the edge of the crate, her posture an automatic imitation of the way she used to perch in the tree house her dad built for her the summer she was ten. She'd sprained an ankle showing him how she could jump down from it like She-Ra: Princess of Power ("For the honor of Greyskull!").

Marley and her mom had been at an audition. As usual. Her father had carried her, dirty-faced and begging for no stitches, to his Oldsmobile for the drive to the emergency room.

Embarrassed at the memory, Meredith shifted her hands into a more dignified position. The crate lid wobbled beneath her, giving her a glimpse of its contents. Spangled costumes.

Intrigued, she looked around. *Scripts* was stenciled on a nearby crate; a cardboard box beside it seemed to contain rolled-up one-sheets — vintage movie posters. Along the wall, dusty movie magazines with Golden-Age-of-Hollywood titles like *Silver Screen* and *Photoplay* were stacked waist-high, a veritable treasure trove of firsthand pop culture references.

Tony had taken her to the Valentine Studios archives, she realized. A place jam-packed with artifacts, reference material, antiques, papers, and the irresistible allure of undisturbed dust. Nirvana, for an academic like her.

Silly man. Didn't he know he'd need a crowbar to wedge her out of here?

Eager to start exploring, Meredith hit upon a new strategy. "Tell you what. I *will* call Marley. I'll get her to agree to a month-long stay at actor fantasy camp, just as soon as she gets back from her honeymoon."

Tony regarded her — and her change of heart — with clear suspicion. "I need a star attraction *now.*"

She sweetened the deal. "A whole month," she reminded in her best QVC spokesperson's voice. "That's double what you're paying for. I'll even throw in autographs for the crew. Signed eight-by-ten glossies if they

115

want. Those are always popular at the 'Fantasy Family' fan conventions."

Meredith waggled her eyebrows enticingly. Beside her, Mr. Pedantic seemed unmoved.

"Right now. Today. This week. My guests will walk if they don't get their star attraction."

"You're not doing this right." Frustrated, she slumped. "I make an offer and you counteroffer. Like this: Tony, I'll trade you one month of the famous Marley Madison for . . . oh, I dunno. Let's see." She pretended to consider it, gazing idly around them. "For two weeks' access to the studio archives."

She drew in a deep breath. Her heart skipped a beat at how much she wanted to delve into the boxes surrounding them. Those film fan magazines, for instance, would have ads in them. Ads she might not have seen before. Ads for long-forgotten totems of popular culture, containing fascinating time-and-place-specific social references. Ads that would enlighten Meredith and help her make important contributions to the museum.

"Then you say: 'Okay. I'll make that trade, Meredith.' And we both walk out of here happy. How about it?"

She waited. Slowly, Tony turned his face to hers. In the shadows cast by the bare light bulb suspended from the ceiling, his expression looked unreadable. No problem.

Meredith had never met a puzzle she couldn't crack. She peered at him, waiting for her usual knack for analysis to take over.

All she saw were rugged angles, dark, straight brows, an inscrutable jaw, and a mouth sensual enough to make her forget what she'd been looking for in the first place. Regrouping, she searched for signs he'd succumbed to her strategy.

Hmmm. There were hints of amber in his dark eyes, she detected. Also faint prickles of beard trying to emerge on his jaw.

No, no, no. That was no use at all. Those details merely revealed that she, like most women, had a genetic susceptibility to testosterone. Tony must be loaded with it. Not even noon yet, and he'd already started in on a five-o'clock shadow? His hormones were obviously hardcore overachievers.

She liked overachievers. She considered herself one. She wondered in what other areas he excelled. What other, more personal and tantalizing areas, he might —

Stop it. She wanted to investigate these archives. That was it. Tony held the key. He just needed a little nudge. A little gentle goading. Maybe some skillful persuasion.

Forget it. *Namby-pamby* just wasn't her style.

"What, are you too macho to negotiate with a girl?"

His face lit with a dazzling grin. He turned

his attention on her with renewed interest. *Uh-oh.* Something about that grin told Meredith she'd chosen *exactly* the wrong tactic to take with him.

SEVEN

*"One morning I shot an elephant in my
pajamas. How he got into my pajamas I'll
never know."*

— Groucho Marx

Her smear campaign clinched it. Pathetic and
ridiculous as it was. When Meredith tried to
drag both his manhood and his business
acumen through the mud simultaneously,
Tony knew exactly how much her *theoretical*
deal meant to her. He also knew he was
going to get what he wanted.

But all he said was, "Your name is
Meredith? It suits you."

Exasperation passed over her features.
Grudging curiosity chased it. He almost
grinned. This was going to be easy.

"Suits me?"

"Sure. Meredith. Meeeee-re-dith." He
rolled the name on his tongue, enjoying the
aggravated look she tossed him. It was about
time *she* was the one off-kilter. "Three syllables. Hard 'M.' Lots of consonants. Sounds
like a girl genius, all right."

"There's no such thing as a soft *M*."

"See? That just proves my point. Meeeee-
re-dith. Meredith the Mastermind."

She didn't know whether to be flattered or annoyed. He could tell. Tony didn't care. It felt good to tip the scales in his favor for a change.

"Well. 'Mastermind' might be overstating it."

He leaned back on his crate, arms propped behind him. "You did say you read books. On purpose."

Her gaze strayed to his biceps. "You don't?"

He shrugged. Of course he did. He had an MBA from Columbia and a truckload's worth of e-commerce research under his belt. He read books on XML, on-line databases, Perl, Internet trends, optical computer chips, and consumer marketing. He'd even launched an e-book venture a year ago.

"I obviously don't read books on negotiating, like you do," he said. "You drive a tough bargain."

That snared her. Meredith's mouth kicked up in a sneaky smile — one that did nothing to diminish her goofball appeal. He actually found her delusional overconfidence kind of cute. God help him.

What he needed was *not* to go all googly-eyed over her, Tony reminded himself. What he needed was to repair the damage her sister's absence would cause his actor fantasy camp. But how?

Dragging his gaze away from her lips might

be a good start. Yeah, that helped. Already he was thinking more clearly.

"I don't know if this deal can wait until your sister gets back from her honeymoon," he hedged. He swept one arm toward the dingy boxes surrounding them. "I was about to have Harry donate all this junk to the Salvation Army."

She gawked. But not for long. Within seconds, she'd slapped her poker face back on. She lifted her shoulder in a move so casual it all but strolled past them.

"You could do that," she agreed with deliberate lightness. "*After* Marley's visit. Who knows? Your altruism might inspire her to extend her appearance another week. Another week would definitely be worth an exclusive look at your archives."

Grudgingly, he admired her guile. Good thing she hadn't been the one to negotiate Marley's actor fantasy camp deal. God knows what outrageous perks he'd have had to provide. But he still wasn't biting.

"Another week." Tony rubbed his hand over his jaw, making an elaborate show of thinking about it. "That's tempting. But the sooner I trash all this stuff —"

"Trash it?" Aghast, she splayed her hands protectively over the crate beneath her.

"— the sooner I can outfit this place like the back lot karaoke bar I've always wanted."

Her eyes bugged. "Karaoke bar?"

121

"Maybe a disco." He brightened, as though a brilliant thought had just occurred to him. "Or a hot tub club! We can dump all this crap and put in Jacuzzis. Hire bikini babes to serve drinks. Like Hooters. Only with bubbles."

She looked ready to choke him. "You can't be serious. You want to trade irreplaceable artifacts for bikini-clad bimbos?"

"And bubbles. Don't forget those."

"How could I?" she muttered. "Your head must be filled with them."

He grinned. Yup, things were definitely turning in his favor. Now if he could just hit upon a solution to the no-Marley problem. The real Marley wasn't likely to call short her honeymoon to make an appearance at Valentine Studios. Which left Tony with . . . Meredith. Marley's less ditzy, less glammed-up, more unpredictable doppelganger.

Of course, *he* hadn't realized the truth about her for over twelve hours. Even though they'd nearly kissed, definitely danced, and come toe-to-toe more than once. Meredith seemed to have fooled the hired paparazzi, the fans, and his actor fantasy camp guests, too. At least temporarily. Was it possible she could fool them for an entire two weeks?

Tony scrutinized her profile, identical to Marley's. He examined her body, identical to . . . Hell, who was he kidding? With her baggy clothes, Meredith could have been

122

hiding a Playboy centerfold's lush curves — plus the requisite bellybutton staple. He had no idea. She dressed like a tomboyish nun with a T-shirt fixation. And an allergy to spandex.

Still, with a starlet wardrobe and a little help from Makeup and Hair, she might actually be able to pull it off. She might actually be able to double for Marley. With his staff, his guests, even his potential investors at the finale taping. It was the simplest, most direct solution to an unexpected problem. But how to convince her?

Considering it, Tony observed her more closely. Meredith sat on the crate beside him, absently patting it in a protective way. He doubted she was aware of the motion. She studied the boxes of archived studio material, the piles of magazines, the tubes of rolled-up one-sheets.

The whole mess of it looked about as useful to him as those fuzzy toilet lid covers his grandma used to have. Which was why it was stored in here, dusty and decrepit. But to Meredith . . . To Meredith, this place was probably pop culture catnip.

He decided to goose his position, to make sure he could read her correctly.

"I like bubbles," he said in his best L.A.-himbo voice.

Her disgusted reaction almost made him grin wider. Bingo. Glancing away, Tony left

Meredith to mull over his hot tub plan for a few more minutes. Given that Hooters-style anti-incentive, he knew she'd make the deal he wanted.

He'd invented the whole thing, of course. Hot tubs at the studios? Hell, Roland would wind up so pruney-fingered he wouldn't be able to dial up his adult film connections. Errol would hire teams of Jacuzzi sanitizers and draw up lists for a hot tub doorman. His aunts would stir things up, too. But Meredith didn't know that.

Besides, this was business. Tony excelled at business.

Or at least he had . . . until recently.

Just the fact that he was here, wrangling with this problem, made him wonder — again — if he was losing his touch. First, that last dot-com debacle. The one with Taryn, which had made him willing to come back to L.A. in the first place. Now this. At this rate, he wasn't sure if resuscitating Valentine Studios would be his salvation or the last nail in his coffin.

Screw waiting. He didn't need thoughts like these messing with his head. Time to put Meredith out of her misery. Tony opened his mouth to offer the deal he really wanted.

"I have a friend who's a contractor," she announced before he could. "He'd probably get you a good bargain on those Jacuzzis you want. You'd have to bypass the Salvation

Army and agree to donate all this to my museum, of course —"

She was calling his bluff. He couldn't believe it.

"— but then we both win. How about it?"

She perked up, delivering him a clear I-dare-you look. Her possessive glance swept over the archival material. Lovingly. He could almost see her cataloging the stuff, mentally arranging it in exhibit halls. In alphabetical order. With a *Thanks to Tony Valentine, Chump Negotiator* plaque on the whole works.

She had to be bluffing. Making a last-ditch attempt to wrest back the upper hand. Automatically, he asked, "Do I still get Marley for a month?"

"Hmmm." Meredith's mouth turned downward. "I just remembered. Marley's taking a *really* long honeymoon. Then after that, she'll probably be busy. Ever since the stint on 'Dream Date' she did last month, she's been more in demand. She's recouping, considering indie film offers and speaking engagements. So come to think of it . . . My sister's probably too booked to squeeze in your actor fantasy camp these days." Meredith tilted her head, putting on a sad face. "Looks like you missed your golden opportunity, doesn't it?"

Sure. Thanks to *her.* Actress imposter. Limousine knee groper. Bewitching bikini top wearer.

Pain in the ass.

Frustrated, Tony clenched his jaw. Her audacity was limitless. "There are lots of museums. What makes you think I'd choose yours?"

She snorted. Clearly, the possibility of him selecting a rival museum hadn't occurred to her.

"I'm an expert in this field. You have to choose mine."

He shook his head. "If you're as lame a historian as you are an actress . . ."

Meredith's mouth dropped open. She crossed her arms defensively. "I'm an excellent historian."

"I can't in good conscience take a chance on that. This studio's been in the family since movies needed a guy on a Wurltizer to add sound. I won't be the one to run it into the ground."

"I'm an excellent historian!"

"You claimed to be a good actress, too. What was that you said? Oh, yeah." He switched to a falsetto, waving one arm girlishly. " 'I'm getting the hang of it, Tony!' "

She frowned. "I *was*."

"Hey, I'm as surprised as anyone," he said in his normal voice. "I'd have thought your superior brainpower would give you an edge in the whole acting department. I guess not."

She narrowed her eyes. "I could act if I wanted to."

"Maybe you'll get a chance someday." He

shrugged. "You could always ask your sister for lessons. Or, you know. Helpful hints."

Her fingertips whitened on the crate beneath her. "I do *not* need Marley's advice. On anything."

"Thinking back on that run-through this morning . . . maybe you do." Tony pushed himself from the crate. "But it's none of my business. I've got all I can handle finding a replacement for my star attraction. I'd better get busy."

He held out his hand to help her down.

She glared at his palm, arms still crossed over her chest. "I could have acted — from childhood, like Marley! — if I'd wanted to. I just had other interests, that's all. I liked fishing, and football, and watching sports with my dad. I liked books, and reading, and climbing trees. I never wanted to be in the spotlight."

"Now you won't be. Sounds like a win-win to me."

She gritted her teeth, unwilling — he figured — to let him see his needling had gotten to her. As much as he admired that resoluteness in Meredith, Tony wasn't about to cop out now. Although he did have a bizarre urge to take it easy on her. To reassure her she hadn't really been that bad on-set today — cell phone snafus and mark missing aside.

"Once you got going, you *did* have a knack

127

for memorizing the lines," he heard himself say.

What? Letting her off the hook now wouldn't help things.

Cautiously, she unclenched. "I've always had a phenomenal memory. My dad said so. So did all my teachers in school."

"Memorizing lines is an important part of acting. Hell, with your memory, you're halfway there already."

Huh? There he went again. It was like touchy-feely Tourette's. He couldn't seem to stop himself from trying to turn her downcast expression sunny again. As sunny as it had been when she'd spotted him backstage.

He had to get out of here before it got any worse. Impatiently, Tony tried to make her get down by waggling his fingers at her.

She ignored them. "You know, you're right. I'm surprised I didn't realize it before. My success here can't be attributed solely to the mass wish-upon-a-star effect."

Gibberish? Now? Tony waggled again.

More ignoring. "Everyone thought I was Marley. I fooled them all. Even you."

That was it. He grabbed her hand and hauled her off the crate. Meredith stumbled, then shoved him away.

"Hey! Watch it, bruiser."

"Why don't you put your money where your mouth is, princess? If you think you're that good, why don't you prove it?"

"Prove it? Prove it how?"

For a smart girl, she could be pretty dense. He'd been hinting at this for, oh, the past eon or so.

"Be Marley," Tony said. "Here, for two weeks. Stand in for your sister."

She blinked up at him. "You're crazy."

He was. This proved it. But he was too desperate to care. "We can pull it off. Together. No one will ever know."

"*Everyone* will know."

Not if he could help it. "Scared?"

"Never."

"Then what's the problem?"

She bit her lip. A belligerent gleam came into her eyes. Whatever was churning around in her head, it wasn't good. He'd have laid odds on it.

"*You need me,*" Meredith observed. "Don't you?"

Damn her. He'd been right. It *hadn't* been good.

"Sure. Like the Clippers need a new owner."

She'd never have a clue he was really agreeing with her.

"No kidding. They're usually ranked as the worst franchise ever. Something's got to give, right?"

Oh, Christ. He'd underestimated her. Again.

Cheerfully, Meredith rose up on tiptoes, bouncing with energy and impending triumph. "If I agree to this, I want full access to these archives. Twenty-four-seven."

"Only with me here with you," he hedged. "Studio policy."

She nodded.

"If I agree, you'll have to do everything I say to emulate Marley," he added. *"Every-thing."*

"I draw the line at fake boobs."

"So do I," Tony agreed.

They shook hands on it. For better or worse, Meredith Madison was about to become her famous sister Marley's double, standing in for the duration of Valentine Studios' actor fantasy camp. It was crazy. Daring. And a little reckless.

But if it was effective, Tony was in like Flynn. The studio would be back in the black, investors would support his new venture, and his uncles' golden years would be secure.

Just like he'd promised.

Beside him, Meredith leaned over. She hiked up her baggy jeans and scratched, revealing a calf hairy enough to rival his. Then she straightened to her full schlumpy posture. She smiled at him, her unmade-up face a beacon of nonstarletlike intelligence.

God. Tony just hoped this worked. Otherwise, he'd know for sure he'd lost his mind — and his legendary business sense right along with it.

EIGHT

*"You think I'm a flapper, but I can keep
house!"*

— advertisement for
S.O.S. scouring pads (1927)

By the time her first official day at actor fantasy camp whirled to a close, Meredith knew
she'd entered an alternate dimension.

After wrangling her deal with Tony — and
agreeing to his crazy scheme — she'd found
herself stuck in the wardrobe trailer for an
hour, trying on overly sexy clothes. Then
she'd been trapped in the hair and makeup
trailer, where a "natural" look apparently required sixty-seven separate products. Plus a
warning not to let her hair get too close to
an open flame.

Next, she'd winged her way through a class
on Star Schmoozing, with eight eager acting
wanna-bes hanging on her every off-the-cuff
word. Finally, at long last, she'd headed to
the studio commissary for a lunch she'd de-
layed much too long.

Tony caught her just as she was lifting her
triple bacon cheeseburger to her lips.

"Are you crazy?" He crowbarred her arm
downward. "You can't eat that."

"But I'm hungry!"

"Starlets eat salad with a little chicken or fish. For the next two weeks, so do you."

He plunked down a plate. It contained a handful of spring greens, two tomato wedges, three peas, and an artistic swirl of grilled chicken.

Meredith poked at a matchbook-size piece of chicken. "In Hollywood, even the chickens are anorexic."

"Eat it. You need to keep up your strength for the eyebrow waxing. The makeup artist told me you blew it off today."

"I can't believe she ratted me out!" She thought she'd dodged waxing for good.

"I guess sisterhood pales in the face of unibrow."

"I don't have a unibrow."

He shrugged. "Like I would know the difference. I'm just the enforcer. The muscle. The strongman."

"The sadist."

"Tell you what. I'll bring you a bottle of whiskey and a leather strap to bite down on. How's that?"

"Positively medieval."

"Then I'll just have to go with my second option and take care of this for you. Wouldn't want you feeling tempted."

With a grin, Tony grabbed her luscious cheddar-and-bacon burger. He took a huge bite, clearly enjoying the meaty taste of its top-quality ground sirloin. He snatched up a napkin, wiped his big dumb mouth, and winked before strolling away with *her* lunch in his fist.

She envisioned creative ways for him to get his comeuppance. A waterfall of heavy commissary trays to the head, for instance. Or a banana peel on the floor. Neither came to pass.

Fake movie stardom sucked.

After "lunch" and two more classes, Meredith had fulfilled her starlet obligations for the day. She decided to go exploring. If she was really going to do this, she reasoned, she needed all the information she could get.

She borrowed a golf cart, one of several the studio management routinely left out for the camp guests' use. It ran like a dream. She chugged it up and over the footbridge in Acajatuba, raised dust in Tumbleweed, navigated past a stunt-class-in-progress in Bayberry. It wasn't long before she'd grasped the lay of the land.

Everywhere she went, groups of camp guests participated in classes and demonstrations. The crowds weren't enormous — six or seven guests per group, max — but they were enthusiastic. Midwestern families, slick eastern urbanites, couples and singles and even one pair of Georgia honeymooners had come. Down to their Valentine Studios security badges, they were uniformly thrilled to be participating in real Tinseltown experiences.

Watching them, Meredith felt a twinge of unease. She didn't want to deceive all these people. They'd invariably be disappointed if they found out one of their mentors wasn't the star actress she'd claimed to be.

But on the other hand . . . by giving them the illusion they expected, she'd also make them happy. That wasn't so bad. Honestly, it wasn't as though Hollywood were jam-packed with authenticity in the first place.

Besides, soon she'd get her opportunity to dig into the studio archives. That was worth a lot. When would she have another chance to scoop the rest of the museum staff like that?

Then there was Tony. He really *had* needed her today. That sensation had been sweet. Meredith couldn't remember the last time anyone had truly needed her for anything — at least for anything more exotic than filing or identifying Gilded Age advertising campaigns in some obscure periodical.

Despite herself, she *liked* that Tony needed her. Only her.

If Leslie were here, she'd have said Meredith was compensating for a childhood of being overlooked. For years of feeling in second place next to her celebrated sister. But Meredith had never been much for psychobabble analysis. As far as she was concerned, Freud had been a misogynistic perv with too much time on his hands. She didn't need anybody else to tell her how she felt.

Aside from all that, Tony had made her mad. Implying that she wasn't *smart enough* to succeed at acting had pushed every button Meredith had. Who did he think he was, anyway? Just a good-looking, burger-stealing, know-it-all studio exec with wandering happy hands. Hands that had nearly pushed *more* buttons within Meredith. Sex-me-up buttons.

Remembering their frisky encounter in the archives building, she shivered. Tony possessed a certain undeniable appeal. Confidence, sensuality, and a way of moving that suggested he knew exactly what he wanted and usually got it. Unlike the men she typically dated, he sported neither a pocket protector nor an eagerness to split the check over dinner. He didn't seem intimidated by her intelligence. He didn't seem interested in comparing Scrabble scores with her, either. He was . . . who he was. When she was with him, she was . . . Marley.

Damn it. Dragged out of her reverie, Meredith frowned. She jerked the golf cart sideways, chugging toward her star trailer. Her next assignment was to study lines for tomorrow. If she didn't stick to the letter of her agreement with Tony, he'd have reneging rights on their whole deal.

She really wanted to explore those archives.

She really wanted to prove she could outdo Marley.

She really, *really* wanted to score that kiss she and Tony had constantly been denied.

Could that kiss have something to do with her interest in pretending to be Marley? Was she just hot to trot, hungry to run her hands over Tony's wide shoulders, broad chest, and bulging biceps? Keen to rub up against him, press her mouth to his, make them both forget their place in the world and their mission for the next two weeks?

If she was, it wasn't a crime, Meredith decided as she pulled up next to her trailer. She glanced at Tony's digs, parked conveniently close to hers. But not doing something about it probably was.

A hush fell over the back lot later that evening. The camp guests took advantage of their open schedules to indulge in spa treatments and commissary dining, or to visit the studio's indoor swimming pool set, originally designed for splashy Esther-Williams-era features. Over on Tony's edge of things, a few hundred yards east of Tumbleweed, the joint was jumping.

He'd envisioned a quiet night. Having finished his nightly videoconference with Jim Woodwiss about the latest business developments, Tony had planned nothing more taxing than a beer, a baseball game, and a bag of Fritos. He'd wanted to put studio-saving strategizing aside and just relax. Instead, his family had descended upon him and blown his plans all to hell.

As usual.

Now, the smoky tang of barbecued ribs floated upward from his battered kettle grill. A trio of wheeled streetlights, cadged from Bayberry's stock, illuminated the post-sunset evening. A breeze fluttered the good-time Corona pennants he'd strung from his trailer like boozy garland, and four won't-take-no-for-an-answer Valentines parked on his Astro-turf lawn as though they belonged there.

"Good progress today, Tony?" Uncle Errol asked, following as Tony descended his trailer's steps with a frozen strawberry margarita in each hand. "Would you say we're off to a promising start?"

"Yeah, what do you think?" Uncle Roland pressed. "Is this actor fantasy thing gonna make millions? Or should I start dialing up the porn people?"

Stuck between one uncle's palpable hopefulness and another's porno back-up plan, Tony hesitated. He wasn't ready to start production on *Studio Sexcapades*, but he didn't want to make promises he couldn't keep, either.

Okay, he didn't want to make any *more* promises he couldn't keep.

"Here. Have a margarita." He gave them

each a drink, then bailed. "Ribs will be ready soon!" he called over his shoulder.

They gave him jointly uncertain looks.

Ugh. This family stuff was killing him.

On his way to mix up replacement margaritas, Tony passed by his pair of lounge chairs. Between them, a beach umbrella kept away the worst of the streetlight glare. Parked in the first chair like a bejeweled queen, his Aunt Esther caught his eye. Then she caught his arm.

"Tony! Come on over here and keep us old ladies company, why don't you? I haven't seen you in so long, I'd almost forgotten what you looked like."

There it was. The guilt sandwich. Not unlike a pastrami sandwich, but twice as likely to give a guy indigestion.

"I look the same as I ever did, Aunt Esther."

She peered at him through her bifocals. "Good enough to be in the movies yourself, just like all the rest of the Valentine men. That's how you look. Heartbreakers, every one of you!"

"That's right," offered his Aunt Nadine, Errol's wife, from her seat beside Esther. She nodded sagely. "It's the family legacy. Charisma is imprinted on the Valentine men's genes. Sort of like the designer label on Roland's butt."

Involuntarily, Tony glanced sideways. Yup.

Roland was decked out in his too-tight vintage men's Jordache jeans again. With a Lurex Hawaiian-print shirt and two gold chains.

"Excuse me," Tony said. "I need to go scour my retinas."

Esther frowned. "Smart alecks never get ahead in life."

"That's right," Nadine said. "And cheaters never prosper."

At a loss as to how that fit into the conversation, he smiled. "More margaritas, you two?"

"We never got the first ones."

"That's right. Never did."

Both women shot accusing looks at Errol and Roland. Roland raised his pink-filled glass in a salute.

Errol winced. "Do turn down your clothes, Roland. They're much too loud."

"Ha, says you. That cute secretary in the business office told me they're retro-chic."

"She also tells me I'm a silver fox, whenever Nadine's out of earshot. The girl is campaigning for a raise."

"Hey, I'll give her a *raise*. Whoa!"

Tony escaped into his trailer. When he emerged with two more frozen strawberry margaritas, Roland and Errol had transferred their bickering to an analysis of Errol's elegant gray suit. Esther and Nadine huddled at the edge of their lounge chairs, murmuring to each other as they scrolled through something on Nadine's laptop.

The portable computer was his aunt's latest obsession. It enabled her to e-mail friends far and wide, to contact members of her reading group, and to badger congressional representatives for the Senior Citizen's Free Jell-O initiative she'd devised.

"I'd settle for the stuff in the box," she was saying. "But the kind in the plastic tubs in the refrigerated section tastes even better. So convenient, too."

"Have you tried the kind in the squeeze tube?" Esther asked. "It's like something Neil Armstrong would eat."

They both gave wistful sighs. Apparently, the astronaut was some kind of heartthrob. Tony didn't get it. For this, he'd missed seeing the Dodgers trounce the Braves?

Esther glanced up. "Ahhh. Perfect. Tony's here with the drinks. Look, Nadine. He mixed them in the blender."

"Just like a Valentine. The Valentine men always did know how to make a tasty drink."

"They're good with grilling, too. Like cavemen, only with a Weber Smokey Joe. When are those ribs going to be done, anyway?"

Tony started to answer. Nadine cut him off with a sigh.

"Probably not for a while. Valentine men have no time sense. They're always late. A day late and a dollar short, that's a Valentine man for you."

More Valentine mythology. For the past thirty years, Tony had been smothered in it — one reason he'd had to leave L.A. to strike out on his own. Feeling neither behind schedule nor broke, he put the second margarita in Nadine's hand. "Enjoy."

Both women beamed up at him. "It's nice to have you back, Tony," Esther said.

A nod from Nadine. "Almost makes you forget how he abandoned us for New York City, doesn't it? Warms my heart."

The guilt bog deepened. Before he got stuck for good, Tony headed for the grill. Heat radiated from the coals, making the rack of ribs drip sizzling juices. He was flipping over the meat, getting ready to brush on some of his special beer-based barbecue sauce, when he felt . . . something. Something indefinable, but real. Something that made the hairs on the back of his neck stand up.

Hand stilled on the barbecue tongs, he glanced up. Wispy smoke obscured his vision for an instant, making his eyes water. He blinked, then looked again.

Like a dream, Marley Madison strolled toward him through the deepening night. Her dark hair skimmed her bare shoulders. Her body moved in hip-rolling slow motion, clad in a red tank top and flowing black pants. Barefoot, she crossed the distance between her star trailer and his, her gaze locked on him all the while.

His family's conversations fell silent. Gradually, Tony realized they were all staring at him, waiting for an introduction.

All except Roland, of course.

"Hey, little lady! Glad you could join us." He took Marley's hand and drew her all the way into the lights. "Now it's really a party, with our star attraction here."

She tucked a lock of smoothly styled hair behind her ear, looking bashful but pleased. "I smelled something cooking, and I was starving. Got room for one more?"

"Of course!" all the elder Valentines chimed in.

"Great." She gestured toward Roland. "Nice shirt. I really like it."

Grinning, Roland slung his arm around her. "A girl after my own heart!"

Everyone else welcomed her. Errol offered a polite handshake and a warning not to turn her back on his brother's "pinch tactics." His aunts waved cheerily from the lounge chairs, inviting her to sit with them. Tony stood, transfixed, as Marley said hello to everyone.

Nice shirt, he remembered her saying. No, she wasn't Marley. She was Meredith. Only Meredith would have admired Roland's bad taste.

But what a Meredith! He'd never seen her looking so . . . bare before. Not even in her

142

bewitching bikini top — which, after all, had had a jacket on top of it. Tonight, he was seeing a different woman. This woman's tank top revealed her shoulders and arms, its thin-ribbed fabric hugging her torso. This woman's tank top highlighted her small breasts more than it covered them, letting her nipples greet the cool night air with a stand-up salute. This woman's . . . eyes were on him, waiting for him to snap out of his tank-top-induced reverie.

She propped her hands on her hips, giving him an amused look. "L.A. man hypnotized by scent of burned ribs. Tape at eleven."

"I like them well done," he told her, meaning the ribs. "And you're . . . *well done*," he added, meaning her. "Good job, princess. Wardrobe, hair, and makeup deserve raises."

"Don't I get any of the credit?"

"Did you *do* any of it?"

"Sure. I'll never be able to duplicate this look by myself, but for now I'm like the Wizard of Oz. Operating the controls that keep everything going. Arms, legs . . ."

"Hey, a movie reference." Dragging his gaze from her, he flipped over a few ribs. "You might pull this off after all."

Meredith looked amazing. Tony couldn't believe how much the hair, makeup, and wardrobe crews had accomplished, especially compared with this morning.

"Right. Next thing you know, I'll actually

143

be *wearing* the cache of stilettos the wardrobe assistant crammed into my trailer," she agreed. Inhaling appreciatively, she moved closer, noticeably more graceful in bare feet. "Don't tell anyone, but I hid them all under the bed."

"Ahhh. You're an under-the-bed person." Tony nodded sagely, using his tongs on the rest of the ribs. "I'm a closet guy, myself. As a kid, whenever I had to clean my room I turned the closet into a head-injury hazard. Did you know if you cram them together hard enough, you can actually make dirty gym socks interlock?"

"Really? Learn something new every day."

"I once wedged a game of Battleship, three G.I. Joes, and a week-old bologna sandwich into a space the size of a shoebox."

"Eeew."

"That was a record, of course."

"Hmmm. I hope you don't still keep petrified bologna in there." She inclined her head toward his trailer behind them, then dipped a finger into the barbecue sauce. She licked it clean. "If so, we'll have to go to my place later instead."

"I've moved on to petrified pizza these . . . days."

The phrase stuttered out, hardly able to make its way from his suddenly diverted brain to his lips. *Her place?* He watched as Meredith gave a little "mmm" sound of pleasure, then dipped into the barbecue sauce again. She licked a trailing drop from her index finger. Her tongue flicked sensuously over the tip, suggesting all kinds of similar activities.

He considered stripping on the spot, picking up the sauce, and dribbling it all over himself. Letting her lick it off him . . . everywhere.

"Mmmm. Good sauce. Is that tarragon I taste?"

He blinked. She peered into the bowl with interest, like a scientist devising a groundbreaking formula. Right. This was Meredith, he reminded himself. Meredith the brainiac. She hadn't really been flirting with him. Had she?

If she hadn't, that didn't really disappoint him. Did it? After all, she'd been flirting with him before because she'd wanted to divert his attention from the fact that she wasn't Marley. Now she didn't have a similar excuse. He ought to be glad.

Keep work and business separate, he reminded himself. They mixed about as well as Linux and Mac operating systems.

"Not unless there's tarragon in beer," he said gruffly.

Why the hell *wouldn't* she flirt with him? Even without the not-Marley-diversion excuse? He wasn't so bad.

"That's my secret ingredient."

"Hmmm. It's good. Got any spares? Brewskis, I mean? I could really use something to wet my whistle."

Hell. She wanted Kryptonite.

He didn't think he could survive another night of chastely tucking her into that pink-pink-pink bed. Especially if he was the only one who missed the flirting.

"I'm out." Surreptitiously, he edged sideways to block her view of his opened beer bottle, sitting on top of the Igloo cooler behind him. "Sorry."

"Have a frozen margarita," Aunt Esther advised from across the Astroturf. "Valentine men mix excellent blender drinks."

"That sounds good. Thanks, Esther!"

"My pleasure, dear."

Both women beamed at each other, obviously striking up a cross-generational friendship. Behind Meredith, Roland edged closer in full pinch mode, his gaze locked on her backside. Errol and Nadine exchanged a look — one Tony recognized as the dreaded matchmaking, meddling-relatives look. His aunt and uncle had practically patented the thing, but it had been a while since Tony had felt it directed at him.

It was definitely directed at him now. Him and Meredith. *Marley,* to his family. Errol and Nadine glanced speculatively between Meredith and Tony. They nodded, sharing a smile.

"This is almost like having a star in the family," Nadine said. "We loved your work on 'Fantasy Family,' Marley."

"Yes," Esther agreed. "Never missed an episode."

"Oh, thank you! That's so nice of you."

With an over-the-shoulder time-to-get-to-work look and a wink at Tony, Meredith schlumped over to their lounge chairs. She sat awkwardly at the end of Nadine's, upsetting the chair's balance. His aunt nearly toppled sideways.

Apparently, you could dress up a tomboy, but you couldn't make her graceful. They'd have to work on that.

"Sorry about that!" Meredith said, steadying Nadine. "I'm not usually so klutzy. I think all this mascara has upset my natural sense of balance." She batted her eyelashes theatrically.

They all nodded. As though that made sense. Feeling uneasy, Tony waited to see what she'd do next. He hoped Meredith would shut up and let his family conclude their star attraction was a little standoffish at barbecues.

No such luck.

"Now, where was I?" Meredith asked brightly. "Oh, right. 'Fantasy Family.' Let me tell you, working with that cast and crew was *such* fun. Just like a real family! When I think back on my first day on the set . . ."

Oh, hell. Fake reminiscences were a recipe for disaster.

"I just remembered. I've got beer inside."

Tony hauled her to her feet, nearly upending the chair again. A confused Meredith leaned down to steady it.

"Careful, Marley," Esther said. "Valentine men have a clumsy streak."

"But they're so passionate," Nadine offered. "There's nothing like a Valentine man to make your toes curl. Just watch out for the headboard-banging thing."

Gross. Legendary Valentine-ness or not, the last thing Tony had in mind was hanging around while his aunts speculated on his skills in the sack. He ignored their bemused faces as he opened his trailer's door and hustled Meredith up the metal steps. He followed, trying not to give his relatives any extra matchmaking ammunition by ogling her butt.

It didn't work. She had a curvaceous, glorious ass. An ass made for a man to get a good handle on. An ass which invited admiration. Reverence. Even cuddling. That was how fine it was. He couldn't imagine why she usually kept a damned sweatshirt tied on top of it. That sweatshirt ought to be ripped into rags. Burned to ashes. Buried in the backyard.

Driven over with a Buick a few dozen times. Just for good measure.

Maybe tomorrow he'd sneak into Pinkville and stuff her sweatshirt into the closet. She'd never look there. On the other hand, Tony considered as he followed Meredith into his trailer, whenever she'd tied on her sweatshirt, she'd flirted with him. Maybe her sweatshirt was some kind of inhibition-releasing aphrodisiac. Maybe if she just *carried* it in her hand . . .

He'd barely shut the door before she whirled on him.

"What do you think you're doing?"

Missing the flirting.

No, scratch that.

"Plotting revenge on your sweatshirt."

"Huh?"

Okay, go on the offensive. That's what he'd come here to do in the first place.

"What do you think *you're* doing?"

Meredith rolled her eyes. "Pretending to be Marley, of course. Like we agreed. I was just getting into it when you slapped your big Cro-Magnon hands on me and dragged me up here."

Oh, yeah. Why had he done that again? Aside from getting a look at her sexy way of climbing a set of stairs?

Tony scowled. "You were about to blow it."

"I was not. I've been thinking about it, and when it comes to trying out my starlet stuff, your family is the ideal group of test subjects. Controlled, limited in size, risk-free, and available for instant feedback. I should spend lots of time with them."

God help him.

As though reading his mind, she frowned and folded her arms. She scanned the small seating area with its leather banquette, fold-out table, notebook computer, PDA, cell phone, and scattered paperwork. He felt an unmacho urge to tidy up.

"What are you looking for?"

"That beer you promised me." Catching on, she swerved her gaze to his face. "That *fictitious* beer you promised me. Tony, you suck. I'm out of here."

He caught her as she reached for the door-knob. "Starlets don't say 'you suck.' "

She glanced over her shoulder. A shadow of doubt flickered over her face. From out-side, the sounds of laughter and tapping computer keys could be heard. Meredith tilted her head as though listening — or con-sidering what he'd said.

"You're not ready yet," Tony pressed.

"Is this because I forgot to tie on my sweatshirt?" She glared at him. "For your in-formation, my butt isn't *that* noticeably bigger than Marley's."

He liked her butt. Telling her that now probably wasn't the best strategy.

"It's not that. You need tutoring. Inside in-formation. Coaching."

She scoffed. "Spare me the Pygmalion routine, Professor Higgins. I've listened to my sister meet the press thousands of times. I know how to handle myself around four elderly Valentines."

"My family's not going to ask you about Captain Crunch."

Indecision loosened her grasp on the doorknob. "Advertising history isn't *all* I'm good at. I did okay playing movie star today. Even before the makeup and without the eyebrow waxing."

"Just bide your time," Tony urged. "Take it slowly. Wait for the right moment. My family might not be geniuses, but they've been in showbiz their entire lives. If they find out who you really are, they'll lose faith in my actor fantasy camp."

She bit her lip. "You mean they'll lose faith in *you*."

Her overly astute gaze met his. Sympathy softened her expression . . . sympathy Tony didn't want or need.

He tried to joke it away. "Girl geniuses suck."

Meredith wasn't having it. She moved closer. Then, to his surprise, she held his face in her palms. Her touch felt as light and lovely as he'd imagined, emphasizing the softness in her — and the roughness in him. He felt ragged all of a sudden. Ragged, and raw. Exposed.

It was crazy. Other people knew him better

than Meredith did. But it was her, Tony would have sworn, who could see inside his head. Who could see his last dot-com merger — the one that had gone belly-up before he'd come to L.A. Who could see that resuscitating the studio was, in a way, his chance for redemption.

"*I* have faith in you," she said, searching his face. "Want to know why?"

He surprised himself by nodding. What the . . . ?

"We're two of a kind, that's why. I'm a hardcore overachiever just like you." Meredith smiled. "I won't let you down. I promise."

I promise. He'd heard promises like hers before. Promises of dedication and diligence and focus. Promises of not letting personal feelings affect business. Promises that never came to pass at crunch time.

He knew better now than to believe in them. But that didn't mean he'd learned how not to want them. Damn it.

"I'm not worried. If you wreck this venture for me, I'll wax your eyebrows myself."

Her expression said she found him about as threatening as a nearsighted puppy. "Ooooh. I'm scared."

"You should be."

"Oh, I am." She nodded, raising her eyebrows in exaggerated certainty. "I'm scared a few more seconds will go by and I'll lose

152

the nerve to do *this*."

Meredith tugged his face lower with her hands. Simultaneously, she raised herself up to meet him. Tony caught her nervous glance, heard her hastily indrawn breath, and realized, *Holy crap, she's about to make the first move*. Just like that, everything inside him stilled.

Her mouth met his, sweet and tentative. She tasted of fruity lip balm. Instantly, he decided he really ought to get more fruit into his life. You know, for good health's sake. On a quest to do just that, he cupped the back of her head in his hand, steadying her for what came next. Her hair felt satiny and loose, spilling over his knuckles as he angled her nearer.

"Don't worry," he promised, fixing his gaze on her mouth. "I've got nerve enough for both of us."

To demonstrate, he began with a gentle brush of his lips against hers. Then a small kiss. He had to pace himself, work up to the really good stuff later. Another kiss, bigger this time. Pacing himself was overrated. He kissed her again, nearly losing himself in the warmth of her mouth, the softness of her skin, the excited energy sizzling between them both.

Pacing himself was ridiculous. Moving in for another kiss, Tony realized lots of other things were ridiculous, too. Like clothes.

153

Meredith's, for instance, could be done away with very easily. He could probably snap those flimsy tank top straps of hers with his bare hands.

Considering it, he leaned back an inch or two. Her face came into focus, flushed pink and filled with . . . bravado. He should have known.

"You call that nervy?" she asked. "Check this out."

She wrapped her arms around his neck, then kissed him again. A plain, relatively chaste kiss — enjoyable, but hardly earth-shaking. Unlike the kisses *he'd* initiated, Meredith's kiss hardly affected him at all. Never mind the pounding of his heart. Or the intense urge he felt to experience it again.

He'd have to call her bluff. "Nice," he said, quirking an eyebrow. "But —"

"But I'm not done yet."

Proving it, Meredith slid her tongue along his lower lip, suggestively flicking its tip partway inside. She traced the same path back again, creating a slippery, hot sensation which rocked him all the way to his heels. Helplessly, Tony leaned forward . . . only to feel her pulling away.

"Can you top that?" she asked.

Her challenging expression dared him to try. Clearly it was time to get serious.

"You tell me." Filled with anticipation, he

wrapped his free arm around her waist. He tugged to pull her closer.

Drawn by the force of his arm, Meredith bumped up against him. Her eyes widened in surprise.

She caught herself just in time. Slapping on a studiously indifferent expression, she winched out her arm from between their bodies and peered at her fingernails. Buffed them on her tank top. Peered again, just as though the two of them *weren't* locked hip-to-hip in a clinch so sexy it made his scalp tingle.

"A man who goes after what he wants," she murmured. "I like that."

Tony nearly grinned. But then he remembered the way she'd taunted him earlier and decided she needed a lesson in first-kiss manners. Rule number one: *Never start what you can't finish.* Rule number two: *Don't waste time talking.*

He lowered his head. This time he took no chances with warm-ups, lingered only a little over teasing her mouth open, and then slid his tongue directly inside to meet hers — exactly the way they both wanted. The result was a kiss unlike any other — hot and intense and unstoppable. Savoring it, Tony spread his legs in a wider stance. He held her tighter, deepening their kiss even further.

Meredith met him every step of the way. She crowded up against him, angling her head to access more of his mouth. She moaned as their lips met, ran her hands over his shoulders, gave herself over to the experience in a way he should have expected — given what he'd learned of the take-no-prisoners way she tackled things — but hadn't. Meredith's answering kiss left no doubt she was enjoying herself. Because of that, Tony couldn't get enough.

Still kissing her, he backed her toward his trailer's seating area. He swiveled, feeling dizzy from more than just the movement. Possibly because all his blood had rushed south. Possibly because they'd barely sucked in a breath since entering his trailer. Possibly because he'd never experienced such an all-consuming kiss. Yeah, it was probably that.

He was enough of a daredevil to want more. Lots more.

They sank onto the leather banquette, Tony pulling Meredith down to sprawl atop him. He ran his hands along the sensuous curve of her hips, traced the outline of her waist, squeezed his palms against her sides. If she'd been wearing a bra, he'd have had his hands atop the band, thumbs below her breasts. But she wasn't wearing a bra. Her taut nipples rubbed against his chest every few seconds, reminding him of all the reasons he was in favor of that decision.

Panting, she reared her head back. "Not bad."

"I know." He barely had breath for the words.

In seconds, Meredith's hands were on his chest. She flexed her palms against the muscles there, exploring him as though she meant to rub away his shirt with her bare hands.

"You're a woman who knows what she wants," he murmured.

"Got a problem with that?"

"I like it."

"Me, too."

They were perfectly matched. Tony pulled her down for another, longer kiss. Leather squeaked beneath them as they moved; a throw pillow slid to the floor. Half on the narrow banquette and half off, they arched to get closer. Nothing had ever felt this good.

He skimmed his fingertips over her smooth bare back, tucked his thumbs beneath her tank top straps, lifted the material away from her soft skin. He kissed the bare spot he'd revealed.

Sliding her hands down his spine, Meredith moaned her encouragement. Tony kissed her other shoulder. A few more inches with those straps and her tank top would fall away completely. He imagined her breasts, soft and naked. He imagined himself licking their pink-pink-pink tips, imagined her breathless cries while he did.

Really, they owed it to themselves to give it a whirl.

Meredith had other ideas. Before he could make another move, she pinned his shoulders to the banquette. Wearing a mischievous grin, she lifted herself up slightly, then straddled him. Her thighs squeezed against his, making him crazy. Her breasts brushed his chest as she flattened sinuously against him, putting as little space between their bodies as possible. She delved her fingers into his hair and tugged gently, making him aware of his scalp as a potential erogenous zone in a way he'd never considered.

"You're pretty good," she said, whispering the words against his ear. "But I still think I'm better."

He heard the teasing note in her voice and returned it in his. "I'll try harder to prove you wrong."

"I hope you do."

Her tongue flicked his earlobe. Tony tensed with pleasure, flexing his fingers helplessly against the leather beneath them. He'd known since the limo ride they'd be good together. But this good? It was unbelievable. He moaned as Meredith kissed his neck, as she released his shoulders and pulled his shirt from his jeans. Another minute and he'd be naked from the waist up. Two seconds later, so would she.

The trailer door creaked open. There was a thud as someone entered. Then, Aunt Nadine's voice.

"Tony! Have you got an extinguisher in here? Your ribs caught on fire! One even exploded. Although Esther thinks that might have been Roland's shirt self-destructing. Anyway, Errol tried to snuff out the blaze with his margarita, and that only made matters worse. I think — *oh*."

She stopped. Reluctantly, Tony transferred his attention from Meredith's shocked-into-stillness body to his aunt.

Nadine gawked at them both from the doorway. Her wide-eyed gaze traveled from Meredith's bare feet to her wild, mussed hair. From the tank top strap that had slid from one shoulder, to her hands grasping Tony's shirt, to his partly bared abdominal muscles. His aunt reddened. She clapped one hand over her eyes, then turned toward the trailer's kitchenette.

"I didn't see a thing. Not a thing! I'll be out of here in a jiff. Just point me toward your fire extinguisher. Have you got one?"

"I do now," Tony grumbled.

Things had gotten pretty fiery between him and Meredith. Until now. Leave it to his family to muck things up without even trying. It was some kind of twisted Valentine knack, not unlike their legendary talent for making movies. Only a lot less welcome.

With an apologetic look at Meredith, he reluctantly prepared to get vertical. "Hang on, Aunt Nadine. I'll get the fire extinguisher for you."

NINE

"A woman is like a teabag. You never know how strong she is until you put her in hot water."

— Mae West

The first issue of *Inside Hollywood* magazine featuring coverage of Valentine Studios' actor fantasy camp hit newsstands on Monday. Meredith learned about it when she arrived on set for the traditional sitcom table read. Instead of finding the camp guests seated at the big rectangular table provided, she discovered them huddled near the doorway, chattering excitedly.

"Maybe some of us will be in next week's issue!" a redheaded Nashville woman exclaimed, nearly jumping up and down with glee. "We could be in *Inside Hollywood*, just like Renée Zellweger!"

Meredith was familiar with *Inside Hollywood*. The weekly magazine was a cross between *US Weekly* and *The National Enquirer*, with a little *Cosmo*-style raunchiness thrown in. It published celebrity pictures, dubious trend reports, gossip columns, and the occasional "news story" — all for a competition-busting ninety-nine cents per weekly issue.

160

Frowning, she slung her script at the *Marley* place at the table and edged nearer to the group.

"At Valentine Studios, camp guests will hobnob with stars past and present, along with other Hollywood experts," a male accountant from Omaha read. "Including such notables as an animal trainer, a former 'Starsky and Hutch' stuntman, director Leon Webster, comedian and 'Hollywood Squares' regular French Smith, popular sitcom star Marley Madison, and more."

"We've met almost *all* those people!"

The six camp guests assigned to the faux sitcom exchanged thrilled glances. Meredith couldn't believe it. The article was non-news, a puff piece designed to tease more than inform. Meant to entice readers into shelling out another ninety-nine cents next week. Apparently, no one cared.

A stylish stay-at-home mom from a Dallas suburb grabbed her husband's arm. "Listen to this! 'Our secret undercover correspondent will have all the details on this exciting actor fantasy camp in next week's *Insider* profile.' " She pointed at the magazine, making the glossy pages wobble with each jab. " 'Remember, if you have information on this or any other story, e-mail us at scoop @insidehw.com or phone 1-800-4MY-SCOOP. Free subscription for every tip we publish. Some restrictions apply,' blah, blah, blah."

"Whoa, cool." A blond and tanned surfer from San Diego nodded. "Like, who has more inside information than us?"

A moment's silence. Then the whole group swiveled to stare at the room's single telephone, like dieters eyeballing the last Krispy Kreme. Clearly, they wanted to call in their own personal *Inside Hollywood* scoops — one of which might be the revelation of a fake Marley Madison.

If Meredith wasn't careful.

Beneath her halter top, coordinating hip hugger pants, and ten pounds of hairspray, she started to sweat. She *knew* she should have allowed the makeup artist to do that damned eyebrow waxing this morning. Marley didn't have a unibrow, and apparently Meredith *did*. What if it gave her away?

But still . . . waxing? Yanking innocent eyebrow hairs out by their roots? It sounded barbaric. If Andy Rooney didn't have to get waxed, neither should she.

"Places, people!" the director snapped, entering the room with a cappuccino in one hand and a clipboard in the other. Like most of the crew — several members of which trailed him — he wore a freebie T-shirt from another production, a pair of khaki shorts, sneakers, and a gimme cap. "Let's get going. We haven't got all day to whip you amateurs into shape. Our show tapes its finale in less than two weeks."

One of the camp guests rolled up the magazine and shoved it into her bulging purse. Everyone scurried to the table. Scripts rustled. Squaring hers like the professional she needed to seem, Meredith folded her hands and waited to begin.

She'd studied her lines backward and forward last night. First she'd helped put out the rib fire, of course. Then she'd shared a make-do dinner of margaritas and chips (Tony had looked at her as though potato salad and side dishes were foreign concepts) and unsuccessfully tried to wait out the night-owl elder Valentines, hoping to get Tony alone again. But to no avail. Esther, Roland, Errol, and Nadine had been as lively at midnight as they'd been at eight. Meredith had wound up in bed at twelve-thirty, with her sitcom script for company instead of Tony.

As a distraction from what she really wanted to be doing — jumping Tony again — script studying had failed miserably. Staring at printed pages wasn't nearly as much fun as enjoying his strong arms around her. Savoring his potent kisses. Undressing his hard-muscled body. Even the fanciest typeface couldn't make her go weak in the knees, and paragraph formatting did not have the power to make her heart pound. She was an academic, sure. But she wasn't crazy.

On the other hand, she now felt more prepared for this fake starlet stuff than ever. Re-luctantly, or not. Studying her lines had helped a great deal, and Meredith had to admit that this morning she felt more com-fortable. An A-student all her life, she'd never entered into any situation as unpre-pared as she had these past days masquer-ading as Marley.

She glanced up to see an assistant passing out sheets of green photocopied paper. Ac-cepting hers, she felt her *uh-oh* sensors kick into overdrive. The same way they did when a troupe of sticky-fingered preschoolers en-tered the museum to "see the exhibits" and be "exposed to culture." Only worse.

"What are these?" the Nashville woman asked.

"New script pages," the director said. "Cooked up by the folks in Sitcom Writing class. Learn 'em, live 'em, memorize 'em. Whenever there's a change in the script, the new pages will come out in a different color. You take out the old ones." He demonstrated by ripping out several plain white sheets. "And slip in the new ones. That way, we can make sure everybody's on the same page. Li-terally. Ha!"

He chuckled, crumpling up the pages which contained the lines Meredith had memorized so carefully. Dispiritedly, she flipped through the green sheets. Her scenes had been rearranged, rewritten, and in some

164

cases, completely revamped.

She'd have to learn everything all over again. Right now, on the spot. For the first time, Meredith felt a glimmer of empathy for what Marley must go through. From a distance, her sister's starlet life looked easy. Up close, things definitely weren't a piece of cake.

Mmmm, cake, Meredith thought distractedly. This morning she'd arrived at the commissary, ready for her usual bagel and shmear, only to be informed that "Mr. V. says you're off carbs, Miss Madison. Sorry about that mix-up with the cheeseburger yesterday. We're supposed to give you this today."

They'd presented her with a rubbery egg white omelet, paired with two pitiful tomato slices and a parsley garnish. No toast. No hash browns. Not even ketchup. Just that sad wedge of flabby egg white and a few veggies.

Meredith had eaten everything. Including the parsley. All the while, she'd dreamed of shoving the whole plate right up Tony's nose. Interfering jerk (with good kissing skills). He was starving her (while turning her on). When she tracked him down today (ready to finish what they'd started) she'd —

"Marley, you're up," the director said, interrupting her reverie.

"Right. Fine. Sorry." Suddenly, nervousness swamped her. Glancing around the table, she saw a sea of expectant faces — okay, about a *dozen* expectant faces, if you wanted to be technical about it. Everyone waited. The room closed in, so silent you could have heard a triple-berry shmear being spread on a sesame bagel.

Focus.

It was only reading. She'd spent most of her life doing that. As a kid, she'd taken books up to her tree house, on trips to the lake ("Look at the scenery!" her dad would gripe. "It's a damned vacation!"), across town to her friends' houses, and even to the movies. She'd found solace, understanding, wisdom, and humor in reading. It wouldn't fail her now.

It didn't. Except for one complaint from the director to "Quit *emoting,* Miss Madison. It's a table read, not a high school play," everything went fine. She read well and managed most of the new lines without stumbling.

Feeling pleased, she spent twenty minutes signing autographs, then headed for her next class: Pilates. This time, she wasn't expected to teach. Instead, "Marley" would be there as local color, showing the actor fantasy camp guests what it was like to sweat Hollywood style — with actors and actresses for company.

She hoped for an easy workout, a minimally comfortable wardrobe, and a super-short session. After all, if starlets were supposed to subsist on rabbit food, they couldn't be expected to perform strenuous activity, could they?

Besides, Marley was a notorious washout when it came to anything sports-related. Her idea of athletic activity was scouring a sales rack while wearing a four-hundred-dollar Juicy Couture cashmere track suit and munching a PowerBar.

Meredith, on the other hand, was an inveterate tomboy. As a kid, she'd played soccer, softball, and basketball, run track, and kicked butt during the occasional flag football game. A wimpy Hollywood-style "exercise class" was probably just an excuse to see and be seen. More than likely, the regulars didn't even take off their sunglasses. It would be no challenge for her. She was sure of it.

"Tony, we have a problem," Errol said, coming into the office.

Ensconced at his desk with Nadine, a chef from the studio commissary, and Harry all waiting nearby, Tony glanced up. He'd been trying to phone potential investors all morning to confirm their attendance at the camp's finale. Instead, one interruption after another had cropped up. In New York where his life was normal (and so were the people around him), he'd have accomplished twice as much work by now.

In some ways, e-commerce and the computers that enabled it were a lot easier to deal with than people were. Microprocessors cranked out calculations. SSL protocols kept data secure. The Internet waited 24/7, ready whenever you were. If any of those components caused problems, they were solvable.

Determinedly, Tony glanced up at his uncle. "What's the matter? Did Roland invade Wardrobe again?"

Errol shook his head. "Worse. He's offering that class of his: Intro to the Casting Couch."

Tony groaned. "Any takers?"

"Trish, the secretary from the business office."

"The one who likes Roland's 'retro chic'?"

"The very same," Errol said. "Fortunately, I took down the sign-up sheet before any more poor, deluded souls registered for the class."

"Good." Tony thanked his uncle, then reached for the phone. "I'll call Roland right now."

"No need." Airily, Errol straightened the starched white square tucked in his suit coat pocket. "I've already ordered security to escort my brother off the lot."

"What?"

If the press got wind of discord at Valentine Studios, the adverse publicity wouldn't do their actor fantasy camp any favors. This was just another gambit in his uncles' ongoing rivalry. Porn versus PBS. Hawaiian-print Lurex shirts versus vintage Armani suits. Casting couch shenanigans versus . . . casting a brother out on his ear. Unceremoniously.

Tony paused in mid-dial. He'd have to phone security instead and revoke Errol's instructions.

"I had to do it," Errol explained urgently. "Roland makes the whole studio look bad. He'll only drag you down, Tony. Take my word for it."

"Thanks, Uncle Errol. But I told you I'm handling everything here. Don't you have a" — he cast about for something that would keep his uncle out of his hair for a while — "golf game to get to, or something?"

Nadine spoke up. "Golf? Don't be silly. Valentine men always overclub. They're notorious duffers. At the club, they call him Errol 'Double Bogey' Valentine."

"That's because of my resemblance to Humphrey Bogart!"

"It's because you whiff so often, dear." She turned to Tony again. "Also, Valentine men get the yips. The silly game gets them coming and going. It's embarrassing." She looked worried. "You don't play, do you? I should warn Marley."

"Marley" — it felt strange now to call Meredith that — "doesn't need to know about my golf status. We're business associates."

Nadine and Errol shared a look. "Certainly. Right *now* that's all you are. But with a little prompting —"

"No prompting." Tony interrupted before she could ride that train of thought much farther. "What did you need? As soon as I get off the phone with security, I'll — hang on."

Security answered. Holding up a hand to halt the buzz of conversation in his office, Tony left instructions for the guards *not* to cart his uncle forcibly from the back lot and asked them to send Roland over to Tony's office later, instead. That accomplished, he gestured for his aunt to make her request.

"Well. The thing is, Tony, I think you're a little detached from this entire actor fantasy camp experience." She folded her hands primly in front of her. "Like most Valentine men, you can lead the troops, but you don't want to get down there with them and fight."

Given her earnestness, Tony didn't have the heart to point out that he'd been fighting for the studio for the past week and a half, abandoning his perfectly good non-Hollywood life in the process. He tilted his head, listening as she went on.

"You're not in New York City anymore —"

Again with the New York City digs? Tony didn't get it.

"— and you can't operate the way you used to."

170

Impatiently, he glanced at the chef and Harry, both still waiting for their share of his attention. "What way is that?"

"Without any *heart*," Nadine said fervently. "Without any personal involvement."

Beside her, Errol nodded. Clearly, they'd discussed this. Come to think of it, Errol was the one who'd busted his chops at the Bayberry reception. *Be easy on her,* he'd said. *You're not in New York City anymore.* What the hell did that *mean?*

"I'm plenty involved. Thanks for your input, Aunt Nadine."

Tony moved on to the chef, a patient Asian man in toque and culinary whites. "What's the trouble at the commissary?"

"Wait!" Nadine cried. "You didn't listen to the rest of my idea. Errol and I think you ought to revamp part of the actor fantasy camp and make a place for yourself in it. Say . . . oh, I don't know . . . at the sitcom taping?"

The sitcom taping. Where Meredith (aka Marley) spent most of her time. Suddenly, his family's meddling MO became clear.

"I'll think about it," he said, suppressing a smile.

"All right." His aunt and uncle shared a conspiratorial look, then left. Tony had no doubt they high-fived each other in the hallway.

Two down, two to go.

"The commissary?" he asked again.

171

"Have you changed orders for the kitchen?" the chef asked. "Somebody phoned our suppliers this morning and cancelled our egg delivery. Instead of eggs, we're getting four dozen sesame bagels and several pounds of triple-berry cream cheese."

"I'll look into it," Tony said, dismissing him. Next, he turned to his ever-patient driver. "What's up, Harry?"

"Not much, Mr. V. Will you be needing my services later this afternoon? My granddaughter's got a school play, and —"

"Say no more. The afternoon's yours."

The driver grinned. "I thought sure you'd say no after that rigmarole with the other Valentines. You're all right."

"Hey. Don't let it get around." Tony grinned, too.

Esther bustled into the office, winded and wound up. " 'Don't let it get around'? Oh, *good*. You *have* heard about this fiasco with the faux press junket." She pressed a hand to her bosom, a fading *grande dame* overcome with relief. "I was so worried you hadn't been informed!"

"Informed of what, Aunt Esther?"

"It would have been *disastrous!* All those people, so disappointed. All that good lighting, gone to waste."

She struck a pose, arm outflung, knuckles against her forehead. Harry hesitated on his way out, clearly intrigued by Esther's dramatic performance.

"Informed of what, Aunt Esther?" Tony repeated.

"You're familiar with the faux press junket? Designed to give our guests the experience of touring to promote a new project, to let them bask in the spotlight, being interviewed and videotaped —"

"It was my idea."

"No need to get snippy." She waved her hand. Noticed Harry standing nearby. Paused. Patting her hair in place, she smiled broadly at him. "I don't think we've met. Esther Valentine, kid sister to the louts who run this place — my dear nephew excepted, of course. And you're . . . ?"

"Harry McIntire. Charmed, I'm sure."

Clearly smitten, he bent to kiss Esther's proffered hand. She giggled. Tony rolled his eyes. Geriatric tiddly winks were the last thing he needed.

"Aunt Esther? The press junket?" he prodded.

She batted her eyelashes at Harry. "The reporter cancelled," she said in an aside, not glancing at Tony. "Just up and quit. Can you imagine that? When the experience might have been so entertaining. I was even going to assist him —"

"I'll do it!" Harry blurted.

He couldn't be serious. Disregarding Harry's outburst, Tony picked up his PDA, looking for a substitute reporter who might accept a last-minute job for extra cash.

"You're *not* going to assist," he told Esther. "You're going to clear out of here, along with Nadine and Errol and Roland, and let me do my job."

"Don't be so *boring*, Tony. I live to help."

Actually, Esther lived to get married. Four husbands so far, and none of them had stuck. By now, Tony figured she ought to have a standing reservation at the church. By the looks of the flirtatious glances his aunt was tossing Harry, his driver was in line to become lucky groom number five.

"You need me," Esther insisted. "The first interview is supposed to start in half an hour. That's not enough time for you to get one of your hoity-toity New York reporter friends out here."

Again? "What's wrong with New York? I like it there. I'm going back there when I'm through with all this." *Before I forget what real, non-La-La-Land life is like.*

Esther pouted. Harry noticed, and leaped to the rescue. "We can do it together! I'll help Esther do the interviews."

Tony shook his head. "Save yourself while you still can."

"There hasn't been much driving to do anyway. I've got to keep busy somehow. Right, Mr. V.?"

"You're crazy, Harry."

174

Scrolling through his PDA's phone list, Tony located the number he wanted. A freelancer who wouldn't mind spending a few afternoons indulging his actor fantasy camp guests' dreams of personal interviews and fawning attention. He dialed.

A weird silence filled the room. He glanced up to find Esther and Harry both skewering him with jointly accusing expressions. Apparently, they *wanted* to collaborate on this crazy scheme.

"Valentine men are very stubborn," Esther told Harry.

Harry murmured his agreement.

That was the last straw. Tony disconnected.

"You want to do this?"

They nodded like kids offered free PlayStations. Tony heaved a sigh. Allowing them to go through with the interviews would keep at least *one* family member out of his hair. It would save the studio one more salary, too. Those were definite pluses.

"Fine." He handed over the sheet of agreed-upon canned interview questions. "But no backing out. If you're in, you're in all the way."

Esther sighed. "Valentine men can be so pedantic."

"I want a commitment," Tony warned.

No problem for Harry. "You got it, Mr. V. So long as I can still have that time off for

175

my granddaughter's play."

Tony agreed.

Esther squealed with delight. "A grand-daughter! Do you have pictures? Let me see. I just love kids, but *certain* members of my family haven't been very cooperative in that department." She leaned nearer to Harry, placing her hand confidingly on his arm. "Tony had a bad breakup with a former girl-friend, you know. His business partner. I sup-pose we should have seen it coming. She was" — her voice lowered to a whisper — "a *New Yorker.*"

Harry raised his eyebrows, stopping in the midst of unfolding his wallet to display the sheaf of plastic-encased pictures within. He glanced speculatively at Tony.

"It was a long time ago," Tony said. "Her New Yorkerness had nothing to do with it."

Esther, predictably, wouldn't leave it at that. "He broke it off with her," she told Harry, "and she got back at him by wrecking some of his dot-com deals. It was all very hush-hush."

"Hmmm." Another speculative glance.

"Aunt Esther —"

"I'm not worried, though." She waved blithely. "Bad karma always comes back to haunt a person. She'll get hers someday —"

"I'm picking up the phone," Tony warned. "Three seconds from now, your interviewing days will be over."

With a huffy over-the-shoulder look at her nephew, Esther quit dishing. Instead, she linked arms with Harry, then accepted the sleeve of photos he offered.

"We'll be in the interview suites," she said, tossing her head. To Harry, she added, "Valentine men are very discreet about their love lives. They always have been."

Harry shrugged and let himself be led away. As they left the office, Tony heard Esther *ooh*ing and *aah*ing over each photograph.

"*I* should live so long to have grandchildren as beautiful as these!" she cried, her long-suffering tone echoing down the building's hallway. "You're so lucky, Harry!"

"I am now," Harry said. "Now that I've found you."

More giggling.

Tony sighed, then reached for the phone to make his calls. If they were *all* lucky, he'd interest enough investors to keep the actor fantasy camp running full-time. He'd already invited several potential backers to the Valentine Studios showcase — culminating in the live studio sitcom taping — scheduled for a week from Friday. When he'd arranged the finale, he'd expected Marley Madison's presence to be a draw. Now that Meredith was here instead. . . .

He flashed on her hairy legs, butt-hiding, hip-tied sweatshirt, and bright, intelligent eyes. Suddenly jittery, he grabbed his cell phone to make calls on the run, then headed across the back lot. If he expected to pull this off, he'd need to get more involved. If Meredith gave herself away by having a unibrow (whatever that was) or acting brainy (God forbid), they were all sunk.

TEN

"Will positively produce a rapid growth of hair on bald heads, where the glands and follicles are not totally destroyed."
— advertisement for Dr. Scott's Electric Hair Brush (1884)

Freshly showered and damp-haired, Meredith stuffed her battered script into her workout bag. She slung the bag over her shoulder, wincing at the soreness in her just-worked-out muscles, then made her way past the locker room's row of lighted makeup mirrors. In front of them, half-dressed female actor fantasy camp guests jockeyed for position.

Blow-dryers whined. Hairspray and powder clogged the air. Chitchat raced from one woman to the next. Supremely uncomfortable in such surroundings, Meredith edged past, her overloaded bag bumping into nearby lockers. She almost clocked a redhead who'd bent over to buckle her sandals.

"Sorry," Meredith muttered, hurrying on.

Every eye followed her. Ducking beneath the scrutiny, she fixed her gaze on the door leading to the now-empty Pilates room. Unlike her sister, she hated being the center of attention. It made her feel overexposed. Uncertain.

179

Right now, on the heels of the difficult class she'd just struggled through, it made her feel foolish, too. She'd thought she'd nail that class. Instead, she'd seen the other Pilates participants nudging each other, pointing out her mistakes. She'd heard them whispering, talking about her thighs and her hair, her exercise technique and her sweaty face.

Be confident, like Marley, a part of her demanded. The rest of her offered a silent (and rude) four-letter-word comeback. She just wanted to forget all this and get away — preferably to the studio archives, where nobody would bother her and nobody would judge her.

Outside, all the studio-supplied golf carts were taken. Swearing under her breath, Meredith squinted toward the business office, where Harry sometimes parked the limo. No dice.

"Hey, Marley. Need a ride?" someone asked.

She looked. A hulking man grinned from behind the wheel of a golf cart, sporting a potbelly, a serious comb-over, and an "Insurance Salesmen are Premium Lovers" T-shirt. He patted the seat beside him. "I've got room for you right here, sweet thing."

She'd just bet he had room. There was always room in the Jerkmobile. On the verge of saying so, Meredith stopped herself. One of her usual smart-mouthed comebacks wouldn't do. *Channel Marley,* she ordered herself. *Be polite. Gracious.*

"No, thanks." She started walking.

He accelerated enough to keep pace. "Come on, Miss TV Star. I'll drive you any-place you want to go." He chuckled. "Just so long as it's my trailer, with me."

Meredith glanced sideways. Subtle, he wasn't. "Gee, that's nice. But to be capable of driving me anywhere, you'd first have to have your gaze surgically separated from my breasts. Are you up for that?"

Whoops. So much for gracious.

"Huh?" He blinked, still staring at her chest.

Boob Guy clearly wasn't quick on the up-take.

"Not interested. Thanks, anyway. See you around."

There. That was better. Pleased with her-self, she waved and headed purposefully into the shadow of a nearby soundstage, still on her way to the archives building. Here in the shade, the air felt cooler. Her damp hair slapped her shoulders, and goose bumps rose on her arms.

Tony would have her butt in a sling if he saw her looking so casual. Meredith just hadn't had the energy to go through the whole hair and makeup rigmarole again. Maybe she could make it to the archives before she ran into Tony. She walked faster.

Putt . . . putt. The golf cart kept pace.

Boob Guy leaned out. "Too stuck up to hang out with the little people? Is that it?"

Heck, she *was* the little people. "No, that's not —"

"I've seen your type before. You think you're too good for everyone else. All I want is an autograph . . . or something."

It was the *or something* that bothered her. Especially given the leering way he said it. Meredith shook her head. "Not right now. I'd be happy to sign an autograph for you during one of my usual post-class sessions, or —"

"Hey! If it wasn't for people like me, you wouldn't even have a job, much less be a star. You ought to be nicer."

This bozo was really pushing it. She stopped, crossing her arms over her chest. "Sorry. In my book, letting you ogle me goes beyond 'nice.' "

He shrugged, now running his gaze across her hips and down her legs. "You're the one who put yourself on display, sweet thing."

Poor Marley. Did she have to put up with this crap every day? "Just leave me alone, all right?"

She started walking again, faster this time. He chugged in her wake, easily catching up. Then passing her. With relief, Meredith watched him go by.

The golf cart stopped, tires squeaking. Boob Guy got out.

"I get it. You're acting, right?" He made his fingers into quotation marks around the word *acting*, comprehension dawning on his face. "You really had me going there, Marley. You're good." Another leer.

"You're unbelievable."

He preened.

"I don't mean that in a good way. Does this approach actually work for you? Ever? Or does it usually get you arrested?" She glanced around for a security guy. Unfortunately, none were in sight. "I'm betting on the latter."

Boob Guy frowned, clueless. "How about that ride now?"

"No." Shaking her head, Meredith walked faster.

An instant later, she'd nearly passed him. God, what a creep.

He grabbed her. "You say no, but your body says yes. *All over.*"

Disgustingly, he scrutinized her again, hand still clamped on her arm. He gave another obnoxious chuckle.

"Oh." She widened her eyes. "You read body language?"

"I read yours, baby."

"Great. Tell me what this means, then."

She kneed him in the groin. He wheezed and released her instantly, crumpling to a

183

hunched-over position with both hands on his family jewels. He gasped for air.

"It means a lady has a right to walk by herself if she wants to." Meredith adjusted her workout bag, then strode to his studio-loaner golf cart. She tossed her bag onto the passenger seat, then got in on the driver's side. "It means I'm taking this, too. I'm sure there'll be another cart along soon. Oh, and thanks for the ride . . . *sweet thing!*"

"You *assaulted* one of my guests?" Tony asked.

He paced the length of Meredith's trailer's seating area. All twenty feet of it. Confined to such a tiny space, he seemed twice as big to her. Twice as imposing. Twice as uninformed about the reality of the situation.

Meredith propped both feet on the banquette table, relishing the clunk of her motorcycle boots. She'd changed into her own clothes after reaching her trailer this afternoon. Sliding into her comfy cargo pants and a T-shirt had felt like coming home.

"He was a slimeball," she argued.

"He was a *paying* slimeball. The kind you — as Marley — are supposed to be nice to."

"Niceness has its limits." She picked up a pair of stilettos, delivered in her absence by the Wardrobe Department. She hurled them toward the bedroom's pink glow. Later, she'd stash them someplace where they couldn't

184

wind up winching her feet into unnatural positions. "I said I'd pretend to be Marley, not morph into a complete patsy. Was I supposed to let him grab me?"

Tony stopped. Looked over his shoulder, eyes narrowed. "He grabbed you?"

She shrugged. "He won't do it again. I promise you that."

A look of disbelief spread over his face. He scrubbed it away with his palm, then shook his head at her. "Jesus. Remind me not to step out of line with you."

"Don't step out of line with me," she teased.

Tony went on pacing, dressed for business in a pair of dark pants and a charcoal gray polo in some expensive lightweight knit. He was bugged by this, she could tell. His shoulders tensed, hard as granite. His expression darkened a little more by the minute.

She tried to ease his mind. "Look, I was having a bad day, all right? My script got changed this morning —"

"I'll help you run lines from now on."

"— I don't like being the center of attention —"

"That's what you — as Marley — are here for!"

"— and I wasn't in the mood for a creep like that. I'd gotten out of Pilates class a few minutes earlier, and" — *I flunked it and the makeup queen routine afterward* — "I felt like

185

kicking butt." She spread her hands. "Boob Guy was in the wrong place at the wrong time."

"Boob Guy?" Tony grinned. "Nice. What's your nickname for me, I wonder?"

"Prince Charming. Duh."

"Ahhh. The limo ride."

They both lapsed into silence. If he was remembering the same steamy, dreamy things she was remembering . . .

"You can't take the law into your own hands, Dirty Harry," he said sternly. "Try to keep your knees to yourself."

"I was provoked!"

"Pilates class is not a recognized defense."

She hadn't meant *that*. The amused look on Tony's face made her forget what she *had* meant, though. Ever since he'd arrived a few minutes ago, Meredith had been too busy defending herself to really look at him. Now, she did.

Swathed in late-afternoon sunlight, outfitted in hard-bodied muscle, and absently smacking his fist into his palm — a motion she doubted he was aware of — Tony looked like a tough guy hero. He looked like a protector of women and children, like a brawler ready to go raise hell . . . one who found her impossibly entertaining. She wished he didn't look so scrumptious. That made it so much harder to be aggravated with him.

"Pilates was *grueling*," she argued, mustering up a little indignation to go with her hormonally driven impulse to just jump him and be done with it. "I'm usually good at athletic things. But they had mats, and machines, and a boot-camp-style instructor. I didn't know what I was getting into."

He scoffed. "Mats. Machines. Big deal."

"You haven't seen *The Reformer.*"

"Who's that? The instructor?"

"It's not a who, it's a what. A torture device with ropes and pulleys and acres of gleaming wood and shiny steel. Kind of like a medieval rack. Only glossier. The Dark Ages, à la Hollywood."

"That doesn't sound so bad."

"Ha! I was on that thing for what felt like *hours*. In super slow-mo! I tried to get through it by pretending I was crushing your head with my thighs —"

"Hey, kinky —"

"— as revenge for the egg white omelet fiasco. But it didn't work. The damned rack just about killed me!"

"It sure as hell made you grumpy."

"Bite me."

Tony grinned. His gaze passed over her speculatively. He rubbed his jaw again. Probably he was still thinking about that head-crushing thigh move. He'd definitely looked intrigued by that. A man who liked to live dangerously. Then his dark eyes softened, just a smidge.

"Tell you what. I know something that'll take your mind off this."

"The archives room." She pumped her fist. "I knew it!"

He gave her a bemused look. "Quit guessing and come on."

Tony's distraction technique didn't exactly get off to a rollicking start. First he had to all but handcuff and blindfold Meredith to get her to agree to come with him without divulging any details in advance. Then he had to endure a nonstop stream of speculation during the walk from her trailer to his.

"I know. You found a first-edition signed copy of Ogilvy's *Confessions of an Advertising Man*," was her latest guess. She looked unbelievably excited at the thought. "It's been out of print for at least a decade. I've been looking for a copy for *ages*."

"That's not it."

She regrouped. "A recording of rare ad jingles?"

"Nope."

"I've got it! A Coca-Cola collectible. That's sweet, Tony. But they manufactured so many of them, everything but the rarest pieces are essentially worthless."

"You can't stand not having all the answers, can you?" He stopped at the foot of the steps. "Just let yourself be surprised," he ordered.

That lasted all of three seconds.

188

Then Meredith piped up from behind him.

"Is it a secret cache of *The World's Funniest TV Commercials You Never Saw . . . But Wanted To Because of the Swedish Nudity They Contain* on videotape?"

Shaking his head, Tony grinned. "Even I'm not that tacky."

He opened his trailer door, motioning for her to precede him inside.

She did. With a sigh. "Then it *must* be the archives room. We're going to your place first for the keys, right? Then we're leaving?"

"No. We're staying here for a while."

That didn't make her happy. She stood beside him, arms folded, tapping her foot impatiently. The motion drew his eye to her boots. Her silly, overcompensating boots. Boots like that belonged on a tattooed biker, not on a va-va-voom woman.

Definitely not on a supposedly Marley-style starlet.

She squinted at him. "This is *not* the archives building."

"I know. It's even better."

"Archives are history waiting to be discovered. Nothing is better."

He raised his eyebrows. Meaningfully diverted his gaze to the leather banquette which had hosted their roly-poly kissing session last night. Waited.

"Okay. So some things are better. But still —"

"You haven't seen what I brought you here for." When she did, she'd be so happy. Tony was sure of it. "Just wait and see."

She brightened. "You're giving me my *own* key to the archives building! Gift-wrapped. Is that it?"

"No."

"Why not? Getting access to the archives is my motivation for doing all this, you know."

For some reason, that irked him. "Later."

"Now. Come on, Tony. I tried to get in this afternoon, but the door was locked." She wiggled her fingers. "Give me the key."

He stifled a sigh. Damn, she was a difficult woman to cheer up. When he'd tracked her down in her trailer, Meredith had looked fit to perform a bare-handed tonsillectomy on the first man who said two words to her. Now, stomping his floor with those boots of hers, she didn't seem much improved.

Except now her ire was directed at him.

Maybe he should tell her he'd already had security escort Boob Guy off the lot. Nah. It was important that she know Tony was in charge here. He couldn't let her think she could ride roughshod over his actor fantasy camp guests. Or him.

The last thing he needed was somebody *else* who thought they knew what was best for him. His family was already working hard at that routine, anyway. They hadn't left him alone for a minute. They wanted to know why most of his clothes were black (the New York uniform). Why he didn't own a car (when taxis worked perfectly well). Why he didn't like burgers with avocado and (God forbid) sprouts on them.

From the moment he'd stepped into the smoggy, welcome-to-L.A. sunshine outside the airport, the Valentine clan had been pestering him, second-guessing him, and doing their best to suck him right back into their close-knit craziness. He'd resisted so far, but —

No. He wouldn't think about that now. Right now, he had a surprise planned for Meredith. When she got a load of what he'd done for her, she'd forget all about that bozo Boob Guy. No woman could resist the arrangements he'd made. Not even a woman as untraditional, outspoken, and brash as Meredith.

"Come on," he said, putting a hand to the small of her back. He drew her toward his trailer's bedroom. There, Tony stopped in front of a covered, shoulder-high, rolling rack. He sneaked an anticipatory glance at her. "Ready?"

She delivered him a killing look.

Oh, yeah. She was ready.

He whipped off the cover. "Ta-da!"

The cover billowed to the carpet. Its passing ruffled the things hanging on the rack, making them flutter in the breeze.

Beside him, Meredith stiffened. Her chin

lifted, and her eyes narrowed. She glanced at him.

Obviously, she was too stunned to realize the full extent of her happiness.

"I smuggled some things out of Wardrobe for you!" he said. "To help you impersonate Marley better. I had to guess on the sizes, but they ought to be pretty close. I've got a good memory."

He curved his hands through the air, demonstrating his masterful recall of her figure. Any minute now, she'd understand that he'd granted her the ultimate female wish — unlimited clothes. Then she'd pounce on him with unbridled gratitude. He could hardly wait.

The bonus of it was, he'd have simultaneously cheered up Meredith *and* made sure she took another step toward transforming into a realistic Marley clone. Congratulating himself on his knack for multitasking, Tony watched her.

"I'm not wearing this stuff," she announced.

He didn't understand. She wasn't thrilled? "Yes, you are. You're wearing it. Any of it you like. Start choosing."

"I can be like Marley in my own clothes," she insisted.

"Sure, you can. Marley looks *exactly* like a pint-sized, badass biker with an allergy to sex appeal."

"Hey!"

"And no bra."

She gasped. Clapped her hands over her chest. "I wasn't expecting company!"

Tony frowned, pissed that she hadn't jumped for joy over his surprise. All women liked clothes. Didn't they? He'd picked out these things at the Wardrobe trailer himself, imagining with every item he grabbed how pleased Meredith would be. Seeing her disgruntled expression now put him on edge.

"You agreed to do this," he reminded her. He jabbed his hand toward the rack of dresses, pants, sexy tops, and — he hadn't been able to help himself — one or two lingerie-type things. "This is your ammunition. Hop to it, princess."

"No."

She glared at a baby blue miniskirt. Her expression suggested the thing might jump off the rack and bite her on the ass. Tony knew that was ridiculous. It would never be able to penetrate the hip-tied sweatshirt she'd put on. Again.

"What is your problem?" he asked, frustrated. She'd reverted to her old slobby ways since the tank top appearance last night, and he didn't know why. He snatched a dress and held it up to her. "This would look great on you."

She smacked it away. "Save it for someone more gullible."

"Or this." He dangled a nightie from his index finger. "I'd love to see you in this."

"Let's keep it PG-rated, okay?"

"How about this? TV starlets wear this kind of stuff all the time."

Meredith scrutinized the low-cut orange shirt and frilly pink skirt in his hands. "I don't think those even go together."

Ah-hah. She *did* have girly instincts. She just kept them under wraps. Certain technophobic clients were the same way. They hid their curiosity about digitizing their businesses, afraid of revealing their lack of knowledge. Once Tony explained the benefits of e-commerce, though, their initial resistance melted. Just like Meredith's would.

If he could somehow combine her know-it-all tendencies with her latent girly-girlness . . .

He added a pair of sequined pants. "*This* matches."

She smirked. "Sure. On stage in Vegas. During a power outage."

He tried to look discouraged. "How the hell am I supposed to see that? I don't know squat about clothes."

"You don't?" Cautious hopefulness entered her expression.

A shrug. "I just know what I like to see on a woman."

"Then we can take away this whole rack. I'm betting on nudity as your hands-down favorite."

And her point was?

"You'd be a million times better at putting together all this stuff than I would be."

"That'd be a switch," Meredith muttered.

"What?"

"Nothing." Contemplatively, she touched a shimmery green top with no back and a plunging front. "I guess I could show you what goes together. You know, like a tutorial."

There it was again. That spark he'd glimpsed. Identifying it now, Tony realized it was Meredith in her element as the one person in the room who knew all the facts. In this case, he doubted she was experienced in clothes coordinating. But she was definitely more with-it than he was. He could see she liked that.

"You're the expert," he said.

Hesitantly, she bit her lip. She scanned the clothes. If he could get her into some of these outfits on a regular basis, it would bolster her appearance as Marley tenfold.

"I'm the expert," she repeated, sounding uncertain. A curious vulnerability softened her face as she grabbed the sleeve of a leather jacket and held it up against her forearm. "The expert in clothes."

More than anything else, her vulnerability clinched it for Tony. He wanted to see her dress up, to hear her lecture him on wearing sequins with silk, to be berated for sporting purple after Labor Day. He wanted to en-

195

courage the sassy, know-it-all part of Meredith . . . the part he'd begun to look forward to tangling with.

"Go to it, expert." He smacked her playfully on the ass. "I'll be out here, waiting."

Left alone with the clothes, Meredith stared at them. Tony had done pretty good, she had to admit. These outfits looked a lot like the ones hanging in Marley's Hollywood Hills closet — the ones Meredith had, on occasion, borrowed (along with Marley's BMW) while house-sitting for her sister.

Hey, there had to be some perks to helping out.

Back to the clothes. Glancing through them, Meredith absently rubbed her derrière. Tony was incorrigible . . . but despite her better judgment, she'd begun to look forward to tangling with him. If nothing else, he definitely kept her on her toes.

However, he was also *way* clueless about clothes. Even worse than she was — which was saying something. The moment she'd realized she could potentially grab the upper hand with him, she'd felt a funny little tingle. A tingle that had intrigued her.

All through this actor fantasy camp experience, Tony had kept her off-kilter. For once, *she* could be the one with all the answers. Sure, they'd be fairly bogus answers. But he wouldn't know that.

The truth was, Meredith had spent her whole life being lectured to. Her mom had meant well, but she'd rarely let up, using Marley as a perfect example of color coordination, of the wonders of abandoning sweatpants, on the thrills of wearing shoes with high heels. Meredith figured she must have absorbed some of that stuff, despite her efforts to tune it out. Right?

Right. Besides, the temptation of seeming like an expert in the one area she'd always blown it proved too much for her to withstand. She had to do it.

Fifteen minutes later, after struggling into a pair of leather bootleg pants and a snakeskin-print silky shirt, Meredith emerged from Tony's bedroom. Her heart pounded as she traversed the trailer's brief hallway. She stepped barefoot into the kitchenette.

Tony had settled on the banquette to wait for her, a Pepsi in one hand and the TV remote in the other. He hadn't noticed her yet. His attention was focused on the TV. On the screen, channels scrolled past at breakneck speed.

She hesitated, struck by how strangely intimate their situation felt. Seeing Tony like this, in his private space with his guard down and his infamous all-work attitude temporarily shelved, Meredith felt as though she'd been given a peek at the man behind the business suit. The guy behind the entrepreneurial ideas and the Valentine family legacy. The real Tony.

Apparently, the real Tony was a lot more laid-back than she'd thought. He was also, it seemed, interested in preserving a full head of hair. A commercial for men's hair plugs had captured his rapt attention.

It was nice to know even the most macho of men had moments of vulnerability.

"Looking to reseed someplace else?" she asked, feeling a teeny wave of tenderness engulf her. "Your chest, maybe? The gorilla chest hair look might come back into fashion. You never know. Your new jungle fur could be braided or dreadlocked or highlighted —"

He jerked. Swiveled guiltily to confront her. "No! I don't need that stuff." He yanked a hand through his — she had to admit — thick, dark hair. "It doesn't hurt to plan ahead, that's all. Besides," he added defensively, lowering his voice a few registers, "the blonde in the commercial looks hot."

"She's a Ph.D. in" — Meredith peered closer — "Hairology?"

"I like smart women."

Again, a tingle raced up her spine. She found herself smiling goofily at Tony, pleased he wasn't scared away by the concept of a woman whose IQ was bigger than her cup size. Even if he *was* capable of being duped into believing Hairology was a real science. It was kind of cute, actually. She sighed.

Oh, God. Was she falling for Tony?

"Nice outfit," he said, switching off the TV. He came toward her, frank appreciation in his gaze. "Turn around."

Mind spinning, she swiveled. Her leather pants creaked in the stillness. Too late, Meredith felt the leather cup her backside and stretch to accommodate her hips. Why hadn't she realized before how tight these pants were?

She completed her revolution and found Tony's attention still locked on her. He swallowed hard.

"Again."

She complied, deciding to take refuge in lecturing. "These pants go with this shirt because, ahh, they're both based on the animal kingdom. Specifically, cows, and . . . um, snakes. That's called BioFashion."

Was he buying it? Meredith peeked over her shoulder.

"Fascinating. Pose like you're having a picture taken."

She propped her hands on her knees and delivered a sultry starlet pout. "Vegetarians are opposed to BioFashion, of course. They prefer, um . . ." Cotton? No, that was plant-based. Linen? Wool? "Polyesteranism."

All this talking. Was she . . . nervous? She did have that tendency to babble whenever she felt nervous.

"Hmmm," Tony rumbled. "Now jump up in the air."

She leaped. Her silky, partly buttoned shirt flowed enjoyably against her skin. The pants might be tight, but the top made her feel downright sexy.

"Orange and pink don't go together," she rambled on, referring to Tony's example outfit earlier, "because they're right next to each other in the alphabet. O and P. They're alphabetically incompatible."

He nodded as though that made sense. Emboldened by his acceptance of her on-the-fly theories, Meredith elaborated.

"The sequined pants didn't match with anything because the . . . sequin molecules only bond with other glittery substances. Like gold lamé or Madonna. Most people don't know that."

God help her, but she enjoyed the way he was looking at her — with a potent mixture of admiration and desire that made her heart pound even faster.

"Mmmm. That's news to me. Bend over," he suggested.

She did. He made a husky, appreciative sound. Meredith caught it and peeked through her veed legs at him. "Exactly what is this supposed to prove, again?" she asked breathlessly.

"Nothing. I just wondered if you'd do it. You look great. Really sexy."

She lurched up and whacked him on the shoulder. He recoiled, laughing. She reached out and pulled his nonhair-plugged hair. He laughed harder. She grabbed his pants at the belt buckle and yanked him nearer.

He quit laughing. His hand curled at her nape, and a heavy anticipation swirled suddenly between them.

"Yeah, that's right." Meredith nodded triumphantly. "Who's laughing now, tough guy?"

"Not me."

Tony wouldn't take defeat lying down, though. She should have known.

"You, either," he said, and kissed her.

ELEVEN

"The play was a great success, but the audience was a disaster."

— Oscar Wilde

"So we're both clear from the get-go — this is just sex, right?" Meredith asked a few minutes later, panting as she unfastened Tony's belt buckle.

She worked at the leather, then pushed him up against his trailer's hallway. In the cramped space, she returned the scorching kiss he'd just given her — the one that had carried them this far toward the bedroom.

"I don't want any misunderstandings later."

"Hey. Isn't that my line?"

"Not with me, it's not."

"Mmmm. I like your way of thinking." He slid his hands eagerly over her hips and along her waist, rubbing her silky shirt against her skin. His gaze lifted to meet hers. "You're one of a kind."

Actually, she wasn't. She never had been, not with Marley around. Meredith paused, uncertain.

Tony took advantage of her stillness to kiss her, then covered her breasts with his big hands. Expertly he palmed her, lifting, stroking, sensitizing. Relaxing again, she closed her eyes. This was familiar territory.

Having Tony's hands on her felt completely natural. His touch — steady, sure, and wonderful — felt amazing. Thank God she'd skipped her bra. There was something especially electric about the combination of his hands, her silky shirt, and her naked skin beneath. She writhed, demanding more.

Purposely — she felt certain — he gentled his touch. Confused, Meredith leaned harder, wondering if she should take off her shirt to keep the momentum going. They'd been frenzied, hands all over each other, panting and pulsing and *needing,* from the minute Tony had kissed her. Why was he slowing down now?

After another kiss, they parted again.

"I won't be spending the night," she warned, a little giddy but still intent on making sure their expectations were identical. "I won't call you in the morning, or — *ooh,* oh my God!" How had he accomplished so much sensation with only two hands? "Or send you flowers as a parting gift."

"No flowers? Not even if I'm very, very good?"

He was already very, very good. His devastating smile promised more of the same, too. Her whole body trembled with delight. Just being this close to him was more exciting than anything she'd ever known.

She had to get on with it. She opened her mouth for her next disclaimer, ready to explain that one romp did not a relationship make. Not in her book.

"Because," Tony added, "I promise to be very, *very* good."

Oh, God. She'd just bet he did. Cradled in the vee of his spread legs, hips touching his, Meredith felt herself turn all hot and impatient. What was he doing still talking? Nobody ever talked during this speech. Nobody except her.

Staunchly, she continued. "We won't be a couple after this. I don't want to meet your friends or your family —"

"You already have." He kissed her neck, then her shoulder.

She shuddered. "That's beside the point. The point is, I don't want anything from you except these" — she covered his hands with hers, as though both of them were discovering her breasts for the first time — "and this."

With unerring surety, she palmed him. His hard, ready erection thrilled her — and, for a shocked instant, amazed her. His size would have given him something *else* to talk about, besides the nonsense he'd been spouting. Clearly, Tony wanted her. Clearly, his pants were too tight and uncomfortable. If she could only get them off him. . . .

"Oh, and these," she added, pressing a soft

kiss to his lips as she unfastened the button on his pants. "I want your lips, too. On me. *Everywhere.*"

He moaned, nodding in agreement. His hand slipped inside her shirt, finding her naked breast; his thumb circled her taut nipple. Breathlessly, Meredith pushed herself more fully into his palm.

She needed more. More touching, more skin-on-skin contact, more of *him*. Temporarily abandoning Tony's pants, she attacked his shirt instead. She tugged it from his waistband, savoring the fantastic view of his sculpted abs, muscular chest, and chiseled arms as she pulled it over his head.

His shirt landed on the clothes rack in his bedroom. Hey, it served a useful purpose after all. Feeling assured, Meredith pushed her hips against Tony. She delivered him her sexiest smile.

"This is all we need. You. Me." She'd said words to this effect before. They'd never failed to elicit a nearly X-rated response. Readying herself, she kissed him. "A pair of hot bodies coming together, feeling good. It's perfect."

"Yes, it is."

At last! He agreed. She wanted to cheer. That, or rip off the rest of his clothes. Hmmm. Decisions, decisions. . . .

"It's perfect," Tony went on, "because it's you."

He caressed her face, gazing deeply into her eyes. Did he think they were embarking on a lifelong love affair? This was casual sex. Casual, casual, casual. Meant to satisfy the need that had been building between them for days. Hadn't she made that clear enough?

"This feels . . . right," he said. "It feels good."

A spark of alarm touched her.

Meredith shrugged it off. "It feels like something I've wanted since our limo ride," she agreed, deliberately sounding as raunchy as she could. "I've wanted to feel your hands on me, to feel your mouth on mine —"

"To see your face, smiling with satisfaction afterward."

He grinned, switching their positions to lean her against the hallway's opposite wall. His palms flattened on the wood paneling, boxing her in. From his now-dominant perspective, he again gave her that affectionate look.

"I can't wait to see that."

Her face? Huh? Once more Meredith stilled, her uneasiness growing. Why was Tony thinking about her face? Until now, his hands had been all over her, for Pete's sake!

"Shut up and touch me," she demanded.

"I'm happy to," he said. He lowered his hand to her hip, making the leather creak faintly as he caressed her there. "Happy to make you feel good." Another hand, on her opposite hip. "So good that you come back for more, and more —"

"That's not shutting up."

"It's close."

"The only sounds I want from you are moans. Let me show you how it's done."

Urgently, she returned her hands to his fly. The rasp of his zipper overrode their racing breath. She caught a glimpse of tight boxer briefs. Yes! Another minute and he'd quit deviating from the script for good. They'd be back in the mindless just-sex zone, where things were safe and predictable. Meredith reached for him.

At that moment Tony leaned slightly, moving himself just out of reach. His knowing smile was the sexiest rebellion she'd ever seen.

"If I didn't know better, I'd swear you were trying to keep this impersonal between us."

Finally! He got it. She offered him a seductive smile. "Does this feel imp—"

He grasped her wrist, inches from the payoff she sought. "I might be crazy, but I'm not an impersonal guy. I want you, Meredith, but not like —"

"Don't say that."

He stopped. An assessing look came into his eyes — followed by a tenderness she'd never expected. "Meredith, Meredith, Meredith," he murmured, touching her face again.

Oh, how had he known that was what she'd meant? Any other man would have assumed she didn't want to hear the no-casual-sex edict he'd been about to deliver. But not Tony. Scared to death by his perceptiveness, she closed her eyes.

That didn't distance her enough. Still his voice found her, strong and unstoppable.

"I want you, Meredith," he told her. "You're beautiful and sexy and funny, and Meredith, *Meredith*, I can't get enough of you."

Her name on his lips sounded like the most perfect of endearments, like the most wonderful of songs. He didn't tease her with it, or even actually sing it (as *Moulin Rouge* as that would have been). But something about the huskiness in his voice as he spoke those few syllables . . . something about *him*, just made her melt inside. All her life, it seemed, she'd waited for someone to see only her. Now that Tony had — well, now that he had, Meredith didn't know quite what to do.

Damn him and his stupid insight. Confused and disgruntled and scared, she cast about for some way to save face.

"Clearly you *can* get enough of me, Tony, because you're half-naked, my shirt is open wide enough for an emergency appendectomy, and we're not horizontal yet."

"Say that again."

"Not horizontal yet," she complained.

208

Geez! No man had ever turned down her straight-up sex kitten routine before. Flummoxed and feeling vaguely rejected, she hugged her shirt around herself. "Not. Horizontal. Yet."

"Not that part. Say my name again."

Warily, she surveyed him. "I've said it before."

"Now. I want to hear it now."

This was silly. So she'd said his name. Big deal. They could still have casual sex together, Meredith assured herself.

Except . . . except it didn't feel quite so casual anymore. Plus, he'd already turned her down. Hadn't he?

Against her will, a tiny part of her admired him for that. He might be a Hairology fancier, but Tony knew what he wanted well enough that he'd take it on his own terms or not at all.

She rolled her eyes. "Tony."

As though she'd done something brilliant, he smiled. He took her hand, used it to draw her closer again, and entwined their fingers like teenaged steadies.

"Again."

It probably wouldn't hurt to play along.

"Tony," she grumbled.

"One more time."

He was making it so difficult to keep up her tough façade. How *could* she be tough? How could she be casual, when Tony saw

209

right through her to what she really wanted?

She pressed her lips together. She shook her head, staring at her bare toes. Closeness. Caring. Recognition. They weren't so much to ask. Except for her, they always had been.

"Meredith, Meredith, Meredith," he coaxed. "I know you can do it. Humor me."

Despite her resistance, a hint of tenderness unfurled inside her. What was it about this man that affected her so much?

He tipped up her chin with his knuckles, giving her a mock-fierce look. "I'm not letting you leave until you do."

Oh, yeah. They were identically stubborn. Maybe that was it.

She gazed into his eyes. "Fine," she said, endeavoring to sound unaffected. "Tony, Tony . . . Tony."

Oh, God. The *Moulin Rouge* sound was in her voice, too! Panicked, Meredith ran, leaving the door to slam in her wake.

Shirtless and confused, Tony stared in the direction Meredith had gone. What the hell had just happened here?

One minute, they'd been close together. Meredith had been saying his name in a husky, sexy voice he could have listened to all night. She'd been holding his hand, gazing up at him. For an instant, her usual expression of stubborn rebelliousness had faded. In its place had emerged a look of . . . Well, he'd have sworn it was *yearning*. Tony couldn't be sure. But then, before he could get a better look, she'd bolted away.

Without so much as buttoning her BioFashion shirt or putting on her motor-cycle boots, Meredith had run. He still felt her hands on him, still smelled the scent of her hair, still throbbed with the arousal they'd shared.

Slowly, his brain ground into gear. Gradually, Tony became aware of himself flattened against the hallway, shirt gone and pants gaping open. He probably looked like the victim of a hit-and-run seduction.

He sure as hell felt like one.

At first, astonishment pinned him in place. Breathing hard, he glanced toward his trailer's door. Part of it was just visible from the hallway where he stood, and the doorway allowed him a glimpse of the rapidly dark-ening back lot beyond. Slowly, slicing off strips of the view by degrees, his front door swung shut.

It pinged against the jamb, then lazily arced outward again. Meredith's slam must've broken the latch.

He'd fix it later. Right now he had a woman to find. Frowning, Tony headed for his bedroom. Atop the rack of Marley-style clothes, he located his shirt. He tossed it over his shoulder, then zipped his pants as he strode to the door.

If Meredith thought she was cutting out just when things were getting interesting, she had another think coming.

Keeping her arms crossed in an X over her partly wrapped snakeskin-print shirt, Meredith hurried toward her trailer. Her mind raced with the enormity of what she'd just heard — from her own lips! *Tony, Tony . . . Tony.* Anyone would have sworn she'd tumbled head over heels for the guy, judging by the wanting, the needing, the *caring* in her voice.

Haven't you? a part of her nudged. She gave it a mental drop kick and stopped for a second, fumbling with her shirt buttons. She wasn't prepared to reveal those kinds of feelings to anyone. Doing so was just asking to get hurt, begging for disappointment. She didn't want to care about Tony. The simple solution was, she wouldn't.

Sure, that would work. Meredith tossed her hair from her eyes and kept buttoning, encouraged by the thought. She'd simply refuse to become any more infatuated with him. She'd . . . boycott him, like consumers objecting to a racy new advertising campaign. Yeah. It was bound to work.

Boycotting was a historically proven tactic, she assured herself. In the 1920s, magazines carrying Lucky Strike ads featuring women engaged in the socially unacceptable pastime of smoking had been boycotted. In the 1950s, there'd been resistance to Foote Cone & Belding's suggestive "Does she . . . or doesn't she?" campaign for Clairol hair color. In the 1980s, networks had refused to air Calvin Klein ads starring a then-teenaged Brooke Shields. Even though *her* boycott of Tony would be strictly personal in nature, it would work. It had to work.

After all, resistance had a long and glorious tradition.

Of course, Meredith recalled dispiritedly as she started walking again, before long millions of women had taken up smoking. Half of all women began coloring their hair. Sales of "Calvin's" jumped three hundred percent. Maybe resistance really *was* futile.

"Yoo-hoo! Marley! Over here!" a voice called.

Brakes squealed a few feet to her right. Before Meredith could get a grip on what was happening, three women piled out of the golf cart those screeching brakes belonged to and surrounded her.

"Come on, we're kidnapping you," Inga — one of the makeup artists — said, tugging at Meredith's arm. Playfully, she giggled. "It's a girls' night tonight, and you're invited."

"We couldn't have a girls' night without you!" her counterpart, Kim, agreed. She grabbed Meredith's other arm. "We were just on our way to get you. And here you are!"

The hairstylist, Salma, nodded, her long, lush hair a testament to her skill. She hurried in the lead as the two makeup artists hustled Meredith toward the waiting golf cart.

"We've been dying to get to know you better," she said, glancing over her shoulder. "We won't take no for an answer!"

Meredith could barely think, much less dredge up a "no." She half suspected her inept hair and makeup had finally proven too much for Salma, Inga, and Kim. Maybe the trio was abducting her for a forced makeover. It was the same tactic her sister had tried — a few times in the past. Marley simply couldn't understand how someone could be happy without a blow-dryer and some nail polish. No doubt Salma, Inga, and Kim felt the same way.

When they reached the golf cart, though, not a word was said about split ends, unibrow, or lip gloss. Bundled into the front seat, Meredith relaxed, feeling herself sucked in by the three women's enthusiasm. Sure, she had a problem with Tony — but maybe a little time away from him would lend her some perspective.

Besides, weren't girlfriends the answer to life's little glitches? With her contact with Leslie limited to one hurried conversation when her friend had dropped off Meredith's stuff — plus the occasional phone call — she *had* been a little lonely. Maybe a girls' night was exactly what she needed.

"We're meeting Becky from Housekeeping at her trailer," Kim said, jumping into the cart's backseat. "She's just past Bayberry. Jennifer and Erin from Wardrobe should already be there. They're bringing the drinks, Inga has the popcorn, and I've got the Russell Crowe videos."

Grinning, she patted her DVD-filled tote bag.

"Hang on," Inga warned, leaning toward Meredith from the other side of the backseat. "Salma drives like a maniac."

"I do not," the hairdresser protested.

She floored it. All the women squealed. Meredith was flung against the golf cart's seat, her hair flying in the breeze. Briefly, she wondered if she should ask Salma to stop at Tony's trailer for her motorcycle boots and normal clothes. Trying to decide, she glanced downward.

Kim saw her. "Fab outfit. You look really cute in that."

Inga and Salma agreed. Weirdly enough, Meredith couldn't detect a hint of sarcasm in their voices. Skeptically, she looked at each of them in turn.

They gazed back, seeming open and friendly. Meredith's heart gave a hopeful little squeeze. Was it possible they would accept her, just like that?

"Thanks. It's BioFashion," she blurted.

215

"BioFashion. Hmmm. That must be the new bridge line from Chloé," Kim said knowledgeably, nodding as she rounded the corner. "I read about that in *Vogue*. Jennifer and Erin will love it. Did you get a preview because of being an actress?"

Meredith gave an uneasy laugh. "Let's not talk about that. Tonight I'm just another one of the girls, okay?"

"You've got it," Inga agreed. The others nodded.

They zoomed into the night, leaving Tony's trailer — and Meredith's feelings for him — far behind.

She hoped.

Rushing down his trailer's rickety steps, Tony stopped on the Astroturf at the bottom and looked for Meredith. A hasty glance took in her trailer, safely parked beside his with all the lights out. The false-fronted buildings of Tumbleweed, just beyond. Night descending on the back lot, with its looming soundstages, additional star trailers, and scattered golf carts.

The sound of one of those carts reached him, engine noise echoing from the buildings nearby. Tony turned his head in that direction. Could Meredith have made her getaway in a golf cart?

No. He couldn't remember having seen one when he'd arrived at her trailer earlier, intending to read her the riot act for assaulting Boob Guy. Had she hijacked *his* golf cart? Nope, it was still parked next to his barbecue grill.

Determined to find her, he headed for her trailer. Probably, Meredith had run inside — breaking her door latch, too, he didn't doubt — and hadn't turned on the lights yet.

No dice. She didn't answer his knock, and he couldn't hear anyone moving around inside. Frustrated, Tony strode toward his golf cart. Ninety seconds later, he navigated the grounds of Tumbleweed, certain he'd spot Meredith stomping around, looking to kneecap somebody.

As he drove, his thoughts churned. So he'd turned down her suggestion of casual sex. So what? That didn't make him some kind of freak. It made him a guy who liked a woman to be one hundred percent with him when they slid between the sheets. Or bumped up against the wall. Or got crazy on a chair. Or balanced in the shower, all sudsy and steamy and wet —

Enough. This was going nowhere. The fact was, Meredith had grabbed his equipment. She'd made her intentions plain. All he'd done was make sure she knew there was a man attached to the hardware in her hand. Was that so wrong?

Swearing, Tony chugged past Acajatuba, the jungle set. Here, encouraged by the automatic sprinkler system, lush foliage grew high, twining around palm trees and rope bridges and exotic-looking huts. No sign of Meredith. Tires squeaking, he flipped a U-turn and sped toward Bayberry.

She wasn't there amid the quaint redbrick buildings, wasn't practicing Tae-bo moves on a wheeled oak tree or taking out her feelings on one of the gazebo walls. He knew she'd been upset when she'd run off. Where could she have gone?

Frowning, Tony accelerated toward the archives building. Maybe Meredith had tired of waiting for him to admit her. Maybe she'd decided to karate chop the door lock and admit herself. She probably thought a little breaking and entering would serve him right for not jumping her bones earlier.

Maybe it would. Tony careened between a pair of outlying soundstages, that dismal thought keeping him company. He peered into the distance, disgruntled. *It's perfect . . . because it's you,* he remembered himself saying. What kind of candy-ass comment was that?

The trouble was, it was true. Holding Meredith in his arms had felt special, unlike anything he'd ever known before. It had felt like *more* than the simple good time she'd insisted on. Tony was a man who called it like he saw it, no holds barred. He just hadn't expected his straight-up philosophy to bite him on the ass, was all.

So he'd told Meredith that being with her felt *good*. That it felt *right*. Big deal. Faced with Meredith's I-want-you-now sex appeal, any man would've found himself waxing poetic. It didn't mean a thing.

Shadows fell over him, turning the evening chillier. Tony kept going, still thinking of Meredith. So what if he'd spent more time with her than he had with any woman since his ex, Taryn? So what if he smiled when he saw her, and thought about her at weird moments throughout the day? That didn't mean he'd gone all gooey over her. That didn't mean a thing.

Did it?

Hell. Was he falling for Meredith?

Unwilling to consider it, he jerked to a stop at the archives building. The door stood closed, the lock intact. Meredith wasn't there. Rubbing his jaw, Tony shoved aside his disappointment. He'd find her — it was only a matter of time.

He considered where else he could look. She couldn't have left the Valentine Studios back lot without clearance; he'd instructed the security crew to contact him if "Marley" tried to leave. So where was she?

Tony climbed back into his golf cart and revved it into motion. He retraced his route, stopping every now and then to ask crew members and guests if they'd seen "Marley."

It was possible she'd walked around to let off steam and was now back at her trailer.

He wished he'd taken her up on her offer. He could have been kissing her right now, hearing that sexy little sound she made when his hand cupped her breast. He could have been laying her down on his big bed, stripping off her clothes and touching every part of her he revealed. Instead, where was he? Freezing his nuts off on a frantic chase through the back lot.

Well, he wasn't making the same mistake twice. When he found Meredith, Tony vowed, he would strip her naked, make her hot and ready, and just go for it. No more fooling around. If she wanted impersonal sex, he was just the man to give it to her. Hell, yeah.

Except . . . in his imagination, the scenario changed. In his imagination, he and Meredith came together on a comfy bed, with romantic soft lighting and lots of sweet words. They moved slowly, tenderly, gazing into each other's eyes. They whispered endearments, held each other tightly, took their time with a lovemaking so pure and meaningful and affectionate that the imaginary Tony was shaken to the core. He *wanted* that. Wanted to be with Meredith, whether he was spooning her close or just lying beside her in the moonlight, sharing a pillow.

Momentarily lost in his fantasy, Tony smiled.

Then he realized what he'd been thinking of. Freaking moonlight? Pillow sharing? *Spooning?*

Christ. Maybe he *had* fallen for Meredith, he realized.

Tony was still digesting this news when a flash of movement caught his eye. Several women were exiting a golf cart parked at a nearby trailer. He recognized them as crew members, part of the Hair, Makeup, and Wardrobe teams. But the third one from the left looked like . . . It was! Meredith. Still wearing her BioFashion clothes, with her hair loose and a tentative smile on her face.

Chattering away, one of the women opened the trailer door. Another preceded Meredith inside. All he could see was her profile, but it was undoubtedly her. He just needed to go over there, find out what had made her run away, and then tell her how he felt. They'd work out their differences, and then —

And then the whole crew would know there was something cooking between him and "Marley." Their relationship would become public, talked about and speculated on with a fervor unmatched in his actor fantasy camp's short history. Hesitating, Tony watched as Meredith ascended the steps. She paused to say something to the woman behind her.

Now was his chance.

He couldn't do it. Not like this. Something

held him back. Clenching his fists on his golf cart's steering wheel, Tony kept his distance as Meredith disappeared inside the trailer. The rest of the women followed. The door swung shut.

That was that. Steeling his expression, Tony turned his cart and headed for his trailer, leaving Meredith — and his feelings for her — behind.

For now.

TWELVE

"The ideal brain tonic. A delightful summer and winter beverage! For headache & exhaustion . . . at soda fountains."
— Coca-Cola (1892)

"We have a confession to make," Salma said, swirling the cocktail in her hand.

She sucked her stirrer clean of the lime, sugar, and rum mixture Meredith had watched her make, then added a mint sprig to her glass. The greenery looked a little worse for the wear, but it contributed a festive touch, all the same.

"We were all too intimidated to approach you by ourselves. That's why we kidnapped you."

"Yeah." The other women nodded. "We were."

"We're lucky you didn't have a bodyguard," Kim said.

Bodyguard. At the thought, Meredith flashed on Tony. He'd been pretty watchful of her body — especially once she'd donned her BioFashion clothes. A little thrill coursed through her, despite her decision to boycott him. Which only proved how necessary it was to go through with said boycott. Who knew

223

how her feelings might run amuck if she didn't?

Besides, Tony hadn't wanted her. His reaction to her offer of casual sex had been more "Hey, slow down," than "Hey, let's go!" That had hurt. It had been embarrassing, too. She'd gone all Cosmogirl and grabbed his package — wasn't that every man's dream? — and he'd felt compelled to remind her there was an actual man attached to it. What a buzzkill.

Although . . . she *had* loved the sound of his voice when he'd said her name in that deep, husky, can't-get-enough-of-you way, Meredith mused. Again and again and again. Hearing that, seeing the affection in his face, had sent a wave of recognition and need clear through her.

Which was part of the problem, wasn't it?

"We hope you don't mind," Becky said. She peeled off her housekeeping uniform's peach polyester zip-up top, revealing a plain white T-shirt beneath. "The kidnapping, that is. But you seemed really nice, not starlike at all —"

Uh-oh. Did the crew suspect her real identity?

"— and we just thought you might like to, you know, hang out for a while."

"I'm glad you invited me," Meredith said. "I don't get to do this very often." Usually, she was working. Or reading. Or house-sitting

224

for Marley. Or researching. "I'm having a good time already."

She hoisted her own cocktail — a mojito, Salma had called it — in demonstration. All around her, the cramped trailer felt comfy and familiar. Meredith breathed in the soothing scents of vanilla candles, Windex, and microwave popcorn. She took in the multicolored throw pillows, the stacks of *Inside Hollywood* magazine, the half-empty Diet Mountain Dew cans.

This could have been any twenty-something woman's apartment, instead of a trailer parked on a studio back lot. Although she'd been here only a half hour or so, it already felt like home. Heck, add some framed advertising prints by Joseph Leyendecker, Coles Phillips, and Laurence Fellows, throw in a clock collection and about six dozen books, and it would *be* home.

Jennifer and Erin — both from the Wardrobe department — looked up with Russell Crowe DVDs in hand. They'd been sorting through the movies Kim had brought, *ooh*ing and *aah*ing over the various "studly Russell" poses on the cases.

"Like I always say," Jennifer announced, "we might as well go out with a bang." She popped in a movie.

"That's why the DVD fest," Salma elaborated. "And the mojitos. Usually we're strictly a Bud Lite kind of crowd."

"But not tonight!" Kim raised her glass, clinking it with Inga's. "Tonight we've got a TV star in our midst and we're doing it up right. Cheers!"

"I don't get it," Meredith said, frowning. "What makes tonight so special?"

"Aside from having you here?"

Uncomfortably, Meredith nodded.

"This might be our last girls' night together," Jennifer explained. "If Mr. V. doesn't make this actor fantasy camp thing work, that is. It's kind of a last-ditch effort to save the studio."

"Yeah. Our days are numbered."

"Only a week and a half left."

Salma sighed. "I don't know what I'll do if Valentine shuts down," she said. "I've been working here since graduating beauty school. My mom used to do hairstyling for all the big stars in the eighties."

"You mean she did *big hair* for the stars in the eighties," Kim said, grinning as she shook her head. "There weren't any big stars here at Valentine Studios by then — it was all cheesy nighttime soaps, workout videos, and sitcom pilots."

"Hey, I liked those soaps!" Inga protested. "They were fun. Don't forget, we filmed 'Fantastic Island' here, too. In Acajatuba, with all those guest stars."

"All those has-beens, you mean," Jennifer grumbled. "This place hasn't been a big draw since the sixties."

They all shifted, trying to ignore Jennifer's pessimism. Meredith didn't know much about movie studios, but she did know that these days, any family-owned company struggled for survival against huge conglomerates. Her empathy for Tony grew. He was in a difficult situation. Helping his uncles wouldn't be easy.

Especially since he'd gotten stuck with a phony Marley.

"How about you, Marley?" Erin leaned forward with an interested look. "What was it like working on 'Fantasy Family'? Your character had the most to-die-for wardrobe!"

"Ummm. It was good. A learning experience . . ."

She went on with the rest of her rote answer. The one she'd heard her sister use, and the one she'd practiced for any fans or crew who might question her. With these openhearted, friendly women, though, pretending to be Marley felt all wrong. It felt like . . . Well, it felt like the lie it was.

She'd come here for a weekend, wanting a Cinderella-style turn in the spotlight. Instead, she'd wound up signing on for two weeks' worth of full-time imposter duty. The worst part was, she sucked at it. She couldn't believe no one had found her out yet. Like the *Inside Hollywood* reporter, for instance. Or the crew. Or the guests.

227

If her family — especially Marley — discovered what she'd been up to . . . God, Meredith couldn't even consider it. Everyone who knew her believed she didn't care about appearances. They thought she openly disdained artifice and loathed traditional girly-girl activities. Admittedly, Meredith had cultivated that attitude. But only because she'd always been so inept at all the things her twin sister mastered so effortlessly.

What choice had she had? She'd had to fill all the specialties — like braininess and rebellion — left vacant by Marley.

Tonight wasn't the time to dwell on her troubles, though. Determined to make friends, Meredith turned the attention away from herself. "So, how long have the rest of you worked here?"

"Five years," Erin said, holding up five fingers.

"Eight," Inga volunteered. "I apprenticed under Julian, one of the studio's last great makeup artists. He could make a hungover starlet look like a million bucks. What a talent."

"Just like you," Kim said loyally. She turned to Meredith. "Four years, for me. I started out doing makeup for catalogs, moved on to ads, editorial, and video shoots, and wound up doing a little bit of everything here. One good thing is, I have lots of artistic freedom."

"And a teeny, tiny paycheck," Inga said with a grin.

"Amen!" Becky put in. "Although lodging *is* included. These trailers, you know. So that makes up for the pay."

"Grazing off the craft services table helps, too," Kim said with a wicked grin. "Where else could we get free sushi, M&Ms, and unlimited San Pellegrino as part of our job descriptions?"

All the women nodded.

"To tell the truth, we're lucky to have jobs at all," Erin confided. "The economy's not that great. If Valentine Studios buckles . . ."

"We're all on the street," Jennifer finished. "Pounding the pavement."

"There's not a lot of work for itinerant beautifiers." Prosaically, Salma took a handful of microwave popcorn and munched. "In this town, it's all about who you know."

The mood in the room turned somber. In the corner, the TV blared out a fight scene from *Gladiator*, but no one paid any attention. Erin's hands went slack on her remaining DVDs; Jennifer set hers aside altogether. Becky absently touched the nameplate pinned to her discarded uniform. Salma nervously twined her hair around her finger. Inga sat with her arms wrapped around her upraised knees, looking worried. Kim picked at a ragged cuticle, a frown on her face.

Terrific. Way to bring everyone low,

Meredith chastised herself. She'd had no idea the crew's futures with Valentine Studios were so tenuous. From the outside, the studio looked glitzy and successful. It had years of Hollywood history behind it. But as Meredith knew all too well — thanks to her meager historian's salary — history didn't exactly pay the bills.

It didn't keep people employed, either.

"I'm sorry, you guys." She reached out to pat Erin's shoulder, her gesture awkward but sincere. "I didn't know things were so desperate here."

"Oh, they're not, really," Salma said, brightening. "Not now that *you're* here. Between you and Mr. V., you'll have this place back to its old self in no time."

"That's right! Everybody knows what Mr. V. accomplished with that MP3 software, M-Tunes. He's good. Famously good."

"So are you, Marley," Inga agreed. "The actor fantasy camp guests *looove* having a chance to meet a real star like you. Everybody I have in my chair wants to know about the famous Marley Madison."

Meredith made a face. "You mean they want to know how awful I look without makeup on."

"Of course," Kim said, shrugging. "But then they start talking about how they love your Diva Dramatics class. Or how they look forward to your Tabloid Tattling class. Or how hilarious they think you are, demonstrating the lessons in dialect coaching. Face it, Marley. You're a hit."

Meredith felt herself blush with pleasure. And embarrassment. Despite that fact, everyone nodded. Jennifer even chimed in with a word of encouragement about Tony's eagerness to choose wardrobe for "Marley."

"Mr. V. *hates* clothes," she added. "So that means something. We outfitted him in a tuxedo for the finale next week, and he threatened to fire us both if we required one more fitting."

Erin giggled, offering a lascivious commentary on Tony's backside. Becky had a story to tell about the guests whose trailers she cleaned, and their enthusiasm for being part of a taped TV sitcom.

"It's real to them, Marley," she said, getting up for another mojito. She passed the rum to Salma, then sat down again. "They talk it up to their friends and family back home."

"They dither over their wardrobes endlessly," Erin said.

"They squeal over every mention in *Inside Hollywood*."

"They practice their lines — really practice! They try new stuff, too. Even that pudgy accountant from Omaha has been getting into the stunt classes. On the way to my trailer, I saw him do a practice fall from a balcony in Tumbleweed."

"Yee-haw," Salma deadpanned.

"All this stuff might be no big deal to you," Becky went on urgently, her eyes wide. "But to the guests here . . . To them, it's the fantasy of a lifetime."

The fantasy of a lifetime. That was the promise from the brochure — the one that had led Meredith on this adventure in the first place. That was what she'd come here looking for. That was what she owed the guests who were depending on her.

More importantly, she realized as she sipped her unfamiliar but tasty mojito, she owed something to these women. To everyone on the crew. They were depending on her to kick start their livelihoods. If she failed. . . .

Scared by the thought, she glanced around the cramped trailer. One by one, she studied the women's shining faces. Becky, Salma, Inga. Jennifer, Kim, Erin. Dozens more crew members just like them were in their own trailers tonight — possibly wondering if Valentine Studios would founder and fail when the actor fantasy camp was finished.

She *wouldn't* fail, Meredith vowed. Whatever it took, she'd turn herself into the best Marley clone ever. She'd impress the actor fantasy camp guests. She'd wow the investors and reassure the Valentines. She'd do her absolute best. If it would help her new friends keep their jobs, it was the least she could do.

It wouldn't be that hard. She'd already nailed learning her lines for the sitcom, and she could hit her mark now, too. She'd successfully bluffed her way through her classes — no harm done there. She'd even managed to appear in public wearing leather pants. As every woman knew, once you'd survived cowhide butt, the sky was the limit.

To pull it off, though, she'd need help.

As the only one who knew her real identity, Tony had been trying to offer her whatever guidance he could. But being around him only stirred an interest in kissing, not in successfully impersonating a TV starlet. What she needed was help from someone less drop-dead sexy, less thrillingly macho, less unsettlingly perceptive.

"Ladies, I need some advice," Meredith said. "I can't think of anyone better to get it from than you, the experts . . ."

Dragging himself back to his trailer, feeling vaguely unsettled and a little pissed, Tony rounded the corner. Ahead, waiting for him beneath his awning, he spotted the last thing he wanted tonight.

Company.

For once, the invaders weren't his uncles, or Nadine, or even Esther and Harry (who, he'd heard, had been getting *very* cozy during their faux press junket duties). Instead, a grip and a camera operator lay on his lounge chairs. A gaffer stood beside his grill. A Foley artist sat beside an AD on his steps, and another crew member waited nearby. He held up a hand in greeting as Tony parked his golf cart.

"Hey, Mr. V.!" the gaffer called. "Did you forget what time it is?"

"Yeah," the camera operator agreed, grinning. "You're late for your regular ass-whupping."

"Scared of a little seven-card stud?" a grip goaded him.

Damn. He'd forgotten his bi-weekly poker game. Putting on a smile, Tony whacked the camera operator on the shoulder, shook the gaffer's hand, and called out greetings to everyone else.

"You guys in a hurry to lose, or what?" he asked.

Guffaws of laughter greeted his comment. That was more like it. Poker and trash talking, he understood. Feeling better, Tony ascended his trailer's steps and reached for the doorknob.

A strip of duct tape caught his eye, slapped over the door and its jamb.

"Your door was broken. I took care of it," the grip said. He hefted a roll of thick silver tape from his ever-present tool belt. "There's nothing duct tape won't fix."

"Damn straight," the gaffer agreed.

The other men murmured agreement.

Tony's grin widened. Duct tape, he could relate to. Maybe some guy time was just what he needed to clear his head.

Back home in New York, guy time — and poker games — was not a regular thing for him. He was always too busy — logging hours at his PC, researching e-commerce leads, putting together dot-com mergers. When business turned demanding, he dreamed in binary code, showered in VBScript, ate HTML for lunch, and breathed number-crunching spreadsheets.

Entrepreneurial success hadn't come easily. But it had compensated him with personal satisfaction, plenty of money, and the ability to say he was the first Valentine in five generations to break out of the movie business. Since that was what Tony had set out to accomplish, he was generally happy with his life.

With his business partner, Jim, in charge of things while he was gone, Tony had expected to miss the daily adrenaline rush, the challenges, the boardroom wrangling. Instead, being in L.A. and helping with Valentine Studios had fueled him, leaving him weirdly energized.

At first he'd wondered why. Given all the years he'd spent building his business on the East Coast, he should have missed it. The more time he spent on the back lot, though, the less Tony worried about it. Jim kept him updated with phone calls and e-mailed status reports. For now, that was enough.

Tony ripped off the duct tape, herded in the guys, and got ready to start taking no prisoners.

Twenty minutes later, the first hand was well under way. The relief Tony experienced upon picking up his cards was profound. His mind cleared. His focus sharpened. He relaxed, fueled by beer and good-natured bad-mouthing.

All the same, he couldn't quit thinking about Meredith. He remembered her emerging from his bedroom in that sexy outfit, giving him lip about that damned hair plug infomercial, twirling around to give him a better look at her.

I don't like being the center of attention.

That was what she'd said, but Tony didn't buy it. As far as he could see, that had only been modesty talking. Or inexperience. How could Meredith know what she didn't like if she'd never experienced it? Once she stood in the spotlight in Marley's place at the actor fantasy camp finale, she'd be hooked. He had no doubt about that.

She'd need more help to pull it off, though — and fast. The clothes he'd brought her were just the beginning. She needed glamour — something Meredith had refused to let the hair and makeup teams give her, thanks to the bare-minimum styling she'd decreed. She needed to burn that ridiculous sweatshirt she tied over her hips, no matter what else she was wearing. She needed to put on high heels now and then, instead of wearing flip-flops or motorcycle boots or ratty sneakers.

Growing up in Hollywood, he'd seen his share of starlets. None of them appeared in public with fake "fun tattoos" (a freebie from a smuggled-in box of Coco Puffs) on their arms. None of them eschewed leg shaving or considered a museum "Dioramas through the Decades" baseball cap high fashion. Meredith did.

On the plus side, she'd nailed all the internals. Skills like script memorization, hitting her mark, and not stepping on another actor's lines had become second nature in only a few short days. Gaffes like coughing during a take, leaving her cell phone on, and arguing with the writers over grammar mistakes in the script had vanished after the first day. Meredith was smart, he'd give her that.

From the feedback Tony had received, her actor fantasy camp classes were a big hit, too. The guests seemed to love "Marley's" contributions. So long as she didn't give away her true identity by not *looking* the part, he figured they were home free until the big finale next Friday night.

Quaffing his beer, he played through one straight, two pairs, and a full house. While the AD dealt a new hand, Tony glanced toward his trailer's hallway, his mind wandering. He remembered Meredith and him in that hallway, pressed up against the wood paneling with their clothes half gone. He remembered her breathless enthusiasm, her sexy smile, her curvy body.

She was something else. If not for the fact that they had to work together, they might have found themselves in that hallway together even sooner.

No mixing business with pleasure, he reminded himself automatically. *That only causes trouble.*

He accepted his cards, fanning them out in his hand. Critically he peered at them, formulating a strategy. Around him, the other guys did the same.

The other guys. Struck by a sudden thought, Tony glanced around the table. Everyone here was someone he worked with. They were all crew members, technically in his employ. Yet he'd been playing poker with them for the past ten days — technically having fun. Mixing, you might say, business with pleasure.

So far, nothing heinous had come of it. No one had quit. Nothing had fallen apart. Business hadn't suffered, and neither had he. Quite the contrary, in fact. Tony believed his regular card games kept him sharp. Hanging with the crew kept him in the loop, behind the scenes, on top of everything.

Jennifer suggested. "Once you go bare, honey, you'll never go back. It *is* swimsuit season, after all."

They were waxing her eyebrows. Eyebrows showed all year, not just during swimsuit season. Meredith frowned as the debate continued. Exactly what was a "Brazilian"?

"We're hardly equipped for that," Erin disagreed.

"Bare? Bare where?" Meredith asked, panicked.

Kim leaned nearer. "These eyebrows look like they belong on Jay Leno. If your agent advised you to grow these for an audition, he should be fired. His judgment is seriously impaired."

The other women nodded.

"You're lucky you changed your mind about this."

"Bare? Bare where?" she asked again.

"*Everywhere.* Men love it," Salma said with a wink. "Trust us. We're professionals."

"I've never even plucked!" Meredith babbled.

They looked horrified. "I should hope not!"

Moaning, Meredith reclined on Becky's banquette with her head on Becky's knee. The housekeeping employee stroked her hair comfortingly. On either side of her, Erin and Jennifer held her hands.

"I don't even shave my legs," she added. "Hardly ever."

The other women exchanged looks.

"She's delirious," Erin announced. "Do it, Kim."

"She needs a facial afterward," Inga said, eyeing Meredith's nose critically. "Those are definitely enlarged pores."

"You'll have to wait until I'm done with her hair," Salma put in, her expression eager. "The color looks surprisingly natural, but there's trimming to be done. Good thing I always carry my shears in my purse."

Yikes. Meredith struggled, trying to scoot off the banquette. All she'd said was that she — as Marley — wanted a new look. Something she could recreate herself. How was she supposed to know the words "new look" were like catnip to this crew?

"Hold her still," Kim ordered, advancing with the wax.

Meredith felt two hands clamp on her head. Jennifer. An instant later, Kim painted on the wax. It wasn't as hot as she'd feared. Fractionally, Meredith relaxed. This wasn't that bad. The warm wax felt kind of soothing, in fact. She released the breath she'd been holding, her body going limp.

Kim smoothed on two muslin strips, one for each eyebrow. "Good-bye, Jay Leno brows!" She leaned closer, her manner confiding. "Feel free to yell if you want," she advised. "Sometimes it helps."

Riiiip.

"Youch!" Meredith flung both hands upward to touch her eyebrows. They felt nearly bald. She screamed.

It really didn't, she discovered, help all that much.

Ten minutes and another hand later, Tony considered his next bet. "I'll see your Barry Bonds, and raise you . . ." His hand hovered over the stack of baseball cards nearest him. "One Rickey Henderson and three bucks."

The rest of his bet clinked into the pot, joining with the coins, dollar bills, and creased collectible cards already there. Like all the poker games they played, this was for low stakes. Nobody wanted to risk too much for the sake of a good time.

The script supervisor anted up.

The stunt coordinator folded. "Too rich for my blood, Tony. You've got that Valentine lucky streak going for you, like always."

Everyone laughed, grousing good-naturedly.

The Foley artist frowned at his hand. "The Valentines owned this damned town. Must've owned half the frigging playing card companies, too. Otherwise, I don't know where all these deuces came from in a single deck."

Deuces were low. More laughter, and pats on the back.

Given an opening, more Valentine legends were tossed around the table. The crew talked about their lucky breaks, being hired by Roland. Their showbiz memories, formed at the studio. Their history-of-Hollywood knowledge, fostered by Errol and encouraged by Nadine's incessant gabbing about "the Golden Era" at Valentine Studios.

Tony grinned. Then he reminisced some, too. Just to be friendly, of course. Looking around the table as the game continued, he had to admit to a weird sense of solidarity. Of belonging. Of having missed . . . this.

Getting together with a crew was something he'd done regularly during his pre-college days while interning at the studio. He'd forgotten how much he enjoyed it.

Being part of the family business was nice. He couldn't, Tony reminded himself, stick around here too long, though. Staying in L.A. would be like ditching an MLB draft to star in Little League. He'd worked hard to become part of the cutting-edge entrepreneurial world. There was no looking back now.

Hanging with a crew, organizing the details of running a studio . . . those things came easily to him. Too easily. He needed a challenge, not camaraderie. He needed bytes and bits and ethernets, not cameras. Not production notes. Not the responsibility of creating Hollywood vacation experiences for TV star wanna-bes from Wichita.

No matter how much he (secretly) enjoyed it.

In the end, Tony won the hand with nothing better than three of a kind. Satisfied, he dragged a fresh round of beers from his trailer's fridge and passed them around. Then he scooped up his winnings.

Energetic trash talking ensued. Grinning, Tony gave back as good as he got. The rest of the crew had had good hands, but sometimes winning was ninety percent mental.

And sometimes, fun was just fun. Low stakes, low risk, high good-time quotient. Now that he and Meredith were on the same page, that was exactly what he intended to start sharing with her . . . starting first thing tomorrow.

Woozily, after an evening packed with laughter, wax, and more makeup (and mojitos) than Meredith had ever encountered in her life, she staggered up the steps to her darkened trailer. Her mind buzzed with the myriad instructions she'd been given. Or maybe that was her scalp, burning from the ministrations of Salma and her assistants. Either way, she was a changed woman.

She paused at her doorway and waved to Erin and Jennifer, who'd dropped her off on the way to their own trailers. They waved back, their smiles giving her a warm, fuzzy feeling. There was nothing, Meredith mused, quite like bonding over shared mascara mishaps to really cement a friendship.

Inside, she carefully put away her mementos of the evening, including three pages of makeup instructions scribbled on a sheet of Hello Kitty stationery. Then she stripped off her BioFashion clothes, washed her face, and brushed her teeth. Finally she stepped into her one secret indulgence — a lacy peach-colored negligee cadged from Marley's closet.

Marley had claimed it was "La Perla" and cost five hundred dollars, but Meredith didn't believe it. Even her sister wasn't frivolous enough to pay that much for something to wear while basically unconscious. Probably her sister had said that only to scare Meredith off. Sort of like the time when they were kids, when she'd claimed the raisins in the oatmeal cookies weren't raisins, but bugs.

Come on — five hundred bucks for a nightgown?

Happily clad in the frothy, silky creation, Meredith slid between the sheets.

She was ready for tomorrow. After all she'd endured tonight, there was no way she was backing down now. She was going to be the best Marley impersonator *ever*. For the sake of all the girls' night women and all the other crew members just like them, she was going to succeed.

If doing that meant resisting one particularly appealing man . . . well, that was just the price she'd have to pay. Otherwise, she'd

246

simply be too distracted to perform. Tony could torture her, he could seduce her, he could even give her that oh-so-sexy smile of his. Meredith wasn't backing down.

No matter what.

THIRTEEN

"The most important thing in acting is honesty. Once you've learned to fake it, you're in."

— Samuel Goldwyn

The next morning, Tony's first knock on Meredith's trailer door wasn't answered. Probably because rap music blasted so loudly from inside that she couldn't hear anything else. Maybe because amid the sound waves shaking her trailer, his knock was just another vibration.

Fighting back a grin at Meredith's choice of wake-up music, Tony considered what the day might hold for them. Now that he'd realized there were no risks in getting close to her, all bets were off. He had an hour before he was expected anywhere. Her first class didn't start until sometime later.

He knocked again, harder this time.

An instant later, the music shut off. Meredith opened the door, sporting a thigh-high pink robe, a vaguely damp, just-showered appearance, and a flustered expression. Her brown hair stood straight up from her head, like a sparrow airport without its early arrivals.

She looked surprised to see him. "Tony! What's up?"

He almost was, looking at her in that short robe. Again Tony congratulated himself on identifying that mixing-business-with-pleasure benefit loophole.

That ranked right up there with his most brilliant business innovations. Downloadable perfume samples. Video games on demand. Virtual home redecorating. He was *good.* There was no doubt about it.

Meredith gave him a curious once-over, unmistakable interest in her expression. It was last night all over again. It was kiss-me-quick, hand-in-the-pants time. It was — it was over, just like that. She abruptly stared at the doorjamb, focusing on the strip of metal there. She ran her thumbnail along it, seeking to push the crooked metal back into place.

Looking as though she wanted to push away the attraction between them in exactly the same way.

"Umm . . . I'm kind of busy at the moment," she said, her tone unfamiliarly crisp and businesslike. "I'm in the middle of doing my hair —"

"I think it's ready to surrender." He dragged his gaze away from her skyscraper 'do. Smiled.

"— and then I have makeup to do —"

"You look terrific without it."

"— and a class after that. So if you could skip to the point, that would be great."

Her impatient look prompted him.

"Do you play poker?" he asked.

"Poker?" She looked confused. "No, not really."

Tony's smile widened. "*Good*. That settles it, then. We'll have to do" — *each other* — "something else together."

He edged past her, entering her trailer.

Meredith tried to stop him, holding both hands out in front of her. She clutched a long, skinny comb in one of them. Probably it was responsible for her squirrel's nest hairdo.

"This isn't a good idea," she protested. "You, being here. Me, being here. Us, together. Privately. All alone."

"I like it." He moved closer. Located a rogue tendril which had escaped the nest and twined it around his finger. Offered her his most smoldering look. "Give it a chance. I can make you like it, too. Together. Privately. All alone."

Her eyes widened. For an instant, Meredith seemed tempted. Then her expression took on the same schoolmarmish cast it had in the doorway.

She stepped away, smacking her comb against her palm, not looking at him. "This is a test, right? You want to see how dedicated I am. Fine." She sucked in a deep breath. "Here it is, then. I know we got off

250

track last night. I know that, and I'm sorry. But I can assure you, it's not going to happen again."

Last night didn't matter anymore. "Things have changed since then."

"Changed? Oh, God —" Meredith grabbed his arm, jostling the things he'd brought with him. She looked worried. "The studio hasn't buckled into bankruptcy already, has it?"

"What? No!"

Disgruntled that she'd even ask that, Tony handed her the motorcycle boots and clothes she'd left at his place yesterday.

"I swear, I'm going to be a better Marley from now on!" she babbled, hardly glancing at the clothes. She hurled them in the general direction of the banquette. "Nothing's going to stop me. Nothing. A lot of people are depending on me, you know."

He was glad she'd realized that. "I didn't come here to talk about that."

"Oh." She straightened. Cast a wary glance at him. Bit her lip. "What *did* you come here to talk about, then?"

"I didn't come here to talk at all."

"Oh." Her eyes widened. "Oh!"

Tony moved to take the comb from her hand, to pull her close. To untie the silky belt on her silky robe and find out if she was as soft and naked underneath it as he hoped.

Before he could touch her, Meredith sniffed the air. Then she bolted down the hallway. "My straightening iron! I think it's melting the vanity!"

As excuses for dodging a guy went, that one was pretty inventive. Tony watched as Meredith vanished in a flurry of fluffy hair, pink robe, and panic.

A few minutes later, she called to him from the bathroom. "Don't worry! The scorch marks rub right off. No problem."

He grinned. "I'm not worried. Leave it. I'll send 'round housekeeping later. It looks like you could use a visit, anyway."

"Oh, no — I don't have them come here. It might blow my cover if they saw all my stuff lying around."

"Suit yourself."

He followed her, noticing the clothes, books, CDs, and soda cans littering her trailer's every surface. An open bag of Oreos shared table space with a copy of the *Journal of American History*. A pair of hoodie sweatshirts with museum logos partially obscured the TV. Obviously, Meredith didn't care about "must-see" TV — or about keeping things neat.

He found her sloppiness hopelessly endearing. Here, at last, was a woman he could relax with. A woman whose high standards were focused on the important things — sex, Oreos, and sex — and not on scouring sample sales or entertaining friends at fancy dinner parties.

Which was more than he'd been able to say about Taryn, for instance. Taryn, who'd blown him away with her Upper East Side classiness, her networking savvy, her business acumen. She'd introduced him to important movers and shakers during his early years in New York, impressing him mostly — he could see in retrospect — by being the opposite of everything he wanted to escape from. Everything Hollywood.

As a New Yorker, Taryn hadn't known who the Valentine family was, or why they were important. That was exactly the attitude Tony had headed eastward to find.

Too bad it had cost him so much. One merger, two new ventures . . . a big chunk of his trust.

But that wouldn't be a problem with Meredith. Meredith, who'd suggested a casual fling herself. Meredith, who'd boldly propositioned him in the limousine and hadn't made a secret of her interest in him since. Her attitude was downright refreshing. Other women could take lessons.

It was such a relief not to have to think long-term.

Long-term was for discussing the Knicks' chances in the playoffs. For outlining e-commerce benefits to skittish potential partners. Not for describing friendly, *non*poker-playing time spent with someone he worked with.

Someone like Meredith.

Tony reached the bathroom doorway and leaned against it. Inside the cramped room, Meredith scowled at her reflection in the mirrored medicine cabinet. Stuck in one corner of it, a piece of cartoon stationery offered scribbled instructions and diagrams. Near her elbow, an unplugged appliance — the straightening iron, he presumed — looked about as useful as a buzz saw during a power failure.

He'd never understand why women needed so much crap to do their hair. Wasn't a simple comb enough?

He asked as much.

"No. This is no ordinary comb, and what I'm doing is no ordinary thing." With dignity, Meredith lifted her chin. "This is a technique I learned last night while hanging out with the girls. It's called teasing."

Teasing. He was familiar with teasing. *Teasing* was the sight of her luscious backside and long legs, visible beneath the hem of her robe. *Teasing* was the tug of silk against her skin, the hint of taut nipple he glimpsed against the fabric, the dewy flush between her breasts.

"Teasing, huh? I think you've nailed it."

"I'm not so sure. My hair doesn't seem to want to lay down again. Salma did something with a flat brush that made all this look normal. Puffy, but normal."

She growled in frustration.

He cocked his head in surprise. "*You've* been taking hairstyling advice?"

"Hey. There were cocktails involved," she said defensively, holding up both hands. "I'm not responsible. After I . . . left your place, I was invited to the other side of the back lot for a girls' night with some of the crew."

Tony pretended he didn't already know where she'd been. And that he hadn't considered baring his soul to her when he'd seen her there.

Squinting in the mirror, Meredith fiddled with the six inches of electroshocked hair above her ears. She held a couple of hairpins between her teeth. A can of hairspray stood at the ready, right next to a zippered bag of makeup.

She was serious about this, Tony realized. She meant to actually style her hair, to put on makeup, maybe even to leave her hip-tied sweatshirt in her trailer today. He boggled. Yesterday, she'd threatened to slug a wardrobe assistant who'd suggested "Marley's" baseball cap clashed with her flip-flops. What the hell had changed since then?

Puzzling over it, he examined her as she raked the comb backward through her dark hair. More of the strands stood on end, hopelessly tangled.

"I don't think you're doing that right."

"Go soak your head."

Ahhh, that was better. That was the

255

Meredith he understood. Reassured, Tony grinned. She raised her arms and went on "teasing," the motion making her pert breasts bob beneath her satiny robe. He forgot all about . . . everything.

Her robe gaped in all the right places. The subtle swell of one breast peeped into view, then vanished. Her nipples puckered against the satiny pink fabric, drawing his attention even more effectively than her aerodynamic hair had.

Loophole, Tony reminded himself cheerfully. Meredith was obviously naked beneath her robe. Or was she wearing panties? Flimsy pink panties made of the same satiny stuff? Surreptitiously, he peeked.

She cut off his view by grabbing a red metallic can. "I'm getting together with the Wardrobe Department later to plan eleven days' worth of Marley-ready outfits," she said, appearing to concentrate hard on spritzing her hair with the can's contents. "I don't want to leave anything to chance."

He coughed. Those fumes were deadly. "Good idea. I'll send over that rack of clothes I picked out. In the meantime —"

"In the meantime, I give up on my hair!" Meredith hurled down her comb. "Damn it! This looked so easy when Salma did it!"

At last. She was holding still. Now, if he could just get her a little less hair-obsessed and a little more naked . . .

He rubbed her shoulder encouragingly. "You'll figure it out. How hard can it be?"

"Oh, I dunno. About as hard as . . . Pilates. Grrr!"

Yipes. Pilates had made her knee that guy in the cojones. Resisting an urge to shield his nuts, Tony smiled.

"I have an idea that'll take your mind off all this," he said, waggling his eyebrows. "Come here. I'll show you."

Oblivious to his innuendo, she squirted a yellow substance out of a nearby tube. With jerky motions, she rubbed it onto her cheeks. "Never mind. I'll just move on to my face."

"Good idea." He was a patient man. He could wait.

"Yeoch!" she yodeled, grabbing her cheeks.

"What's the matter?"

"It's this." She indicated the tube. "The special secret ingredient in this cream Inga gave me." Hopping up and down, Meredith flapped her hands in front of her face as though encouraging the cream to dry. "I forgot how much it stings."

Tony scoffed. Women were always complaining about the price of beauty. As near as he could tell, slathering on antiwrinkle cream wasn't nearly as arduous as strapping perfectly appealing breasts into uncomfortable bras. But women insisted on doing that every day, didn't they?

"If only you'd go braless more often," he began.

Her exasperated look cut him off.

"Was there something you needed from me?" she asked. "I have a class to conduct soon, and a full schedule after that."

"Your schedule today consists of one class." Tony checked his watch. "About forty-five minutes from now. Followed by one turn through the press junket with Harry and Esther, and a session on horseback riding with the stunt coordinators in Tumbleweed. Until then, you've got plenty of time. Time for —"

Casual sex, was what he'd planned to say. It was the cornerstone of his big seduction pitch. In the bright fluorescent light, though, surrounded by styling products and makeup and pink satin, "casual sex" sounded kind of crass.

Time for nookie? Tony substituted silently, testing it out. *Time for the mattress mambo?* Neither of those was very romantic.

No. Screw romantic. He was here for a fling. He had to remember that.

"Time for . . . ?" she asked edgily, eyebrows raised.

Maybe *time to get lucky?* Sure, that was good. He glanced at Meredith, feeling unaccountably nervous, mentally winding up for his big pitch. Sticking his arm out the bathroom doorway, he pumped up his biceps a few times. Repeated the motion on the opposite side. That was better. Studlier.

"You've got time," he repeated, "to get luc— hey, are you all right? Your eyes are watering."

"I'll be fine." She sniffed, blinking through her tears at the tube. "It's just this cream. It has AHAs in it. Plus beta-hydroxy acids, vitamins C, E, and B12, and a secret exfoliating ingredient. Inga said I need a skin care regimen."

"You bought into that BS?"

Meredith shrugged. "Sometime between the third mojito and the Russell Crowe video film festival, it started seeming like a good idea." She sniffled again, eyes still watering. "I've never been very good at froufrou stuff, though."

"Give me that." Frowning, Tony snatched the tube. He wanted to throw it out the window for interfering with his casual-fling plans. If he did that, though, Meredith would probably just dive after it. "It can't be that bad."

He squeezed out a generous portion. Slapped it onto his freshly shaved mug like a guy in an Old Spice commercial. Gave her a big macho grin.

"See? I'm fine. You just need to toughen up a little."

"Hmmph." Her skeptical gaze swept over his face.

"Now, why don't you come on over here

—" He stopped, feeling a bizarre prickling on his cheeks.

"Yes?" she inquired.

"And let me show you what I came here for. Ouch!" He peered at his face in the mirror. Was it his imagination, or was he developing an instant heat rash? "I thought that stuff was just vitamins."

"Vitamins, secret ingredients . . . girly stuff. Why?" Meredith asked, all innocence. "Is it too much for you?"

"No." The burning intensified. "Of course not."

"I have matching body lotion. In the same formula."

He warded her off with both hands. "No, thanks. I wouldn't want to look *too* good. It might cause a stampede or something."

"A stampede. Right." Obviously fighting back a grin, she grabbed a makeup brush from the counter. She swabbed it in something pink and fluffed it over her face. "Look, I really need to get busy here. So if there's nothing else . . . ?"

That was a brush-off if ever he'd heard one. What the . . . ?

He tried another tactic. "You look *really* good today."

Compliments were always worth an A-plus, right?

Or maybe a small kiss? He waited hopefully.

Meredith rolled her eyes. "Uh-huh. Really good." Brush, brush. Peer. Frown. "I look like Quasimodo after a bender. But thanks for the pep talk."

"No, you don't." He rubbed his palm over her back, encountering slippery robe atop warm, sleek muscles. "See? Not a hint of a hunchback, that I can tell."

"Har, har."

Suddenly, a thousand pinpricks jabbed his face, tingling all over — and not in a good way. Tony grabbed the edge of the counter. Maybe he'd applied too much cream.

Manfully ignoring the sensation, he mustered up a secondary tactic. "Is this a new robe? It looks good on you."

"It's straight from Marley's closet." Meredith snatched a smaller brush. Squinted at the taped-up diagram. Started in on her eye makeup. "I packed up all my own stuff. I've decided to wear nothing but starlet clothes from now on."

Starlet clothes. He envisioned micro miniskirts. High heels. Skintight everything, and more super-sexy bikini tops.

"Sounds like a good idea," he said.

"I'm dead serious about impersonating Marley."

"I'm getting that."

He should have been thrilled. He should have been delighted his erstwhile star attraction was finally giving the job one hundred percent. The trouble was, Tony wasn't thrilled. He was, in fact, becoming increasingly frustrated.

What had happened to the Meredith he was used to? The one who put her hand on his knee, who grabbed his crotch, who kissed him as though oxygen was an afterthought? He wanted that Meredith back. He could think of only one way to get her.

"Hey!" Emitting a surprised squeal, Meredith jumped. Her makeup brush clattered into the vanity sink. "Did you just grab my ass?"

Tony froze, both hands still cupped in ready position. He hadn't expected her to freak out. He'd touched her for only a nanosecond. It had been so sweet . . . until she'd screamed.

"Uhhh . . ."

She glared at the tube of beauty cream. "Did that stuff damage your brain cells, or what?" Then she glared at *him*. "Putting on three kinds of eye shadow is a delicate operation. You could have blinded me!"

They glowered at each other. Tony, through his watering eyes. Meredith via the mirror. A few moments ticked past.

"Last night you liked it," he finally said.

"Last night was a mistake," she replied.

Coolly, she resumed her makeup. Dumbfounded, he watched her. She raised a tube of red lipstick, nearly smeared it all over her eyelids, and then jerked it away. Flushing a little, Meredith dusted a sponge applicator with blue eye . . . stuff . . . and applied it with a shaky hand.

Tony frowned. "You don't mean that."

"Oh, yes. I do. Also, if it's all right with you, I think we should spend less time together. The makeup and hair and wardrobe crews gave me some advice last night. I'm pretty sure I can handle everything on my own. You don't need to baby-sit me anymore."

Baby-sit? "Baby-sitters don't grab your ass."

Slowly, her gaze roved over him in the mirror. "Actually, if I'd ever met a single dad who looked like you when I was babysitting, I might have grabbed yours."

A grin wobbled onto her face. Instantly, she squashed it.

"I mean, if you're finished, I have to get dressed."

She hurled the brushes into the sink. Meredith headed for the bedroom, her businesslike gait barely managing to fluff up her shortie robe.

Tony followed her into Pinkville, nonplussed. That was the second come-hither look she'd given him since he'd arrived this morning. He knew he hadn't mistaken the interest in her expression *or* the longing in her eyes. She still wanted him. Just as much as he wanted her. Except she was denying it.

"What gives?" He scowled, disgruntled as a new thought struck him. "Are you playing hard to get? Because I've got to tell you, I'm not a game-playing kind of guy."

"Except poker, apparently."

"You don't even play poker!" he said accusingly. He'd been so happy to hear it. How had everything gone wrong since then?

Meredith faced him, her arms outflung. "What is *up* with you today? Cut me some slack, will you? I'm trying to concentrate. This girly-girl routine might look easy to you, but it's difficult for me. Trust me."

Her voice cracked. Blinking hard, she turned away.

"Awww, Meredith . . . hang on. I didn't mean —"

"Button it. I don't want your pity."

She was really upset, Tony realized belatedly. "Is this something about your hair?" he asked gently.

She blinked harder, then rolled her gaze to the ceiling. She sucked in a deep, shuddery breath. She shook her head.

It *was* about her hair. He knew it. Despite her apparent — wordless — denial. Women were completely undone by bad hair days. Wondering what the hell to do about it, Tony peered at her.

She'd managed to stripe her eyelids with blue, he noticed. Her cheeks were as rosy as a serious sunburn. Despite all the hairspray, her hair hadn't tamed itself a bit. It still drew his eye with its gravity-defying height.

She didn't look like a TV starlet. She looked like a televangelist's QVC-addicted mistress. Or maybe Bad Girl Barbie. He found it kind of cute. Underneath everything, he could still see the same gutsy, funny, pain-in-the-ass woman he loved. To be with. Loved to be with.

He had to face facts. As a Marley clone, she was a complete washout. As Meredith, though, she was . . . undeniably appealing. In a war painted, barely dressed, I-dare-you-to-ridicule-my-hair kind of way.

"So you need a little practice," Tony told her in his kindest voice. "That's no crime."

She did *not* find that as encouraging as he'd hoped. Ignoring him, Meredith slid open her bedroom's built-in closet door. Three mismatched stilettos tumbled out. With a sheepish look, she kicked them back in.

"If it wasn't for the actor fantasy camp, you wouldn't need to do any of this," he added. "I loved the way you looked in the limo on that first night. All fresh and clean and *real*. Do you know how rare genuine beauty is here in La-La Land?"

She sniffled, raking clothes across the rack. "I'll bet you say that to all the girls who grab your knee."

Tony grinned. "Only the ones who pass out on our first night together, defy me at every turn, and manage to look dead sexy in a sweatshirt."

At his mention of clothes, her despairing gaze whisked over the choices in front of her. "I *knew* I should have asked Jennifer and Erin for a crib sheet! I don't have any idea what to choose. Do you think they make Garanimals for starlets?"

"What the hell are Garanimals?"

"Line of children's clothes," she enthused. "Marketed in the seventies. Ads featuring pandas and tigers and giraffes. The concept was brilliant — everything coordinated by the tags, so kids could match —"

Undoubtedly seeing his blank look, she stopped.

"Never mind." She turned to the closet again.

"How about the BioFashion clothes?" Tony suggested, spotting the leather pants and snakeskin-print shirt hanging within reach. "Those looked great on you." *And partway off you.*

No dice. With precision, Meredith selected a flower-patterned skirt and a pale green halter top. She flung both onto the bed with a defiant look.

He glanced at her legs. "If you wear that skirt, all those Band-Aids on your legs will show."

She froze. Tightly, she said, "I shaved my legs this morning. It's . . . been a while since I attempted that."

"You should do it more often," he advised.

She glared.

"Because it will give you practice. And show off your legs. You have really sexy legs."

"Nice try, Einstein."

She did have sexy legs. In the nonbandaged places. "So you have a few nicks. Big deal. Happens to everyone."

"I'm lucky I didn't slice off a — a kneecap!"

Her voice quavered on that last, breaking as she tried to continue. Keeping her back to him, Meredith kicked a few more tumbled stilettos back into the closet, then slid it shut before any more could escape. Shit. She was upset again.

"Who am I kidding?" she asked. "I'll never pull this off."

Her hands went slack on the jeweled flip-flops she'd selected. Apparently, high heels were the last frontier — territory she wasn't willing to totter into yet.

"Sure you will." She had to.

Her frustrated gaze met his. "No, I won't. I'll never be like Marley. I'll bleed to death first, or give myself lipstick poisoning. On my stupid eyelids."

Okay, Tony amended. She wasn't just upset. She was seriously upset.

He gestured toward his still-tingling cheeks. "All you've done so far is give an innocent bystander a permanent heat rash. That's not

267

so bad." He pulled a face, hoping he could make her smile.

Instead, her eyes filled with tears. "Sorry about that," she sniffed. "I didn't mean it."

Oh, Christ. One look at her plaintive expression made him panic. He wasn't thinking about getting lucky anymore. All he cared about was making sure she didn't cry. Desperately, he cast about for distraction.

"Hey, what's this?" Tony strode to the wall beside the closet, upon which hung a taped-on cardboard star. "I don't remember seeing this before."

Meredith sniffled. "It's a dressing room star. The girls gave it to me last night. I was supposed to write my name on it, but . . ." She shrugged helplessly, her gaze on the homemade star. "I couldn't do it. It didn't feel like me."

"Awww, come on." He looked over his shoulder at her. "It could feel like you, if you wanted it to."

"You're just saying that because you need me to be a star," she accused. "You need me to be like Marley."

He did. But looking at her now, with her half-assed attempts at glamour and her defiant posture, Tony realized there was more to it than that. He wanted Meredith to feel like a star . . . just because she deserved it.

"Maybe. Or maybe I see something in you that you don't."

"Sure." She rolled her eyes. "Inner beauty, right? And a nifty personality? I've heard it before. Save the rah-rah routine. I know exactly what I'm like."

Tony shook his head. "No, you don't."

"I'm the tomboy. The troublemaker." She ticked off each description on her fingertips, her old rebelliousness back in spades. "The smart girl who wanted to read all the time, and who didn't get a real date to the prom."

So? He'd figured out that much on his own. Well, not the prom thing, but the rest of it. It didn't take a rocket scientist to realize that a historian probably grew up as a bookworm. That a woman who wore motorcycle boots had probably been a little girl who climbed trees. That outspoken Meredith had probably been defiant since her days in Pampers.

Tony shook his head. "There's nothing wrong with reading or any of the rest of that stuff. That's not what I'm talking about."

But Meredith was on a roll, and she wasn't stopping. In fact, she was pacing.

"It's true!" she cried. "Do you know who asked me to my senior prom? Tommy Winkleman. I was so happy. Until I found out he pocketed all my used fruit punch glasses and sold them afterward as 'Marley Madison souvenirs.' The rat fink. So don't tell me *I* could be the star. I know better. I always have."

Tony frowned. Was that jerk Winkleman registered on LongLostClassmates.com? He had a sixty percent interest in that site. Probably enough to enable him to track down the guy and teach him a lesson about —

"Are you even listening?" Meredith threw up her hands. "Forget it. I don't have the 'star quality' you need. But I can learn to fake it, and I'm going to. For the next week and a half, I'm Marley. That's all there is to it."

Her obstinate gaze challenged him to disagree.

"Okay," he said. "It's a deal. But for right now, you're Meredith."

She sighed, as though he just didn't get it.

Tony knew he did. He also knew more was required here than mere talking. Women always overrated the talking thing. He was a man of action.

"You're Meredith, who's going to be late to her first class," he added, unable to hold back a grin. Then he grabbed the flip-flops from her grasp, tipped them both onto the bed behind her, and cradled her head in his hand. "Because you'll be too busy being kissed to realize what time it is."

FOURTEEN

"You press the button; we do the rest."
— advertisement for Kodak cameras
(1888)

The good news was, Meredith's romp with Tony had managed to squash down her out-of-control hair and rub off just enough of her makeup to make her appear normal for her Diva Dramatics class and the faux press junket afterward. The bad news was, she'd caved.

Why hadn't she been able to resist Tony?

Just because he'd been sweet? Just because he'd been caring and sexy and hadn't taken no for an answer? Just because she'd been dying to kiss him from the moment she'd opened her trailer door this morning and found him on the steps?

Well . . . yes. Yes to all those reasons. And more. Meredith had tried to tell herself that any woman would have fallen into Tony's arms and forgotten her mission. Not to mention her supposed boycott. But the truth was, she wasn't just any woman, and Tony wasn't just any man.

He was the man who'd heard her Tommy Winkleman prom story and had still wanted to kiss her afterward. The man who'd witnessed her Band-Aid-covered legs and still admired them. The man who'd seen her with authentic Bride of Frankenstein hair . . . and had still insisted he saw beauty in her. That made him special. Really special. Also, possibly unboycottable.

Whenever she was around Tony, Meredith turned to mush. That was all there was to it.

At first she'd tried to laugh it off.

"Of course you want me! Now, when my hair and makeup is all done," she'd groused when he'd come up for air after that first kiss. "You guys always wait until we're completely ready to go out, and *then* you find us suddenly irresistible."

"I find you irresistible all the time," Tony had said.

Then his mouth had met hers, and . . . whoosh. Instant fireworks.

"Especially when you're in my arms," he'd added, smiling.

Mush, mush, mush.

In her defense, Tony had exercised an unfair amount of understanding, coupled with a smidge of machismo and a hefty dose of sex appeal. No wonder she'd crumbled. Given the science of it, who could blame her?

It made a lot more sense than Hairology.

Now, a few hours later, Meredith perched on a sofa on the faux press junket set, wired with a clip-on mic and armored with Soft &

Dri. A Valentine Studios poster hung behind her. A table accessorized with tulips sat beside her. A battery of set lights shined down on her, and an enormous camera recorded her every word and gesture — and Harry's, in the armchair opposite her.

She should have been concentrating on the questions Harry was asking her from his clipboarded list. Instead, she'd been unable to quit thinking about Tony.

She needed a new strategy for dealing with him. For making sure she didn't succumb to his obvious charms again and forget her duties here. But on the other hand . . . she was here, wasn't she? At the faux press junket? That meant Tony's effect on her wasn't *too* mind scrambling. Maybe she could handle it.

After all, if they kept things casual between them, that shouldn't put her Marley masquerade at risk. She could compartmentalize her relationship with Tony, just like Madison Avenue compartmentalized potential advertising markets. She could keep her heart uninvolved. She could keep her mind focused on surviving the transition to Starletville and enjoy a harmless fling at the same time.

Because a fling was all she was looking for anyway, right?

Harry cleared his throat, calling her attention back to their interview in progress. Meredith glanced at the mini tape recorder balanced on the arm of his chair, reminding herself it was logging their entire conversation. As was the camera.

With relish, Harry poised his pen over his reporter's notebook. He was really getting into his new role.

On a nearby set, Esther was doing the same. Only she'd added glittery cat's-eye sunglasses and a leopard-print jacket to her faux press corps ensemble. Clearly, Esther was channeling Joan Collins. Or maybe one of the women from "Ab Fab" on BBC.

The actor fantasy camp guest Esther was interviewing caught Meredith's eye. Excitedly, she gave "Marley" a thumbs-up. Meredith smiled and waved. She liked seeing the guests enjoying themselves. That was definitely one of the perks of this gig.

Harry leaned forward. "How long have you wanted to be an actress, Marley?" he asked.

"Oh, um . . . forever, I guess," Meredith answered, snapping herself into her starlet role. "I've always been interested in performing. Ever since I was a little girl."

She forced herself to concentrate and went on explaining, spinning the story she'd heard Marley give over the years. She covered the auditions, the lessons, the tutors. Omitted the unknown twin sister who'd been left behind at home, doing homework and sharing Hamburger Helper dinners with her dad.

"What was your first acting job?" Harry asked, his kindly face encouraging her to confide in him. "Did you enjoy it?"

"Absolutely!"

Meredith detailed Marley's first lucky break in a Kool-Aid commercial at the age of four. She went on to describe her sister's various bit parts, then her work as a regular on the kids' series "Playtime."

All the while, she recalled Tony's smoldering look as he'd trailed his fingers over her robe earlier, capturing its loosely knotted belt in his hand. She remembered how she'd ached for him to untie it. To part the silky fabric, bare her naked body, touch —

"You did a lot of pilot work then?" Harry asked. "Before finding your big break?"

Meredith coughed. She crossed her legs. "Yes. Several pilots, some for series which wound up running for a few episodes. Some for series which never aired."

She detailed a few of the pilots' plots, their titles and characters. All the while, her imagination wandered back to her and Tony on that bed. Again she felt him kiss her neck. Felt him wedge his knee between her parted thighs, encouraging her to arch against him. Felt their heartbeats racing, her robe coming dangerously close to slipping aside completely. If only —

"What were you like growing up?" Harry asked.

"Bookish," Meredith answered distractedly. "I practically lived between the pages. I read

Black Beauty when I was eleven, and for a whole month afterward I pretended my Schwinn was a horse. Complete with a clothesline 'bridle.' My dad was sure I'd break an ankle practicing 'jumping.' "

Harry smiled, looking charmed. "You always had a big imagination, then?"

"I guess so." Belatedly, she remembered she was supposed to be answering questions as Marley. Thinking about Tony was sidetracking her — just as predicted. "It's really been useful for my acting career."

"I'll bet." He consulted his clipboard. "What about your family? How do they feel about your success? Are they thrilled?"

"They are." Meredith managed a nod and a smile, but inside, a tiny part of her chafed at the admission. Everyone had always raved about Marley. "My mom keeps a scrapbook of all my press clippings. She drags it out at family gatherings — Christmas, birthdays, the Fourth of July. In the Madison household, every day is Marley Day!"

Her voice wobbled. Clearing her throat, she shifted in her seat. It wouldn't have killed her parents to make a fuss over some of *her* accomplishments, Meredith thought now. Her published articles. Her job at the museum. Her Historian of the Month plaque. Without the gloss of Hollywood on them, they didn't mean a thing, she guessed.

She lifted her chin, determined not to

dwell on that. She smoothed her pastel-print skirt, ready to go on.

"A scrapbook, huh?" Harry asked. "That's a pretty heartwarming story."

"Isn't it?" Her smile felt brittle.

"You must feel very lucky."

"I do. Sometimes even *I* don't realize how lucky I am."

Come on, she chided herself. It wasn't as though Marley had asked Meredith to hijack her starlet identity for a couple of weeks. Meredith had done that all by herself. It was up to her to escape this mess. Unscathed. And undetected.

She ought to play fair. What would Marley *really* say right now?

"I have to admit," she continued, "that the fans, the adulation, the awards — much as I enjoy them — don't mean nearly as much to me as the people I love do. They're the ones who matter most. The ones I couldn't do without."

It was true, she realized with surprise. She really did believe her sister felt that way. Especially now that she'd found Jake and Noah. Meredith smiled.

So did Harry. He looked delighted with her answer.

"When it comes down to it, life is all about finding people to share things with," he agreed. He winked at Esther.

Esther wiggled her fingers in a flirtatious

277

wave, then blew a kiss. Harry's smile broadened.

The camera and sound operators rolled their eyes.

"Back to the questions." He consulted his clipboard. "About your current project, Marley, here at Valentine Studios. I know you've been involved in something special here. How's that coming along?"

"Really well, I think. I'm enjoying it."

That was an understatement. This morning with Tony, she'd gone beyond enjoying . . . all the way to succumbing. If not for her demanding schedule, she'd have lingered on that bed with him for hours. Kissing. Touching. Rolling atop the blankets with their bodies tangled together, unable to get close enough.

She'd been nearly crazy with desire by the time Tony had untied her robe. She'd held her breath as he'd slowly parted it. The pink satin had slid over her skin, revealing more of her with every inch. He'd smiled, stroking her tenderly as . . . as the wardrobe assistant knocked on the door, arriving with the daily delivery of stilettos.

Meredith had never loathed high heels more.

She swore she was never wearing them. Just as a matter of protest. The starlet clothes, the hair, the makeup — they made her feel awkward enough. She didn't need any libido-busting footwear to compound her troubles.

Although without them, she thought wickedly, she'd have been *much* later to her Diva Dramatics class.

"Tell us your thoughts," Harry prompted.

As if. She'd probably be arrested.

"It's been a lot of fun here at Valentine Studios," she compromised, doing her best to put forward her charade. "I feel lucky to be working with all my costars on the sitcom. The crew, too. It's been a once-in-a-lifetime experience."

She smiled at the guys behind the camera. They grinned back. Nearby, Meredith recognized Nadine hovering around the craft services table which had been set up for the press junket. She selected a cupcake, licked the icing from her fingers, then waved.

Meredith waved back, out of camera range. It amazed her that she even recognized how to do that — or that it was necessary. Maybe this experience *was* changing her a little. . . .

"Well, I think those are all my questions," Harry said. "Thanks for talking with me, Marley. You've been great."

Whew. She'd made it.

Harry leaned forward and shook her hand, adding his other hand to cover hers in a warm-hearted gesture. His eyes twinkled, and his face creased in another grin. Harry was really enjoying himself. She was glad.

279

She liked him a lot.

The camera and sound operators stepped back, taking a break before the next interview subject was seated. At their cue, Meredith unclipped her microphone. She tugged it carefully from beneath her halter top, then stood and dropped the mic onto the sofa cushion.

"Oh, one more question," Harry said as she turned away. "Where should we mail your souvenir videotape? From the finale sitcom taping? They'll be duped and sent out at the end of the month to all the actor fantasy camp guests."

Meredith rattled off her address. Dutifully, Harry wrote it on the paperwork attached to his clipboard.

"Thanks. Now we're really done. First, a break." He eyed Esther, who was also wrapping up her session with the actor fantasy camp guest assigned to her. "Then another few interviews. This beats waxing the limo any day. Have a good afternoon, Marley."

"You, too, Harry!"

Relieved to be finished — and off camera — Meredith headed to the craft services table. She planned to say hello to Nadine and possibly score a handful of Fritos. Although the caterers always provided healthful options like tropical fruits and crudités, junk food proved most popular. It also proved best at soothing Meredith's rattled nerves. No matter how often she did the fake-starlet routine, it never seemed to get easier for her.

She and Nadine chatted. Before long, Meredith felt even better about things. Sure, she'd slipped up on her resolve not to be with Tony. But she'd found a way around that — keeping things casual between them. And okay, so she'd accidentally revealed her bookworm childhood to Harry. But he'd added that actressy spin about "imagination" himself, which proved he hadn't noticed anything amiss.

All in all, she figured, she was doing really well today.

Still, something nagged at her. Was it lipstick on her teeth? Spilled coffee on her skirt? Either one could have impaired her Marley impersonation, but Meredith didn't think they were the problem. Quickly, she reviewed her morning.

She gave a mental shrug, unable to pinpoint anything potentially damaging. Aside from arriving at her first class a little late, of course. That was Tony's fault. Satisfied, she popped a corn chip in her mouth.

"If I'm not mistaken, that's not a Hollywood Hills address you gave Harry," Nadine commented. "I'm surprised you live in such a working-class neighborhood."

"Hmmm?"

"I overheard you. I didn't mean to, dear." Blithely, Nadine waved her arm. "I couldn't

281

help it. All the Valentines are notorious eavesdroppers, you know. It runs in the family."

Still chewing, Meredith wondered how Nadine had inherited one of the infamous Valentine qualities she was always going on about. She'd married into the family when she'd hooked up with Errol.

"So does a curiosity about real estate," Nadine continued. "Hence, my question."

She gazed at Meredith expectantly.

Meredith tilted her head, confused. Then it hit her.

Oh, no. Her address.

Gasping, she clapped her hand over her mouth.

"What's the matter, dear?"

I wish I could take back that stupid address. That's what's the matter. Tony was going to kill her!

"Corn chip down the wrong pipe." She coughed.

Helpfully, Nadine pounded her on the back. "That better?"

Meredith nodded gamely. But she didn't mean it. How could anything be better when she'd made another mistake?

She'd given Harry her real address. Not Marley's Hollywood Hills address. Not an equally fashionable phony address in Malibu. *Her* address, for her own modest apartment. If Harry recognized it as being in a completely unlikely zip code to house a famous former sitcom star. . . .

"Good!" Nadine chirped, taking Meredith's arm and leading her away from the Fritos. "Because I have a plan for your afternoon of horseback riding lessons . . ."

Tony strode along the back lot, wearing his cell phone's hands-free headset. Still talking with a potential investor, he punched in a text message for Jim Woodwiss, responding to an e-mail his partner had sent this morning.

Things were going well in New York. Given the additional responsibility of running things in Tony's absence, Jim had flourished. It was almost as though he'd been waiting years for the opportunity to show what he could do. Tony felt relieved to know his ventures were in capable hands.

He felt a little more relaxed, too. California was working its magic on him. Sunshine warmed his shoulders and the top of his head. A light breeze ruffled his shirt as he passed between the soundstages. It was barely June, but it was a perfect seventy-five degrees outside.

The amazing weather was one thing he'd missed about L.A. It was also one thing that had lured him out of his office to make phone calls on the run.

The other was Uncle Errol, who Tony spied headed his way from the distant business office. Errol had asked Tony for a meeting, but he hadn't said what the agenda was. Tony held up a hand in greeting. His uncle waved in reply.

Walking to meet him, Tony finished his phone conversation and hung up. One more potential investor down . . . only a few dozen still to go.

The pressure of getting the studio's actor fantasy camp off the ground weighed on him. If he didn't secure enough investors to attend the finale, he wouldn't be able to line up enough capital to finance more sessions. If he didn't line up more sessions, the camp wouldn't flourish. If the camp didn't flourish, his uncles would be in the poorhouse . . . and Tony would have proven himself incapable of bouncing back from his recent dot-com setbacks.

He'd be damned if he'd let that happen.

His uncle reached him. "Walk with me, Tony."

With an elegant gesture, Errol motioned toward Tumbleweed. They strode together, side by side — much as they had when Tony had been a teenager. When he'd been new to working at the studio, Errol had advised him. More than likely, he had more advice in mind now.

But Errol Valentine had never been a man to rush into things. Hell, according to family legend, he'd taken two years to propose to

284

Nadine. For him, Tony was willing to wait. He put his hands in his pockets and kept moving, walking at a pace his uncle could easily manage.

All around them, activity ranged on the back lot — activity Tony surveyed with approval. He sidestepped assistants ferrying wardrobe and props between sets, construction workers carting lumber and equipment to the soundstages, camp guests strolling between classes.

Errol nodded, watching Tony maneuver along the lot. "You still belong here, Tony. No matter what you say, Hollywood is in your blood."

Oh, Christ. So much for feeling relaxed. It looked as if his uncle had called him out here for Family Argument Number Six: You Oughtta Be In Showbiz.

"I know you want to believe that, Uncle Errol. But just because every Valentine before me worked in the biz doesn't mean I should, too."

"No, your aptitude means you should, too," Errol said firmly. "So does your zest for this work. I've been watching you. You come alive when you're on the back lot."

"What, I was a zombie before?"

"You could say that. Yes."

Tony had been kidding. His uncle wasn't.

"Is this about my black clothes again? I know you're into the whole style routine, but

285

I don't care about that stuff. This T-shirt" — Tony plucked a handful of the black cotton snugged up against his chest — "is not a symptom of anything except a need to not get arrested for indecent exposure."

"I'm not talking about your clothes. I'm talking about *you*. I've known you your whole life. New York changed you."

"Jesus. That again?"

"Yes, that again. Tony, we all see it. Me, Nadine. Esther. Even Roland. You left here ten years ago with big dreams, full of heart, ready to take on anything — so long as it wasn't Hollywood."

Tony frowned. He hadn't thought his family had realized his true motivations for leaving. Hadn't thought they'd understood any of it — his frustrations with being "just another Valentine," his need to strike out on his own, his hunger to learn about more than soundstages, studio sets, and back-end percentages.

"Now you're back," Errol continued, "and you're . . . tougher. More distant. All work."

He'd been right. They hadn't understood.

"Work is what will save this studio," Tony said tightly. "*My* work. If you don't like what I'm doing —"

"No, no." Errol raised his hands, as lined and pale — and as dignified — as the rest of him. "I'm in favor of your actor fantasy camp plan. I hope it succeeds — we all do.

But when this opening session is finished —"

"When it's finished, you won't have any worries. I'm already talking to potential candidates about running things here. You won't have to deal with a thing. I'll set up all the details before I go back to New York."

Errol looked appalled. "You're still going back?"

"That's been the plan from the start." Tony veered sideways to allow a golf cart of costumed camp participants to drive past on their way from the wardrobe trailer. "I work my magic on the studio, get some investors, set things up —"

"But we need you here."

Tony shook his head. "You think so now. All my clients do. But —"

"We are family," Errol interrupted, voice shaking. "*Not* clients."

"You're right. But the dynamic remains the same," Tony explained patiently. "You'll be a little nervous at first. Then you'll get used to the new guy. Before you know it, things will run like clockwork."

"We don't run a clock factory here! We run a family business," Errol disagreed. "A business which hasn't had anyone but a Valentine at the helm since 1922."

With dawning comprehension, Tony stared at his uncle. "You thought I'd stay," he said. "If you got me back in L.A., you thought I'd stay for good."

Mulishly, Errol shut his mouth. He frowned, squinting beneath the bright sunlight like a designer-dressed Clint Eastwood. Struggling for patience, Tony took a minute to look closely at his uncle. Possibly for the first time in years.

Errol's hair was completely white now, not brown streaked with gray. His face was lined with a lifetime's experiences. His shoulders — although rigidly straight — were thin beneath the fabric of his suit coat. Undeniably, Uncle Errol was an elderly man. But he was still proud, still vigorous, still distinguished — right down to the tidy white hankie peeping up from his breast pocket.

The sight of it made Tony smile. He remembered using Errol's ever-present hankie to wipe his bloody knee when he'd skinned it coasting down the banisters at the Tumbleweed Hotel. Remembered borrowing it as a makeshift parachute for his G.I. Joes. Remembered Errol using it to rub away Nutter Butter crumbs on Tony's nine-year-old face, and later tucking it into Tony's teenager-size tuxedo before a Valentine Studios premiere.

At those memories, affection swamped him. He loved his uncle. He wanted to make him happy. He wanted to make sure Errol lived out his golden years in comfort and security . . . free to frustrate the bejeezus out of his nephew at every turn.

But if doing that meant turning his back

on everything he'd worked for all these years . . . Tony couldn't do it.

"I work in the dot-com industry now," he said. "It's what I'm good at."

Errol's stubborn expression didn't waver. *You're good at this,* it said silently. *You belong here.*

Tony wanted to shake him. "Come on, Uncle Errol. Didn't you ever want to do anything else besides work at the studio?"

"Yes." Errol drew himself up to his full height, focusing on something in the distance. "On certain occasions, I've wanted very much to sock my brother in the nose. As it happens, we've stumbled upon one of those occasions today."

He nodded toward Tumbleweed's main street. In the center of it, Roland zoomed toward them in a golf cart. He swerved between the saloon and mercantile, kicking up dust. Cheerfully, he honked at the camp participants he passed. They waved back at him.

When he saw Tony and Errol, his whole face lit up.

"Hey!" he yelled. "Just who I've been looking for!"

Errol stiffened. "More than likely, he's come to announce his participation in something dreadful," he muttered in an aside to Tony. "Like an all-nude revival of *Grease*."

Roland climbed out of his golf cart, his vibrant Hawaiian-print shirt casting an orange-tinged glow on everything nearby. He waved a script in his hand.

"Check this out, Tony," he said eagerly. "I couldn't wait to show it to you. It's going to be Valentine Studios' salvation, I swear. A guaranteed direct-to-video money maker."

Tony looked. "*Cheerleader Hot Tub Boinkathon?*"

"Yeah. It's about this cheerleader. Honey is her name —"

"Naturally," Errol sighed.

"— and she's bored one night, see? So she calls up all her hot cheerleader friends, and they come over to her place in their little skirts and sweaters."

"With their pom-poms, I imagine?"

"Of course with their pom-poms, Errol." Roland rolled his eyes. "What kind of porno would it be without those? Anyway, they fire up the hot tub, but it's not working right. That's the first plot twist —"

"Plot twist?" Errol marveled. "I can't believe they even have scripts for these. Where did you get this?"

Roland ignored him. "So the cheerleaders have to call up the lonely hot tub technician guy," he explained with enthusiasm. "When the hot tub guy gets there —"

"Did you write this?" Errol asked, eyes narrowed.

"Sure. From personal experience." Another eye roll. "Don't I wish. Anyway, after the hot tub's fixed, it's *hot,* see? So all the cheer-leaders start stripping off their uniforms. Some of the zippers are broken — that's plot twist number two! — so they have to help each other get undressed."

"No," Tony said emphatically. He started walking again, led by Errol toward the out-skirts of Tumbleweed.

Roland followed. "But there's already a se-quel in the works! *Honey and the Sorority Sis-ters.*" He held up his arms, as though seeing the title in lights. "A Valentine Studios pro-duction. Give it a chance, huh, Tony?"

"No," Tony repeated. "For the millionth time, Uncle Roland — we're not filming pornos. We're running an actor fantasy camp."

Roland sagged, clearly dispirited. He snatched the script. "Maybe with some re-writes. I'll keep you posted."

He hurried away, good-naturedly waving to still more camp guests and studio employees as he passed them. Gregariously, they waved back. Shaking his head, Tony watched as his uncle stopped a nearby stunt man to share a joke. Both men laughed uproariously.

Thoughtfully, Errol watched his brother.

"I do believe you inherited your stubborn-ness from him," he said from beside Tony. They both leaned on the fence at the Tum-bleweed corral, arms on the top and feet propped at the bottom. "Your entrepreneurial streak, too. Roland has never been satisfied with the status quo."

Neither had Tony. But he refused to believe he owed any part of himself to his Valentine heritage. Sure, it'd had its perks, especially when he was younger. Being a Valentine had meant entrée to the best parties, access to the wildest entertainments, and opportunities to carry on the legendary family legacy at the studio. But it'd had its drawbacks, too. For Tony, feeling pigeonholed into a career and being judged on his last name alone had been chief among them.

He shot his uncle a warning look. "My entrepreneurial streak is all mine."

"I'm just saying, there's a lot of Valentine in you," Errol protested with a shrug. "You can't escape it."

Yes, he could. "I already did."

Errol gave a noncommittal sound. Clearly, he didn't believe it.

On the verge of disagreeing, Tony glimpsed movement inside the corral. Two chestnut horses, saddled and bridled, entered on leads held by the riding instructor.

"Look," Errol exclaimed, peering beyond the horses, apparently surprised. "There's Nadine. And Marley Madison, getting ready for her first horseback riding lesson. Imagine that!"

Gleefully, his uncle rubbed his hands together. He shared a coconspirator's smile with Nadine, who'd just led Meredith into the dusty corral, then addressed Tony again.

"I'm sure there's room for one more student," he said. "Why don't you get in there and give it a go?"

FIFTEEN

"There's two theories to arguing with a woman. Neither one works."
— Will Rogers

Tony stood in the Tumbleweed corral beside his assigned horse, one hand on the reins. To his right, the trainer held the leather lead snapped onto the bridle, waiting for his signal to begin the lesson. To his left, Meredith nuzzled her horse, talking nonsense to it. In the distance, his aunt and uncle leaned on the corral's split-rail fence, watching avidly.

Nadine waved. He raised his hand begrudgingly.

"You realize they've set us up, right?" he asked.

"Who?" Meredith said. "Nadine and Errol?"

Tony nodded.

"Let's put it this way. Does Joe Camel have a hump?"

"Uhhh —"

Meredith grinned wider. "Of course I know. I figured it was no coincidence Nadine already had an *ensemble* picked out for me." She said *ensemble* with an exaggerated French accent, twirling to show off her clothes and boots. "Or that she kept encouraging me to unbutton my shirt to show 'a little cleavage.' If I hadn't had a Marley-style push-up miracle bra handy, the jig might have been up right then. There's no way I'd measure up to starlet specifications."

Tony lowered his gaze. "Oh, you measure up, all right."

She preened. "Like I said, the bra's a miracle."

"So are you."

He meant it. Not just because she looked good. Also because Meredith was miraculously smart, funny, and resourceful. She took no crap from anybody. Tony admired her for that.

But he was still a guy . . . so he also admired her in that outfit. For the umpteenth time since meeting her in the corral, Tony felt his gaze drawn to her. To her blue jeans, which fit like a second skin. To her boots, which lent her a daredevil air. To her matching western-style shirt, which hugged every inch of her torso. Ordinarily, he didn't go for the whistlin' Dixie look. But on her. . . .

"It ought to be illegal to put innocent pearlized snaps under so much pressure," he added, grinning.

She tipped back her straw cowboy hat. Squinted. "That sounds like a complaint, pardner."

"No, ma'am." Tony's best drawl brought a smile to her face. "My only complaint would be if I didn't get to undo a few of those snaps later."

"I see." Meredith petted her horse's muzzle. "Interested in checking out the engineering wonders of a miracle bra, are you? Here I thought you were strictly a high-tech guy."

"I guess all this sunshine's gone to my head." *So has your smile.* When she turned it on him like that, he felt the breath knocked from him. "I'm considering dabbling in some low-tech entertainment."

"You don't say?" Calmly, she patted her horse's forelock.

Tony leaned closer, ducking to fit his head beneath the brim of her hat. In the meager waffle-weave shade it provided, he placed his mouth beside her ear.

"Yeah. I'm considering pulling those snaps apart with my teeth, unzipping those jeans, and kissing you from here" — he touched her jaw — "to here." He nudged her knee with his.

Her startled gaze swerved to his face. Meredith swallowed. "What about lower? Aren't you going to kiss lower? Ankles need attention, too, you know."

He should have known she'd argue with him. Truth be told, he didn't mind. Her protest only allowed him to reveal the rest of his plan.

"Nope. I won't be kissing your ankles."

She frowned, looking disgruntled. He'd offered to lavish kisses on ninety percent of her body, and she still wasn't satisfied? Greedy, greedy, greedy.

"Your boots stay on. I like the idea of you naked, except for those boots."

Meredith sucked in a breath.

"Yeah, you can leave those on," he announced.

He sauntered back to his horse. *That* ought to let her know who was in charge of things between them. Satisfied, Tony reasserted his grip on the reins. He prepared to signal the riding instructor.

"Hey, Prince Charming!" Meredith called.

Tony turned. She motioned him across the few steps that separated them, a devilish expression lighting her face. That expression should have warned him. It didn't.

"You can leave your boots on, too," she said magnanimously. "In fact, for the kiss I'm thinking about giving you right now, you can leave everything on. All you'll need to do is . . . unzip."

Giving him a wink, she swung into the saddle.

It was a long time before Tony could comfortably do the same.

After an hour of cantering around the Tumbleweed corral with Tony, Meredith discovered several things about her hunky actor fantasy camp exec. First, that he was an inexperienced rider. Second, that he didn't allow mere inexperience to stop him from challenging her to a corral-bound race. Third, that he was an excellent loser.

His graciousness extended right down to his congratulatory kiss . . . stolen beneath her hat brim while Nadine and Errol conveniently looked skyward. Meredith still felt a buzz from that kiss's impact. Sweet. Sexy. Inherently unforgettable.

"Well done," he'd said. "You're good."

She *felt* good. At the hot, approving look in his eyes, she felt her knees turn to jelly, too. Or maybe that was the effect of his kiss making her feel all dizzy and flushed. She couldn't be sure.

"So am I," he'd added. "Out of the corral, that is."

Meredith had nearly buckled right into the dust.

"I can't wait to find out," she'd managed, proud of herself for summoning up speech. Especially when her body was ordering her to strip him naked and kiss him now, kiss him *now!*

Tony's knowing look had made one thing clear — he'd meant to make her feel all those things. Dizzy. Hot. Turned on. She had no doubt he knew he'd succeeded.

Now the two of them stood together in the

studio stables, surrounded by the earthy smells of horses, leather, and hay. Brushes in hand, they tended to their mounts the way the instructor, Franco, had shown them.

Grooming, it seemed, was the price to be paid for a lesson at Franco's expert hands. He'd led each mare into the largest stall, secured them there, and offered detailed instructions. Then he'd lingered just long enough to make sure Meredith and Tony weren't going to dreadlock the horses' manes or weave ribbons into their tails.

Finally, satisfied, he'd left them on their own.

"Where did you learn to ride like that?" Tony asked. "On a horse, you're a different person."

"A graceful person, you mean?"

Meredith saw Tony open his mouth. She waved away his inevitable protest, then went on brushing. "Don't bother being polite. I don't mind. You've mostly seen me tottering around in high heels. They're not my natural element."

He nodded and remained silent, reaching across his horse's broad back. He brushed the animal with gentle, careful strokes, waiting for the rest of her answer.

She liked that he didn't rush to speak. The other men she'd known (and dated) had rarely shut up. They'd wanted to tell her all about their 401(k)s or their stock options, their published articles in research journals or their stints as keynote speakers at historian conferences. Tony was different.

"I learned to ride when I was nine," she said, encouraged by his easy acceptance. "Marley was taking tap-dancing lessons. My parents thought I needed something similar to 'help my coordination.'"

"Why not tap dance? With your sister?"

Meredith glanced up, aghast. "And risk my status as her complete and total opposite? No way!"

He laughed.

"What else could I do?" she asked. "For our entire lives, my sister soaked up the spotlight. Competing didn't work" — she cringed, remembering that disastrous soliloquy — "so I had to spend all my energy becoming the anti-Marley."

"Thereby proving that Marley's success didn't threaten you in the least. Am I right?"

Meredith pursed her lips. She went on brushing, carefully not meeting his eyes. Maybe if she pretended to be really interested in her horse's sweaty hide. . . .

Okay, so Tony found her completely transparent. That fact should have left her annoyed. Vulnerable. Disconcerted. Instead, Meredith merely felt . . . understood. When it came down to it, there wasn't anything "merely" about something so monumental as that.

"Am I right?" he repeated.

Stay casual, she told herself. *Be cool.*

Meredith shrugged. "Were you right," she repeated. Stalling. After all, it was totally obvious. Just like . . . "Come on. Was the first TV ad broadcast in 1941?"

Tony straightened, shaking his head. "You're going to have to quit doing that."

"Doing what?"

"Answering me in advertising trivia."

Gazing into his bemused face, Meredith realized what she'd done. Advertising trivia was her life. So was answering a question with a question. It was a habit of hers. A little like babbling when she got nervous. Or putting black pepper on her popcorn.

"Yes, it was broadcast in 1941," she told him.

Graciously, he didn't stomp all over being right. Instead, he simply went on brushing. "I thought most people didn't even have TV sets then."

Meredith relaxed. Now she was in her element.

"Less than five hundred were in use at that point. Enough to make the ad — for Bulova watches, by the way — a practical trial run. It was broadcast during a baseball game on an experimental NBC-TV station in New York."

He nodded. "In other words . . . yes. I'm right. Marley's success never bothered you."

Rats. She thought she'd sidestepped that one. Dazzled him with facts. Blinded him with detours. "Damn, you're persistent."

He grinned. "That's what led me to develop the first wireless Internet stereo network." He paused. "So?"

"Mmmm?"

"You never answered my question."

He was right. She was trapped. "Your question. About Marley?"

A nod.

"Hmmm." Pretending to think about it, Meredith bent over to choose a different brush. In the process, one of her shirt's little pearl snaps popped open.

"Whoops." She widened her eyes and tucked her finger inside the opening, as though confirming her neckline had just lowered by an inch. "How'd that happen?"

As she'd expected, Tony forgot all about his question. He didn't appear interested in discussing the relative merits of snaps versus buttons, industrial sewing thread, or the tensile strength of the average women's western shirt, either. His attention snapped straight to her chest.

"You didn't say that mambo bra was red lace."

"Miracle."

"Huh?"

It was hard not to grin. "It's called a miracle bra."

"Miracle, mambo . . . whatever." Tony tossed down his brush and edged past his horse. He pulled Meredith into his arms, both of them disheveled, windblown, and a little sweaty. Neither of them caring. "Either way, you made your point."

"My point?" Meredith raised her eyebrows.

"I'm not feeling much like talking right now, either," Tony said, and kissed her.

Four and a half minutes later, they sneaked past their horses and strode up the stable's central aisle.

"I knew that was a bad idea," Meredith grumbled.

"How was I supposed to know my horse had gotten attached to me?" Tony asked. "Who knew horses got jealous?"

Meredith took another swipe at her hay-covered behind. She marched ahead of him. "By now, both of us. See you at the sitcom set in fifteen minutes?"

"Better make that half an hour." Dourly, Tony craned to examine the wet, water-trough-shaped imprint on his butt. "At this point, a real shower wouldn't hurt."

Meredith was climbing the steps to her trailer when she felt it first — a sensation of being watched. One hand on her doorknob, she glanced around the back lot.

Tony's trailer came into view, its awning

fluttering. The false fronts of Tumbleweed rose in the distance, sheathed in a small cloud of dust. Huge, boxy soundstages marched along the myriad pathways, casting shadows on the golf carts parked near them. Closer to her, a sparrow flew past. It landed at the edge of a puddle on the asphalt to steal a drink.

Hmmm. Nobody in sight. Obviously, no one was watching her. Despite that fact, the sensation remained . . . exactly as it had several times over the past few days. Puzzling over it, Meredith cocked her head. Her imagination must be getting the better of her. Either that, or Boob Guy had returned to the back lot with a pair of binoculars.

Unlikely, given that Tony had ousted him. Esther had told her as much while they'd chatted before her press junket interview. Apparently, "Marley's" street-fighting moves were the talk of the crew. Several female staffers had been the unhappy recipients of Boob Guy's unique brand of noncharm and were glad to be rid of him. According to Esther, they'd actually cheered upon hearing the news he was gone.

Meredith scanned the back lot again. Then, brushing off her backside once more, she shrugged and entered her trailer.

Freshly showered and dressed in a pair of jeans and a white button-up shirt, Tony climbed into his waiting golf cart. He glanced at Meredith's trailer. They were due to meet at the sitcom set for a line reading rehearsal — part of his promise to help her impersonate Marley — but he was tempted to blow off work altogether and meet her inside her trailer instead.

The sound of hip-hop music thumping from within changed his mind. That was her getting-ready music. Undoubtedly, Meredith was concentrating on repairing the post-riding-lesson damage. Fluffing her hair, putting on makeup, beating the crap out of any stilettos that dared to fall from her closet. He didn't want to risk a rerun of this morning's meltdown. Plus, Tony wasn't sure he could cope with another run-in with her face cream.

Besides, he had another plan. Wheeling the cart into motion, he zoomed toward the studio commissary. By the time Meredith was ready to meet him, he'd be ready for her.

When Tony arrived at soundstage 23, the sitcom set was quiet. He strode past the bleachers, empty now of their live studio audience. He glanced at the multiple monitors and the "applause" sign, all of them turned off and temporarily abandoned by the crew. A single row of lights beamed onto the set's fake living room interior, illuminating the scrounged-up furnishings, the lumpy cast-off sofa parked in the middle . . . the woman studying her script in its center.

Meredith didn't see him. Head bowed, she read silently. She'd curled up against a flowery cushion and crossed her legs beneath her. One of the lights angled over her, just like a spotlight. Inside its glow, she looked completely natural. Not because she reminded Tony of Marley that way — just because she looked perfectly herself. Luminous. Relaxed. Singled out.

He didn't know how long he stood there, watching her. Didn't know how he'd never noticed exactly how beautiful she really was. How adorable, with her forehead crinkled in concentration. How memorable, with her feet unconsciously tapping on the sofa cushion — as though a part of her really wanted to be running or jumping or shooting hoops. He only knew he could have stayed there all afternoon.

She looked up. "Oh. You're here."

A wide smile spread across her face. Seeing that smile, something happened to Tony. Something new and giddy and best left unexamined. He left the edge of the bleachers and crossed to her, his footsteps clunking on the concrete floor.

"Have you got a spare script? I didn't have room to carry one. Not with all this other stuff I wanted to bring."

He moved his arms from behind his back, where they'd been hiding his surprise.

Meredith saw the bouquet of carnations in his left hand and the handful of candy bars in his right.

"For me?" She threw down her script and hurried over, grabbing the flowers first. She buried her nose in the red blooms. "Nobody's *ever* given me flowers before. Unless you count Tommy Winkleman's lame corsage, of course. But that was only meant to lull me into complacency so I wouldn't notice his Marley scheme. Besides, the orchid was limp, so that doesn't count."

She beamed at him. That giddy feeling tweaked him again.

"There's nothing *limp* about anything I'll ever give you," he boasted. He enjoyed the unabashedly greedy look on her face. She'd looked at him exactly that same way this morning when they'd been tangled together on her Pinkville bed.

"Promises, promises." Meredith rolled her eyes, then turned her attention to the candy. There was nothing coy about her interest in that, either. "Hang on. What's this? Snickers? Reese's Peanut Butter Cups? Twix?" She wrinkled her nose. "Don't you have an artistically carved celery stalk or something? I can't eat any of this."

"Why not?" he asked, feeling stupidly disappointed.

"Starlets don't eat anything normal, that's why."

Tony nodded. "I guess you're right." He started to tuck the candy bars in his shirt pocket for later.

"Gotcha!" Meredith made a grab for a Snickers, a smart-alecky grin on her face. Stuffing her bouquet into the crook of her arm, she unwrapped the chocolate and took a bite. "I really had you fooled, didn't I? I'm not *that* much of a born-again starlet. As if I'd actually pass up chocolate." She chewed happily. "Life wouldn't be worth living."

With a new swing in her hips, she crossed to the set's kitchen area and grabbed a prop vase. She plunked the carnations inside it. Admired the flowers again. Smiled at him over their bright red tops. One side of her cheek bulged with candy, her demeanor completely unaffected and one hundred percent Meredith.

She was barefoot again, Tony noticed. Without her fancy shoes — which lay kicked off beside the set's sofa — Meredith moved easily and lithely. Not with a starlet's coquettish, artificially sexy wiggle, but with a woman's physical grace.

He liked it. He also liked the way she looked in her pink fluttery skirt and white shirt. Even her Band-Aid-covered legs added to her tomboy-meets-girly-girl appeal . . . as though she'd shaved her legs while pulling an Ollie on her skateboard.

Marching on those legs, Meredith headed

to the sink. She turned on the taps, holding the vase expectantly beneath the faucet. Nothing happened.

"That's a prop sink," he reminded her. "It's not plumbed."

"Right. Of course." She smacked her forehead. "I keep forgetting everything here is fake."

"Yeah. It looks real. It feels real. But it's not."

Meredith paused. Her quizzical gaze rose from the flowers to his face. It didn't take a genius to read the question in her eyes. Or to know Tony wasn't ready to deal with it yet. Hell, flowers and candy said enough, didn't they?

He strode to the sofa. He picked up the script. "You ready to do this?"

Meredith's expression changed. Apparently, she thought she had her answer — and she wasn't entirely happy with it, either. Damn it. That was the trouble with women. You were screwed if you talked to them (and messed up the conversation), and you were equally screwed if you just shut up.

"Sure," she said crisply, taking brisk steps to the sofa. "Of course I'm ready. Let's get —" She paused halfway to him, head cocked to the side as though listening.

She put down her Snickers. This was serious.

"What's the matter?"

"I thought I heard something. A click. Like a camera shutter." Seeming to shake off the sensation, she strolled into the living room. "Probably just more of your hired paparazzi. Nadine and I saw some of them on our way to the corral this afternoon."

Tony stilled. "Paparazzi?"

"Yeah." Distractedly, she squinted over his shoulder at the script, her hair falling onto his sleeve. "They took pictures of us on the lot today. Yesterday, too. I'd swear I saw a flash as I got into my golf cart to go to class."

"I didn't hire any more paparazzi. Just those few for Marley's — your — entrance. They were booked for that night and for the camp guests' arrivals the next day, but that's it. Until the finale, there won't be any more paparazzi on the lot."

"Then who did I . . . ? Oh."

Real paparazzi.

Their eyes met. "Did the *Inside Hollywood* reporter bring a photographer?" Meredith asked.

"No." Tony shook his head, frowning. "The reporter's undercover. Toting along a photographer would blow it."

"Then who's been taking my picture?"

They both knew the answer to that.

Real paparazzi.

This wasn't good. Especially if someone had sneaked onto the soundstage with them.

If word got out that Marley Madison wasn't Marley but Meredith. . . . Tony grabbed his cell phone. He punched the number for Valentine Studios' security office.

Meredith put her hand on his arm. "It's probably nothing. Maybe a camp guest who wants souvenir photos?"

"Right. Or maybe it's a freelancer looking to score big with the tabloids. I'm taking no chances."

He issued orders for security to do a sweep of the studio grounds. He also asked the staff to review the admissions records and video footage from the gates. Then he snapped his cell phone shut. He stalked past the sitcom set, looking for the source of that *click*.

Meredith dogged his every step. She crouched beside him, furtively tiptoeing over thick cables and the tangle of equipment behind the set's false walls. She peered behind cameras and light stands. She hunkered down to examine the underside of the craft services table.

"Do you really think they're still here?" she whispered.

"If they are, we'll find them. This place isn't that big."

"What are you going to do if you catch them?"

"I'm going to whisper a lot so I *don't* catch them."

Catching his drift, Meredith pursed her lips.

They searched the entire soundstage. They looked behind the scenes and up front on set. They roved from one end of the place to the other. Tony saw nothing out of the ordinary.

Frustrated, he stopped in front of the sitcom sofa. They'd made a complete circuit and come up empty. He rolled his shoulders, trying to relieve the sudden tension there.

"Looks like they're gone," Meredith said.

"For now," he agreed. They'd have to be more careful from here on out. Thoughtfully, Tony examined her. "It's a good thing you're getting the hang of this. That's one factor in our favor. Even if someone snaps a photo, you definitely look the part these days. Exactly like Marley."

"Sure. But everything around here is fake, remember?"

She arched her brow and crossed her arms, delivering him a pointed look. Uh-oh. That look said Meredith wanted something from him. Tony would be damned if he knew what. Reassurance? He'd just told her how terrific she looked. An apology? He couldn't think why.

"Fake or not, we've got to work with what we have," he said. "It's our best tactic."

"Even if it's less than optimal?"

He blinked at her, only to encounter another condemning look. He shook his head. "Are you having a sugar high from the

312

Snickers? You're not making sense."

A moment passed. Then . . .

"You're *happy* I'm more like Marley now!" Meredith blurted, her tone accusing him of something truly heinous. "You just said so. Admit it."

"So?" There had to be more. Tony waited.

Stubbornly, she buttoned her lips. He'd have sworn she was waiting for something, too. He scratched his head.

"You being more like Marley is what we're both here for. Speaking of which, we're wasting time." He caught hold of Meredith's elbow to lead her to the sofa. He plunked her down on the center cushion, then scooped up the script and tossed it to her. "Ready for that line reading?"

She gawked. "We're still going to do it?"

"You still need the practice, don't you?"

Her eyes narrowed. "Evidently."

That *had* to be her museum voice. The one she used on miscreant teenage visitors and coworkers caught cataloguing Victorian data in the Swinging Sixties wing. What the hell was her problem?

Only one way to find out. "What the hell is your problem?"

"Nothing."

"Are you mad I didn't find the photographer? Because I will. It's only a matter of time."

She waved away his assertion. Was she

trying to aggravate him on purpose?

She crossed her legs — and pulled down her skirt. She was!

"Like I said," Meredith explained airily, "I'd just forgotten how fake everything is here. How . . . illusory. I got caught up in believing some of it was real." Her gaze flickered to the carnations on the kitchen counter. Swerved away guiltily. "I won't make that mistake again."

Clearing her throat, she paged through the script. She found the dialogue exchange she wanted, then thrust the whole mess at Tony.

He glanced down at the lines she'd indicated.

" 'You're a dirty, rotten scoundrel, Cassandra,' " he read aloud. " 'You wouldn't know honest emotion if it bit you on the' — hey. These are your lines."

"Oh, that's right. They are." Sweetly, Meredith glanced at the script. "My mistake."

Now he knew something was up. Maybe he could fix it before it mushroomed into something bigger. Tony searched his mind for a strategy. Thinking of his observations earlier — and the mushy, head-over-heels feeling he'd experienced while making them — he settled on, "I've been meaning to tell you. You look really natural in the spotlight. Really good." Her expression was unreadable. He decided to up the ante. "Exactly like Marley."

That ought to do it. Pleased, he waited for Meredith's reply. It wasn't long in coming.

"If you knew me at all," she said, clutching her script tightly, "you would never say that."

Thirty seconds later he was alone on the set, listening to the soundstage door thud closed behind her. He frowned.

Thirty seconds after that, the door squeaked open. Meredith marched in, her chin held high. She stopped in front of him, not meeting his eyes.

"I forgot these." She plucked the remaining candy bars from his shirt pocket. "And this." She grabbed the vase of flowers from the kitchen and hugged it against her chest. Then she spotted her half-eaten Snickers bar, still on the counter where she'd left it.

Her gaze shifted toward him. With both hands full, she hunched her shoulders self-consciously.

Then she bent down and bit into the candy bar. She straightened with it — wrapper crackling — stuck between her teeth. With dignity, Meredith faced him.

"Thank you," she said, speaking around her mouthful without biting down. "From now on, I'll ask someone else to run lines with me."

Then, again, she was gone.

SIXTEEN

"An amazing new way to make toast! You don't have to watch it — it comes out automatically when it's done."
— advertisement for Toastmaster pop-up toasters (1927)

No one else was as good at line reading practice as Tony was. It took Meredith only a few tries to discover that. Nadine gave it a shot, but she couldn't resist sending instant messages on her notebook computer at the same time ("Valentines are famously impulsive," she said). The various dings and dongs of her chat software drove Meredith to distraction, and she couldn't remember a single word.

She moved on. Esther boomed the lines in her most dramatic voice, flinging her arms around and striding spectacularly across the set. Unfortunately, she believed all lines were meant to be revised. In her hands, no script was safe. Neither was Meredith's sanity.

Errol couldn't read the lines without his bifocals and was too (secretly) vain to be seen in public wearing them. Roland tried to rehearse, but spent most of his time pinching her butt and pitching her parts in movies (all of which starred someone named "Honey"). Harry did his best, but kept being called away to chauffer guests to Rodeo Drive.

In the end, there was no hope for it. Meredith was back with Tony as her line reading partner the following afternoon, driven to it by sheer necessity.

She needed to be good. Otherwise, the actor fantasy camp would fail and the studio staff would lose their jobs. To be good, she needed to practice. To practice, she needed a partner. Ergo . . . three o'clock found her slinking back to soundstage 23 with a truce-engendering bribe in hand.

To get it, she'd stopped by the gift shop next door to the commissary. Its limited options had included a Valentine Studios souvenir keychain, a fanny pack emblazoned with the "Fantastic Island" logo, and a plastic screw-top container filled with three pounds of gourmet jelly beans. Since Tony didn't seem to own a car — or keys for one — and fanny packs were a step backward in the evolutionary chain, she'd chosen the beans.

"Sorry about yesterday." She handed them over.

Tony pretended to stagger beneath their weight. Hefting the container, he studied the multicolored candies inside. "Bubble gum flavor." He pointed to one. "My favorite. And grape. Look! Root beer, too."

Meredith took in his bright eyes and

cheerful grin. "You're just a big kid at heart, aren't you?"

"I dunno. Maybe."

But he wasn't even looking at her. He'd already unscrewed the lid and had scooped out a handful of jelly beans. He popped them in his mouth and chewed happily.

"Want some?"

Meredith shook her head. A weird sense of relief lightened her. In guy speak, she was forgiven. She knew that. She'd spent enough time with the neighborhood boys — climbing trees, playing baseball, and learning to master a frontside 180 on her skateboard — to make her familiar with the local customs.

Pretending it never happened was as good as if it really had never happened. At least if you were a guy. She had to admit, the theory held a certain appealing simplicity.

As planned, she and Tony ran through her lines. Then they tried a full rehearsal, complete with Meredith hitting her marks. They stopped only occasionally for jelly bean breaks.

"There's a mythology to jelly beans, you know," she volunteered during one of those breaks, sitting on the floor beside Tony as she watched him cup a sugary handful. "If two people reach in and choose the same kind of bean at the same time, they're meant to be together."

"Oh, yeah?"

She nodded.

"Sugarholic's destiny, huh?" He shook the candy, then peered inside the container. Cupping it in one strong palm, he held it out to her. "Let's try it."

She couldn't. It was ridiculous. She wasn't even sure what had made her blurt out such a corny idea. For all Meredith knew, some confectionary company's advertising agency had dreamed up that piece of folklore for a campaign — which would explain why she'd remembered it.

"It's silly," she said, shaking her head.

"If it's so silly, it shouldn't bother you to do it."

"That philosophy explains a lot about you."

"Har, har." Tony rattled the jelly beans. "Come on."

She wasn't going to. Finding a soul mate in a jelly bean jar was beyond absurd. All the same, just as though she was seriously considering it, Meredith found her gaze traveling from Tony's long, strong fingers to his muscular forearm. Across his chest and up to his chin. To the sexy stubble darkening his jaw. There was no point tempting herself by going any higher . . . say, to his lips.

Despite all her best, secret hopes, Tony wanted her to be like Marley. He did. Yesterday had been proof enough of that. She still had the hurt feelings to prove it. Meredith didn't know how it could be possible, but even though her sister wasn't here, she was *still* laying claim to everything Meredith wanted for herself.

In this case, what she mainly wanted was for Tony to want her. For herself. Casual fling be damned.

"Fine," she surprised herself by saying. "Close your eyes. We'll draw on the count of three. One — two — three!"

An instant later, she opened her eyes. Tony did, too. Their combined gazes went to the jelly beans held aloft in their fingers — a purple one for Tony . . . and a red one for Meredith.

"Cherry," she announced, blinking in disbelief.

"Grape." His voice sounded subdued.

A stupid sense of disappointment gripped her. They weren't meant to be together. They'd failed the jelly bean test.

For the first time in her life, Meredith renounced the concept of truth in advertising.

"We'd better get back to those lines." Grabbing her script, she pushed up from the floor, where she'd been sitting with her back against the sofa. She brushed off her legs, unwilling to look at Tony. "They're not going to practice themselves, you know."

He grabbed her hand. "It doesn't mean anything."

Then why did she feel so let down? "I know that."

Frowning, he got up, too. He looked as though he'd like to punt the jelly beans across the set. Meredith imagined him holding the container in front of him, giving it a hearty boot-fortified wallop, watching it fly end over end.

"Go ahead," she said, nodding toward the jelly beans. "I'd say you're good for a solid fifty yards, at least."

Tony cocked an eyebrow. "A fifty-yard punt?"

"I told you I'm a football fan."

A funny expression crossed his face. "How'd you know I was thinking that? About punting, I mean."

She shrugged, afraid to wonder.

He rubbed his jaw thoughtfully. "You know what? I'd say that's a better indicator of compatibility than any old jar of jelly beans."

"What, the fact that I like football?"

"That, too."

He smiled. The knot of wanting inside her squeezed just a little tighter. He was trying to cheer her up, Meredith realized. Did that mean Tony *wasn't* just interested in her as a Marley clone?

The extent to which Meredith hoped that was true astonished her. She didn't know when it had happened, but she'd gotten herself completely infatuated with him. With his sparkling eyes, his off-color jokes, even his occasionally swaggering macho stance.

Tony was smart, funny, kind to his family and his staff. He knew when to take charge and when to relax. He was (with the small exception of his admiring Marley) remarkably wonderful. When it came to him, Meredith was a goner — putty in his hands — and she knew it. Despite his Marley-centric gaffe yesterday and the jelly bean disaster today, she really cared for Tony.

The real question was . . . how far should she take those feelings? How far *could* she take them?

Oblivious to her thoughts, Tony slung his arm around her shoulders. He hugged her close, murmuring something naughty in her ear.

Her eyes widened. She felt her cheeks heat. "I'm pretty sure that option's closed to everyone but members of the Cirque du Soleil," Meredith demurred. "And Gumby."

His laughter carried all across the set. He walked them both toward the sitcom kitchen, leaning close to whisper another suggestion. Shocked — and thrillingly, surprisingly interested — Meredith shivered.

"You really think you're burly enough for that maneuver?"

"For you?" Tony asked. "Anything."

Then he took away her script. He let it flutter from his hand as he kissed her. Meredith kissed him back.

Left behind them, the jelly beans stayed on the floor.

Forgotten.

Mostly.

"You're really good at this," Meredith said, watching Tony.

He sat back, drippy paint brush in hand. He smiled at her, taking a break in the set decorating they were helping with.

For three days now, they'd been honing her Marley impersonation. They'd run lines, argued over wardrobe, and rehearsed autograph sessions. They'd met covertly with the dialect coach (Meredith's delivery of Marley's "Fantasy Family" Southern belle catchphrase definitely needed work). They'd even held "Jeopardy"-style quiz sessions on all the various jobs involved in a studio.

"On a TV or movie set," Tony had begun, "this crew member is the head of the lighting crew."

"Who is the gaffer!"

"This crew member moves scenery, sets up flags, fingers, and scrims" — he paused to make sure she was following his use of the specialized terminology — "and handles production equipment like cranes and dolly tracks."

Meredith knew this one, too. "Who is the grip!"

"He could be referred to as the gaffer's

323

right-hand man, but this crew member —
also known as the assistant chief lighting
technician — isn't usually described in such
'grown-up' terms."

"Who is the best boy! Yahoo!"

Triumphantly, secure in her knowledge of
Hollywood facts and figures, Meredith
danced a jig around Tony. Unfortunately, that
only prompted him to sign up the two of
them for high-intensity lessons with the
dance instructor. They had to get ready for
the finale's after-party, he'd explained. Before
she knew what had hit her, she'd been mam-
boing, waltzing, and cha-chaing her feet off.

Which explained why she was here now,
willing to sacrifice some of her preparation
time for the sake of giving the sitcom's
kitchen table a fresh coat of paint in readiness for the finale. That, at least, could be
done sitting on the newspapers they'd spread
protectively over the floor. Her classes were
finished for the day, and so was her (gradually easier) Pilates session. For the afternoon,
at least, she was free.

Until now, she'd been driving herself hard.
Every time she saw Inga or Salma or any of
the other crew members, Meredith wanted to
redouble her efforts. Being like Marley was
exhausting. Dressing in figure-revealing
clothes, applying attention-getting makeup,
vamping up her hair . . . all of it still felt
vaguely threatening. It felt alien. Unlike *her*.

324

More than once, she was tempted to back-track. To pull on her comfy cargos, to whip out her Dodgers cap, to retire her Lady Bic and shaving cream and Band-Aids. To go back to her old self. That self might have been less noticeable, less dazzling, less than Marley — simply *less*, to everyone else — but to Meredith she'd been comfortable. Safe.

Embracing the feminine, girly-girl parts of herself was terrifying at times. Somehow, it felt as though she was courting disaster. Every time Meredith stepped outside her trailer in another glammed-up outfit, she expected to find herself ridiculed, exactly the way she had been during her youthful attempts to emulate Marley.

Her family — the people who unquestionably loved her best — had found the notion of Meredith stepping outside her usual role unthinkable. If it weren't for the fact that no one at the actor fantasy camp knew her as Meredith, she might have found the whole charade impossible. As it was, her anonymity added a necessary level of bravado. She could do it, and would.

Besides, in the end, Meredith had had a realization. Scary as her experiences had been, they were better than standing still. Better than staying the same, better than camping out on the sidelines her entire life. Whether she liked it or not, finding herself at Valentine Studios had exposed unexplored parts of her personality. It had catapulted her into a whole new way of looking at things.

She'd always thought she was pretty tough. Fairly brave. Reasonably invulnerable. Now she knew the truth. Her cherished cynicism — her *rebelliousness* — had all been an act.

How did she know that? Because at heart, she was just like any other woman. She wanted to love and be loved. Seeing Tony took her breath away. Feeling his hand on her arm, hearing his laughter, sharing an afternoon with him . . . all of those things swept right past her defenses. But Meredith couldn't help wondering . . . what if he, like everyone else, let her down?

The risk inherent in her Marley charade made the stakes all too clear. If she went all the way with it, and Tony reacted the same way her family had — by laughing — Meredith didn't know how she'd survive it.

But that was a worry for the future. Right now, she needed to think about painting the next chair leg. Applying the perfect coat of Sahara White. Avoiding the drippy dangers of Tony's brush, which he wielded with a combination of finesse, skill, and sheer recklessness.

"I can't believe this," she said, leaning sideways as he dabbed at a spot she'd missed on her chair. "You, Mr. Fix-It. Mr. Handyman. You're supposed to be a high-tech guy."

"I like working with my hands. Using a

paintbrush, using a PDA, typing an e-mail . . . they're not so different."

They were different. Starting with the fact that Tony looked happier when he was wielding the paintbrush. But Meredith knew he'd never listen to some cornball follow-your-bliss career counselor routine. For that matter, neither would she. She might as well save her breath.

Instead, she gestured toward the painted chairs. Then toward the props Tony had repaired when they'd arrived. Up close, the items looked hard-used. At best. But on camera, they looked as good as new — Meredith had seen the test footage herself. Such was the movie magic he knew how to employ.

"How'd you learn to do all this?" she asked.

"Work on set?" Tony looked around, taking in the bustle of crew members intent on their tasks and the eager passing of actor fantasy camp guests. He shrugged. "I grew up here. The back lot was my playground; the soundstages were my training ground. I apprenticed under just about everyone who works at the studio. You pick up a lot that way. Including complicated techniques like chair painting."

He winked and applied more Sahara White.

Meredith wasn't fooled. "It's more than

that. You're like a part of this place."

"Hazard of growing up a Valentine." He slapped on more paint, looking dismissive. Sounding guarded. "My family's practically a Hollywood institution."

"I sort of figured that out," she said dryly, "once I saw the pictures in the archives. Eight presidents, countless foreign dignitaries, every movie star under the sun . . . all of them photographed with your uncles or Esther or some other Valentine honcho. It's amazing. I had no idea."

He gave a noncommittal grunt and went on painting.

Tony had granted her admission to the archives yesterday. So far, she hadn't had a chance to sort through much of the materials they contained. But what she had seen was impressive.

Meredith nudged him. "What a life. I can't believe you don't hang around here hobnobbing with the rich and famous full time."

"And risk my status as the only Valentine ever to escape Hollywood? No way!"

His denial sounded suspiciously close to the one she'd made about Marley. It seemed they had more in common than they'd expected.

"It wouldn't be so bad to work here," she said.

"Says you." Tony shook his head. "For my whole life, everyone assumed I'd take over

328

the studio. Everywhere I went, people recognized my name. 'Oh, you're one of the *Valentines*, they'd say. As if that explained everything anyone needed to know about me."

Meredith understood what that was like. Anyone who learned she was Marley's twin immediately assumed she was a carbon copy of her famous sister, with no identity of her own. She'd had to go pretty far in the opposite direction to escape those comparisons.

"You could always change your name," she mused. "Stanley Twimblewhistle. Burt Goobersnatcher. Arnold Zephyrnoodle."

"Mmmm. Tempting. With one of those names, I'd get all the chicks."

"Yeah. Especially if you called them 'chicks.' " She rolled her eyes. "What are you, straight out of 'Starsky and Hutch'?"

"I've got my suede jacket and Gran Torino out back."

"I recommend you keep them there."

He pretended to be disappointed. He looked so cute, Meredith couldn't resist leaning over to kiss him. Bracing her fingertips on the paint-splattered newspaper, she pressed her mouth to his. In moments, she forgot where she was altogether.

The sound of throat clearing nearby reminded her. She and Tony broke apart to find Nadine and Errol standing on set, watching them with expressions of beaming approval.

"Aren't they cute?" Nadine asked.

"I knew they'd suit each other perfectly," Errol agreed.

Tony glanced at Meredith, then at his aunt and uncle. "You two are going to take all the credit for this, aren't you?"

"Of course! Valentines are wonderful matchmakers!"

"Why wouldn't we?"

"It will be nice to have a TV star in the family," Nadine continued. "Not that that's the only reason we're interested in pairing you with our Tony, Marley."

Beside her, Tony stiffened. *Marley* echoed through the room. Meredith felt a little queasy. She hated deceiving such nice people. When this was over with and the coast was clear, she'd come clean to all the Valentines, she decided.

"Not at all," Errol confirmed, oblivious to the tension *Marley* had engendered. "We're not hangers-on, although we are fans. And the union of a Valentine and an actress is certainly a natural marriage of archetypes."

Marriage. That made Meredith and Tony spring apart. Busily, they started painting again. By tacit agreement, each pretended not to have heard the "M" word. Mentioning it too soon in a relationship could be deadly. Everyone knew that.

All the same, she saw Tony sneak a speculative glance at her. A glance she noticed because she, coincidentally, happened to be doing exactly the same thing.

Nadine and Errol left, satisfied with their matchmaking. In their wake, Meredith lifted her paintbrush. Carefully she pushed away a stray lock of hair with her forearm, trying to regain her equilibrium.

Whew. For a minute there, she'd been seduced (again) into believing what she and Tony had together was real. Into believing she could live happily ever after on the back lot, with friendly Valentines all around, kissing Tony whenever she pleased. Nadine's use of her sister's name — and Errol's mention of marriage — had brought her plummeting back to reality.

She had to keep her wits about her. Not get carried away. Because the truth was, she didn't really belong here. No matter what changes she made on the outside, she probably never would belong here.

But all of a sudden, Meredith realized . . . she wanted to.

SEVENTEEN

"You can fool all the people all the time if the advertising is right and the budget is big enough."

— Joseph E. Levine

That Monday, the next issue of *Inside Hollywood* hit the stands. It arrived at Valentine Studios courtesy of an actor fantasy camp guest who spotted it during a Krispy Kreme run and subsequently smuggled it in. By late morning, Harry had obligingly fetched an entire shrink-wrapped bundle of glossy issues. They spread across the studio's seventy-acre Burbank lot like the low buzz of a catchy tune. No one was immune to humming along.

Tony didn't realize it at first. He'd spent part of the morning jogging around the back lot with Roland — who, like the rest of his meddling family, never seemed to leave the studio — and the rest of it helping with a class on stunts. He'd already been wearing workout gear. He'd figured, why not?

In his ordinary New York life, he'd never have been in sweats and a T-shirt at ten o'clock — much less have conducted serious business in them. But more and more these days, his East Coast life seemed to recede. Today it had felt perfectly natural to talk with his actor fantasy camp guests, to gather informal feedback from them, to help them suit up in safety harnesses and helmets. The sun had shone down on him, the breeze had ruffled his hair, and the smiles and excited chatter of his guests had made stepping outside of his usual routine more than worthwhile.

Of course, it had also made him late. Which explained why it was nearly eleven o'clock before Tony realized the crisis that had befallen them.

Having changed into an open-collar shirt and a pair of casual linen pants — his suits were getting pushed farther and farther into the recesses of his trailer's closet, just like Meredith's stilettos — Tony arrived at the business office to find no one around. The receptionist, Penelope, wasn't up front at the studio's circular granite-topped desk. None of the admins were at their stations; neither were the accountants. The entire staff seemed to have vanished.

Puzzled, Tony turned right at a potted ficus. He passed more offices, all of them furnished in the last remodel's early "Ozzie and Harriet," their Atomic Age accents unmarred by the twenty-first century. He peered into conference rooms. All were unoccupied.

This was seriously weird. Valentine Studios had fallen onto hard times, but the studio was still a going concern — especially with the actor fantasy camp now in full swing. Someone on staff should have been there.

Then he heard voices. Following the sounds, Tony strode to the business office's kitchen-slash-copy-room. The conversation continued, overlapping itself like waves in Santa Monica, growing in volume as he neared.

"Can you believe . . . an item . . . secret?"

"Without any makeup . . . !"

"Must've hung upside down from a soundstage ceiling to get a shot like that. Who would have thought . . ."

"Wonder who the . . . correspondent . . . next week?"

Tony rounded the corner. Scattered around the break room, eight startled employees glanced up. Issues of *Inside Hollywood* lay open all around, being shared approximately in twos and threes. One atop the copier. One propped up against the coffeemaker. One in Penelope's hands, and one beside the fruit basket Nadine ordered regularly from GetFruit.com.

He was nearly deafened by the rustle of magazines being closed, shoved behind backs, hurled under tables, stuffed into purses. Eight pairs of guilty eyes stared back at him.

"Good morning, Mr. V."

"Nice day today, Mr. V."

"Mr. V! Cup of coffee?"

Tony declined the inky brew Penelope held out (noticeably one-handed). He reached around her and pulled out the magazine someone had stuffed haphazardly into the crack between the mini fridge and the cabinet where the copier paper was kept.

"What page?" he asked.

His staff blinked at the fluorescents overhead. They kicked at stray paperclips, rearranged the packets of artificial sweetener at the end of the counter. A bookkeeper coughed.

Fine. He'd find it himself. He flipped through blurry shots of celebrities in bikinis, beneath headlines that screamed, "Lose the lard! Star ordered to shape up or ship out." He scanned red carpet pics of movie premiere arrivals, telephoto shots of stars doing ordinary things like guzzling a Starbucks or squeezing melons at Ralph's. He perused columns of breathless gossip and fashion tips, ads for the Hollywood Grapefruit Diet, a "Where Are They Now?" feature on the stars of "Melrose Place." He began to believe he'd caught his employees red-handed . . . at an innocent coffee break.

Then they began slinking away, mumbling excuses about "spreadsheets" and "guest services." No one here enjoyed work *that* much. Tony knew he was on the right track.

The truth — and the "Insider" column — were worse than he'd expected. First, there were three grainy photos of Meredith. One he recognized as her glancing over her shoulder as she entered the makeup artist's trailer. Given an *Inside Hollywood* spin, her girls' night out looked a lot like a clandestine affair-in-progress.

The second he identified as Meredith flubbing take after take on the first day of sitcom filming. That one — picturing a less-than-glamorous "Marley" with bedraggled hair — made her look hungover. Or depressed. Or maybe a little crazy.

It got worse, though. The third picture . . . The third he looked at with his fingers clenched on the pages, hardly able to believe he was seeing a picture of himself kissing Meredith after their riding lesson. Her cowboy hat hung down her back by its stampede string. Her hand caressed his cheek. His arm was around her, holding her close.

Tony remembered that moment. That kiss. It had been sweet, tender, irresistible. In that moment, he'd realized he *wanted* a woman like Meredith — someone who was independent, gutsy, unafraid to get her hands dirty and her pants covered in horsehair if the occasion demanded it.

He recalled thinking that he couldn't have imagined Taryn on horseback — unless there was a networking opportunity in it for her.

He recalled realizing then that what he'd had with Taryn had been mutual advantage, not love. Not true partnership. He recalled believing that with Meredith, things might be different.

All the while, some paparazzi scumbag had been snapping photos. Taking advantage of a personal moment to sell magazines. At the realization, Tony suddenly understood why Hollywood relationships were legendarily tricky. He could hardly wait for Meredith's stint as Marley to be over with so they could just be themselves.

That thought was fleeting, though. What lingered was anger. Anger and disbelief, as Tony skimmed the *Inside Hollywood* article.

The Insider *has to wonder . . . is former "Fantasy Family" star Marley Madison hiding something? This reporter thinks so. Two and two just don't go together. Famous for her sense of style, Marley seems to be slumming it at Valentine Studios' actor fantasy camp. And there's something fishy about the details in the "press junket" interview she granted early last week, too. Describing herself as having grown up "bookish," — a misnomer if the* Insider's *ever heard one — Madison confessed to hating stilettos and craving Oreos. Marley, Marley, Marley — your public might feel that way, but a star like you should not. For shame!*

"Jesus. Did Boob Guy write this piece of crap?"

"We don't think so, Mr. V.," one of the admins said. "We're pretty sure that Neanderthal can't wield a pencil."

They all giggled. Tony didn't. There was more.

The conundrum continues. While wanna-bes do their best star-in-training impersonations at Valentine Studios, our favorite former Southern belle has "declared" her residence in a certain decidedly unglitzy zip code. Could Marley be trying to relate to her regular-Joe actor camp constituency by dumbing down her digs? Or have her post "Fantasy Family" fortunes really declined that much?

Even juicier, the scuttlebutt around the back lot is all about Marley and studio exec Tony Valentine, the original prodigal son returned from the Big Apple. They've been spotted canoodling (pic above), but what's the real story? Only the Insider *knows . . . and we'll give you the shocking scoop next week! All the scandalous details about the real Marley Madison, only in* Inside Hollywood!

Appalled, Tony gaped at the two-page article. There were insinuations that Marley had gained weight, colored her hair, even joined a cult. Allusions to temper tantrums

338

(Boob Guy), romantic flings (Tony), and divalike behavior (his staff). He'd expected and hoped to find coverage of other camp guests. But that reporting was cursory at best — mostly limited to anonymous guests' speculations on everything from Marley's penchant for flip-flops to her mistakes in Pilates class.

Damn. Whoever the *Insider* correspondent was, that person clearly got around. Tony glanced at the article again, looking for clues to the mystery reporter's identity. His gaze snagged at the bottom of the page, on the routine trawling-for-submissions flash the magazine included with every article:

Remember, if you have information on this or any other story, e-mail us at scoop @insidehw.com or phone 1-800-4MY-SCOOP!

It could have been anyone. Anyone with access to a computer or a telephone. He ground his teeth, wondering how many of his guests and staff had turned in tips. Wondering which of them was really the *Insider* in disguise.

He should have insisted on knowing the reporter's identity. But the column's authenticity depended on absolute anonymity for the *Inside Hollywood* correspondent. The editor in chief had assured Tony of that when they'd discussed the feature. At the time, it had seemed worth the risk to garner useful press coverage.

That had been before he'd had an imposter Marley on board.

Damn, damn, damn.

Tony reexamined the article. Some of its information was true — but presented in a deliberately misleading way. Some of it was pure fabrication. All of it could be potentially damaging to Valentine Studios' actor fantasy camp. What good was a tourist attraction featuring a supposedly whiny, unglamorous, affair-having sitcom has-been? That would hardly draw tourists away from Disneyland, Sea World, Universal Studios, and all the rest of California's famed tourist traps.

All the scandalous details about the real Marley Madison, only in Inside Hollywood!

Christ. This might get even more disastrous when next week's issue was published, Tony realized. "The real Marley Madison." What other big secret could the article be hinting at, except a revelation of Meredith's presence at Valentine Studios?

Of course, by next Monday when another issue of *Inside Hollywood* hit newsstands, the actor fantasy camp finale would be finished. His investors would be secure. But Valentine Studios' future guests . . . they'd read that coverage. Reservations would take a hit if the camp's main attraction was uncovered as a fraud.

Frowning, he glared at the article. He should have known better. He was a business professional. An expert acknowledged for reimaging tired companies and giving them a dot-com-age boost. When *Inside Hollywood* had offered to send one of their undercover correspondents to write a feature on his inaugural camp session, he should have recognized the potential PR pitfalls. What the hell had made him allow it?

"Here you are!" Errol announced, coming into the room wearing a dapper suit and a curious expression. "I was wondering where everyone was. Tony, I have a proposition for you. I've been thinking . . . If your actor fantasy camp fails, there's another way to save the studio. If we lease out some of our unused soundstages as office space —"

"You!" Tony said, advancing on his uncle. "You're the reason *this* happened!"

"I beg your pardon?" Startled, Errol glanced at the magazine. He recognized the *Inside Hollywood* masthead and blanched. "Now wait just a minute —"

" 'Chester Dodge is an old friend,' you said. 'It won't hurt to give him an exclusive,' you said." Tony smacked the magazine in his palm, frustrated beyond measure. "*This* is what happens when you do business with friends, Uncle Errol. Even friends who are major magazine editors. They stab you in the back."

"Now, Tony. That's not strictly true. Just because that New York girlfriend of yours

341

turned on you —"

"Don't even go there." The last thing Tony wanted was a reminder of Taryn's betrayal. Summoning up some semblance of calm, he continued. "I tried to accommodate you, Uncle Errol. I hired the old-timers you recommended for the security crew. They let in paparazzi. I used your buddy Carl's agency to screen headlining attractions. They dropped the ball, leaving me to scramble to sign up Marley Madison at the last minute."

With a hesitant smile, Errol held out his palm in a *stop* gesture. "If you'll let me point out how nicely that worked out for you both . . ."

"No."

His uncle had *no* idea what a headache hiring "Marley" had been, at least in the beginning. As though finally getting some inkling, Errol closed his mouth.

Tony paced, slapping the damn magazine against his thigh. "I used your friends, the geriatric set designers. They gave me two soundstages filled with relics, some of which I've already had to repaint. I gave the account for actor fantasy camp advertising to the agency you suggested. They erected exactly two billboards. What about radio? What about cable TV spots? What about bus ads, Internet promotions? Market research and target audience identification? What about partnerships with the tourism board, outreach

342

to travel magazines?"

"Some of those things aren't proven to work," Errol pointed out, looking a little miffed. "And you're forgetting the newspaper advertisements."

"Oh. Right." Tony smacked his forehead, still pacing. "A one-column drive-by in the *Times* and a few classifieds in the alternative weeklies. How could I forget those?"

"I'll admit Neville's techniques aren't exactly cutting-edge," Errol agreed stiffly. "But you should give them more of a chance. They've been effective in the past."

"*In the past.* Exactly."

That was the trouble with Errol's cohorts. They'd all enjoyed their heydays twenty, thirty, fifty years ago, but were still being subsidized by buddies like Errol.

"New and flashy isn't necessarily better," his uncle said. "There's something to be said for consistency. For loyalty."

"Unless it interferes with sound business practices."

"You don't mean that."

"The hell I don't! I'm not like you. I'm not like any of the Valentines."

"I wouldn't sound so proud of that if I were you."

"Oh, yeah? Well, you're not me. That much is obvious. Because of your overly sentimental, let's-help-out-a-friend, complete-pushover 'management style,' this studio is on the verge of bankruptcy. And unless I can pull off a miracle, I've got a whole new disaster on my hands."

In demonstration, Tony threw down the *Inside Hollywood* magazine. It flopped open to the well-creased centerfold article about Marley. Errol's gaze darted to the pictures. Uncomfortably, he looked away. He'd already seen the article, then. Or had he perpetrated it?

Was Errol the mystery reporter?

"I'm sorry about the article," Errol said. "No one meant for this to happen. You look upset."

"Upset?" That was the understatement of the century. "This is the last straw," Tony warned, biting off each word. "From here on out, I'm running things *my* way. Efficiently. Progressively. Intelligently."

"Coldly."

His uncle's steely look was a revelation. So Errol *was* capable of something more than a good-natured Cary Grant impersonation. Perversely, Tony took encouragement in that fact.

"If that's what it takes," he agreed. "Coldly. Absolutely."

From the doorway, Roland spoke up. "I guess that's how they do it back there in New York, eh, Tony?"

In no mood to be ganged up on by his errant relatives, Tony turned. He had no idea how long his uncle had been there. Or what

Roland might have overheard. He didn't much care.

"That's how *I* do it. That's how I get results," he said. "That's why you hired me to save this studio in the first place."

Roland blinked. "You think that's why we 'hired' you? Why we wanted you back here in L.A.?"

He shared a telling glance with Errol — a look that didn't, for once, appear to signal the onset of another brotherly feud. In this, Tony was amazed to discover, both elderly Valentines seemed in complete agreement.

"We wanted you here running the studio because it's your legacy." Roland's voice sounded as though the truth should have been obvious. "And because you're family."

"Because I'm family?" Stunned, Tony quit pacing. He gawked at his uncles. "That's it?"

Wearing mystified expressions, they nodded in unison.

Tony couldn't believe it. After all this time, all this effort, it turned out he'd been nothing more than the latest recipient of his uncles' misplaced altruism. To them, he was just another charity case. Like Chester, the Machiavellian tabloid editor. Or Neville, the stuck-in-the-Stone-Age ad man.

What about his acclaimed entrepreneurial skills? Tony wondered. What about his business connections, his computer expertise, his knack for coaxing a good performance out of staff members? What about the non-Hollywood qualifications he'd spent *years* honing? Didn't they mean anything?

Staring at Roland and Errol, he realized for the first time that no, they didn't mean anything. To his uncles, all that mattered was that his name ended in Valentine. That was the beginning and the end of who he was. No amount of success in New York had changed that, or ever would.

Too filled with fury and disappointment to stand still any longer, Tony grabbed the magazine he'd slapped onto the table. Then he grabbed another, and another. Soon, he had every issue held in a tight, angry bundle against his chest. He didn't spare a glance for his uncles. He didn't think he could look at them without hitting something.

First, he'd find as many magazines as he could, before Meredith got hold of one. Seeing that issue was bound to hurt her. Then he'd get back to work. Given what Tony had just learned, he felt more determined than ever to make this venture succeed.

He'd show his family he was more than just another Valentine, damn it. Or he'd go down fighting.

"Hold up there a minute, Tony," Roland said.

"Yes, wait, Tony. You've misunderstood us," Errol urged.

But Tony couldn't listen.

"I've got an actor fantasy camp to run," he said. "For your own sakes, I'd suggest the two of you stay out of my way while I do it."

Considering the lies, half-truths, and damning insinuations contained in that *Inside Hollywood* article, if Meredith had seen it Tony expected to find her sobbing. Or unleashing wicked left hooks on everything that wasn't nailed down. He wasn't sure which. Knowing her, he figured it could go either way.

Instead, after roving the back lot searching for her, he finally located her in the archives, amid boxes and crates and stacks of movie magazines. Dressed in her own museum T-shirt and a pair of jeans with Tevas on her feet, Meredith looked much the same as she had when he'd picked her up in the limo.

Natural. Unspoiled. Unreasonably appealing. He couldn't help thinking it. Much as Tony appreciated her starlet impersonation, he found the real Meredith most attractive.

Not that he'd ever tell her that. What woman wanted to hear her primping and pampering was unnecessary? If he knew women, that would take all the fun out of it. Kind of like removing the beer from the ballpark. It wasn't strictly necessary to the game, but a man enjoyed it.

He stood just inside the door, watching her. Her casual clothes — practical as they were for rummaging through the dusty archives — could have tipped someone to her non-Marley status. Tony knew he should mention it to her. But with all that had happened, he found himself absurdly happy just to be in her presence. Just seeing her, he felt a thousand times better.

She glanced up and smiled, the same way she always did. Tony accepted that smile for the clue it was. Either Meredith didn't know about the *Inside Hollywood* article or she didn't want to talk about it yet. He decided to keep quiet for now.

He came nearer, letting the door swing shut behind him. As he got closer, her smile faltered. A crease appeared between her brows.

"What's the matter?" she asked.

"With me? Nothing." Tony stuffed his hands in his pockets like a ten-year-old, determined to shove aside the troubling events of the past hour. "What have you got there?"

Meredith looked at the vintage magazines sorted in mostly orderly piles all around her. "Lots of period advertising content. Several pounds of dust bunnies. The usual."

Tilting her head to the side, she peered up at him. Something in his expression seemed to lead her to a decision. She sucked in a deep breath and gestured toward her finds.

"Maybe you can help me make heads or tails of some of this stuff."

A weird sense of gratefulness overtook him. He'd have sworn he was glad to be needed . . . or glad she understood him well enough not to push him into unburdening his troubles. Both were crazy ideas. Shaking off the feeling, Tony toed aside an empty cardboard box and found a place on the floor beside her.

"Looks like you're making good progress."

"I am." She drew up her knees, going back to the magazine she'd been reviewing. "If you'll lend me some of these materials for the museum, I can make a fascinating exhibit. With Valentine Studios as the sponsor, of course. It'll be good public relations."

Public relations. His least favorite phrase of the day.

"You can use whatever you need."

He leaned forward to heft a cardboard box from the nearest pile. When Tony opened it, the unfamiliar smells of yellowed paper, dried ink, and aged fabrics drifted out. Within moments, he was engrossed in sorting through the things inside. The decades-old magazines he set aside for Meredith. The tissue-wrapped costumes he stacked nearby. The photographs —

On the verge of picking up a pile of studio shots, Tony glimpsed something beneath them at the bottom of the box. He reached for it.

"Glamour!" he said, surprised.

"That again?" Meredith muttered absent-mindedly. "Look, I already headlined two classes today. Now I'm working. Fancy clothes and makeup would just be a distraction."

"No, not you — this. This bottle." He showed it to her. "Glamour. It was Esther's idea. Valentine Studios' version of those early eighties designer fragrances."

"Ahhh. The ones with one name and a lot of attitude. Obsession. Opium. Poison. Eternity. Those were a goldmine for advertisers. They really heralded the beginning of lifestyle advertising. No hard sell — just ambiance without content." Meredith nodded knowledgably. "Those techniques practically invented yuppies."

He opened the top. "Smell it."

She did. "Oh, my God! It's like, like . . ." She shook her head, obviously working to conjure up a suitable description. "It's a collision of bad taste. That's what it is."

"I know." Smiling broadly, Tony took a big sniff. "This really takes me back. I was about nine years old when this stuff debuted. My mom, Aunt Esther, and Aunt Nadine wore nothing else for years. I think they did it out of sheer, stubborn Valentine loyalty. I'm surprised there's any of it left."

Meredith fluttered her fingers, motioning for him to recap the bottle. "It's making my eyes water. I think my lips are burning."

"Yeah. That was a drawback. Every time I hugged my mom good night, I had a coughing fit." Filled with nostalgia, he shook his head. The bottle still had that absurd neo-modern shape, created by a designer friend of his father's. He traced the exaggerated glass curves. "Because of Glamour, I could detect any female member of my family at fifty paces."

She blew her nose. "Touching."

"I must've snitched a million dollars' worth of quarters for the Pac Man game outside the commissary from my mom's purse. Got away with it, too. Glamour was my early-warning system."

"It's a perfume . . . *and* a juvenile crime aid!" she said chirpily, mimicking an advertising pitchman. "Step right up, folks. Glamour will polish your floors, clear your sinuses, and make your teeth whiter than white! It'll make your husband crawl on his knees with desire — or the last remnants of his strength to escape."

"Har, har."

Tony took one more fond sniff. Reluctantly, he began tucking the bottle back into the box. Meredith leaned over and snatched it.

"What are you doing?" she blurted. "I need that!"

"What for? Your exhibit?" Of course. Until Glamour's demise in the grunge wave of unisex fragrances, it had been a smash hit. "Come to think of it, I'm pretty sure we did advertise this . . . something about sequins —"

"No, not for my exhibit." She grinned. "To ward off muggers. That stuff's more powerful than pepper spray any day."

"Very funny."

But he didn't really mind her jabs at Glamour. If Meredith had taken to the perfume, it would have seriously messed with his head. He wasn't sure he could get it up for a woman who smelled like his mother and aunts. It was for the best, really.

Hesitantly, Meredith took another sniff. She screwed up her face in mock horror, then thrust the bottle aside.

"It smells like feet."

"It does not." Tony rolled his eyes, amazed he still had the capacity to be surprised by the outrageous things she said. "It smells sophisticated."

"Sophisticatedly stinky."

He shook his head. "You just had to push it, didn't you?"

"I wouldn't be me if I didn't."

"No," he said, thinking he wouldn't want her any other way except one hundred percent *her*. "You wouldn't be. Give me that bottle back. I think you need another sample sniff."

"Sorry," she said, not sounding the least bit remorseful. Primly, she squared off her stacks of museum-ready acquisitions. "The bottle's already in the exhibit-possibilities pile. It can't possibly be moved. *Especially* for another sniff. That might be deadly."

"Have it your way. But I've got to warn you. At this rate, you're not on the short list to sample Arrogance, 'the fragrance for men,' when I come across it in this mess."

"Awww. Darn it."

Smiling over her excellent sham regret — whether she'd admit it or not, Meredith had a knack for acting — Tony went back to the pictures he'd initially been interested in. Within minutes, he found himself fully absorbed in the photos. In the stack, he found studio publicity shots of all the Valentines — including his parents, the often-absent "location scouts" of the clan.

Meredith looked over his shoulder with interest.

"They seem happy," she said.

"They were. They were doing what they love to do — travel and drum up production deals. The original location for 'Fantastic Island' was some place they'd visited in the South Pacific while wining and dining an expatriate director."

"Nice work if you can get it."

He gazed at the picture. "As long as they were together, they didn't care where they were. Still don't. My parents have one of the few thriving Hollywood marriages. And a record number of frequent flyer miles to go with it."

Meredith peered closer. "Why aren't you in this picture with them?"

"I was probably here. In L.A., in school." He shrugged, then moved on to the next photo. "Sometimes I traveled with them in the summertime, but the rest of the year I stayed with various aunts and uncles."

"What, on a rotating basis?"

She'd been kidding, he could tell. He wasn't.

"Sort of," Tony agreed. "When I was younger, you couldn't pry me off the back lot. I was enthralled with everything here. Compared with dropping water balloons off the Tumbleweed saloon or exploring the jungle in Acajatuba, being stuck in a hotel someplace didn't hold much appeal."

He lapsed into silence, remembering. He *had* loved it in L.A. Had loved it most of all here at the studio. Why had that changed? Just because he'd needed to prove himself?

If so, fine, Tony decided stonily. He still did.

Her voice was soft. "You must've missed them."

He wrenched himself back to the conversation. "Sometimes," he admitted. "But they were here a lot. And hey — what other kid had a half dozen attendees at parents' night? Six emergency phone numbers? A whole troupe of advocates for parent-teacher conferences?"

Meredith nodded. "I sure didn't. My dad was it. My mom was usually ferrying Marley someplace to audition or take a lesson. My parents are happily married, but they've definitely never spent much time together." She scrunched her nose. "Maybe that's *why* they're happily married . . ."

"See? I was lucky. The Valentines definitely know how to band together for a cause. Especially if it concerns someone they care about."

In the midst of putting away the pictures, he glanced up. Despite his explanations, Meredith's brown eyes were filled with empathy.

Tony frowned. "Don't look at me like I'm Little Orphan Annie. I'm fine."

Dubiously, she examined him. Then she flicked her gaze sideways, to the next closest box. "Hey, what's that?"

It was clear she was changing the subject. That she believed him when he said he was fine. Tony didn't buy it.

"Hang on," he said. "Don't you want to psychoanalyze me? Delve into my childhood for clues to commitment issues? Explore my *feelings* about things?"

Her answer was matter-of-fact. "If you had

issues, you wouldn't be so close to your family now. You wouldn't talk about them with all that affection in your voice."

It was that obvious? Embarrassed, he grumbled to himself. He hauled over the box she'd mentioned and flipped it open, waving away the increasingly familiar odors of items stored for a long time.

"In fact, you probably wouldn't have come back here at all if you had *issues* with them," Meredith continued, undeterred. "That's all I need to know."

Hmmph. He had "issues" with a select few of his family members right now. But those would be solved after he'd made a success of his actor fantasy camp. Tony was convinced of it.

Besides . . . at least one person here was on his side. Meredith. She didn't see him as "just another Valentine." She believed in him. She knew how much making the camp succeed meant to him, and she was prepared to help make it happen. That was important to Tony — really important.

He studied her, amazed.

"You missed out. When they took the girls aside in sixth grade to teach them how to tease boys, be obsessed with shoes, and give future boyfriends the third degree, you must have been climbing a tree someplace."

She grinned. "Probably. Or reading a book."

At the sight of her smile, lightness filled him all over again. Meredith was like magic. Somehow, being around her eased all the burdens he shouldered. It didn't stop there, either, Tony realized. He wanted to do the same thing for her — wanted to comfort her, protect her, cheer her up. He'd never experienced all that with Taryn.

Back to the box. From inside, he pulled out another pile of wrapped, spangled costumes. Then a second batch of photos. Ready for another nostalgia trip, Tony sifted through them. Images flashed past of Nadine. His mother. His dad and Esther at a ribbon-cutting ceremony. His uncles, caught at a table at The Ivy in the middle of one of their famous feuds.

His uncles. At the sight of Errol and Roland's bickering faces, all the anger and disappointment Tony had felt earlier rushed right back to him. Why wouldn't *they* see he was more than just another Valentine?

Frustrated, Tony averted his gaze, searching for a new distraction. He'd make a success of his actor fantasy camp. He'd show his family there were other ways of doing business besides offering charity to old friends and running a studio into the ground. Besides hiring any old down-on-his-luck pal who happened to need work. Then they'd realize —

Wait a minute. Was that an issue of *Inside Hollywood*, stuffed between *Photoplay* and

Silver Screen on the floor beside Meredith? He peered closer.

It was. It was the current issue, too. She'd seen it.

She just hadn't told him.

Tony frowned. How the hell was he supposed to help her, to console her, if she didn't even confide in him? A little irked — but mostly concerned — Tony pried the magazine out of the pile.

He held it up. "Is this part of your exhibit, too?"

"Hmmm?" Meredith turned, looking engrossed in her work. She blinked, bringing the magazine into focus. An odd look suffused her face. "Oh, that." She glanced away. "Actually, I was really hoping you wouldn't notice that."

EIGHTEEN

"Always a bridesmaid but never a bride."
— advertisement for Listerine
"breath deodorant" (1925)

"Wouldn't notice it?" Tony waved the *Inside Hollywood*, making the pages flap. "How could I *not* notice it? You're the worst magazine hider in the world."

He looked at her semiaccusingly. Meredith would have sworn she glimpsed something serious in his expression, something hurt in his dark eyes.

She must be mistaken. Probably, he pitied her. Then again, maybe he just didn't want her mixing up archival and current materials. Maybe that wasn't pity but annoyance she saw on his face. She wasn't sure. She'd always been better at reading reference materials than reading people.

She'd always been better at acting tough than playing it straight, too. Blithely, so Tony wouldn't guess how she really felt, Meredith waved her hand.

"I wasn't exactly expecting company."

His eyes widened. "You weren't expecting company."

"That's right."

He made a sputtering sound of astonishment. Uh-oh. Acting tough was going to be twice as hard if Tony didn't buy it. Hastily she looked down, pretending to be busy sorting. Her hands shook on the next magazine, though, and her heart pounded.

She'd been reading the stupid tabloid when she'd heard Tony's footsteps outside the archives building. She'd barely had time to shove the issue beneath a copy of *Photoplay* before he'd opened the door. Once inside, Tony had stood there for the longest time, just watching her. Meredith had been certain he'd been too disappointed in her to come any closer.

But when he had . . . Well, when he had, she'd forgotten all about her troubles. One look at Tony had told her something else was bothering him. She'd wanted to help. Since he hadn't wanted to talk about it, Meredith had tried the next best thing: action. Doing something together tended to work well with men. Tony was no exception.

It had been nice. Reminiscing over his childhood at the studio, looking at family photos, being nearly asphyxiated by Glamour . . . together. They'd shared a mini reprieve, and Meredith had learned a little more about Tony in the process. She'd felt closer to him than ever.

Until now. Now the jig was up, and she mostly felt scared. What if Tony looked at her differently after reading the *Insider* column? What if he was disappointed she'd almost blown her Marley cover? What if he realized exactly how un–Marley-like Meredith really was, despite her best efforts, and quit wanting her?

"You know what they say," Tony mused, lifting his gaze from the magazine to her. "You should only start worrying when they *quit* talking about you."

"Hollywood truism?"

He nodded.

"Figures. It's about as whacked-out as everything else in this town." She rolled her eyes, still trying to maintain some semblance of tough-gal cynicism. "Who wants people talking about them?"

"Movie stars. TV stars. Screenwriters. Executives." Tony ticked off more possibilities on his fingers. "Camera operators. Caterers. Agents. Bodyguards. Personal trainers."

"Okay, okay. I get it." Morosely, Meredith held up her hands to make him quit. "I'm sorry, Tony. About the article. I should have mentioned the photographers I saw earlier. Plus, I didn't want to tell you, but I blew it in the faux press junket interview with Harry. I was a little distracted. I let slip a few details that contradict Marley's life — as you no doubt read in that article. I'm just lucky nobody knows she's really on her honeymoon right now."

She glared at the magazine. When she'd found an abandoned copy at the commissary this morning, it had seemed a harmless diversion to browse over her coffee and bagel with shmear. How wrong she'd been. Seeing herself inside those pages had been an awful shock. Stealth photography ought to be a crime — especially when hat head was involved.

"I was distracted that morning, too," Tony said. "After you left to go to your interview, I wandered around for ten minutes trying to remember where my next appointment was."

"Did you find it?"

"Sure. After I accidentally wound up in a Movie Makeup For Dummies class. Turns out I'm a natural at inflicting fake black eyes, Dracula fangs, and imitation bruises."

Who was he kidding? Tony could never hurt anyone — not even artificially, and especially not when that "anyone" was Meredith. She understood that now. Now that he hadn't freaked out over all this.

Cautiously, she looked at him. Maybe Tony was someone she could count on. Someone who would understand her. Someone for whom being Meredith — just Meredith — would be good enough.

He nudged her. "Hey, Brainiac. Did you know you can make pretty passable fake blood with corn syrup and food coloring? It's cool. Just like a horror flick from the pre-CG days."

She studied him. "You know, for a supposed business genius, you have a major childlike streak."

He shrugged. "You have a major babealicious streak."

Meredith almost laughed. Who could remain cynical after a cheesy comment like that? But whatever else happened, she didn't want Tony to know that article had hurt her feelings. Letting down her guard now — even to laugh — would only be the beginning of the process. And it would only lead to trouble. Vulnerability always did.

She tried to shore up her reserves. Tony's grin unraveled ninety percent of them. When he covered her hand with his and squeezed, the remaining ten percent flew the coop. If Tony was going to be *nice* about this, she didn't stand a chance.

Crossing her arms, Meredith hit him with her last-ditch effort: her best curmudgeonly voice. "You're impossible."

"And you're stubborn," he said easily. "The point is, you make a mistake, you move on. No big deal. That's what we're going to do here. Move on."

"Just like that?"

A nod. "Just like that."

But all of a sudden, Meredith wasn't quite ready to move on. She kicked at the *Inside*

Hollywood issue with the toe of her Tevas.

"They implied I was a mentally unstable cult member," she grumbled. "A fat one!"

Tony's grin widened. "Given the choice between loony, cult-following, and chubby, you take offense at chubby?"

"I grew up a tomboy. But I'm still a woman."

He arched his eyebrow. "Meaning?"

"Meaning, no woman wants the size of her butt to be the subject of national speculation." She patted her hips, searching for the reassurance of her usual hip-tied sweatshirt. As always lately, she was surprised to find it missing. "It's embarrassing."

With a casually powerful movement, Tony scooted closer. Distractedly, Meredith watched his biceps flex as he steadied himself on the floor, watched his naked chest whoosh into view and then disappear as his partly buttoned shirt fell forward. It settled against his body again, hugging the width of his shoulders and the sculpted muscles of his torso.

Hey, this was working. Just looking at him, she felt a little better already. Interested in finding out how far the distraction process could take her, Meredith contemplated Tony in more detail. His forearms, lean and tanned in contrast with his rolled-up shirtsleeves. His bent legs, clad in summery linen pants that made him look like a vagabond beachcomber.

His dark hair, his clean-shaven jaw, his overall don't-argue-with-me demeanor.

If she didn't respond to his attempts to move on, she didn't doubt tickling was next on his agenda.

He smelled of soap and sunshine, emanated a crackling kind of expectancy which Meredith sensed but didn't understand. Was he that sure he could humor her into becoming vulnerable? That certain she, as a woman, needed to release all the feelings she'd kept pent up since reading that article?

Knowing Tony . . . probably.

Readying herself for a joke, another bit of dubious Hollywood wisdom, a review of the latest episode of "SpongeBob SquarePants" on Nickelodeon, Meredith raised her face to his.

"You don't ever need to be embarrassed with me," he said, his face utterly — surprisingly — sober. "Because there's nothing you could ever *do* that would change who you *are*. And who you are is someone I really, really like."

Meredith opened her mouth to protest — and found herself being kissed instead. Tony delved both hands in her hair to hold her to him; then he showed her with his kiss everything he'd just told her with his words.

The pressure of his mouth on hers was certainty; the sweet slide of his lips was discovery; the combination of their breath and warmth and need was affirmation. *Here is what you need,* his kiss said. *I want to give it to you. Take it, revel in it, give it back and find it multiplied a thousand times.* When their lips met again, it was completion . . . When their hands touched it was invitation.

How a simple brushing of fingertips could have conveyed all that, Meredith didn't know. She only felt that it did, and believed. She lifted her hands to touch Tony's as he cradled her face, and he curled his fingers around hers in a gesture that welcomed her. She opened her eyes to find him gazing at her with such concentration, she felt as though she had been invisible before and had only now become perceptible.

Given that look, there was no holding back. The worries she'd tried to hide crept from their corners. As though they, too, had become tangible in an instant, they flowed from her hands to Tony's — and were gone a heartbeat later, absorbed into his greater strength. He smiled and stroked her hair, and a completely unreasonable peacefulness stole through Meredith.

This was what it felt like to be naked, she thought. Without a barrier of sloppy clothes and museum-speak, without a book to bury her face in and a sister to be the opposite of. It didn't matter that she still wore her jeans and T-shirt, that her sandals remained strapped to her feet. With Tony she was her

hadn't been naked lust that had brought them together. It had been naked need. Need to be held, to be understood, to be happy.

Tony angled his head, drew back, smiled at her. He trailed his fingertips over her cheek, along her jaw . . . lightly flicked the pad of his thumb over her lower lip. His eyes were filled with tenderness — that, and recognition.

"Meredith, Meredith, Meredith," he murmured.

This time, she didn't object. She wasn't afraid, and she wasn't trying to remain unmoved. She smiled, remembering her earlier insistence on casual sex every other time they'd been together. She might have known nothing could be casual with this man. Not when he knew her heart so well.

"Tony, Tony, Tony," she returned.

He closed his eyes, briefly, as though savoring the way she said his name. The gesture let her admire him openly — the straight line of his brows, the assertive angle of his nose, the sensual shape of his mouth. If a man could be said to be gorgeous, that description definitely applied to Tony. Meredith found him wildly appealing — even now, when he watched her with a knowing gleam in his eyes.

Rats. When had he opened them?

Caught, she diverted him with a kiss. Their mouths met, their tongues slid together, their moans rose in unison. It wasn't enough. Tony caught the back of her head in his palm and deepened the kiss, running his free hand along her arm, her waist, her hip. Arching to be nearer, Meredith wriggled against him, kissing him with all the fervor she could muster.

In an instant, their togetherness morphed from cozy to heated, from gentle to needy. She grabbed at his shirt, blindly trying to unfasten the buttons. Instead, she encountered fistfuls of fabric and what felt like a few extra pairs of arms as Tony similarly strove to grab her T-shirt and lift it over her head. They maneuvered in new directions, each fumbling with the myriad zippers, buttons, and rivets on the other's pants.

A button popped into the air. "Woo-hoo! Success!" Meredith said as it pinged to the floor. "There's no stopping me now."

Laughing, Tony stood. "Oh, yes, there is."

A moment later, he'd scooped her into his arms. Meredith shrieked, clinging to him. Breathing heavily, he balanced her there, his hair in his face and his eyes dark with desire. She looked up, and knew her own expression must match his. She'd had enough of waiting.

"I was thinking the floor over there might be good," she suggested, hearing the huskiness in her voice as she spoke. She angled her head sideways, making her hair spill over his biceps. "If we spread out some of the costumes for cushioning —"

"You deserve better than a floor."

He strode to the archive building's door. Opened it.

"Wow, one-handed. I'm impressed."

Daylight spilled over them, along with the faint sounds of activity on the back lot. They both squinted into the sun.

Feeling surprisingly comfortable held in his arms, Meredith glanced up. "Your place or mine?"

"Yours is fifty yards closer."

"Mine."

Tony walked, his gaze fixed on their distant destination. It was just like *An Officer and a Gentleman*. Only without Louis Gossett, Jr., a soundtrack, and that white Navy officer's hat. Meredith didn't figure she could pull off the hat, anyway.

"As incredibly romantic as this is," she said, "we'd probably be less conspicuous if you put me down."

"Right."

With a decisive movement, he set her on her feet. They linked hands and walked together, then shared a glance and started to jog. Their breath panted into the sunshine.

A golf cart of actor fantasy camp guests chugged past.

"Just out for a jog," Tony assured them.

A pair of stunt coordinators happened by.

371

"Just rehearsing!" Meredith called to them, waving. "Bye!"

Esther and Harry turned up, walking hand in hand near Tumbleweed.

"Boring business meeting," Tony told them. "Gotta run."

"*Really* boring," Meredith emphasized.

But Esther and Harry seemed perfectly content not to be drawn into conversation. Suspiciously content, in fact. Meredith craned her neck as they passed the twosome. They'd just ducked behind a wheeled oak tree, and she'd swear Harry had stolen a kiss from a giggling Esther.

She stifled a grin and moved on.

"Hey, I think Pilates class is making me fit or something," she commented. "This jogging stuff isn't even all that tough."

"Not with the proper incentive," Tony agreed.

Still jogging, he unbuttoned his shirt. The tails flapped in the breeze. A second later, Meredith got an armload of white linen. Nude from the waist up, Tony sprinted ahead.

"Hey!"

He grinned over his shoulder. "This is the incentive."

And how. One look at his naked chiseled arms, broad shoulders, and muscular back told her that. Another look told her he was reaching for his fly, even as he kept moving.

Would he really drop his pants, right here on the back lot?

Meredith never found out. Never one to sidestep a dare, she'd grabbed the hem of her T-shirt and was about to lift it over her head when her trailer came into view. A final burst of speed brought her all the way there.

They slammed inside, laughing and giddy. The whole place rocked as they raced to the back, shedding clothes as they went. Meredith dropped Tony's shirt on the banquette, then added her own museum T-shirt beside it. Hopping on one foot through the trailer's minuscule kitchen area, she wrenched off one Tevas, then the other.

At the end of the hallway, Tony appeared. Clad in nothing but a pair of sexy boxer briefs, he reached both hands to the top of the doorjamb. He regarded her from that pose with affectionate impatience.

"I win. You suck at getting undressed on the run."

Meredith's jaw dropped. He looked incredible. Not too muscular, not too lean . . . just right. She'd forgotten how tight his abs were, how intriguing his narrow hips . . . how promising the rest of him, confined in those briefs. Yowsa.

Two, Meredith figured, could play at this game.

"Oh, yeah?" she asked. "Watch this."

She shimmied out of her jeans in two seconds flat, leaving them in a puddle on the floor. Wearing her skimpiest white panties and a matching bra, she lingered at the opposite end of the hallway. She struck a pose.

Tony's face brightened with a satisfying amount of interest. His gaze skimmed over her ankles, her legs, her belly, her breasts . . . focused on her face. At the appreciation she glimpsed in his eyes, Meredith felt a distinct tingle race through her. She'd never felt sexier.

But he still hadn't moved, and she wanted him to come to her this time. With that thought in mind, she mustered all her remaining self-restraint and stayed where she was. Giving Tony a seductive look, she ran her hands over her breasts, feeling her nipples pucker against her palms. She traced a path to her hips, rotating them slightly as she gave each curve a leisurely caress. She dipped her fingers to the vee of her legs, then spread them wide over her thighs, as though savoring their feminine shape.

And she did savor it, Meredith realized. For her entire adult life, she'd obsessed about covering her hips, hiding her thighs, denying her womanly curves. But now, given the glazed look in Tony's eyes and the unmistakable signs of approval he displayed elsewhere, she reveled in every part of herself. She was made just as she'd been meant to be, strong and soft at the same time. She wouldn't hide that fact anymore. Here in the clear daylight, she'd embrace it.

"You're beautiful," Tony said, moving nearer. "Beautiful Meredith."

Proudly she met him halfway. Her limbs trembled and her heart raced, but only because she wanted this — wanted *him* — so much. Tony held out his hand and she took it. Another kiss later, they landed on the cotton candy bed she'd found so silly and so pink before.

Today, she didn't. Today, sunshine warmed the pink, illuminating Tony's face as he joined her on the comforter. Today, softness surrounded them both, making the pink seem cozy and sensual as they came together. It was the perfect setting for the love they shared . . . but truthfully, Meredith wouldn't have cared if they *had* wound up on the floor of the archives. So long as she and Tony were together, that was all that mattered.

He stretched out beside her, propping his head against his crooked arm ("The better to see you," he told her). He kissed her, making her dizzy with wanting. He told her how incredible she looked to him, how much he wanted her, how he'd looked forward to this moment for days. Meredith had, too.

With reverent care, Tony stroked her from head to heels. She quivered and moaned beneath his touch, impatient for him to go faster . . . faster. Still, he wouldn't.

"I want this to last," he said. "Even if it kills me."

She sampled a little stroking of her own, filling her hand with the smooth, hard length of him. He groaned.

"Never mind. It *is* killing me."

They rolled over together, tangling the bedclothes. Meredith lost herself in explorations of him. She learned the muscles of his forearms and shoulders, wrapped her arms around his middle and squeezed his butt, rubbed herself against the crisp dark hair on his chest. She wiggled her bare toes and slid her foot along his calf, loving the fact that beneath all the macho leg hair and muscle, Tony was still susceptible to being ticklish.

"Hey! Quit it."

"If you're trying to look fierce, give it up. You don't scare me."

"Oh, yeah? Watch this."

"Nope." Laughing, Meredith shook her head, half on and half off the piled pillows. "Although that's a pretty funny face. You should try it out on door-to-door salesmen. They'd laugh themselves right out of the neighborhood."

"How about this one?"

"Careful. Your face might freeze that way."

"This one?"

She considered him, feeling her heart squeeze with happiness. She was glad they could be open like this — even here, in bed.

"Oscar the Grouch called. He wants his face back on Sesame Street. Pronto."

With a mighty grumble, Tony pulled her back into his arms. Meredith gasped to find herself a little more naked when she got there. How had he whisked off her bra so quickly?

Soon, though, she didn't care about the mechanics of it. Not when Tony's hand closed possessively over her right breast. Not when his head lowered to her left. He sucked her nipple into the soft, wet heat of his mouth, flicking her with his tongue.

She squirmed, breathless. She clutched his head, arching her toes into the mattress.

"I'm not sure how I goaded you into this . . . but please, keep going."

"My pleasure."

He loved her thoroughly and well, paying exquisite attention to her breasts, her mouth, her belly, her thighs. He brought his head to the junction of her thighs and offered a soft kiss through her panties, one which made her shake and moan. With infinite care, Tony slipped off those panties. He gazed at her nakedness, an expression of absolute wonder on his face, then kissed her again.

Meredith had every intention of giving as good as she got. She made it only as far as wrenching off Tony's boxer briefs and closing her hand around him before he deftly moved away to continue with what he was doing.

Hazy with desire, she slid sideways and stroked him again. He felt wonderful in her hand, all warm and hard and ready, and she wanted to make him shudder the same way she did. Except every time she tried, she got distracted by another caress, another kiss, another lick to a sensitive place. Very soon, all she wanted was for the good feelings to go on and on.

Panting, she told him so. "Please, Tony. Don't stop."

"Never."

He levered upward and kissed her, looking masculine and perfect and absolutely, positively delighted to be loving her. In every move he made, Meredith detected happiness. In every word he spoke, she heard love. Buoyed by the realization, she *did* give as good as she got — this time, in more than a physical sense. When she kissed him, she did it with all her heart. When she held him, she put her whole self into the embrace. It was the least Tony deserved . . . just for being himself.

Finally, *finally* he poised above her, bracing himself on his strong arms. Heat poured from their bodies. Meredith felt herself slick and ready for him, but still he waited.

His dark-eyed gaze met hers, filled with need and something else . . . something special and unmistakable. Meredith knew it was love. What else could it be? She felt exactly the same way. On the verge of confessing her feelings to him, she drew in a breath — only to release it in a whoosh as Tony entered her.

Their union was as incredible as she'd ever imagined, and twice as meaningful. Even as he thrust forward and retreated, Tony kept his gaze locked on her. Even as she pulsed around him, Meredith looked deeply into his eyes. Theirs was the most intimate connection she'd ever experienced, the most passionate she'd ever known. She wanted it to go on and on.

It did. Not even the toe-curling orgasm that shook her next could dispel the magic which seemed to surround them. Tony yelled aloud and quaked with his own release, and all Meredith could do was hold him close and marvel at the miracle that had just occurred.

She'd fallen in love. With someone who loved her back. Someone who thought she was wonderful, someone who smiled when he saw her, someone who lingered in bed with her long after their lovemaking was over. What were the odds of that?

Pretty damn slim.

About as slim, Meredith thought, as vulnerability being as safe to her as it suddenly felt. And yet, it did. She didn't know why she'd guarded against it for so long. If letting herself be vulnerable led to "trouble" like this . . . whoopee! Bring on more. She was ready for it.

After all, she had a lot of lost time to make up for.

Absolutely, positively . . . with Tony.

NINETEEN

"When a girl goes wrong . . . men go right after her."

— Mae West

Tony rolled over in bed next to Meredith, smiling, one forearm flung over his face against the brilliant sunlight pouring inside the trailer window. Loving her was going to kill him for sure. But what a way to go.

For days they'd been together. At his place. Her place. And on one (memorable) occasion, on the exotic, *Arabian Nights*-style set from *Love Ever After*. They spent the nights together, sneaking back to their individual trailers at sunrise. They talked and laughed, planned and reminisced, worked on the actor fantasy camp and spent as much time in each other's arms as possible.

There was nothing, Tony discovered, like being completely in sync — personally, professionally, sexually. For the first time in his life, he'd fallen crazily in love — and he'd fallen hard. Suddenly, with Meredith by his side, he felt ready to take on even the goofiest things. Hikes to the Hollywood sign. Dinners with his family. Even deep, meaningful conversations.

381

Meredith had changed him. With her courage, her intelligence, and her incredible lack of inhibition (he especially liked that last one), she made him see there was more for him than business success. More than another deal, another e-commerce innovation, another conquest.

Another Taryn. Another betrayal.

He told her about that, too. He hadn't meant to, but his guard had been down. It had all started with mind-blowing sex, followed by beers and a ball game on the tiny TV in his trailer . . . So who could blame him? When Meredith had turned to him with the requisite past-relationships question, Tony had blurted out the truth.

"Six serious girlfriends, starting with Cynthia Witt in third grade. I buried her shoes in the sand near the monkey bars."

"And that endeared you to her?"

"It was a symbolic gesture. I buried them right next to *my* shoes."

"Deep. Especially for an eight-year-old."

"Yeah. I was always ahead of my time." He chugged some beer, paused to watch a line drive to left field, then put his palm on her knee. He frowned, thinking. "After that, I played the field for a while. Scattered serious girlfriends, one live-in girlfriend —"

"I hope you'd at least made it to college by then."

"— and several flings. And no, I wasn't

382

shacking up in middle school. My parents were liberal, but not *that* liberal."

"Okay." She sounded like someone checking off a mental to-do list. They both paused to watch the next pitch; then Meredith turned to him again. "So you were a player from the get-go, then."

"Not necessarily. Women come on to *me*."

"I'll bet." She licked an imaginary pencil, then poised it over her hand as though it were a notepad. "Average relationship length?"

"What is this, a *Cosmo* quiz?"

He'd had a girlfriend — a fling, really — who'd loved subjecting him to those pieces of crap. By the end, he'd taken to choosing "C" almost exclusively. Inevitably, she was classified as a "sex-crazed diva who really knows what she wants. Favorite wardrobe item: red bustier."

"My average is six months," Meredith offered.

She chomped a potato chip, not the least bit deterred by his deliberately grouchy rebuttal. As inconvenient as it was, that was one thing he loved about her. She was fearless. She saw right through him — and wanted to be with him anyway.

"Six months is long enough to get to know someone," she continued, "but not quite long enough to get bored by them. *If* you choose carefully in the first place, that is."

383

He might as well give in. "Three years."

"Three years? Wow!" She felt his pulse. "Are you sure you didn't turn fifty without realizing it? Your commitment quotient is way too high for a young stud like yourself."

Tony didn't know whether to be mollified by her "stud" comment or miffed at her wiseass pulse-checking routine. He settled on putting down his beer . . . and ending the conversation. He was an action — not words — kind of guy.

Right now, his action of choice was to grab Meredith's thighs and tug her sideways on the narrow banquette. Potato chips flew everywhere. An instant later, Meredith was sprawled on her back beneath him. In the background, Bob Costas raved about a home run, but Tony's mind was focused on scoring of an altogether more interesting nature.

Slipping his hands beneath Meredith's shirt, he grinned. He loved the way she felt, all soft and warm and feminine. Her breasts were the loveliest he'd ever seen. They called for delicate treatment . . . and lots and lots of attention.

"Here," he said, settling in. He gazed at her from his conqueror's position atop her, his forearms propping him up. "Let me clarify things for you."

"Clarify things?"

She blinked innocently.

Her nipples hardened beneath his hand in

384

a not-so-innocent way.

"In the stud department," Tony explained seriously.

"Ahhh." She smiled.

One kiss led to two, two kisses led to four . . . four kisses led to an hour spent ignoring the baseball game while they invented new banquette positions. Afterward, Tony stretched and pulled Meredith into his arms, content that he'd asserted his mastery over studliness.

He nudged her onto his shoulder, then tucked her head into the special nook where she belonged. Drowsily, she curled up against him with one hand spread over his heart. The gesture felt right to him. Meredith did have his heart. In that moment, he knew he'd have done almost anything to make her happy. Even things that didn't involve sexual acrobatics and a lifetime supply of Reddi Wip.

That was true romance.

They lay that way for a long time. Tony stroked her hair, letting himself go. He felt Meredith's caring warm him, felt her trust in his grasp as surely as if it had been a fly ball in an outfielder's mitt. He felt her admiration and loyalty, steadfast and deep, and counted himself lucky to have found her when he had. She was a woman in a million.

Probably, that was why he knew he loved her.

Possibly, that was why he told her as much as he did.

"So . . . about the live-in girlfriend," she said, angling her head to look up at him. "Who was she? Did you love her? Were you going to get married?"

Taking a cue from her casual tone, Tony answered. Some women might have been bugged by discussing the past. Obviously, Meredith wasn't one of them.

"Her name was Taryn, I thought I did, and everybody believed we would. Yeah."

Meredith grew still. "Even you?"

He shrugged and changed the channel to ESPN. "For a while, I guess I did. We worked together, we lived together, we spent most of our time together — it seemed like a natural evolution."

A recap of the day's games was on. Dividing his attention between the score ticker and the sportscasters' reports, Tony scanned the TV. Absently, he squeezed Meredith's shoulder.

"Are you hungry? I could really go for one of those triple bacon cheeseburgers from the commissary."

Steely silence met his question.

He guessed she wasn't hungry. Exhaling, Tony pressed a kiss to the top of her head. He was glad Meredith liked sports. It was one more thing they had in common. One of the many things. He'd never felt happier with another woman.

"Wow, the Diamondbacks got shut out again," he said.

Now the silence felt deliberate. Ominous, even.

He backtracked, reviewing their conversation. Was it his burger suggestion?

"Have you become a vegetarian? Because I have to say, that's taking the whole fake starlet routine too far."

She rolled her eyes. Progress. Now he knew it wasn't a craving for Tofurkey that had made Meredith shut up. Tony tried again.

"Six months isn't such a lousy average relationship length," he told her with a reassuring hug. "Don't feel bad about it."

That did it.

"I don't, you lunkhead!"

Meredith wrenched from her nook. He felt bereft without her hand over his heart. She got up and started gathering her clothes. The fact that she was (gloriously) naked distracted him for a minute. Or two. Then . . .

"Is this about Taryn?"

His answer was the angry tug Meredith gave her Marley-style one-shoulder top as she pulled it over her head. She thrust her arm through the single sleeve, not looking at him.

It was *definitely* about Taryn. Jesus. The woman had been out of his life for years, and she was still screwing it up.

"You asked me! I thought you could handle it."

"Me, too."

Meredith zipped up her orange miniskirt. Picked up her handbag. Jabbed her feet into a pair of sequined flip-flops.

"Still boycotting the stilettos, huh?" he asked.

She looked as if she wanted a stiletto right now. To hurl at his head. Propping both hands on her hips, Meredith stared at him.

"Look. If what you had with Taryn" — she said the name as though it might skitter up her leg and sting her — "was so special you can't even talk about it, that's fine. It's better I know going in what I'm really up against."

"What you're up against?"

"Every guy has some dream woman in his past, some perfect girl who makes all the rest of us look like scum." Meredith paced, tossing her arms around as she spoke. "Obviously, Taryn" — again with the skittering, stinging thing — "is yours."

"Is *that* all this is?"

Her eyes bugged in surprise, then narrowed. Uh-oh.

Rapidly, Tony pushed off the banquette. He went to her, putting both hands on her shoulders. He gazed into her stubborn, defiant, beloved face, knowing he absolutely should *not* feel glad she was jealous of his ex. It was childish and stupid. But he couldn't help it. There it was.

"Taryn and I were business partners. We ran in the same crowds —"

"Supermodel crowds?"

He almost grinned. "No, dot-com crowds. In New York. I was new in town, Taryn was from an established family, she knew a lot of people . . . To make a long story short, we had a fling."

"A live-in fling." Suspicion clouded her features.

"Essentially. We were already spending a lot of time together. Rents were high. It was expedient. I was wary of mixing business with a relationship —"

"Sounds familiar." She crossed her arms.

"— and I was right. In the end, Taryn and I didn't want the same things."

"Two-point-two children and a wireless home network?"

Of *course* a wireless home network. What was this, the Stone Age? Shaking off the thought, Tony doggedly continued.

"So we split. Or I should say, *I* split. We broke up. I thought it was amicable . . . until she sabotaged all our joint business accounts. She told everyone I was from a famous Hollywood family and was just dabbling in e-commerce. She took credit for a few of my ideas, sold them as her own, and made a killing. She did everything she could to ruin me. She almost succeeded."

"I can't believe it," Meredith said indignantly, uncrossing her arms. "Doesn't anybody in New York have any sense? You're a dot-com whiz!"

He shook his head. "You're only as good as your latest deal. Taryn made sure I didn't have too many of those."

Meredith's muttered epithet made her opinion of his ex plain. Despite himself, Tony felt warmed by her loyalty.

"You're better off without her," she said.

"Believe me, I know. I trusted her with everything, and it was a mistake. A mistake it's taken the last several years to recover from."

Another dubious look. "She meant that much to you?"

"No, she wrecked my business that much." Patiently, he pulled Meredith closer, enfolding her in his arms. He rested his chin on the top of her head. "It took a while to rebuild, to find another partner, to come up to speed. Of course, then the dot-com boom went bust . . ."

Meredith squirmed — about to offer a rebuttal, Tony was sure. He paused, considering things. Right now, the woman in his arms probably didn't care very much about the economics of Internet retailing and all the rest of the things he usually spent 24/7 immersed in. He took another stab at explaining himself.

"So if you're worried I'm hanging on to

some long-lost mushy feelings about Taryn . . . don't be. The only emotion I have left for her is regret." He sighed, raising a hand to stroke Meredith's hair. "Even that's faded since I met you."

It was true, Tony realized. He didn't feel so hurt by Taryn anymore, didn't get pissed just thinking about the way she'd turned on him. Now, with the actor fantasy camp occupying his professional life — and Meredith sparking up his personal life — he had everything he'd ever wanted.

"So are we good?" he asked, hunching down to examine her face. "Everything settled? Ready for that triple bacon cheeseburger now?"

"Men," she grumbled, rolling her eyes good-naturedly. "You're all led by your stomachs."

Her smile told him they were square. "With me that's not strictly true. I'd say it's more of a seventy-thirty split."

"Seventy-thirty?" Meredith stepped backward to glance up at him, her mouth twitching with amusement. "What, seventy percent stomach and thirty percent . . . ?"

"*Thirty* percent stomach," Tony corrected. He took hold of her hand and guided it to the front of his jeans. "Seventy percent —"

"Ahhh. Of course." Seductively, she caressed him. Speculatively, she surveyed the results of that caress. "Hmmm, look at that.

A one hundred and twenty percent size increase."

"You've got a wicked head for numbers. Have I ever told you how much I love that about you? Brainy girls are the best."

"Yeah, we are. Don't you forget it."

Tony knew he never would. He also knew they were both wrong. Despite all the time they'd spent in bed, what had really led them here was one hundred percent love. Before too much more time went by, he intended to tell Meredith exactly that.

Maybe over that cheeseburger he'd mentioned . . .

Two days before the actor fantasy camp finale, Meredith hurried into the Valentine Studios business office, intent on finding Tony. Sappy as it was, being with him was the best part of her day. All during her hours spent masquerading as Marley, she looked forward to meeting him. This time, though, her visit was a surprise.

She'd already attended the usual round of rehearsals for the faux sitcom. After that, Meredith had taught one Diva Dramatics class, followed by one session of Star Schmoozing 101. All the camp guests were becoming remarkably adroit at behaving like real celebrities. One, she'd heard, had even demanded a dressing room stocked with San Pellegrino, sour Skittles, and gift certificates to a nearby Tan By Mist salon.

Meredith had never been so proud.

Her day hadn't ended there, though. She'd also kicked butt at a Pilates class, held an autographing session (this time, helping camp guests devise appropriately starlike scrawls), and attended a wardrobe fitting. She'd conducted a seminar on surviving beauty treatments — that one had felt particularly apt.

Then, finally, she'd absconded with a golf cart for an impromptu joy ride around the back lot with Salma, Inga, and Kim. They'd all been gratified to see Acajatuba receiving preliminary treatment from the set decorating department — in anticipation, they'd learned, of what everyone hoped would become the second session of actor fantasy camp.

That *had* to mean things were going well. Pleased with her part in that success, Meredith popped through the double doors in the Valentine Studios reception area. She waved to Penelope, who was on her way out with her purse and a Big Gulp in hand. A few more staffers rushed past, all of them carrying assorted purses, reports, and — in one case — a prop which needed repairing.

Calling out more good-byes, Meredith felt like a salmon swimming upstream — with a similarly single-minded objective. She grinned, keeping one eye on the office clock's five o'clock reading. Six minutes from now, the place would be deserted.

"Yoo-hoo! Marley! Oh, Marley!"

At the sound of a familiar feminine voice, Meredith skidded to a stop. Literally. She'd never get used to these damn high-heeled shoes. She still found stilettos too scary, but she had progressed to sturdy two-inch heeled sandals.

"What's the matter with you, dear?" Nadine asked, leaning out of a nearby conference room. Her omnipresent notebook computer yawned on the table behind her, casting flickers of light onto the chair she'd abandoned. "I called and called your name, but you just kept right on going."

Damn. It was so hard to remember to respond to *Marley*. "I'm sorry, Nadine. My head's in the clouds today."

"Probably because you're thinking about my nephew, aren't you?" Nadine's sweet, lined face brightened with a smile. "You two certainly seem to be hitting it off. Are you here to meet him?"

"Ummm . . ."

"It's okay, dear." Nadine waved off Meredith's hesitation. "You don't have to be shy with me. Why, a person would think you believe *I'm* that dastardly *Inside Hollywood* reporter."

She tittered. Meredith froze. *Was* Tony's aunt the mysterious *Insider* columnist? The reporter's identity had been discussed far and wide over the back lot, but no one had suggested Nadine. Even though she obviously possessed the know-how to e-mail scoop @insidehw.com at the drop of a hat.

"Yes, I . . . Tony and I have some things to discuss," Meredith hedged. "He's probably waiting —" She gestured toward the end of the hallway.

"Pish. Does a man good to wait. I want to show you something."

Eyes twinkling, Nadine led the way to her computer. She leaned over it, rapidly typing something. Then she clicked the mouse. A web page loaded onto her screen.

"Is this something about your Senior Citizen's Free Jell–O initiative?" Meredith asked, leaning closer. "Or is this a site for one of your e-mail groups? Hang on . . . this is —"

"Tony's company. I Googled the URL myself."

Meredith glanced at Nadine, impressed. Then she studied the Internet site for Tony's dot-com business, equally impressed. A few clicks told her he'd been too modest. The company looked very successful. She was relieved to notice that his partner, Jim Woodwiss, looked very trustworthy, too.

"Tony's the first in the family to strike out on his own," Nadine said. "Valentine men are notoriously independent, you know. But he's the one who's most demonstrated it."

At the note of affection in Nadine's voice, Meredith transferred her gaze from the screen to the older woman's face. What she saw there gave her pause.

"You're very proud of Tony, aren't you?"

"Of course! We all are." Nadine scrunched her nose as though the information should have been obvious. "He struck out on his own and he made it."

A small frown marred her features. "Of course, I do worry about him there in the big city. I've never been to New York, but it seems *so* impersonal. Valentine men don't do well without people they love nearby."

"Well, he's here in L.A. now," Meredith offered reassuringly. It was sweet of Nadine to worry about her nephew. "You don't have to worry about Tony anymore."

"I suppose you're right. At least for now. It's just that —" Nadine's computer dinged. Immediately, she perked up. "Whoops! That's Errol's special chirp. He must be IM-ing me from his new cell phone. He's a little reserved in person, but is that man ever a typing demon! The things he sends me . . ."

Distractedly, she examined the message. Meredith didn't need to be told twice to look away. This sounded *way* too personal for her to see. Nadine flushed, then snapped her notebook closed with a flourish.

"Well! That'll have to be continued elsewhere!" She fanned herself, giving Meredith a saucy smile. "Enjoy your meeting with Tony, dear. And remember — Valentine men are good for a lifetime! I'm certainly proof of that."

With a cheerful wave, Nadine skedaddled out of the conference room. A few seconds later, Meredith heard the reception area doors whoosh closed behind her. If Meredith was lucky, the coast was finally clear.

She cocked her head, listening. All around her, the powered-down office equipment hummed in its mechanical slumber. The air-conditioning whined, betraying its near-antique status. Driven by the cool current, a pink "while you were out" slip fluttered across the conference table.

What was she still doing here? Clearly, everyone was gone for the day — everyone except Tony. Smiling all over again, Meredith strode down the hallway to his office.

She found him working, typing something into his notebook computer. He swiveled in his midcentury modern office chair without looking up, then scanned a report on his desk. In Tony's masculine hands, the PDA he picked up next looked absurdly delicate. He frowned at it. Keyed in some data. Set it aside to examine something on another notebook computer propped on the opposite edge of the desk.

She loved watching him. He hadn't noticed her yet — thanks, probably, to the hands-free headset he was speaking into. He said a few words, leaned back in his chair, grinned at whatever the person on the other end of the line said. Geez, he was handsome. Charming, smart, innovative . . . Meredith couldn't get enough of him. In fact, ever since their official relationship talk, she'd felt more head over heels for him than ever.

She turned and shut the door. The tiny *snick* of the lock tumbling into place gave her a whole new shimmer of anticipation. Meredith turned.

"That sounds good," Tony said, raising a hand in greeting as he continued his conversation. He pressed a button to mute his headset. "This'll just take a minute," he promised.

"That's fine."

Arching her brow, Meredith strolled across the office. She paused at the window. The parking spaces reserved for Valentine Studios' office employees were empty. Behind her, Tony's voice rumbled on, talking about technical innovations, investors, and . . . apartment leases? She shut the blinds.

In the light filtering between their nearly flattened slats, Tony absently pulled the chain on his retro desk lamp. Squinting against its forty-five watts, he glanced up.

It was the moment Meredith had been waiting for. Holding his gaze, she untied the fabric belt on her close-fitting wrap dress. She shrugged and let her outfit fall to the floor.

Tony stared at her, eyes widening.

"Gotta run," he blurted into his headset. "We'll talk soon. Bye."

Wow. A Marley-style wardrobe *did* have its advantages, Meredith discovered. It was easy to get out of, for one thing. For another . . . For another she forgot as Tony's phone clattered onto the desk, spinning with the gratifying force of his movement. His hands-free headset followed in short order.

"Why, Miss Madison," he drawled, steepling his fingers like a hunky executive. "You're completely naked under that dress."

"Yes. I am. Good of you to notice."

"My pleasure."

Feeling a rush of purely feminine vitality, Meredith stretched her arms to the sides, as though shaking off the cares of a difficult day. Casually, she let them drop.

She looked Tony straight in the eye, a small grin on her lips. "I guess that observant streak of yours explains the enthusiastic smile you're wearing."

"Partly." His smoky gaze traveled over her body, touching all the places his hands, his mouth, his tongue had touched so many times before. "I'm also smiling because I know something you don't know."

"Oh? What's that?"

"The leather sofa over there unfolds into a *very* comfy bed." Tony stood. Slowly. As though anticipating what was to come . . . or being careful not to injure his one-hundred-

and-twenty-percent size increase. His smile widened. "Apparently, one of my Valentine predecessors fancied himself something of a ladies' man."

"The casting couch is real, then?"

"In your case . . . absolutely."

Smoothly, he moved them both to stand beside the worn leather sofa in question. It looked perfectly ordinary — like something out of a Pottery Barn catalog. But when Tony pressed a hidden switch with his foot. . . .

"Wow!" Meredith exclaimed as the furniture mechanically morphed itself into a bed. "Go, go, Gadget Bed!"

They laughed. Smiling, Tony pulled her into his arms.

"I hope you like expensive sheets," he said, nodding toward the immaculately made up sofa bed. "I slept here until I found other accommodations. I dropped an obscene amount of money on those sheets."

Was he kidding? Aside from so-called five-hundred-dollar nightgowns from Marley's closet, Meredith's only other indulgence was ultra-thread-count sheets.

"The way I see it," she mused, "a third of your life is *way* too great a quantity to spend with anything less than the best."

Tony framed her face with his palms. He gave her a tender look. Then he gave her a kiss.

"There's that math whiz stuff again. I knew you were perfect for me."

For the next hour and a half, Tony made it a point to show her exactly *how* perfect he thought they were together. And Meredith? She wasn't so much of a math whiz after all. She completely lost track of all the different reasons she loved him back. There were just too many to count.

TWENTY

"Edison's greatest marvel . . . the Vitascope! Pictures life size and full of color. Makes a thrilling show."
— advertisement for Vitascope motion
picture projector (1894)

It was hunger that finally roused them. Meredith stirred first, untangling herself from the sofa bed's sheets. She stretched out her arm in a languid movement and made contact with Tony.

Intimate contact.

"Mmmm," he murmured, blinking up at her from his neighboring pillow. "*Yeah*, right there."

She smiled. "I seem to have unerring aim."

"I love your aim. Love, love, love it. And lots of other things about you, too."

"Awww, Tony."

"It's true."

She believed him. *Love, love, love.* Looking at him now, Meredith realized that while Tony had said he loved things *about* her, he might just as well have said he loved *her*. Because that was the sentiment in his eyes, in his touch, in his smile.

She could hardly believe it. Most men were

notoriously closemouthed when it came to discussing their feelings. But Tony . . . Well, he clearly wasn't that way.

Of course, it might have been the sex hangover talking. But Meredith didn't think so. They'd connected on too deep a level to dismiss it now.

Should she tell Tony she loved him, too? The moment was right. Suddenly nervous, Meredith hesitated. She needed to compose herself first — not an easy task, especially while she still had one hand wrapped around the intriguingly warm, hard length of him.

After one more sensual stroke, she reluctantly released him. There'd be more time for that later. Right now, she had an announcement to make. Quickly, before she could lose her nerve, Meredith flopped onto her belly. She propped herself on her elbows and looked into Tony's eyes. She drew in a deep breath — which failed to calm her heartbeat even a little bit.

She was ready. *I love you,* she thought.

Before she could speak, Tony did.

"Your courage," he mused, his tone thoughtful. "That's one of the things I love about you. You're brave."

Okay, so maybe she could wait just a *few* seconds longer. Just long enough to find out all the other specifics he loved about her.

"You didn't want to do this whole Marley impersonation thing, but you did it," Tony continued. Fondly, he gazed into her eyes. He stroked her hair from her face, then tucked a lock of it behind her ear. "You kicked ass with it, too. I don't know what I would have done without you. This place wouldn't be gearing up for another actor fantasy camp session, that's for damn sure."

Inside, she beamed. Outside, she modestly shrugged one shoulder. "I'm just happy it worked."

"Worked? It's been phenomenal."

Meredith remembered her closetful of stilettos, her history of flubbed lines, her Pilates disaster. Boob Guy. The faux press junket interview with Harry and the awful tabloid reports in *Inside Hollywood*.

"It's had its rocky moments," she admitted.

"Sure. But you hung in there. And now . . ." Tony paused, his eyes searching her face. In his expression, she glimpsed wonder. Contentment. Gratitude. "Now you've nailed it. I'm proud of you. Hell, even the *real* Marley will be amazed when she gets a load of you."

Meredith waved off his assertion. "She'll never see me this way. Trust me. My sister would have a heart attack if she knew I put on so much as a swipe of lipstick, much less full-on makeup and a killer wardrobe. By the time I get back, I'll have shed every particle of this experience."

She caught Tony's odd expression and hurried to squeeze his arm. "Except you, of course. I'm hanging on to you for as long as possible."

His features still didn't relax. Maybe he'd just realized exactly how momentous the words he'd said to her were . . . and was wondering where the return sentiment was.

It was her perfect opening. She'd been yearning to tell Tony how she felt. Now she could say it. Now, before they got off track — or headed to the commissary for that triple bacon cheeseburger he'd mentioned so long ago. Feeling vulnerable and nervous — and yes, wildly excited — Meredith took his hand.

I love you, she thought. *Say it. Just say it!*

Tony gave her a puzzled frown. "No. I mean, Marley will be amazed when she sees you *here*," he said. "At the finale."

"What are you talking about? Marley won't be at the finale."

"Sure, she will. Along with the rest of your family. I was just reviewing the guest list on my PC when you came in." He squinted, re-membering. "Your parents, Imogene and Frank Madison. Your sister, of course. We'll have to arrange a low-key entrance for her. Maybe your Dodgers cap and a pair of sun-glasses, right? She can pretend to be you, for a change." He grinned, obviously excited as he anticipated a successful finale. "And Marley's new husband, of course. Jake . . ."

"Jarvis," Meredith supplied woodenly when he paused. "Jake Jarvis and his son, Noah."

Tony snapped his fingers. "Yeah, that's it. Jake Jarvis and your new nephew, Noah." Smiling, he gave her a quick kiss. "Leave it to my own personal genius to come up with the right answer."

Her whole family was coming to the finale.

Frozen by the thought, Meredith stilled. Her hands felt numb. Her heart seemed to have stuttered to a stop. Even her brain locked up for a minute. Blithely, Tony went on talking.

He yammered on about how fortunate it was that Marley and Jake were returning from their honeymoon right before the finale. About how confirmations had already come in. About how stunned the Madisons would be to witness Meredith's transformation.

"They might not even recognize you at first," he said, looking pleased. "*That's* how well you've done. You're a big hit, Meredith. I can't wait to see their faces when they get a look at you on set, performing."

Apparently, he had no idea how devastating this news was to her. She failed to see how he couldn't.

Okay, don't panic, she told herself. *Gather more information.* Her knack for analysis had never failed her before.

"I thought only actor fantasy camp guests were coming to the finale," Meredith said with a weird sense of detachment. "Drama actors to the sitcom taping, musical performers to the one-hour drama taping, sitcom people to the variety show taping, et cetera."

"They are," Tony agreed. "All the camp guests are invited to the tapings and the party afterward. But everyone's allowed to invite personal guests, too. Our soundstages have seating for lots of people."

"But — but — *I* didn't invite anyone!"

"Sure, you did." Again with the bewildered look. "As part of your initial paperwork. Remember? You filled out the personality profile, the permission forms and waivers, the emergency contact information, the guest list questionnaire . . ."

He kept talking, but Meredith couldn't listen. With a surge of dread, she remembered completing that paperwork. At the time, Valentine Studios' actor fantasy camp had been a lark; staying until the finale had seemed a remote possibility at best. She'd dutifully listed her family members as potential attendees, just like the form had suggested, and then hadn't given it a second thought.

Her whole family was coming to the finale.

A rerun of her mortifying childhood soliloquy popped into her head. Only this time it happened beneath the bright lights of a sitcom set. Hundreds of people witnessed it.

Including those people whose opinions meant most to her.

Meredith nearly groaned aloud.

"I don't want anyone to come!" she blurted.

"It's too late. Penelope already sent the invitations. Didn't you hear me? Everyone's already confirmed."

Confirmed. Someone on Marley's "team" — her personal assistant, Candace, probably — must have intercepted the Valentine Studios invitation and relayed it to Marley. Just as Marley's last-minute instructions had stipulated. Why, oh, why, did she have to have such an efficient staff? After all, her "house-sitter" had been playing hooky for almost two weeks now.

Reassuringly, Tony patted Meredith's hand. "Don't worry. All actors are nervous about performing. You'll feel better once you're actually on set."

She felt leaden with dread. Like a person in one of those dreams where it's only possible to move in slow motion. She'd spent her whole life building an anti-Marley façade, trying to distinguish herself by being different. Trying to pretend she didn't want any part of her sister's fame. Now her entire charade would crumble in a single night.

Her whole family was coming to the finale.

Tony caressed her cheek, turning her face to his on the pillow. As soon as he caught her wide-eyed, petrified gaze, he gave a gentle smile.

"You look like I just suggested tap-dancing in a chicken suit on 'American Idol.' Relax. You'll be terrific. I probably haven't told you this before, but Marley's not the only actress in the family."

Oh, yes. She was. Meredith knew that. Marley might as well have been the only *daughter* in the family, so brightly did her personal spotlight shine. Meredith would be insane to try to compete. That's why she never had.

Couldn't Tony see that? He knew about her anti-Marley routine. He knew *her*. What was wrong with him?

Suddenly, being naked felt way too vulnerable. Meredith got up, dragging an armload of sheet to cover herself with.

"I won't do it," she said in the most reasonable voice she could muster. Wringing her hands, she paced around the silent office. "I just . . . won't do it. You'll have to run the sitcom taping without me."

She glanced at him, hoping for confirmation. Tony gawked at her, dark and brawny against the pristine sheets. God, he looked terrific. *Was* terrific, ordinarily. Desperately, she averted her eyes. Grabbed her cast-off wrap dress. She was stupid, *stupid* to have gotten into this mess. . . .

"Without you?" he asked, befuddled.

409

"You're the star! We're not doing it without you."

She couldn't speak. Couldn't explain, couldn't be rational, couldn't get past the terror of what he'd proposed. Couldn't find her shoes.

Tony continued. Confusion sounded plain in his voice.

"Look, nerves I can understand," he said. "I've been involved in showbiz all my life. You acting types get tense before a performance. But ditching the whole taping —"

" 'Acting types'? I'm *not* an acting type!" How could they have spent so much time together and still seen that one significant detail escape his notice? "I'm . . . just me."

"You," he said confidently, "are going to be terrific."

"No." She shook her head. The whole idea terrified her. "I'm not. Because I'm not going to do it."

"You have to do it. Contractually."

Meredith wheeled sideways, a sandal in her hand. She felt her mouth drop open in astonishment.

" 'Contractually'?" He could not be serious.

"Okay, not contractually. Not technically. We both know your sister's agreement doesn't apply to you. But the spirit of that contract, of our agreement —"

"Does not involve wholesale personal hu-

410

miliation. At least it didn't the last time I checked."

For a long moment, Tony only stared at her. She could see the bafflement in his face, could feel him trying to make sense of her refusal. That only upset her more.

They'd *connected.* They'd fallen in love! Didn't he understand her better than this? Didn't he know that performing on set while the people she loved laughed at her — or worse, pitied her — would be her worst nightmare come true?

"Of course it doesn't." He'd adopted his e-commerce voice, the same one she'd heard on the phone. *Let's be reasonable,* his tone said. *We can work this out.* "But still, there is a contract to be fulfilled. If you won't do it —"

"Are you threatening me?"

"I wouldn't call it a threat."

But Meredith would. She certainly *felt* threatened. By the look in Tony's eyes, the disappointment at the edge of his expression . . . the possibility he really didn't understand her at all.

Wanting to deny what was right in front of her face, Meredith reconsidered. Maybe she could do it. She'd been practicing. She knew her lines backward and forward, knew how to hit her mark, knew what clothes to wear and (almost) how to tease her hair into that sexy style Salma had created. Thanks to all the effort she'd expended, the entire actor fantasy camp believed she was Marley.

But her family knew the truth. Marley *definitely* knew the truth. It was bad enough that Meredith would have to come clean about swiping that Valentine Studios "fantasy of a lifetime" invitation in the first place. Did she have to add complete mortification to the package, too?

Briefly, she closed her eyes. She pictured the scene: Her family, in the front row. Her tomboy self, pretending to be sexy and feminine and talented. Pretending to be someone special, like Marley . . . pretending to be a star.

No. She couldn't do it.

"Okay," Tony said in a gentler tone, still watching her from the sofa bed. He waited as she jammed one shoe on her foot and then searched for its mate. "No threats. How about this? I'm asking. Please perform in the finale. For me."

"No," Meredith said. "No. I'm sorry."

"You're *sorry?*"

His disbelieving tone followed her as she put on her other shoe, untwisted its strap, blinked through a haze of tears to retie her dress's slipping self-belt.

The damn thing wouldn't cooperate. Just like her stupid heart. It persisted in believing she must be wrong about him. Tony did understand her. Any minute now, he'd tell her that. He'd pull her into his arms and her crookedly tied belt wouldn't matter because her dress would be coming off again soon. He'd love her. Everything would be okay. Any minute now.

Except Tony didn't do any of those things.

"Yes, I'm sorry," Meredith croaked out, not trusting herself to elaborate. "I just can't do it."

Disbelief emanated from him. "Not even if I ask you to?"

Especially if you ask me to, she thought.

"If you understood the real me," she managed, "if you cared about me at all . . . you'd never ask me to do this."

Then she opened the office door and slipped outside, desperate to get away.

Tony gaped across the room, at the office doorway through which Meredith had just left. He glanced at the crumpled sheet she'd abandoned on the edge of the sofa bed, took in the pillow where she'd laid her head to receive his kiss less than an hour ago.

If you understood the real me — if you cared about me at all — you'd never ask me to do this.

Of everything she'd said, that demanded a rebuttal the most. The notion that he didn't understand her was admittedly likely. He was a man, she was a woman — confusion was bound to result. Right now, for instance, he was befuddled as hell. But to suggest that he didn't care about her . . . now *that* pissed him off.

He threw off the sheets. He caught up to her just as she passed the office's kitchen-slash-copy-room.

"If you cared about *me*," Tony said, grabbing her by the arm, "you would never refuse!"

"What?" she demanded.

Turning, she whipped her gaze over him. Belatedly, he remembered he was still naked. Obstinately, he didn't care. The office was deserted anyway. Besides, in his current mood, he'd probably deck anybody who dared to confront him about it.

"I've worked my ass off to make this actor fantasy camp a success," he said, feeling himself shake with pent-up emotion. "To make the studio turn a profit, however I could. Now you come along, refusing to finish the job on a *whim?*"

"It's not a whim."

He paced, unable to believe it. Meredith stood in the hallway, one hand on her hip. Her eyes were red-rimmed, her posture as hunched and protective as it had been on the night of the welcome party. Clearly, she felt she was the wronged one.

"It's not a whim," she repeated.

"Then I'd like to know what it is. Because from where I'm standing, it looks a

414

lot like blowing me off."

That hurt. It hurt more than Tony could believe. Damn it, Meredith *knew* how much making a success of the studio meant to him. To his life. She knew how hard he'd worked, how much of himself he'd invested, how many promises he'd made. She knew this was the key to proving he wasn't just another Valentine.

She didn't care. She didn't care about him or the two of them together. Didn't care enough, despite everything — he'd thought — they'd shared.

What a sucker he'd been. Again. He'd broken his rule against mixing business with emotions, and it looked like now he'd have to pay the price: another failed venture . . . another failed love affair.

He wanted to break something, punch something, throw back his head and howl. How could Meredith just *stand* there? Tony stalked to her, staring her down, needing to get some reaction — any reaction — out of her.

"You've mastered your starlet routine a little too well, princess. Now you're every bit as egocentric as your famous sister. Twice as flighty, too. At least with Marley I would have expected this. You took me by surprise."

And how. Furious, he looked down at the crooked part in her hair. He couldn't believe Meredith was submitting to this so meekly, with her head down and her mouth shut. Where were all her snappy comebacks? Her karate kicks? Her wiseass comments?

He guessed she reserved those for people she didn't plan to stab in the back. Unbeknownst to him, he'd just been booted into the pile marked Men To Betray Today.

He waited, hoping like an idiot for an explanation. Any explanation besides the one screaming through his head — that she didn't care. That she'd used him for sex or companionship or hell — he didn't know — maybe just for plain old amusement.

Finally she raised her face to his. Everything inside him stilled, waiting for Meredith to say that she hadn't meant any of it. That of course she was doing the finale. That she knew how much he was depending on her performance there to impress his investors, and that their whole argument tonight had been some colossal, badly timed joke.

She remained silent . . . but her eyes shimmered with tears.

At the sight, something inside him softened. Deliberately, Tony hardened himself against it. Unlike honesty, feminine subterfuge was cheap — but he wasn't buying it. Taryn had cried, too — right before she'd tried to ruin him. Now it looked as though Meredith was doing the same thing.

"What's your game?" he goaded, too frustrated to think about what he was doing. All he knew was that he needed her. "Are you trying to sabotage me? To blackmail me into staying here in L.A.? Because you knew going in I never intended to stick around."

That did it.

"You're leaving?" Meredith's lips quivered.

He couldn't believe she had the gall to pretend to be surprised.

"You know I never meant to stay. Why would I? Blowing off my dot-com business for this" — he gestured around himself at the studio offices — "would make me just another sloppily sentimental, family-before-business failure like the rest of the Valentines. Wouldn't it?"

"You don't see them that way," she protested softly.

Damned if he didn't. Weirdly enough, he couldn't say so out loud. Fisting his hand, Tony paced again.

I won't let you down, he remembered her saying. *I promise.*

It looked like her idea of a promise meshed perfectly with her idea of giving a damn. Both lasted only as long as they were convenient.

"I'm going back to New York," he said. "But first I'm seeing this through." He stopped in front of her, willing her to change back into the person he knew. Willing her to love him. "For better or worse, you're the star of this thing. *You're* the one people are coming to see —"

"You mean Marley's the one they're coming to see."

He waved off her assertion. "Same thing."

The minute the words left his mouth, he knew they were a mistake. Meredith's eyes narrowed, and her whole face flushed.

"I'm *not* the same as my sister."

"More's the pity. Maybe *she'd* keep her word."

"Maybe *she'd* tell you to f—"

Tony held up his hand to cut off the obscenity he knew was coming. "Uh-uh, princess. Hollywood starlets don't swear."

Her eyes transmitted the sentiment just as surely as the words themselves would have. He'd hurt her, Tony knew. He guessed that made them even.

"I want you to keep your word. Appear at the finale."

"I'm sorry." She straightened. Clear-eyed now, she kept her voice subdued and certain. "I can't."

She meant she wouldn't. He knew it. Her refusal, soft-spoken as it was, cut him to the quick. Meredith knew what she was doing, and it felt like nothing so much as a betrayal. She didn't understand him, didn't love him, at all.

"Get out, then."

Her eyes widened. Tears brimmed in their depths, but this time Tony looked away before they could affect him . . . much.

"Stop pretending," he rasped. "Stop pretending you —"

"I thought it was more than that!"

"— care about me, and just *get out*."

"It was real," she said.

He'd have sworn he heard pleading in her voice. It had to be a trick — a trick of the heart, designed to keep him confused. Designed to make him play the fool until he had nothing left to lose at all. How long would it take to rebuild his life again? A year, two? Five? He didn't want to do it. Determinedly, Tony turned away.

"Just go."

Meredith touched his arm. "Tony . . . I never meant to hurt you. You must know that. If there was another way —"

"Give me what I need."

Tentatively, her hand fluttered. After a heartbeat, it moved away. She lowered it to her side, empty.

"I thought so," he said. He glanced over his shoulder, giving her the cruelest smile he could muster. For some reason, though, it only made him ache all the more. "Don't forget to phone in an *Insider* scoop on your way out. You might as well finish the job. I've never known you to do anything halfway."

She sucked in a breath, but Tony couldn't take any more. He wasn't sticking around for more heartache. He strode down the hallway, hungry for the solitude his office promised. He'd just reached it when Meredith's voice carried to him.

"Nope, nothing halfway," she confirmed, her words a hoarse whisper. "Not even loving you."

He paused with his hand on the doorjamb, his heartbeat thudding with the impact of her words. Then he realized he was about to weaken, all over again.

"Damn, you smart girls are heartbreakers," Tony said, and shut his office door.

TWENTY-ONE

"Fasten your seat belts. It's going to be a bumpy night."

— Bette Davis

Meredith didn't sleep at all that night. She tossed and turned in her lonesome pink bed, alternately blowing her nose and swiping away tears. They dribbled into her ears, onto her pillow, into the corners of her heart, until she knew she couldn't possibly contain any more. And yet . . . she did.

Tony didn't love her. How could he? He didn't really *know* her. Despite everything they'd been through, he hadn't cared enough to realize the changes she'd made as Marley's stand-in were temporary — the real her was underneath. The real her was overlooked. The real her was scared.

The real her was lonely.

At sunrise she dragged herself from her bed's nest of tattered tissues, kicking aside an empty box as she made her way to the bathroom. She switched on the light and looked in the mirror. Those dark circles wouldn't have dared to appear on Marley's face; those spotty red blotches wouldn't have had the temerity to mar her sister's cheeks. Meredith sighed.

Just more proof she wasn't cut out for this. And never had been.

By rights, Meredith knew she probably should have left Valentine Studios last night. She should have packed up her things, reverted to her trusty cargo pants, museum T-shirt, and hip-tied sweatshirt, plunked on her Pumas and made tracks back to her own low-rent neighborhood. She hadn't been able to muster the energy, though. Maybe a part of her was still in denial. Maybe a part of her still believed in Tony.

Yeah, right, she told herself as she left the bathroom. Dispiritedly, she scraped the clothes hangers across her closet, looking for something to wear. *The gullible part.* The part that had actually believed he might be her Prince Charming, come to sweep a certain punk-historian Cinderella off her feet.

Things like that happened only in fairy tales. In real life Cindy got dumped, the prince took off after a busty blonde, and the wicked stepsisters launched a successful reality TV show based on the whole saga. In real life, true love never conquered all.

So how come she was still gullible enough to hope it would?

With another sigh, Meredith got dressed in a brilliant yellow skirt, wildly patterned top ("Inspired by Versace," Erin had confided), and low-heeled ankle boots. She did her hair and makeup by rote, trying not to wince as she applied eyeliner to her puffy, bloodshot eyes. She still had classes to teach. If nothing else, she didn't want to let down her actor fantasy camp students.

Won't bailing on the finale let them down? a part of her jabbed.

Meredith frowned and pushed the thought aside. For her role on the faux sitcom there was an understudy of sorts — a camp guest, Eve, who looked a little like her and whose job it was to serve as stand-in while the lighting and camera crews set up. Eve knew "Marley's" lines, too. With a little advance notice, Meredith figured Eve could handle starring in the sitcom.

Heck, she'd probably enjoy it! It would be Eve's turn in the spotlight, her chance to shine. Wasn't that what every understudy wanted?

By the time Meredith grabbed her handbag and headed outside to her golf cart, she'd convinced herself. She'd be doing everyone a favor by not appearing at the finale tomorrow. In the meantime, she'd just have to do her best to avoid Tony.

She could get through this. She had to. Her pride — and her sense of obligation to her friends at the studio — demanded it. Once she had, Meredith promised herself, she'd retreat to her own life with its books and its dust and its take-out Kung Pao chicken for one, and she'd never look back.

At least . . . not too often, she wouldn't. If she could help it.

Tony strode through the back lot the morning after his argument with Meredith, cooling down from his run. Driven by anger and frustration and disappointment, he'd pushed himself harder than usual. Now he dripped with sweat. Breathed like an old man. Hurt like the victim of a runaway truck.

None of that had to do with the exertion he'd just put himself through. All of it had to do with Meredith. With Meredith, and the way she'd wrenched out his damned heart and stomped all over it. Jesus, but he should have known better.

Moving onward, Tony felt his quadriceps ache in protest. On either side of him, camp guests and staffers parted like waves at the prow of a particularly big and pissed-off boat, scuttling to the side to get out of his way. He glowered as he passed them, too torn up inside to muster a smile.

It would only be a false one anyway.

False, like Meredith's feelings for him.

Hell. He'd thought she was better than that. Stronger. He'd thought she was different. All last night Tony had replayed their argument in his head, only to come to the same conclusions. If Meredith didn't believe in him, he couldn't believe in her. Couldn't believe she loved him the way she'd claimed to.

Nothing halfway. Not even loving you.

He'd be a moron to buy into it. The five and a half hours he'd spent last night sleeplessly surfing through infomercials, C-SPAN, and ESPN — not comprehending any of it — hadn't changed his mind. The only thing left for him now was to finish what he'd come to L.A. to do: save Valentine Studios. He'd made promises. He intended to keep them.

He intended to prove himself, as much as he ever had.

What else did he have left?

Shaking out his tense shoulders and arms, Tony kept going. He surveyed the studio back lot as he moved through it, needing to feel the pride, the determination, the *excitement* that had fueled him until this point.

He breathed deeply of the sawdust in Tumbleweed and the fresh jungle green paint in Acajatuba. Squinted against the glare of sparkling windows in a rejuvenated Bayberry. Ran his hand along the sham brownstone stoops in little New York and skimmed his fingertips over the engraved brass plaques at the entrances to every soundstage he passed.

He remembered loving all those things. But in defiance of reason and past experience alike, no excitement gripped him today. No sense of urgency compelled him to work harder, harder, *harder*. Instead, a weird sense of unreality stole over Tony as he made his way back to his trailer. All around him, the studio bustled with activity and life . . . but none of it had ever felt more artificial.

How had he never noticed how insubstantial all this was? How fleeting? Valentine Studios was the perfect Tinseltown illusion. The people buzzing around it didn't seem to realize it, but that didn't change the truth. The place was all appearance with no substance behind it, all activity and movement with no basis in reality.

Just like his relationship with Meredith.

Even calling it that — a *relationship* — was ludicrous. Like going on-line with an ancient, 9600-baud modem and calling it web browsing. Or booting up a circa 1996 PC and expecting it to perform as anything more than a bulky doorstop.

Time had moved on. Tony had to, too.

He should have called in a replacement for Meredith last night. Should have begun strategizing, laying groundwork for her eventual no-show at the finale tomorrow. Doing damage control, the same way he'd have had to if her real identity had become known, thanks to those *Insider* columns. Tony hadn't been able to muster the energy, though. Maybe a part of him didn't want to accept reality. Maybe a part of him still believed in Meredith.

Yeah, right, Tony told himself. He crashed up his trailer's steps and slammed inside. Within minutes, he stood beneath the shower spray, feeling hollow and bereft. *The gullible part.* The part of him that had actually believed he might have found a woman who'd stand by him. Who'd believe in him, renowned Valentine or not. Who'd help him, partner with him, *love him.*

Things like that happened only in sappy chick-flick movies. In real life, girlfriends turned on you, families performed useless acts of charity in hiring you, companies went on in your absence as though you were never needed to run them at all.

Reminded of that, Tony stepped out of the shower with a frown. He toweled off. After his last e-mail from Jim Woodwiss, Tony had realized exactly how efficiently his partner had been operating the business. He'd begun considering the logistics of dividing his time between the coasts, merging both halves of his life — East Coast realism and West Coast razzle-dazzle. Business and pleasure.

Tony had even gone so far as to consult a realtor about leasing an apartment here in L.A. — the better to keep an eye on the studio. The better to be close to Meredith. The better to love her and find out if they could have a future together.

Of course, that had been before he'd realized her feelings for him were just another acting-and-artifice illusion. Before he'd known that she'd let him down. Before he'd remembered that in real life, true love never conquered all.

Too bad he was still gullible enough to hope it would.

Damn. With a fierce yank at the clothes in his trailer's closet, Tony grabbed a suit and shirt from their hangers. After he'd dressed, he plucked a tie from its place and draped it around his neck. No point in continuing to loosen up. Before very long he'd be back in New York, the way he'd initially planned — the way he'd told Meredith he would be. There was nothing here for him to stay for.

Not now. From the looks of things, not ever.

He only wished the prospect of returning to dot-com networking, his austere, modern apartment, and the usual take-out Kung Pao chicken for one sounded more appealing. It had suited him in the past. Now Tony was changed.

Now he'd given his heart away. No matter how hard he tried, he didn't seem able to reclaim it, either. It was firmly in Meredith's grasp.

Maybe, he thought as he headed for the business office to make phone calls, it always would be.

Or maybe he could go on without it. Given the job that remained to be done, that looked like Tony's only hope. Steeling himself for encounters with Meredith, confrontations with his uncles, and all the other problems which awaited him, Tony drove toward his office. It was past time to move on.

Grabbing a moment between her Tabloid Tattling class and her usual Pilates session, Meredith hunched into the passageway that divided the exercise room from the studio swimming pool. She cradled her cell phone to her ear.

On the other end of the line, her best friend Leslie's voice brought a welcome wave of relief. It was so good to hear the rational sound of someone from her *real* life — not the false one she'd been carrying on these past two weeks.

"I don't know, Meredith," Leslie was saying, backed up by the faint strains of the classical music the museum favored as background ambiance. "Maybe you should consider doing it. The finale, I mean. It would be good for you to stretch yourself a little."

"What are you, nuts? The finale?" Meredith shuddered. "Hel-lo, shades of the soliloquy fiasco."

"Come on." Leslie chuckled. "You were what — twelve years old when that happened? You've grown up since then. Besides, you said everyone there believes you're Marley. What's the risk?"

Did she have to repeat herself? Clutching the phone more tightly, Meredith closed her eyes. They'd already been over this during the first twenty minutes of their heart-to-heart. But she guessed Leslie hadn't gotten it.

"The risk," Meredith said again, "is my —"

"Parents, I know. And Marley, too. You told me. But honestly, they'll love you no matter what. That's what families are for."

"Not my family."

Leslie exhaled in obvious skepticism. "I've spent innumerable dinners, sleepovers, and homework sessions at your house, remember? I spent Christmas there the year we went off to college and my parents got divorced. I know your family."

Not like Meredith did, she didn't.

"Besides, I don't think that's what's bugging you," Leslie continued. "I think it's the guy — Tony — who's bugging you."

At the mention of his name, a lead weight of sadness pooled in Meredith's belly. She'd felt queasy all morning, a wreck of sleeplessness, heartache, and nerves. She couldn't speak.

But her best friend was never at a loss for words.

"You've already survived your family's reaction to You as Performer. And you've already staked your claim to non-Marley-hood. Right? So I think what's really got you freaking out here is that you're mad."

"Mad?" The idea was idiotic. "At whom?"

"Tony, of course."

Meredith froze. Then she scoffed. "Yeah, right."

Undeterred, Leslie shifted the phone. Through the receiver, Meredith heard the familiar jumble of museum Mozart, exhibits being erected, and screaming school groups. A powerful wave of homesickness washed over her. She wanted to be back there in her own life, where things were predictable and happened exactly the way she'd constructed them to.

Where a manicure wasn't needed to prove your point and combat boots were acceptable attire.

"You're mad because Tony still wants you to be like Marley," Leslie said, scholarly patience in her voice. "You want him to accept you the way you are. Cargo pants, hat head, thunder thighs, and all."

At that last, Meredith smiled faintly. She and Leslie shared their phobia about baring any body parts south of the waist. They owned identical baggy surfer-boy shorts for the beach, bonded over dressing rooms filled with pants whose waistbands gaped if the hips fit, complained with equal fervor over J-Lo's ballyhooed booty — which they both swore had shrunk drastically, a betrayal to pear-shaped women everywhere.

Unbidden, a memory zipped into Meredith's mind. Her, standing in her star trailer wearing only a bra and panties. Tony, admiring every curve of her naked form.

"I thought he *did* accept me the way I am."

"Then what's the problem?"

"He didn't." Uncomfortably, Meredith wiggled in her nook. She pressed her back against the pale mauve wall and propped her feet on the glass facing the pool area. Inside it, camp guests frolicked in the azure water. "Tony thinks I'm someone who wears lipstick and miniskirts. Someone who wouldn't leave home without her push-up miracle bra. Someone who understands what 'teasing' means."

"Well . . . aren't you? After all this?"

"No!"

Leslie gave a disbelieving sound. "Not even a little bit?"

Prodded by her friend's insistence, Meredith glanced down at herself. At her yellow skirt and the hint of cleavage bared by her "Versace inspired" shirt. She did kind of like this get-up. Absently, she raised her hand to her shampoo-commercial-worthy hairstyle. Another surge of unease filled her. Staunchly, she tamped it down.

"This stuff is all temporary," she assured Leslie. "It's not me at all."

Silence carried down the line. Then, "It could be."

"Not you, too!" Meredith shook her head, filled with indignation. "It was bad enough when my sister was constantly trying to make me over. Now you're getting in on the act, too? What next? A stiletto intervention?"

"Calm down. I'm sorry. I'm not trying to make you over." Leslie sighed. "I just . . . I just think you might be selling yourself short. There's more to you than cynicism, cargo pants, and an aversion to combing your hair."

"Har, har. Very funny."

"I'm serious."

Meredith went quiet. This wasn't the kind of support she'd phoned Leslie to find. Didn't anyone understand her anymore?

Maybe you don't understand yourself, that pesky part of her piped up. *Maybe that's the problem.*

"Look, I'd better go. Thanks for the pep talk."

"Come on, Meredith. I didn't mean to make you mad. I'm sorry." A pause. "Do you want to talk some more?"

"Okay." Deliberately, she lightened her tone. "How's that new Alka-Seltzer ad exhibit coming along?"

"Fine. Don't talk to me, then. I've only been your best friend since we swore an oath on Strawberry Shortcake to never kiss a boy."

Meredith rolled her eyes, feeling her mood

lighten. "Umm, I have a confession to make . . ."

Leslie laughed. "Me, too. Although not recently. Finding a worthy single man while working in a museum is like going fishing for sharks in a pond full of geriatric goldfish."

"That's for sure."

Smiling, Meredith relaxed her grip on the phone. Men might let a girl down, but good friends never would.

"So . . ." Leslie continued, a quirky catch in her voice. "Got an extra invite for that finale thing? I'd like to see you perform, too."

Putting her head in her hands, Meredith groaned. It was official. The whole world had gone crazy.

Tony stood backstage at the Valentine Studios sitcom set, crew members moving lights and scrims and cameras all around him. The bustle was comfortable. The terror in the eyes of the woman he'd been talking with was not.

Eve, Meredith's stand-in, had just learned she might be the star of the show during the finale. Now she looked as if she might keel over at any second. She clutched her throat and stared at him with eyes gone big, the most petrified vacationer the state of Texas had ever unleashed.

"I never thought I'd actually have to *perform!*" she said in her honeyed drawl. "I just wanted to see what it was like on set. As Marley's stand-in, all I had to do was be about the same size as her and have the same color hair" — she held up a brunette hank in demonstration — "and that was it! I'll admit, it was enough to make me something of a celebrity back home in Amarillo, especially after everybody got a load of those *Inside Hollywood* articles. But *performing* . . . I just don't know."

"Calm down," Tony told her. "You'll be fine."

"I don't know. I just don't know." Eve wrung her hands, glancing nervously toward the set. "I mean, I learned some of Marley's lines — I couldn't help but pick up on them, seeing as how I watched the rehearsals every day. But to actually say them in front of an audience! Why, I think I'd be too nervous."

"All actors are nervous. Don't worry."

Eve leaned forward. "I'm very worried," she confided.

He gave her what he hoped was a reassuring smile. Tony couldn't be sure. He'd practiced the same move on a wardrobe girl on the way over here, and she'd crossed herself.

It could be that his heartache still showed on his face. He sure as hell *felt* like the walking dead. But since Eve hadn't yet whipped out a garland of garlic and a crucifix, he figured he was okay.

435

"If you forget your lines," he said, "just read them from the TelePrompTer."

"TelePrompTer?" Eve blinked, then squinted toward the set.

Gently, Tony turned her by the shoulders until she directly faced the unit attached to a nearby camera. The whole works stood shoulder-high. She couldn't possibly miss it.

Eve shook her head. "What TelePrompTer?"

"It's right there." He pointed. "See?"

"Oh, well. That's the problem, then." With a bright, apologetic smile, Eve glanced over her shoulder at him. "Unless something's smack in front of my face, I can't see it. I'm just about as blind as a bullfrog without my glasses."

"Maybe you could put them on, then."

Her mouth dropped open. "On TV? Heck, no! I don't want to be captured on that souvenir videotape for all posterity with my glasses on." Decisively, Eve squinted harder. "Don't worry, I see it now. I can read it."

Mumbling something, she moved forward. Then she moved a little closer. Closer still.

"There. That's perfect," Eve said.

"Hey, watch it!" the camera operator protested, leaning sideways. "Your nose almost smudged my lens."

He looked at Tony for help. Tony squeezed his eyes shut and shook his head. The finale was doomed. That was all there was to it.

★ ★ ★

"Mom . . . Mom, listen to me," Meredith said, urgently speaking into her cell phone. She'd finished her Pilates class and, freshly showered, was crossing the back lot on her way to a session of Diva Dramatics (today: handling the *de rigueur* pint-sized "sooo cute!" pooch and all its accessories). "I don't have time to talk about your Rubber 'N Me fashion design class. I have a problem!"

"Well, now, I don't doubt you have a problem, with an attitude like that, young lady." Imogene Madison exhaled, the sound of movement jogging across the phone line. Chirpily, she continued. "Most people don't know this, but rubber is a very underrated design material. It's surprisingly comfortable to wear, too."

She nattered on about rubber bracelets, a lace-up corset her design partner had created, a "charming" pair of flip-flops that would be perfect for her younger daughter. In resignation, Meredith let her continue. When her mother pontificated about one of her lessons, it was better just to roll with it.

Everyone in the family knew the craze would run its course. Imogene was an inveterate self-improver, addicted to classes and coaching of every kind. Invariably, though, she moved on quickly. One month it was classical guitar; the next, glassblowing. On a whim, Imogene had once tried skydiving.

437

"So, your father and I are looking forward to the Valentine Studios shindig tomorrow," Imogene suddenly said. "It ought to be a hoot."

Great. Already it was a joke to them.

"Actually, Mom, that's what I'm calling about."

"Who would have thought *you*, of all people, would get up on stage and perform?" Imogene gabbed on, amusement in her voice. "I thought you'd had your fill of the spotlight in fifth grade. You know, when you jumped on stage at the Girl Scouts benefit to protest the commercialization of the local troop?"

Meredith groaned. She'd worn a costume made of Thin Mints boxes and a pair of thrift-store Ugg boots. She'd carried a protest sign. It hadn't been her proudest moment.

"Mom, listen. You and Dad don't have to come to this finale thing, especially all the way from the Valley. It's not a big deal. You're probably busy taking a class —"

"No . . . I don't have one that night."

"— or watching a rerun of 'Fantasy Family.' "

A snort. "We've got the collector's edition DVD set of your sister's sitcom now. Occasionally your father TIVOs an episode, but that's just because he wish listed 'Marley Madison.' He gets a big kick out of seeing all your sister's entries on-screen."

Meredith just bet he did. The whole family

had always been proud of Marley. Now digital video recording technology allowed them to follow her career effortlessly. Super.

"I don't want you to come," she blurted.

Shocked silence filled the line.

Then, "Frank! Meredith doesn't want us to come to her performance tomorrow," Imogene called, sounding hurt.

Oh, God. Now she'd done it, Meredith realized. Her mother held a grudge like a master. She didn't want to be deprived of her Night O' Laughs — courtesy of her daughter — and the whole world was going to know about it. Starting with the man of the house.

"We're coming," Frank boomed, his voice muffled. "Tell her we're coming. To the thing. At Valentine Studios."

At the decisive sound of her father's voice, Meredith nearly burst into tears. Her dad had always stood by her. Through sprained ankles, Hamburger Helper dinners, and the intricacies of Geometry homework. Gratitude filled her.

"Besides," Frank continued, obviously having come closer to the phone, "we're meeting Marley there. And Jake and Noah. Haven't seen them since the wedding. We can't miss that."

"No, we can't," Imogene agreed. "Did you hear that, Meredith?" she asked, returning to their conversation.

Crushed, Meredith nodded. She stared, unseeing, at the closest soundstage. Her parents just wanted to see Marley. No matter what else Meredith did, she'd forever be in her sister's shadow.

Unless you make a change, a part of her whispered. *How can they see who you really are if you stay on the sidelines?*

God, this shtick was getting old.

"Meredith? Meredith? Arrgh, these stupid cell phones." There was a dull thud as Imogene performed her usual ritual — beating the phone against her palm. "Frank, I think we got cut off!"

"I'm here, Mom," Meredith mumbled. "See you tomorrow."

Show them who you really are, something inside her urged.

Giving whatever it was a mental drop kick, she hung up the phone. Meredith strode to her next class, heartily sick of living with a damned Jiminy Cricket in her head — a conscience who smarmily delivered one-liners just when she least needed them.

She knew what she wanted out of life. It wasn't to stand in the spotlight. Not tomorrow, not ever, and especially not as Marley. She was more than a carbon copy of her sister, damn it.

Yeah — you're scared. She's not.

"Bite me," Meredith muttered, aiming a kick at a nearby stoop. She didn't need to change. She sure as hell didn't need to traipse all over a sitcom set looking like an idiot — acting unlike herself. No matter what anybody thought, she knew who she was, inside and out.

Right. You're the anti-Marley.

It was true. She was proud of it!

So how come, Meredith wondered with a sinking heart, being her sister's opposite in all things . . . didn't quite feel like enough anymore?

TWENTY-TWO

"Peel off your inhibitions. Find your own road."
— advertisement for Saab automobiles
(1995)

The morning of the finale dawned bright and smoggy, the sun shining through that uniquely L.A. mixture of oxygen, exhaust, and suspended dreams. As the guardian of one of those dreams — running a successful studio — Tony wasn't happy to find half his staffers lingering outside when he arrived at the business office.

They stood in clumps of twos or threes, talking. They leaned against parked cars, faces turned to the sun. They cradled chai lattes or sipped Ultimate Iced Blendeds as they traded industry gossip, not the least bit interested in getting down to work.

If the truth were told, Tony felt the same way. Being without Meredith had stolen all the sparkle from rejuvenating Valentine Studios . . . all the sparkle from his life. But that didn't mean he was ready to quit. Far from it.

"We've got a studio to run here," he snapped as he strode past the nearest group

442

of slackers. "Doesn't anybody have anything better to do?"

"Aww, come on, Mr. V. It's a nice day," a gaffer said.

"Yeah," one of the sound operators piped in. "We're in the homestretch now. We can kick back a little."

"Kick back after the finale," Tony commanded. "Right now, get back to work."

General grumbling ensued. One of the prop guys kicked a potted oak tree. An eyebrow-pierced admin slurped her coffee.

"Do I have to spell it out for you?" Tony asked, letting slip the leash on his bad mood. "Double-check the set dressing. Make sure there's enough film. Run another rehearsal with the actor fantasy camp guests. And Penelope — confirm the caterers for the after party. There'll be several important industry people at this event. Things *will* run smoothly."

Frowning, he went inside. The arctic chill of the air-conditioning hit him first. The outdated system always worked best in the morning, before it got hot out. Good thing he was wearing another suit today. Tony headed for his office.

Halfway there, voices reached him. Errol and Roland, squabbling again. From the sound of things, Roland had devised a new porno opportunity, and Errol was protesting. As usual.

"Another one of your lowbrow 'Honey' movies?" he asked from a nearby conference room. "Over my dead body!"

"Oh, yeah? I think that can be arranged!" Roland returned.

"I was speaking metaphorically, you imbecile."

"That makes one of us."

A chair scraped. "If you were as punctilious as you are pugnacious, *I* wouldn't be looking into leasing our unused soundstages as office space."

Silence. Probably, Roland was trying to figure out what the hell "punctilious" meant. The gist of it should have been pretty obvious, though — and was, an instant later.

"Take that back!" Roland yelled.

"If you can spell it," Errol replied in his most cultured, most taunting tone, "I will."

"Why, I oughtta —"

By the time Tony burst into the room, Roland had Errol in a headlock. His uncles grappled their way around the conference room, bashing into chairs. They slung insults at each other — pointed ones, borne of several decades' experience in brother baiting. Breathing heavily, Roland landed a punch. Errol retaliated with a fencing-style jab with a ruler.

It was like watching "WWE Smackdown" . . . on PBS.

"This doesn't look much like staying out of

my way to me," Tony said. "What the hell is the matter with you two?"

Guiltily, both his uncles swerved their attention in his direction. Roland straightened his pineapple-print shiny shirt; Errol moved to adjust his necktie and nearly jabbed himself in the throat with his ruler. Swiftly, he tucked it behind his back.

"I can't deal with a last-minute tiff today," Tony told them, aggravated that he was even expected to try. "I have a finale to produce. You two aren't helping. If you can't get along, then leave my studio."

His uncles exchanged a look. With it, some of their ire seemed to drain away. Errol even went so far as to put down his ruler and prop his hip on the edge of the conference table. He gave a faint smile — one that had Tony completely befuddled.

"I won't call security," Tony warned as fiercely as he could. He didn't have time for this bullshit today. "I'll drag you both out of here myself. Don't think I won't."

Clearly, Roland thought *exactly* that. He crossed his arms carelessly. In a conversational tone, he remarked, "That's the first time you've said that."

Tony clenched his fists. "Said what?"

" 'My studio,' " Errol supplied helpfully. His speculative gaze passed over Tony, then swerved to Roland. "You owe me twenty dollars."

Grumbling, Roland dug into his wallet to pay up.

"Hang on a minute." Tony couldn't believe it. "You had a *bet* about me?"

"Sure. More than one." Roland handed over a twenty.

Errol tucked the cash into his money clip. "Don't take it too hard, Tony. At least I always wagered in your favor. Roland didn't think you'd ever claim ownership of Valentine Studios."

"Why should I?" Roland asked with a defensive glare. He nodded toward his nephew. "He doesn't even claim his name. 'Mr. V.,' they call him around here. It's just plain disrespectful. That's what it is."

Roland frowned at Tony, as though freshly hurt by his remembrance of it. Beside him, Errol delivered an equally accusing look. Trapped beneath their disapproval, Tony felt ashamed, like he had as a kid when caught snitching all the chocolate chip cookies from craft services. Then, he just felt pissed.

What did they know about him, anyway? Not enough to realize *why* he was "Mr. V." to the staffers at the studio. Why it was important to distance himself from this place.

"If either of you knew me," he said, "you'd understand."

A moment passed while they digested that.

"Understand what?" Errol asked.

"Yeah, what?" his other uncle echoed.

"How are we supposed to understand something you've never told us? I don't remember Tony explaining about that 'Mr. V.' business. Do you, Errol?"

"No, Roland. I don't."

Skewered by the hurt and high-handedness directed his way, Tony frowned. Jesus. Apparently, his uncles could agree only when it came to dissing him, their nephew.

"You might as well explain yourself, Tony," Roland said. "We've got all day."

Errol nodded, brushing a piece of lint from his suit coat.

He shouldn't have to explain himself, Tony knew. Shouldn't have to spell out everything there was to know about him. Wasn't family supposed to know that stuff already? Wasn't that what families specialized in?

Unbidden, a memory of Meredith returned to him.

If you understood the real me — if you cared about me at all — you'd never ask me to do this.

Hell. Did Meredith feel as misunderstood by him as he did by his uncles?

Tony jutted his chin forward. "We don't have all day. I have a studio to save." *And a former star attraction whose absence at the finale might make the whole thing crash and burn.* "If you'll excuse me, I'm going back to work."

"Okay. Thanks anyway, Candace. I appreciate your help."

Hanging up the phone after her conversation with Marley's loyal personal assistant, Meredith rolled the kinks from her neck. She frowned. She was just going to have to accept it.

Her whole family was coming to the finale.

Between classes, she'd been trying to track down her sister. She'd hoped to persuade Marley (at least) not to come to the finale tonight. Unfortunately, she hadn't been able to reach her. According to her entourage, her sister and her new husband were largely "unavailable" except for messages, still honeymooning. They weren't expected back until hours before the Valentine Studios finale.

In fact, when Meredith had called Marley's manager, Brian, he'd mentioned that Marley would probably travel from the airport directly to the finale. She'd apparently asked her driver, Hugh, to pick up Noah from his grandmother's and then meet her and Jake with her BMW — plus a separate hired limousine "for the luggage."

Meredith guessed some things never changed.

Some things . . . just like her. The anti-Marley.

Shrugging off the thought, she headed to the final rehearsal for the actor fantasy camp sitcom. She arrived early on purpose, intending to give Eve the good news. But when she did. . . .

"Oh, Marley," Eve drawled, eyes shuttling right and left, hand on her breastbone. "Mr. V. told me I might have to stand in for you, but I just didn't think . . . I mean I hoped . . . oh, no."

Oh, no?

"I just don't think I can do it," Eve confided. She squinted in the direction of the TelePrompTer, then shook her head more decisively. "I tried rehearsing last night with my husband, Bill — we share one of those star trailers, you know — but I kept forgetting the lines! I'm just not cut out for stardom. Not like you."

If she only knew. "Sure, you are, Eve! You can do it," Meredith urged. "I have complete faith in you. It'll be fun!"

But no amount of encouragement was enough. Eve staunchly insisted she'd be too nervous to perform. In the end, Meredith was forced to admit defeat. No one else would take her place.

And she still didn't have the courage to do it herself.

What was she going to do? Work harder at persuading Eve? Enlist another stand-in? She couldn't bring herself to perform, but she felt guilty about letting down all the actor fantasy camp guests, the crew — even Tony. If she ruined this for them, they'd never forgive her. Acajatuba would never get its day in the sun. The studio might even shut down.

Surely all of that wasn't up to her! Sitting in one of the director's chairs, Meredith plunked her chin in her hands. Nobody who *really* knew her would expect her to go through with this. The idea was ridiculous — a tomboy historian turned starlet for a night?

"What's the matter, Marley?" someone asked from nearby.

"Yes, what's with the long face on our star performer?"

Meredith glanced up to find Esther standing on set with Harry arm in arm beside her. Compassionately, they *tsk-tsked* and moved nearer. Both of them fussed over her, advising a sweater for the chilly set, a comfier chair, a shot of whiskey for nerves (Esther's contribution, of course).

At the sight of their friendly faces, Meredith experienced a nearly overwhelming urge to spill everything. To unburden herself to no-nonsense Esther and kindly Harry, and hear someone say everything was going to be okay.

She looked up. "I don't know what I'm going to do," she blurted. "Everything's gone wrong."

"Tell us about it," Esther prompted.

So Meredith did.

The logistics of pulling together four video-taped performances on a single night were tricky. Tony had a lot to keep track of —

which should have meant summoning up some of his legendary business focus to do the job. Instead, as he made his usual round of meetings, check-ins, and soundstage visits, he found himself distracted.

"Mr. V." It's downright disrespectful.

That's the first time you've said that. "My studio."

Hell. A little slip of the tongue, and they'd never let him live it down. It was just as well he was returning to New York. Staying here would drive him crazy.

Especially without Meredith.

Frowning, Tony strode onward, intent on double-checking the preparations for the after party. It didn't matter what people called him, he knew. Or what possessive phrases happened to drop from his lips. All that mattered was getting the job done.

After which they'd all celebrate here, in soundstage 14.

Several of Valentine Studios' most successful movies had been filmed here. For tonight, the party planner had transformed the space into a winter wonderland of white walls, pale flower arrangements, ice sculptures, "frosted" bare tree branches, and millions of twinkling lights. Given the L.A. summer they'd had, the chilly theme was bound to be popular.

Several people milled around, setting up the bar and arranging chairs. Many more labored on the sidelines, affixing mirrors and lights to the walls and erecting portable Grecian-style columns. In the middle of all the activity, Tony spotted Nadine in a nearby chair, busily tapping away at her laptop. She seemed engrossed. He was surprised when she glanced up, swiveled around, and smiled at him.

"There you are, Tony!" Cheerfully, she looked him over. Her smile faltered. "My, don't you look formal in that suit?"

So she'd noticed he'd returned to his usual New York wardrobe. Big deal. Why that should make him feel as though he'd betrayed her somehow, Tony didn't know.

Lightly, he hugged her hello. "You have eyes in the back of your head, Aunt Nadine."

"Necessary feminine equipment, dear," she replied, waving one hand. The other she kept poised in readiness over her keyboard. "I'm just taking notes on the décor. If we have a lot of these shindigs, I don't want to repeat anything."

He didn't have the heart to tell her there probably wouldn't be more parties. "That's why we hired someone. To keep track of the details."

A snort. "You can't have too much supervision."

At last — someone around here who saw eye to eye with him. Surprised to find himself grinning, Tony held up a hand in fare-

452

well. "Try not to wear anything too scandalous to the after party. Uncle Errol's heart isn't what it used to be."

"Says who?" Nadine winked. "I'd say your uncle's ticker is working just fine."

And on *that* note . . . Tony pushed aside a heavy linen curtain to enter the VIP area — a requisite for any self-respecting L.A. party. This one contained a private bar, cozy white leather banquettes, a gleaming glass cube to set drinks on . . . and two elderly Valentines, duking it out over the slender buffet table.

"Onion dip," Roland said.

"Sashimi," Errol countered.

"Budweiser."

"Salon Blanc de Blancs Brut."

They yanked a printed menu card between them, as though trying to force the issue with sheer stubbornness. Nearby, a harried-looking member of the catering staff dithered over his set-up, clanking cutlery and dropping napkins. Another employee dodged around him, balancing a stack of trays. Clearly, Roland and Errol's latest squabble was unnerving the party staff.

"That's it!" Tony roared. At his uncles' surprised expressions, he felt his blood pressure rise even further. "Both of you — *out!*"

Roland pouted. "We were just trying to improve the menu."

"Yes," Errol agreed. "It needs some refinement."

"Out!" Tony pointed toward the exit.

Grumbling, Roland headed in that direction. Errol, however, stayed put. With his hands on his suit-jacket-covered hips and his chin held high, he gave Tony a critical once-over.

"I've had just about enough of this, young man."

Tony sighed. "Uncle Errol, don't give me a hard time about this. It's been a long day."

"It's about to get even longer." With a steely expression, Errol marched away from the buffet table to confront him. "Sit down."

"I have work to do." Feeling hassled and bereft, Tony dragged a hand through his hair. He glanced around. "Uncle Roland went that way. So I'd suggest you go that way."

He indicated the opposite direction.

"I said . . . *sit down*." Errol gave a two-handed shove.

To his absolute shock, Tony found himself pushed forcibly onto a waiting leather banquette. He lurched upward.

Errol — with utterly unexpected strength — shoved him downward again. This time, he kept one hand on Tony's shoulder.

"This has gone on long enough," his uncle said. "It's time I enlightened you about a few things. I'll thank you to stay put while I do."

When Meredith finally started talking, it *wasn't* about the performance she was

454

dodging. It was about Tony.

She told Esther and Harry about all the time they'd spent together. About the way they seemed to mesh so well. About her feelings for him and the feelings — she'd thought — he had for her. About the way he'd encouraged her to give her all at the actor fantasy camp.

About his leaving L.A. for New York.

"I thought Tony had changed his mind," Meredith said, shaking her head. "He was enjoying running the actor fantasy camp so much. I figured he'd want to stay. He says his partner is doing a great job managing their company in New York. So why does he have to leave?"

Esther patted her hand. "You have to tell him how you feel about him. That will make him stay."

"That's right," Harry agreed. "But first of all, you have to tell him the truth about yourself."

They looked at each other. Nodded.

Meredith felt more skeptical. "Do you really think telling him how I feel will — *hang on*." She examined the pair with dawning dread. "Did you just say . . . 'the truth about yourself'?"

They nodded.

"True love can only be based on the truth," Esther said.

"He's got to know," Harry added.

"Know . . . what?" It couldn't be what she thought it was.

Harry glanced around, then leaned closer. "That you're not Marley Madison, of course. You're Marley's twin sister."

"Meredith," Esther supplied. "It was naughty of you to fool us." She gave a mock censorious finger waggle. "Sounds like something I would have done myself, once upon a time."

Meredith's mouth dropped open. A denial sprang instantly to mind. After one look at Esther and Harry's trusted faces, though, she couldn't keep up her ruse any longer.

"How did you know?"

Harry shrugged. "Your interview."

Esther sighed. "Your shoes."

Damn. She should have known ditching those stilettos would catch up to her sooner or later.

"Esther and I got together after the press junket to talk about it," Harry said, "and two and two just didn't add up. Your childhood. Your address. Once Nadine got in on the conversation, she said —"

"I *knew* it!" Meredith crowed, relieved to be in the know about one thing at least. "Nadine *is* the *Inside Hollywood* reporter!"

Esther and Harry exchanged a puzzled glance.

"No, she isn't." Esther shook her head. "Harry is."

"*What?*" Meredith stared at him. "He can't be. Nadine is. She's the one with the computer — the one e-mailing *Inside Hollywood* all the time. Isn't she?"

Harry gave an uncomfortable cough. "'Fraid not. Sorry about those pictures, though. The photographer was a newbie. He turned in his whole roll of film. Usually I have more say about what winds up with my articles."

At his matter-of-fact tone, Meredith boggled. Harry was the *Insider.* Sweet, unassuming, gruff-but-kind Harry?

"But . . . how?" she asked. "Why?"

"Money, partly. Limo drivers don't exactly make bucketsful, and I've been thinking about retiring."

That made sense. Meredith nodded, helplessly drawn into sympathizing with him.

"Opportunity, too," he went on. "People tell me stuff while I drive them around. Producers, actors, executives. Camp guests. It's like I'm a combination shrink, long-lost pal, and invisible man."

"I had no idea."

"After all these years in the limo, I've got tons of material. When *Inside Hollywood* came knocking, I couldn't say no."

"I can see why," Meredith admitted. "Still . . ."

"Don't worry. Your secret's safe with me," Harry assured her. "Getting a big scoop is less important to me now." He aimed a loving look at Esther. He squeezed her hand. "After this assignment, I'm quitting."

"We're going to Spain to run with the bulls," Esther announced. She gave Harry an equally besotted look. "We're going to live abroad, and Harry's going to write his auto-biography, *My Life with the Stars*. I'm going to proofread and bring him sandwiches."

"And do all the typing," Harry reminded her.

"Exactly." She kissed him, then rubbed away a lipstick smear. She patted his cheek. Sighed. Turned to Meredith. "All this time, I've been chasing something that didn't exist. Looking for men to complete me. But I'm through with that now."

Meredith couldn't believe it. Esther was one of the most self-assured women she'd ever met. It didn't seem possible that she'd tried to find herself in the arms of her hus-bands.

Some of Meredith's incredulity must have shown on her face, because Esther went on.

"I know, I know. I look like I've got it all together." Her smile flashed. "But looks can be deceiving. You're proof of that one."

Meredith nodded, caught. "Sorry about that."

Esther waved away her apology. "It's all right, hon. Someday I'll buy you a mai tai and you can tell me the whole story. In the meantime . . . just remember this. Nobody else can give you what you need. Only you can do that. If you're looking on the outside, you're looking in the wrong direction."

As Esther's words hit her, Meredith stilled. Was that what she'd been doing? Looking on the outside?

You're mad because Tony still wants you to be like Marley, Leslie had said. *You want him to accept you the way you are.*

On the face of it, that had sounded reasonable. But was it possible, Meredith wondered, she'd been using Tony as an excuse? Using him as a scapegoat to blame for the things *she* was afraid to confront?

For instance . . . not wanting to be the anti-Marley anymore?

"Don't waste time like I did," Esther said, giving Meredith a sharp look. "If you care about Tony, do something about it *now*. Before it's too late."

"This studio was founded on two principles," Errol began, apparently assured he had Tony's full attention. He placed both hands on his suit jacket lapels, looking for all the world like a championship orator. "Those two principles were honor and hard work."

Tony stared at him, still stunned that his cultured, urbane uncle had forcibly jammed him into a seat.

"In the beginning, we had to scrape to get

459

by. We filmed our silent pictures on ramshackle sets. We counted our pennies. Soon enough, though, we progressed to 'talkies.' By dint of thrift and industry, we managed to get a toehold in Technicolor and Cinemascope. In musicals and dramas. We diversified. Valentine Studios flourished."

At last, Tony snapped out of it. "I've heard all the family lore before, Uncle Errol. Right now, I have a finale to produce. So if you don't mind —"

"Along came new innovations," Errol said, raising his voice. Clearly, he was unwilling to stop now. "Smell-o-vision. 3-D. Those ghastly beach bunny bingo movies. Still, Valentine Studios thrived."

"Cut to the chase," Tony said, sensing a lecture in the making. After all he'd been through over the past few days, he didn't have the patience to traipse down Memory Lane.

"Fine," Errol said. An unreadable look crossed his face. "Here's my question for you, then. Given our knack for adaptation, our yen for *honor* and *hard work* here at Valentine Studios, isn't it a puzzle we've wound up here? On the edge of bankruptcy?"

Crossing his arms uncomfortably, Tony shrugged. He understood why Errol needed to get this off his chest. Probably, his uncle sensed the impending downfall of the studio. He wanted to remember their successes one final time. That didn't mean Tony had to, too. He was a forward-looking man. Always had been.

"What do you think," Errol demanded, "made this studio finally falter?"

"I don't know," Tony said, feeling trapped beneath his uncle's gimlet stare. "Poor management. Unsound investments. The usual. I never really thought about it."

"Never really thought about it." Errol looked incredulous. "In that case, I'd better return Roland's twenty dollars to him. I didn't win that wager after all. You never did accept ownership of this studio."

Defensively, Tony elaborated. "It never mattered to me why the studio was in trouble. Only that I could help. That's what was important."

Errol nodded, his expression softening. "You *have* helped unstintingly. As soon as we called you, you came to L.A."

"Of course I did!"

"The fact that you did gives me hope right now. It's what assures me the family legacy still lives on in you."

Shifting uneasily, Tony looked away. As though sensing his discomfort, Errol paused. Then he pulled up a nearby chair. He sat across from Tony as the caterers and laborers milled inside the soundstage, as the bustle of preparty activity continued. He sat and he waited, as though gathering strength. Finally,

461

he drew in a breath.

"I can see I'm going to have to tell you everything," Errol said. "I didn't want to, but I can see you don't understand."

Ordinarily, Tony might have taken offense at that. Not this time. The ominous tone in his uncle's voice made his stomach flip over in dread. Whatever this was, it wasn't good. Without thinking about it, he leaned closer to Errol.

"I was sick, Tony. About four years ago, I had a series of transient ischemic attacks — mini strokes, the doctors called them. The episodes happened weeks, sometimes months, apart, and at first we weren't sure what was happening. I tried to convince your aunt my slurred speech was due to one too many martinis, but Nadine wasn't buying it."

An uneven smile flashed over Errol's face. Folding his aged hands over his knee, he darted a quick glance at Tony.

All Tony could do was breathe. Anything else felt unreal. How could this be happening? He hadn't thought, hadn't known. . . .

"Don't look so shocked," his uncle said. "TIAs are a frighteningly common experience among men and women my age. But they can be treated. Even prevented, by people wiser than me."

"Why didn't you tell me? Call me?" Tony shook his head, still in shock. Thinking of all his uncle had gone through, he felt sick at heart. "I would have come."

"I know you would have." Errol nodded. "But the TIAs happened so far apart, so erratically . . . I couldn't see dragging you from your life in New York. I told Nadine not to call you, and forbade the family to mention it. I didn't want to worry you."

"Worry me?" More upset now, Tony drove a hand through his hair. He gave Errol a nononsense look. "What worries me is that you could keep any of this to yourself! Am I part of this family or not?"

A faint smile. "Certainly, you are."

"Then in the future, I want to know these things. You're going to tell me if you so much as sneeze." He frowned at his uncle, so Errol would know he meant business. Then a new thought struck him. "Are you all right now? How do you feel?"

"I'm fine."

Tony got to his feet. He gestured toward the banquette he'd been sitting on. "You look pale. Here, lie down."

"Honestly, I'm fine." Now Errol's smile was a full-blown grin. Affection shone from his eyes. "My therapy worked, my prescription medications were successful, and my two surgeries nearly performed miracles."

"Two surgeries!"

"There's no need to worry, Tony. The point is . . . when that time came, Roland

463

was here. He took profit we'd earmarked for studio improvements — improvements that would have moved us into twenty-first century filmmaking — and spent those funds on my medical bills instead. For that, I'm forever grateful. Because of it, though, we're in trouble now. That's why we needed your help."

Tony sat down with a thud. After all his uncles' bickering, after all their ups and downs, the fact that Roland had stepped up and helped his brother . . . Well, now that he thought about it, it really wasn't all that surprising.

"Uncle Roland is a good man," he said.

"He's a loyal man," Errol agreed. "Through and through."

Tony glanced up. *That's* what loyalty means to you? What Roland did?"

Errol looked bemused. "Naturally. Loyalty means believing in the people you love. You, of all people, must know that. You believed in us enough to come here."

"Yeah, but I . . ." At a loss for words, Tony hesitated. First, Errol's news about his illness. Now, this revelation. "You only did that because I'm a Valentine."

"Tony, Tony." Affectionately, Errol shook his head. "Is that what this is about? I thought you'd left that notion behind you years ago."

"I —"

"Ahhh," Errol interrupted, nodding sagely. "The 'Mr. V.' business makes sense now, too. Roland will be glad to know it's nothing more serious. He was worried."

His gruff, happy-go-lucky uncle, worried? Tony couldn't quite picture it.

"About 'Mr. V.,' " he began. "Let me explain —"

But before he got very far, Errol leaned forward and raised his hand to stop him. He seemed at peace somehow. Whether that was because he'd finally told his secret or because he was relieved the actor fantasy camp experiment was nearly finished, Tony didn't know.

"You don't have to explain," Errol said. "Don't you think all of us went through the same thing you've gone through? Hated being 'just another Valentine'? Hated having to follow in the footsteps of all those studio moguls who came before us?"

Tony had never thought about it before. He said so.

"Well, think about it now," his uncle advised. "While you're at it, think about *why* you're here, and where you really belong." He stood, preparing to leave. "*You* define your work, Tony. None of us would have thought of actor fantasy camp. We made the right choice in bringing you here — and *not* just because you're a Valentine."

They were the words Tony had waited a lifetime to hear. Strangely enough, he had a whole new perspective on them now. For the first time ever, he didn't need them.

"There's no better kind of person to be," he said.

He meant it.

He only hoped that tonight, Meredith would agree.

TWENTY-THREE

"If you can dream it, you can do it."
— Walt Disney

The live studio audience filled in quickly that night. They packed the bleachers and overflowed into the standing-room-only space, eager to see their friends and loved ones perform. The sounds of murmured conversation and muted laughter rose to the rafters of soundstage 23. Backstage, Tony shook hands with crew members. He reassured jittery actor fantasy camp guests. He looked for Meredith.

She was nowhere in sight.

Disappointment thrummed through him. Had she left without telling him? Caught that bus back to her own neighborhood after all? He hadn't been able to find her earlier today. . . .

"We should get started," the first AD said, consulting his clipboard. "We're already ten minutes late, Mr. V."

"Valentine," Tony corrected, finally at peace with his family — and his place in it. Through the behind-the-scenes bustle, he looked at the director. "Mr. Valentine."

"Oookay. Whatever you say."

"Or Tony. Tony would be fine, too."

"Right. About the taping —"

"We're waiting." Tony consulted his watch. "A little longer."

It was the fourth time he'd made that announcement. This time, as before, the harassed-looking director frowned.

"We have an understudy," he urged. "Let's put in Eve. You know as well as I do that Marley Madison is notoriously flaky. She might not show at all."

"She'll show."

She had to. Meredith, that is. There was so much he had to tell her . . . so much he had to make her understand. Thanks to his family, Tony had a new perspective on things. If he could have misread Errol and Roland so thoroughly all these years, he could have misread Meredith the other night, too. In fact, given what he knew of her, he was certain he had.

But misunderstandings could be worked through.

If only she'd come.

Fifteen minutes and one more request to start later, Tony was still waiting. The set lights were on, the crowd was growing increasingly restless . . . There was still no sign of Meredith.

Where was she?

Throwing her borrowed overnight case on

her trailer's pink-covered bed, Meredith winced at the weight of the thing. Added to the packed suitcase Leslie had brought her almost two weeks ago, it made for a substantial quantity of luggage. More than the duffel bag she usually traveled with, at least.

It looked as though she was leaving Valentine Studios with much more than she'd arrived with. But Meredith didn't need luggage to tell her that. Her heart whispered it with every beat.

She glanced at the clock. Atypically, she was late. But one more thing still remained to be done — one more thing before she left.

Drawing in a deep breath, she crossed the bedroom. For the last time, she nimbly side-stepped the tumbled stilettos, then stopped at the opposite wall. She raised her hand. Touched the homemade cardboard star taped there at shoulder-height. Smiled.

Once upon a time, a crew of five women had believed Meredith deserved that star. Tonight, there was every risk she might disappoint them. Certainly, what she was about to do wasn't what they'd tutored her to do. But it felt right, in her heart. For now, that was all that mattered.

Raising her other hand, she readied the Sharpie permanent marker she'd brought. She focused on the star and, with a trembling hand, wrote on its face.

Meredith.

She'd never expected the limelight would be her destiny. Had never thought it would be possible to break away from Marley's shadow. Or even, to diverge into more mundane matters, to consider going onstage with her stomach in knots and her knees too wobbly to hold her up with anything close to grace. But that's exactly what Meredith was doing.

She just hoped she didn't hurl in the midst of her opening bow. The possibility seemed distinctly likely — that's how nervous she was. Until tonight, she hadn't known teeth could actually lock up in terror.

With a final pat to her star, Meredith turned. Unsteadily, she made her way to her trailer's door. This might be the craziest thing she'd ever done. It was definitely the bravest.

But the truth was, she'd finally had enough of being the anti*anybody*. For better or worse, starting tonight, Meredith meant to be the one hundred percent *her*. Given all the years she'd wasted already, she figured it was about damn time.

Tony felt the change in the air first. It crackled from backstage to the front of the set — where he'd moved to make a crowd-calming announcement — in a single current of expectation.

It zapped him just as he finished speaking.

"So if you'll give us a few more minutes," Tony told the audience, "I know you won't be disappointed."

Out of the corner of his eye, he glimpsed movement in the wings. The second AD, who'd been standing at the edge of the set having an apoplectic seizure over the idea of delaying the sitcom taping to wait for "Marley," now beamed with obvious delight and relief. He held up both thumbs in the signal they'd agreed upon.

Their star was here.

Meredith.

Instantly, Tony's heart lurched. His mouth went dry. His palms curled into involuntary fists at his sides. He wished he'd had a chance to prep her, to give her a final word of encouragement . . . to tell her he loved her, no matter what else happened tonight.

But there hadn't been time for that. Hadn't been time for anything.

As though sensing something had changed, the crowd hushed. In the resulting quiet, Tony leaned toward his microphone.

"Ladies and gentlemen . . . the star of our show!"

At her cue, Meredith appeared. She took a single hesitant step from backstage, her gaze locked with Tony's, then walked faster. Nervousness radiated from her flushed face and her unsteady smile, but as she grew closer

471

. . . as she grew closer, Tony could not take his eyes from her.

She was afraid, he realized. Afraid to be here, afraid to perform — and still she'd come. For him. Humbled by her courage, he waved his arm toward her in a showy gesture. Meredith deserved the spotlight. For all the beautiful things she was, for all the wonderful things she did, she deserved it.

She was dressed for it, too. Her slinky, punk-rocker red skirt and shimmering white halter weren't the clothes Tony had seen during dress rehearsals — but they were perfectly Meredith. Her black leather high-heeled boots weren't the daring stilettos she'd been assigned — but they allowed her to move with her characteristically athletic grace. Almost a hybrid of her trusty Tevas and the towering stilettos she'd been avoiding, those boots suited her.

Meredith came to a stop beside him, her head held high and her posture confident. Gone were the stooped shoulders she'd sported before. In their place was a smile and a wave for the audience, just as though Meredith had been inhabiting the spotlight for years . . . belonged in it.

Tony stared at her, awestruck. There was something different about Meredith tonight . . . something not quite Marley, but not quite the hip-hiding tomboy historian he'd come to know, either. Tonight, her hair was sleek, not pouffy. Her makeup was subdued, her clothes sensual, her demeanor straightforward.

This Meredith was entirely new, Tony realized. She was beautiful in a way that was uniquely hers, inhabiting — at long last — the most stunning version of herself. When she smiled at him, she took his breath away.

God, but he loved her.

In that moment, Tony made his most radical decision ever. Meredith's courage deserved more of a reward than he could ever give her. But as a start. . . .

He held out his palm. To his immense relief, Meredith put her hand in his. He returned her smile with a heartfelt one of his own. Then, Tony turned to the audience.

"Let's hear it for Valentine Studios' latest star attraction," he urged. "Meredith Madison!"

"Meredith? Meredith Madison?" one of the crew members asked, just off-set. "What the . . . ?"

On the sidelines, Esther and Harry grinned. Elsewhere on the soundstage, gasps of surprise were heard. Excited murmurs rippled through the audience. Flashbulbs popped. Nobody seemed to know what was going on — but everyone recognized a scoop when they heard one.

Amid the din, Meredith's wide-eyed gaze met Tony's. She squeezed his hand hard, then hustled them both out of microphone range.

"What are you doing?" she asked hoarsely, her eyes searching his. "I didn't come here to see you sabotage your studio!"

"And I didn't come here to see you denied all the credit you deserve," Tony returned. "Just trust me."

"I do." The truth of her avowal was there in her face, in the pressure of her hand in his. "But revealing my true identity was never part of our plan. What about your studio? What about your work? What about all the success you wanted?"

"I had it the minute you took my hand tonight," he said. "I had it the minute you came back to me. Being with you is all the 'success' I need."

Her eyes misted. "Oh, Tony —"

Before she could finish, a reporter stood, tape recorder in hand. "Mr. Valentine! Chip Estevez from the *Times*. Did you just say *Meredith* Madison?"

"Yes," Tony said proudly, leaning toward the microphone with Meredith in tow. "Yes, I did."

The uproar escalated. Several spectators adjusted their camcorders, eagerly filming. Another journalist rose.

"Meredith Madison," he repeated. "Any relation to Marley Madison?"

The crowd hushed expectantly.

"Yes," Tony told them. He moved again, so his words would be sure to be heard clearly. "But as you'll all find out when the sitcom taping gets under way, there's no one else in the whole world as unique as Meredith."

Beside him, she stilled, obviously surprised. Her gaze met his again, and this time, one of those tears fell. Meredith swiped it away.

"Thank you," she whispered. A squeeze. "You're pretty special yourself."

"You ain't seen nothing yet." He grinned.

"And now," Tony said, speaking into the microphone, "as they say in showbiz . . . on with the show. Ladies and gentlemen, Meredith Madison!"

She took her final bow before joining the rest of the cast. Standing in the spotlight, Meredith smiled, still holding Tony's hand.

She leaned toward the microphone. "Thanks, everyone. And get ready for a good time, because this sitcom cast kicks butt!"

From the sidelines, the rest of the players applauded. Eve blew a kiss. Meredith's "leading man" gave her a bow.

From the bleachers, six people suddenly rose. They whooped and hollered, stamping their feet and clapping their hands. One of them — a middle-aged man in a golf shirt — waved his Dodgers cap.

"Go, Meredith!" he shouted. "Go, Meredith!"

She blushed, turning her face toward

Tony's shoulder. She offered a weak wave as the two of them walked off stage.

"My dad," she mumbled. "Oh, God."

Tony peered toward the bleachers. "Then I guess that's your mom with the — what is that, a rubber trench coat? And I recognize Marley, even with her starlet shades on. Who knew she could wolf whistle like that? The tall, suntanned, crazy-in-love guy must be Jake, and the kid on his shoulders must be your nephew, Noah."

Meredith gave them an anxious, flustered glance. "Uh-huh."

"But what I can't figure out," Tony said as they reached the edge of the sitcom set, "is who the woman in glasses is. You know — the one with the frizzy hair and the 'Historians do it with Dates' T-shirt?"

"That's my best friend, Leslie. I sent her a comped ticket via messenger."

"Ahhh. Indulging your superstar powers already, I see." Tony glanced toward the bleachers again. His grin widened. "Look. They've started a 'wave' for you."

All six of Meredith's biggest fans performed the maneuver flawlessly, rising from their seats in succession with their arms in the air. The audience members nearby joined in.

Tony had never been happier to have invited guests to a studio taping. It looked as though Meredith's friends and family were prouder of her than she realized.

"Places, Miss Madison," the first AD said.

They were off to the show.

Meredith had never felt more impatient to have a performance finished in her life. There were so many things she wanted to tell Tony, so many things she wanted to explain.

Starting with *I'm sorry* and ending with *I love you*.

Fortunately, the sitcom flew by. There were a few gaffes, a couple of flubbed lines, and one case of camera fright — but that was handily solved when a half dozen crew members helpfully leaped up to point to the TelePrompTer. Everyone — cast, crew, actor fantasy camp guests, and business office employees — pulled together to create a real team.

In the end, they created a bona fide hit, too.

Afterward, Meredith felt elated. Not just because she'd tackled one of her biggest fears and survived — also because Tony had been there for her. He'd taken her hand, smiled at her, jeopardized the success of his actor fantasy camp for her. Compared with what he'd risked, her decision to finish her sham-Marley charade seemed downright insignificant.

Her family didn't think so, though. They swooped upon her the minute Meredith entered soundstage 14 for the after party. She stepped into the luxuriously white space, accepted the flute of champagne one of the waiters pressed into her hand, and was instantly engulfed in hugs.

"Meredith." Imogene clapped both hands on Meredith's cheeks and grinned at her, shaking her head. "I can't believe it. We're so proud of you."

Frank cleared his throat. Then he hugged her, too. "Nice work, kiddo. Easier than falling out of a tree house, eh?"

Next to step forward was Jake, the former "studliest sportscaster" in L.A. "Just don't let them put your picture on the side of a bus to advertise the studio," he advised with a good-natured roll of his eyes. "You wouldn't *believe* the kind of trouble that can cause."

Marley, glamorous in a fuchsia dress with skyscraper heels, elbowed her new husband. "Hey! It's that kind of 'trouble' which brought us together, buster."

They traded a loving, teasing smile. Then Marley nudged her sunglasses to the top of her hair, headband-style, and hugged Meredith. For a moment, Meredith only clung to her sister, feeling the connection they'd always shared. At long last, they separated.

Marley stepped back. She whisked her gaze over Meredith with assessing thoroughness.

"I always knew you had it in you," she announced. "To be the *real* you. Congratulations, Meredith. You're fab."

Embarrassed, Meredith felt herself flush. All this praise was completely unexpected — and a little overwhelming.

Suddenly, two small arms clamped around her middle.

"Arrgh!" she cried, catching on quickly. "I'm being squished to death by a monster hug!"

A husky laugh was muffled by her midsection. She glanced down to see Noah, just as she'd expected, hugging her with all the brawn his four-year-old's arms could muster.

"It's just me, Aunt Meredith." He released her, his little face bright. In both fists, he held plate-size chocolate chip cookies. "See what the caterers gave me?"

"Yum. I'll bet those are terrific."

Noah nodded and munched, scattering crumbs. Marley and Jake watched him. They looked the very picture of newlywed bliss . . . right down to the rhinestone-leashed Yorkie — Marley's dog, Gaffer — in her arms. He gobbled a piece of cookie, too.

It was all too much. The performance, the congratulations, the excited crowd milling around the after party. And Meredith still hadn't managed to reconnect with Tony. To her chagrin, he'd disappeared after the last curtain call and hadn't been spotted since.

But when she raised on tiptoes to scan the crowd for him, she caught her parents watching her.

She'd never seen so much pride in their faces. The shock of it completely made her forget what she'd been doing.

Imogene smiled knowingly. "We were sure you'd come into your own sooner or later," she said. "My fortune-telling classes predicted it."

Frank nodded. "You seem real happy, honey."

"Oh, look, Frank!" Imogene pointed to a passing waiter. "Crab cakes. Let's go try out the food. I see cooking lessons in my future!"

As quickly as that, they were off. Meredith watched them go with a bemused smile. She still couldn't believe her parents hadn't laughed themselves silly over this whole spectacle.

Marley, too, watched them weave through the crowd.

"I'm in for it now," she said with a wry look. She accepted some champagne and took a sip. "Now they'll *never* quit talking about you."

"Me?" Meredith gawked. "All they do is talk about you!"

Marley looked astonished. "Me? No, way!"

"Way."

Speculatively, both sisters watched their parents. Imogene and Frank fed each other

480

crab cakes, then headed to the dance floor. Meredith couldn't believe she'd ever been more than a blip on her parents' Marley-centric radar screen.

According to Marley, she'd been the blip.

"Mom never quit talking about *you*," Marley explained. " 'Why can't you be sensible, like your sister?' she'd say. And then Dad would chime in. 'Meredith meets professors at her job.' " Marley's Frank impersonation was pitch perfect. " 'Not frivolous pretty boys and unemployed musicians.' " She rolled her eyes. "Sheesh. It really got to me sometimes."

Marveling, Meredith sipped her champagne. Someday, she'd definitely have to compare notes over this whole parental pride issue. But in the meantime . . . she had a man to find.

Meredith wove her way through the party, standing on booted tiptoes every now and then to see over the heads of the revelers near her. There was no sign of Tony. Probably, he was working — talking with investors and sealing Valentine Studios sponsorship deals. To be fair, she told herself, she ought to be patient.

She snorted. Yeah, right. *That* was going to happen.

Setting down her empty champagne flute, she edged along the white fabric-covered walls. All around her, actor fantasy camp guests and visitors mingled and chatted, ate and drank. Servers glided through the crowd bearing trays; musicians played on a temporary bandstand. The swanky affair was everything Meredith had imagined a Hollywood shindig would be.

Everywhere she went, people congratulated her. Becky, Salma, Inga, and all the rest of the girls raved about her success and, to a woman, claimed to have guessed her secret. Not that they minded. They made her promise to keep in touch — and to come back for their Colin Farrell "Hunk of the Month" movie-watching party next week.

Finally, at a loss as to where Tony might be, Meredith slumped beside a fancy Grecian pillar. An instant later, someone grabbed her arm and yanked her sideways. She wound up beside one of the luxe white velvet curtains in the VIP area . . . staring up at Tony's face.

"Damn. I thought you'd never quit gabbing," he said, and kissed her.

The moment their lips met, Meredith felt complete. Tony cradled her head in his palm and held her close, and their kiss went on and on. Thrilled, she buried her fingers in his hair and pasted herself up against his body. There was no place she'd rather be — in that moment, or ever.

Too soon, they parted.

"Oh, Tony. I'm so sorry. About everything."

"*I'm* sorry, too. I didn't mean a word of it. Not a word," he said at the same time. He touched her hair as though reassuring himself she was still there, in his arms. "Watching you leave was the worst moment of my life. I didn't realize —"

"*I* didn't know," Meredith babbled. "Didn't know what I really wanted or how to get it. Not until I was without you. Without you, everything was so —"

"Insubstantial. Dreary. Lonely and —"

"Meaningless. But then you were there on-stage, and you were waiting for me."

"How could I not?" Tony smiled. He kissed her again. "You're the star attraction of my heart."

Awww. That was so sweet. Feeling her grin helplessly widen further, Meredith squeezed her hand on his.

"Thank you for believing in me," she said. "Even when I wasn't sure I believed in myself."

"Always." His eyes promised he meant it. "And in the meantime . . . I've got something for you."

Mystified, Meredith watched as he reached behind a fold in the curtains. At the same instant, Roland and Errol appeared. Roland clapped his nephew on the back, interrupting his gift retrieval.

"Big success, Tony. Big success! I've gotta say, I'm a little disappointed — this probably means my 'Honey' movies will be put on hold for even longer now. But if it means the studio's survival —"

"We're *both* in favor of it," Errol said. "We've been swamped with members of the press and potential investors. After seeing Meredith, they're crazy for the actor fantasy camp concept. 'We love the Cinderella aspects of all this,' they're telling us. 'Love how you turned an ordinary woman into a star.'"

"They're sure guests will be lining up to repeat the process," Roland added. "They can't wait to move forward. With funding, sponsorships, joint advertising ventures —"

"Deals are definitely in the works," Errol confirmed, nodding. "But we had to come congratulate you two, before finalizing anything."

His gaze swerved to Meredith with clear affection. "A splendid job, my dear. You're excellent, just like a Valentine, born and bred."

Coming from him, that was a high compliment, Meredith knew. Just as she knew, a little while later when Nadine appeared, that it would be a long while before she and Tony had any more time alone together.

"Thrilling, just thrilling!" Nadine said. "You had us all fooled, Meredith. We should make a movie of your story. I'll e-mail a producer friend of mine . . ."

The gabbing continued. At long last, the three elderly Valentines wandered off in search of more drinks — and a rhumba. Left alone with Tony in their secluded corner, Meredith moved into his arms.

"Now . . . where were we?" she asked.

"Opening my surprise."

He pulled something from behind his back. Offered it to her. Meredith nearly staggered under the weight of the enormous jar.

She cocked her brow. "Jelly beans?"

"Look closer," Tony advised.

She did. "*Red* jelly beans. Thousands of them."

"All identical." His grin harkened back to the jelly bean mythology she'd shared with him. "This time, I'm taking no chances. You're mine."

"Forever," Meredith agreed.

"That's touching," Esther said, arriving with a drink in hand and Harry in tow. "How about cracking open those beans, anyway? Woman doesn't live by gin alone."

Tony rolled his eyes. "There's a buffet, Aunt Esther."

"Wonderful sitcom performance," Harry said. He smiled at Esther, then gave Meredith a wink. "I can almost guarantee *The Insider* will give it — and the whole actor fantasy camp — a rave review in next week's *Inside Hollywood*."

Meredith grinned. One of these days, she'd

have to tell Tony all about his driver's secret life. But in the meantime . . .

The Madison and Jarvis clans joined their corner. The rest of the Valentines crowded around, gossiping about the sitcom performance and getting to know Meredith's family. Leslie dropped by to congratulate Meredith, shyly introduced herself to Tony, and wound up being offered a starring role ("She's a cheerleader named Honey, see . . .") by Uncle Roland.

Mayhem ruled. Meredith attempted to talk with Tony, attempted to share her jelly beans with him, endeavored to tell him all the things she'd been keeping inside for so long. But every time she tried, another family member butted in.

Tony experienced similar frustration. Finally, he abandoned his drink and climbed onto the nearest banquette, waving his arms.

"Hey!" he shouted, clearly at his wit's end. "Can't you people see I'm trying to talk to Meredith about something *important?*"

Everyone clammed up. Several dozen expectant gazes swerved toward Tony and Meredith — who stood frozen in the corner. She glanced up at the man she loved.

"Looks like *you're* the star of the hour now," she said, grinning. "What's on your mind?"

He scowled at the crowd. Flexed his fists. Swallowed hard. Whatever he had to say, it was . . . making him nervous, she realized. Suddenly filled with anticipation, Meredith waited.

"Oh, the hell with it," Tony said, breaking into a grin. "You're all going to find out sooner or later, anyway."

He jumped down from the banquette and turned to Meredith.

"I'm staying in L.A. to run the actor fantasy camp. It looks like the studio is in my blood, after all. And you —"

"Oh, Tony! That's wonderful!"

"— you are in my heart."

She stilled, gazing into his eyes. What she saw there mirrored everything she felt. Beginning with love and ending with . . . love.

"From the moment I saw you," Tony went on, "I knew you were special. You touched me, and I needed you. You talked to me, and I heard. You laughed with me . . . and I swear, my heart grew two sizes at the joy in your face. Without you, even showbiz loses its magic. With you, I'm whole."

"Oh, Tony." Meredith felt the tears on her cheeks, sensed the people around them — quieter now — heard the quaver in her own voice. Nothing else mattered except the man whose hands she held in hers. "I can't imagine going on without you. You're stubborn and determined, brilliant and sexy and funny —"

"Not all at the same time, I hope."

"— and you're absolutely, positively, the only man for me."

"That makes us even, then." He thumbed away the tears from her face, then kissed the places he'd dried. "Because you're the only woman for me. I love you, Meredith. With all my heart and soul."

"I love you." Helpless affection welled inside her, making her voice turn husky and her heartbeat quicken. Drawing in a breath for courage, Meredith gazed steadily up at him. "I know now that I'll never stop. How could I? You're my perfect Prince Charming."

Tony smiled. "Then let me take you away, princess. Please, say you'll be mine."

"I'm yours," Meredith said instantly. "Any time. Any where."

"Come on. That was way too easy." Tony grinned. "You do realize this is an official proposal, don't you?"

She blinked. "Ummm . . ."

Tony got down on one knee. From someplace behind him, a Valentine Studios prop master pushed forward. He bent beside Tony and handed him a box. With utmost care, Tony opened it.

Meredith gasped at the ring inside.

"When I ask you to be mine," Tony said seriously, "I mean forever."

"When I say yes," Meredith answered with equal gravity, "I mean forever, too."

And once he'd slipped the ring on her hand, once the crowd began cheering, once Meredith and Tony indulged in a perfect, earth-shaking, knee-rocking, sweet-hot kiss . . . their combined *forever* began. Just like in the fairy tales. Just like in the sappy chick flicks, the steamy novels, and the stories whispered from one romantic to another.

In Tinseltown — as in everywhere — true love was hard to find. But Meredith and Tony took their cues, played their parts, and uncovered their own true selves in the process. With that kind of magic at work, it's no wonder their love began as a perfect switch . . . and ended as a perfect happily-ever-after.

About the Author

When she sat down to write her first book, **Lisa Plumley** expected the process to be easy. Three tries and several years later, she realized it's not easy — but it is the most fun to be had outside of shoe shopping. Now the bestselling author of more than a dozen books, Lisa lives in sunny Arizona with her husband and two children. She invites readers to visit her Web site, www.lisaplumley.com for previews of upcoming books and more.

The employees of Thorndike Press hope you have enjoyed this Large Print book. All our Thorndike and Wheeler Large Print titles are designed for easy reading, and all our books are made to last. Other Thorndike Press Large Print books are available at your library, through selected bookstores, or directly from us.

For information about titles, please call:

(800) 223-1244

or visit our Web site at:

www.gale.com/thorndike
www.gale.com/wheeler

To share your comments, please write:

Publisher
Thorndike Press
295 Kennedy Memorial Drive
Waterville, ME   04901

DATE DUE

79			97